THE GAUSS FACTOR

THE GAUSS FACTOR

To Gary & Mandy & family

with love & best wishes from

Steve

Stephen Tasker   28. 8. 97

The Book Guild Ltd
Sussex, England

The Book Guild Ltd
25 High Street
Lewes, Sussex

First published 1997
© Stephen Tasker, 1997
Set in Baskerville
Typesetting by Raven Typesetters, Chester

Printed in Great Britain by
Antony Rowe Ltd,
Chippenham, Wiltshire

A catalogue record for this book is
available from the British Library

ISBN 1 85776 235 5

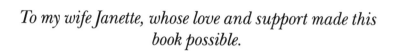

To my wife Janette, whose love and support made this book possible.

PART ONE

Jim had long had a fondness for Cornwall. It went back to his honeymoon days. There was a quaintness and character about it that put to shame other locations supposedly more exotic or romantic. He loved the narrow lanes, the steep-sided seaside villages, the temperate climate and, not least, the friendly people with the easygoing twang. Within all that, to find the perfect retreat, well, it was just idyllic. Jim was immersed in a feeling of total contentment as he lay staring up at the misshapen ceiling of the tiny bedroom. The bed was old, iron and immensely comfortable. The furnishings were basic, adequate and perfectly acceptable. All was simple yet serene.

His lover and companion lay motionless beside him. She was still submerged in that deep sleep of pleasure and fulfilment that follows a night of lovemaking and passion. Their loving was always uninhibited and frequently reached the ecstatic. He was lucky. Not every husband and wife could reach and sustain such levels of satisfaction as they had consistently for so long and every time they went away together they seemed to achieve new heights; and especially in Cornwall, in their heavenly hamlet.

Carol would be waking soon but there was time enough for Jim to have a shave and a shower, then downstairs, via the narrow winding stone staircase, and into the tiny kitchen to get preparations underway for a hearty English breakfast. He rose and made his way nakedly towards the adjoining bathroom door.

Emerging smoothly from her slumber, Carol knew

3

instantly that she had enjoyed a deep and contented sleep and she knew why. She felt for her partner almost instinctively. His absence prompted a flutter of disappointment and an inquisitiveness which was soon to be answered by the muffled noises from downstairs. Like Jim, she was still naked from the night's activity and she looked around for the silk dressing gown that Jim had bought her some years ago. It was draped on a chair near the window and she made her way towards it, her arms outstretched above a taut body in the way that you do after a good night's sleep and secure in the knowledge that her exercising was in private. Suitably robed, she drew the curtains covering the small wood-framed window, to be confronted by a sight she had seen before. The narrow lane passing the cottage was filled with sheep. Such a road block had few implications for traffic flow because there was little to speak of, just the occasional tractor and a handful of cars belonging to the inhabitants of the hamlet. Some of those, like Jim and Carol, were temporary. But whatever the category, the pace was leisurely. Carol made her way barefooted and noiselessly down the stairs, crept up behind her husband and embraced him tightly.

'Mornin', lover,' she sighed.

'You sneak,' said Jim, playfully reprimanding. 'I wanted to surprise you with breakfast in bed.'

'Don't worry, my darling,' replied Carol. 'I can soon return there. I like nothing better than to be surprised by you in bed.'

Jim had turned round and his eyes were smiling as he returned his wife's embrace and added a deep passionate kiss for good measure.

'Off you go then before your bacon frazzles.'

'OK, but give me five minutes first to have a quick shower,' said Carol as she slinked off provocatively, allowing her silk robe to fall tantalizingly off her shoulders. With an exaggerated teasing expression, she finally got to the top of the stairs again and was out of sight.

'I love you,' she shouted.

'I love you too, sweetheart,' called back Jim, whose mind

was by now elsewhere than on the hard crispy bacon pieces spitting at him from the frying pan.

A few minutes later Jim was nudging open the bedroom door with his foot, his hands occupied with the tray containing his breakfast masterpiece. Carol was just emerging from the connecting bathroom but, to Jim's surprise, she was fully clothed.

'That was a quick shower and change,' he said, placing the tray down on the barely wide enough bedside table. 'I'd half expected that you'd still be in a state of undress.'

'And hoped, no doubt,' retorted Carol, still mindful of her husband's voracious appetite not many hours previously. 'I would have been but for the dreaded Cornish water supply,' she said.

'Oh no. Not again.'

'I just about managed a quick rinse and a rub down this time.'

It wasn't the first time that week that the vagaries of the local water supply had interrupted their ablutions. Still, Cornwall was not noted for its plentiful water resources, particularly at this time of year when there was an abundance of temporary inhabitants, and it did add to the quaintness and character that Jim and Carol so much adored.

'Still, no excuse now,' remarked Carol. 'A quick breakfast and then off to Looe for a proper look in that gorgeous clothes shop we noticed the other day. Remember? The one you said we'd come back to,' she teased.

Jim sensed that it was not going to be his day: spat at by his breakfast, teased by his adorable wife, then the water supply cut off; and now he was developing a pain in his wallet.

'OK, then, but two conditions,' he said.

'Oh, yes.'

'Firstly, that we do justice to my breakfast, with due deference to the amount of time and loving care spent in preparing it.'

'Agreed,' said Carol, 'and second?'

'That we nip over to Polperro for lunch in The Smugglers' Arms.'

5

'It's a deal,' said Carol and they sealed it with a hug and a kiss before tucking into Jim's culinary offerings with a vengeance.

Jim had escaped the Looe shops without too much financial damage being inflicted, for which he was grateful but, anyway, he would not have let it worry him unduly as he strolled down the narrow street towards the centre of Polperro blissfully hand in hand with Carol. One of the things they loved about the place was the almost traffic-free environment. They could have taken one of the horse-drawn carriages but it was a beautifully sunny and pleasantly warm late morning and they preferred the gentle walk after leaving the car in the obligatory car park. On the way down they passed a newsagents and *The Western Press* billboard caught Jim's eye:

WATER SHORTAGE CRISIS NEARS

Jim mentioned it to Carol.
'There, that's why you didn't get your shower this morning.'
'Fine,' said Carol, playing along with Jim's oversimplified linkage of the two events. 'Of course,' she continued 'you know what that means, don't you?'
'What, darling?'
'It means that we shall have no option but to shower together tonight, water permitting, to conserve resources, of course.'
'Mmm …,' approved Jim. 'Rain, rain, stay away. Come again another day,' he sang quietly but gleefully as they wandered off hand in swinging hand in the direction of the narrow alleys around the harbour.
The stream that emptied into the harbour had all but dried up. No one could remember it at such a low ebb.

It had been a relaxing day for Jim and Carol, aided and abetted by the slow pace that prevails in this part of Cornwall in advance of the main season. After the leisurely pub lunch that Jim had light-heartedly demanded from Carol, they walked up the path to the cliff top where magnificent views of Polperro were laid out below them at every twist and turn. It had been another warm and cloudless day and on the return journey to the car park this time they felt the need to avail themselves of the equine transport. They completed the afternoon with a visit to nearby Fowey, courtesy of the car ferry, to avoid the long drive round the inlet.

When they got back to the cottage they slumped into the deep armchairs, tired but exhilarated and, above all, content. They debated the options for the evening. A meal at The Jubilee Inn was tempting but they decided to leave that until the following night, which was due to be their last before returning home. Instead, Carol cajoled Jim into making the short trip to the local store for two steaks and a bottle of claret. He just made it before the small but always excellent butchery section closed down for the day. Carol had the remaining ingredients for the meal already and it would nicely use up most of their remaining fresh produce. She hated waste. It went back to her childhood. Her parents, whilst not poverty-stricken, had always had to be careful. At school, whenever they studied the harsh realities of life in the less prosperous parts of the planet, Carol always used to regard the waste and destruction of perfectly good food as nothing less than obscene. In her brief flirtation with politics in her mid-teens she constantly denounced the indefensible European Community food mountains at all her local party meetings. Jim must have had sympathy with these views because he never left a morsel on his plate; or was it simply that she was such a good cook, which she undoubtedly was?

It seemed no time at all before Jim was back, mission successfully accomplished, with a copy of the local paper also tucked under his arm. Its lead story betrayed another doleful message about the continuing drought and the ever-dwindling water supplies. Jim made a mental note that when he got back home he would speak to his pal at the Met Office.

After completely devouring the excellent meal, Jim and Carol settled back to finish off the wine. It had been a perfect day in perfect company. Yet it was still not late and their minds were coming round to the same conclusion about how to round it off perfectly.

'Ready for that shower yet, darling?' ventured Jim.

'I thought you'd never ask,' replied Carol with an almost nervous edge of anticipation to her voice. She walked over to Jim and began to undo the top button of his trousers. It was a bit tight, no doubt as a result of the evening's consumption and her slender, delicate fingers had a little difficulty. That achieved, however, she then proceeded slowly to lower the zip. Then, with just a little push the cotton trousers dropped to the floor. Jim eased out of his shoes and, his sense of excitement by now considerably heightened, stepped out of the trousers. Before he could make a move to return the compliment Carol was already pulling her T-shirt up over her head, to be followed almost in the same movement by release of the bra that held her beautifully shaped breasts. As always, Jim could only gaze in wonder at the smooth sensuous quivering objects of desire as he slowly divested himself of his own shirt. His only remaining garment was scarcely able to conceal his almost uncontrollable throbbing. Carol by now had reduced to her briefs but teasingly admonished Jim as he moved towards her.

'Shower first, darling. Remember?' she said and before Jim could grab her she was scampering up the staircase. Jim followed on behind just within arm's length, as Carol discovered when she felt his hand slip past the elasticated top of her briefs. With knickers almost down to her knees she stumbled to the top of the stairs and got free into the bedroom with Jim in hot pursuit.

'Now steady on, darling,' she cautioned. 'Patience is a virtue, you know.' She went into the bathroom and turned the shower knob. Nothing came. She turned again but there was no water to be had. This was becoming ridiculous, not to mention frustrating. Carol had a thing about cleanliness. She was more than willing to yield up her body to the man she loved so deeply, every nook and cranny of it, and in all manner of contortions and forms, so long as it was mutually agreeable, but she had to be clean and sweet-smelling. Without that it distinctly affected her enjoyment and commitment, and no more so than in these hot, sweaty days. Jim knew this and, sensing disappointment ahead, he fiddled with the shower controls himself, to no avail. From neither shower nor sink taps could a drop of water be gleaned. Water was something that was always taken for granted. What was going wrong? Was it just a local problem? What was being done about it? Was this the crisis reported on the billboards? The whole business was becoming increasingly annoying.

Carol, meanwhile, had slipped away downstairs and when Jim, still in his state of undress, came down to join her, she was almost fully clothed again.

'Come on,' she said, 'we'll pop over to Hope Cottage and see if they're having the same problem. I fancy a bit of mild night air, anyway,' she added, 'and by the time we get back you can bet your life that the supply will be back on. We could even call in at The Jubilee for a nightcap if you're up to walking a bit further.'

Jim dressed with disappointment but did not find Carol's suggestions totally without merit. He knew, in any case, that they would have no pressing reasons for rising early in the morning or, indeed, all day for that matter. There would be plenty of opportunity to satisfy his temporarily subdued libido. This business of the water shortage was beginning to niggle him, though. It was, after all, almost the twenty-first century. The privatized water companies were swimming in pools of profit, if not water. There could be no excuses.

It was not a long drive home on the Saturday. Mostly by motorway, the greater volume of traffic was on the opposite carriageway, thundering down to the South West in ever larger numbers as the calendar progressed deeper into summer. Not even the perpetual road-widening works could stem the constant flow. Carol was at the wheel. She enjoyed motorway driving more than the twisty-turny roads that she preferred to leave to Jim. He could admire the scenery instead, except that the English landscape nowadays seemed to lack the beauty of days gone by. Or was he just getting older and nostalgic? First it was the rape seed turning England's green and pleasant land into great swathes of swaying yellow and now even the remaining verdant bits did not have the same lush quality that they used to have. Increasingly, in the more populated areas, an arid landscape was becoming evident, facilitated, no doubt, by the hosepipe bans now becoming more widespread and backed by stiffer penalties for breaches. Still, it was a beautiful day with a cloudless blue sky and he was in the company of the woman he loved. He was relaxed after a wonderful week. What was there to worry about other than a return to work in two days' time?

Bill Gittings had known Jim Webb as a near neighbour and friend for about six years. They had struck up an almost instant rapport when they first met and they found that they had a lot in common. They were about the same age with a similar outlook on life. They played golf together at the local course, with handicaps that were not too dissimilar. They both had the immense good fortune to be married to highly attractive and vibrant wives and they too got on like the proverbial house on fire. They even had jobs not totally unconnected, Bill being employed at the regional Met Office where he had been in one capacity or another for twenty years and Jim being an insurance claims investigator. Jim often joked that he had to deal with the mess caused by Bill's bad weather. The joke was wearing a bit thin this year, though, since so far it had been a year notable for the dearth of large-scale weather-related claims. There had been no hurricanes, gales, floods or heavy snowfalls, although a couple of long periods of heavy frosts early in the year had spawned a spate of burst pipe claims. It would be later when the weather was expected to exact its revenge, through a surge in subsidence claims as a result of the long dry spell. This would not involve Jim too much, though; firstly, because the bulk of the problem would be in the clay belts of mainly south east Britain and, secondly, because Jim invariably had to give way to more expert investigators in that field.

'There we are then,' said Bill, returning from the bar with two pints of Theakstons Best. More often than not they would have a drink in the clubhouse after their midweek nine holes but now and again they felt the need for a change of scenery, especially now that The Crown had Theakstons on draught and was only a short diversion off the road back to Lichworth.

'Cheers!' said Jim.

'All the best,' responded Bill. 'So you had a good holiday then.'

'Fabulous, Bill. It gets better every time we go down there. Carol and I love it. It's perfect. Away from it all, but not too far away, if you see what I mean.'

'Mandy and I really must try it sometime.'

'You'll be too late now for the summer. There are only six cottages in the hamlet and they get booked up months in advance, usually with repeat bookings. Why don't you try for an autumn or winter break? Get the old log fire going. Very cosy. You can't beat it.'

'We might just do that,' mused Bill.

'Only slight problem we had this year was the water supply. Kept cutting off. There seemed to be a general problem in the area, but then I suppose that's Cornwall for you at this time of year. In a way it adds to the peculiarity of the place, but you'd think they would have got it sorted out by now, wouldn't you? Still, you'll know all about that, Bill. Just you make sure you get the reservoirs topped up before you go and then order yourself a week of warm sunshine.'

'If only it were that simple, Jim. It's like you asking your policyholders not to have any accidents for a week so that you can have a week off.'

'Chance would be a fine thing,' responded Jim, knocking back a fair portion of his best bitter.

'But seriously, though,' said Bill, 'there is a real problem developing, and not just in Cornwall. Believe me, you're going to see some serious repercussions soon if something isn't done. There's no sign of the drought ending and things are going to get much worse before they get better.'

11

'So it is a drought then?' asked Jim. 'Officially I mean.'

'Drought is one of those emotive words that conjures up fear and dread,' answered Bill. 'In fact, there are several definitions of it. When I started it was a scientifically based term, but I won't bore you with the details.'

'No, please do, if you know what I mean, and if you don't mind talking shop. It's a subject that is beginning to interest me. But hang on,' added Jim, 'do you fancy a top-up first?'

'Sounds like a good idea,' enthused Bill. They usually limited themselves to a pint and a half, especially with it being Theakstons. They valued their driving licences, particularly Jim, for whom it was crucial to his job. Jim returned swiftly with two halves and Bill resumed.

'The definition of drought or, to be more precise, the term is "absolute drought," was first given in 1887. It meant a period of at least fifteen consecutive days without rain, or technically "less than nought point two millimetres of precipitation". The present drought exceeded that the Monday before last and there is no end in sight over the next week.'

'But fifteen days doesn't seem very long,' responded Jim, 'when you think of the connotations of the word drought, not to mention all the rain we must get at other times to make up for it. Why worry unduly?'

'Well, you're right up to a point,' agreed Bill, 'but it's no good looking at drought periods in isolation. Climatologists used to use other measures as well.'

'Now don't get too technical for me,' joked Jim.

'Dry spells they call them. Now that's not too difficult for you to understand, Jim.'

'And no doubt you had a definition for them as well.'

'Certainly did: fifteen consecutive days with no more than one millimetre of precipitation.'

'So what is all this leading to?' asked Jim.

'Simply that you have to take a long-term view. A drought needs putting in the context of dry spell frequency over a period and we're not just talking summers. It can happen in winter too. And you need to look at the trend over several years.' Bill sipped his beer and then continued. 'Of course, the situation is further complicated by wide regional variations. Then again, if you are talking about storage of water that's a whole new ball game. There's evaporation and run-off rate to consider, for a start, and they can be significantly different according to the time of year. Then you need to consider the type of rain...'

'Now hang on, Bill, just a minute. This sounds like the British Rail wrong type of snow scenario all over again.'

'Well, it could be cyclonic, convective or orographic. Honest!'

'OK, Bill, now just keep it simple. How long does a drought or series of dry spells, or however you want to define it, have to last before we run out of water?'

'It all depends,' said Bill thoughtfully, after first downing a fair proportion of his remaining beer.

'On what?' prompted Jim.

'Depends what you mean by run out and at what location you are talking about. The amount of usage also comes into the equation, including conservation measures.' There was a brief pause and then Bill added more quietly, 'I'll tell you something though, Jim. There were some top-level discussions going on at our place today with the regional water company. It looks as if they're about to apply for some stringent use restrictions, cutting off the supply at certain times, or standpipes, something like that. In fact, our feeling is that they are already a bit late. There may have been some complacency.'

'But how and why?' asked Jim. 'Surely these things are monitored. You know, the number of days' supply left. How much is in the reservoirs, and so on.'

'Well, yes and, of course, supposedly by a body that is totally independent. But you still have to rely on the cooperation and actions of the water companies and quite frankly, Jim, profit is king. It's all about meters, increasing demand, pushing up dividends and share price nowadays. Water is a commodity. They might as well be selling baked beans. That's why capital investment's never been enough. And as far as the long-dreamed of National Grid is concerned, taking water from where it falls to where it's needed, that's as far away as ever. After all, everybody knows that we'll never run out of water, don't they? The minute you start panicking and appointing Ministers for Drought, it pisses it down, if you'll pardon my French. No one believes that a country like ours, surrounded by water, on a planet which is seventy-five per cent water, can possibly run out, that is until the stand-pipes go up and the water wagons go out. And as for the monitoring, well that's another story. Have you got another hour, Jim?'

'Did I touch a raw nerve by any chance?' asked Jim. 'Bill, I promised Carol I wouldn't be late tonight. Do you fancy a game at the weekend?'

'Sorry, Jim, I can't this weekend. We're going up to my mum and dad's on Friday night and won't be back until late on Sunday. How about next Wednesday again?'

'You're on. In fact, any chance of Wednesday afternoon off? Maybe we could fit in eighteen holes.'

'I'll work on it' said Bill. 'I'll give you a ring.'

They made their way out through the main entrance and as they walked towards their respective vehicles Jim couldn't help but cast a glance towards the canal that ran alongside the car park. The water level was as low as he could remember it.

'Looks as though someone's pulled the plug,' he called across to Bill.

'Yeah, and to make matters worse, there's nothing in the tap to fill it up with. See you.'

'Have another drink, Carol,' said Mandy. 'I'm driving tonight, remember.' They often took the opportunity to go out for an hour or two when their husbands were in golfing mode. If they were to be golf widows they would make the best of it. They took it in turns to be the driver and one of them limited alcohol consumption accordingly.

'Go on then, Mand, if you insist,' responded Carol, using an abbreviated name that emphasized their friendship. They had had a good old chinwag about Carol's holiday and Mandy had brought Carol up to date on the latest gossip. Apparently there had been an amusing incident at Mandy's next door neighbours' house a few nights before. Steve and Karen, a young and somewhat immature couple, had had another in a series of flaming rows. This time it ended, much to the delight of Mandy and those other neighbours not averse to parting their curtains, with Steve battering on the door shouting, 'Let me in, let me in,' attired only in the briefest of underwear. When his remonstrations brought no response and when alternative entry via a locked garden gate failed, he had no option but to clamber over the garden fence. His embarrassment was complete when a protruding nail snagged his only item of clothing, catching it on the fence whilst he vaulted over and into the garden. He then made for an unlocked rear door, a forlorn and slightly ridiculous looking figure, stripped of credibility as well as clothing.

'What a scream,' exclaimed Carol. 'How is he ever going to show his face again?'

'I don't suppose it's his face that he is worried about,' laughed Mandy. 'Still, it won't bother me. I've seen it all before. In my job you take men's private parts for granted. Most men look pretty ridiculous without clothes, don't you think?' Mandy was a nurse and Carol envied her for that. She had always wanted to go into the profession herself but never did for one reason or another. It seemed such a worthwhile job and even the pay had improved recently. Instead, she had enjoyed, if that were the right expression, a series of office jobs, culminating in her present position at Gumblatt Spratt and Philips, solicitors of utmost repute.

'Mind you,' continued Mandy, 'I must say that Steve was one of the better specimens I have seen recently. And how fortunate that I just happened to have the camcorder charged up and handy. You must come round one night this week and watch the video.' The story ended in a fit of giggles. Before the evening was out Carol had fixed up a time for a viewing, but not that night. She had promised Jim that she would be home at a reasonable hour.

*　　*　　*

As they came round the corner into The Close with Mandy at the wheel, Carol got a shock. There was a police car parked outside the house and her heart went into her mouth. Her first thoughts were that something had happened to Jim, a car crash perhaps. This fear was quickly relieved when she noticed almost immediately that his car was not only in the drive but also seemed to be intact. A burglary perhaps? This was always a fear with the both of them out at work. Mandy shared her concern. They would find out soon enough.

Jim had heard Mandy's car pull into the drive and was at the front door, a policeman and woman behind him in the hall, just as Carol approached it. He looked grim and this confirmed Carol's anticipation of bad news.

'What is it, Jim?' she asked, but Jim was silent.

'I'll go now,' said Mandy. 'I'll ring you later.'

'No, please. what am I thinking of? Come on in for a few minutes,' said Carol.

'Come and sit down, love,' said Jim. 'It's bad news I'm afraid.'

'It's Dad, isn't it? Something's happened to Dad. Tell me, Jim.'

'Dad was involved in a car crash late this afternoon,' said Jim quietly, as he faced Carol, holding her gently by the arms. Carol looked him in the eyes seeking reassurance and a glimmer of hope.

'How bad is he?' she asked.

'I'm afraid he's died, sweetheart.' They collapsed in a tearful embrace. Mandy moved across to provide another comforting arm. After a few moments Jim looked up at the two police officers and nodded. They took their cue and left quietly. They were only young and they hated these next of kin jobs. They had stood quietly in the background out of respect but it was time now for them to leave. Jim had been informed of all the details and he would tell Carol when the time was right, but not just then. She was more in need of his physical support.

16

'I'll put the kettle on,' said Mandy after a short while, aware that no one was really listening but conscious of the need to leave Jim and Carol alone for a few moments.

Carol took the death of her father badly. She coped, mainly through Jim's unerring sympathy and support. Friends and family rallied round too, particularly after Jim had returned to work, two days after the funeral. She had been so close to her Dad: in some ways she had been like the son he had never had, and closer than her sister, Anne. It was the manner of his death, too, that was grievous. George Martin had been driving home that early evening from the supermarket, *en route* to his small bungalow not that many miles up the road from Lichworth, in the small village of Needlewood. He had lived there alone since his wife Elizabeth had died seven years earlier, having succumbed finally to the effects of multiple sclerosis. But he had been comfortable, mobile, in receipt of a good company pension and still looking forward to many more years of retirement in the knowledge that his two daughters, families and friends were all close at hand. A pall of black smoke had been visible from a long way off but he was drawn to it because that was the direction in which he needed to head. About half a mile from the village the country lane develops a series of twists, turns and undulations, mirroring the contours of the land as it wends its way through a heavily wooded area. It was to be part of the new national forest, begun earlier in the decade, that would eventually see an area of hundreds of square miles designated as woodland, as indeed much of this area had been in the Middle Ages. George loved the woods and had spent many happy hours there with Elizabeth and the girls, when they were younger. They used to go for picnics, or sometimes to escape the heat of a summer's day. Woodland had an atmosphere and a biosphere, as daughter Anne's eldest daughter called it, that was uniquely natural. But, like many of nature's wonders, there were forces lurking within that were capable of great menace and disaster. The long dry spell had left them like a tinder box, just waiting for ignition.

No one knew how the fire started, whether by a carelessly discarded cigarette or the combination of a strong sun on a piece of broken glass or whatever. George knew that he was heading towards the smoke but he was in the part of the road where the forward view was obscured, and direction became confused by the bends. He had reduced his speed but was still taken aback by the wall of thick black smoke that hit him as he rounded the blind bend. The woods reached out over the road at that point as branches from each side shook hands to form a leafy tunnel. George knew nothing about the huge burning ember that smashed through the windscreen and rendered him unconscious. The car, unable to cope with the loss of control and the adverse camber, careered off through a small gap and into the burning trees, to be enveloped by a roaring furnace. It flipped onto its side and when it slid and then thudded to an eventual stop a deluge of flaming branches fell onto it. It was a bonfire that George would not emerge from and everyone had prayed that he had not regained consciousness before finally succumbing to the fiery tomb. It was a horrid end and a cruel waste of a good man who still had much to contribute in his later years. Carol would miss him dreadfully. Although she had a happy life and a wonderful husband, she had lost the man who had guided her through many of life's crises. With her mother and her father now both gone she felt a part of her had died. Jim had tried to convince her that a part of them would always be within her, but he knew that it would take time for her to appreciate this.

It was no consolation to either of them that Carol's father's death was not an isolated occurrence. Others had suffered in various parts of the country from raging fires brought about by the parched conditions. Devastation could spread so quickly and firefighters faced a never-ending and impossible task.

'How's Carol?' asked Bill.

'A lot better,' answered Jim closing the car boot and then transferring his fully-laden golf bag onto the trolley.

'Mandy thought that she was a bit more like her normal self when she saw her yesterday,' said Bill.

'Thanks for all that you and Mandy have done, Bill.'

'We've not done much really. I think that with these things it's time that is the healer.'

'I'm sure you're right,' said Jim, 'but thanks for being there. Now come on. Let's go and smash a few golf balls.'

Carol had insisted that Jim gave Bill a call. It was nearly two weeks since Dad had died and she knew that Jim was making sacrifices to be supportive. Jim took it as a sign that Carol was beginning to come to terms with her father's death.

They gave the practice ground a miss, preferring to go straight to the first tee whilst it was vacant. Jim's swing was a bit rusty and his direction was somewhat wayward but he surprised himself with the distance he got from his first drive. It was Bill's turn on the tee, and he walloped his Titleist straight and true and seemingly for many a mile at this longish opening par four.

'Great shot,' said Jim. 'That must be one of the longest you've ever hit at the first.'

'I think it's the course that's playing shorter and shorter,' said Bill, modestly, picking up his tee and then returning his driver to the bag. They set off after their balls, towing their carts behind them. 'I mean,' continued Bill, 'just look at how brown and bare it is, and hard as concrete.'

'I thought it was dry last time we played,' said Jim, 'but it seems an awful lot worse.'

'Talk in the clubhouse last week was that this is the worst anyone can remember; worse even than seventy-six or ninety-five for so early in the summer. The committee are worried about how bad it will get and how long it will take to recover.'

'Were you able to reassure them from your inside knowledge?' asked Jim.

'On the first point, it could get very bad. There is no end of the drought in sight and there are bound to be further use restrictions. On the second point, how long will it take to recover? Well, who knows? If previous experience is anything to go by we'll have a few weeks of heavy downpours and things will recover fairly quickly.'

'Nature does seem to have a balancing mechanism, doesn't it?' asked Jim.

'Does it?' replied Bill as Jim veered off towards his ball. They joined up again a short time later on the green, Bill having pitched on comfortably with an eight iron and Jim having had two further strikes and still being further from the hole.

'I'll hold the flag for you,' said Bill, as Jim parked his cart between the green and the second tee. They putted out: a five for Jim and a par four for Bill, who cursed his putter as they made their way to the tee.

'So what were you implying back there?' Jim picked up their conversation about the drought where they had left off. 'That Mother Nature isn't in equilibrium? That this dry spell won't end with the usual deluge from the heavens? I thought you said that was what usually happened.'

'My job has taught me two things about Mother Nature,' responded Bill. 'Firstly, that over a given period there does tend to be a balance and whilst we never stop grumbling about the weather in this country – too wet, too dry, too hot, too windy, etc. – nature is actually quite fair with us. We have an equable climate.'

'And secondly?' asked Jim.

'Never, ever underestimate the forces of nature. Never take anything for granted. Never assume that you can always forecast the future from the records of the past. In short, respect her, because you can never be quite sure what she is going to do. Now keep quiet whilst I negotiate this tee shot,' added Bill, half-jokingly. 'You know what a balls-up I usually make of this hole.' The second was a short part three, but with a postage stamp of a green which was at a lower level than the tee, and it was surrounded by hazards. It was not Bill's favourite hole. The only consolation was that today the brook in front of the green had dried up, another victim of the drought. True to form, though, he landed in it and, even though it was waterless, he dropped a shot escaping its

20

clutches. Jim parred the hole to even up the contest, for a contest it always was, though indubitably played in good spirit.

Today, though, as they accompanied each other down the fairways from tees to greens, not always taking the same line, their talk amidst the brown and increasingly barren surroundings kept on returning to the drought. Jim had developed an interest in it extending beyond just normal curiosity. It had started as a holiday inconvenience. Then there was the death of Carol's father, a tragic accident, but arising from the freak weather. It was a topic that dominated conversations as concern rose about the effects on everyday life: daily water supplies that everyone took for granted, the elderly, the sick, the effect on industry and people's livelihoods and, not least, the effect on the environment. He knew that with Bill he could tap in, as it were, to the latest and most accurate professional opinion and forecast. Of course, the summer of 95 was still fairly fresh in people's minds, the dried-up reservoirs and rivers and so on. Bill still reckoned that 76 was worse, or was that partly nostalgia? Bill and those at the Met Office still regarded it as the year of the 'Great Drought'. By the end of July that year reservoir capacity in Devon and Cornwall was below a quarter, the Thames had dried up for the first nine miles from its source, and standpipes were being made ready. In June, the death rate had been as high as in a harsh winter. To make matters worse, the record-breaking summer came after another exceptionally dry year in 75 and the combination was said to be as rare as one in two thousand years. But it ended with the wettest September and October ever recorded, so no doubt the same would happen this year and everyone would wonder what all the fuss was about, just as in 95, just three short years ago, when the land seemed to turn from brown to green in about 48 hours, and in no time at all people were grumbling about the cold wet weather again.

And yet, Jim got the impression that Bill was unconvinced. They paused for a while after holing out at the long par five fifth.

'So is this worse than 76 then, Bill?' said Jim as the two of them parked themselves on what used to be a grassy hump behind the green.

'No doubt about it,' said Bill, 'and worse than 95, too. Over fifty days without rain already in parts of the south and east, and much earlier in the summer than ever before. And have you noticed how it's started getting hotter in the last few days?'

'You're telling me,' said Jim, wiping his brow with his handkerchief.

'Now do you want the bad news?' asked Bill. Jim turned his head to face him. 'It's going to get much, much hotter according to our latest forecast.'

'Yes, I read the forecast in the paper this morning,' said Jim.

'No, I mean the long-range forecast; you know, the one we stopped publishing years ago because it wasn't accurate enough.'

'So is it more accurate now then?' asked Jim.

'We have a computer enhancement that we've been refining for the last few months,' replied Bill, 'and it seems to be working very well. We're still not ready to go public on it yet. The boys from Bracknell are being a bit cautious. But from what I can gather it's a major breakthrough. What's more, I've seen the projection for next month.'

'And?' enquired Jim.

'Hot! It's forecasting the 100 degree Fahrenheit mark will be beaten. No rain, anywhere, apart from maybe the Orkneys and Shetlands.'

'I can see why they don't want to broadcast it,' said Jim. 'One botch of that magnitude and it's back to the drawing board.'

Jim had the honour at the sixth and he went to tee-up. Their paths diverged quite a lot over the next few holes. It was behind the ninth green that they allowed themselves the next break and another little chat. They shared a canned drink in a vain attempt to quench the thirst engendered by the hot, still early evening. After a brief compliment to Bill about his immaculate pitch at the last that ringed the hole, Jim's conversation returned to the familiar topic.

'So let's take stock about this drought then, Bill,' he said, in an almost business-like fashion. 'It's started earlier in the year than the previous great summer droughts.'

'Correct, if you mean "absolute drought",' agreed Bill.

'Second, it's part of a longer dry spell that again goes back for as long as any previous period.'

'Right.'

'And this "absolute drought", as you call it, that has also lasted as long as any on record.'

'Not quite, except in one or two places, but rapidly approaching a record.'

'With all the forecasts pointing to no change whatsoever.'

'Correct,' said Bill.

'So, assuming that the forecasts are correct, where will that leave us?' asked Jim.

'In uncharted waters,' replied Bill, 'or not, as the case may be,' he added, subconsciously reviewing his choice of phrase.

'So what is anybody doing about it?' asked Jim.

'Oh, the usual things. Use restrictions. Pleas for conservation. Rationing. Drought orders. Eventual political intervention. The privatization issue will be reopened. The National Grid idea will be resurrected. Desalination plants will get talked about again. And amidst all the talk everyone will expect the heavens to open.'

'Meanwhile,' said Jim, 'people will be inconvenienced, some will be impoverished, and some will even die.'

'More than likely,' agreed Bill. 'It all depends on what we find in those uncharted waters. Just make sure that you've got a life belt with you, that's all.'

'What do you mean?' enquired Jim.

'There could be panic, you know. Water rationing, food hoarding and sky-high prices for what food there is on the supermarket shelves.'

'Surely it couldn't get that bad, Bill. Not in this day and age with the European Union, and international transportation and support systems.'

'Don't you believe it. If we were to reach a situation where the fresh food supply dried up, it wouldn't take long to run down what was held in store. Then the imports would start to get sucked up by the hoarders and the wealthy. And don't assume that there would be an increasing and never-ending flow of imports. Food production in The States, the world's breadbasket, is well down this year, again due to a long series of dry years, not to mention their pollution problems. In Europe, food surpluses are a thing of the past after the measures to reduce capacity. What's more, the drought is getting a grip on the continent too. So where would you look for emergency supplies? Africa? Asia? They haven't got enough to feed themselves. Australia? They haven't recovered from their record drought last year. Need I go on?'

'Maybe we'd just have to change our diets,' suggested Jim.

'What to?' asked Bill. 'Fish stocks are severely depleted. Rice production is well down. No one will eat beef after the latest health scares. Our cows are not producing milk. Need I go on? Are you worried enough yet?'

'Bill, I'm frightened to death.'

They set off on the back nine. The thought had occurred to Jim that if the worst predictions did come true, one of the victims could be his beloved golf. It was hardly likely that the watering of sports grounds would receive any kind of priority. They might as well enjoy it whilst they could and Jim launched a huge straight drive down the middle of the tenth fairway and marched off with Bill, for once heading in the same direction.

'Did you win, darling?' asked Carol as Jim came through the already open door.

'Yes, by two strokes surprisingly, despite a poor start. Have you had a nice day?'

'Yeah, fine. Relaxing.'

'Did you call round at Mandy's?'

'No, I'd forgotten that she's on the late shift this week. So I just had a quiet afternoon sat out in the garden with this old Desmond Bagley,' she nodded in the direction of the paperback by the armchair, 'then I had a pizza before settling down in front of the telly. Would you like me to rustle you up something to eat?'

'No, stay where you are. I'll pop something in the microwave. Shall I make you a drink while I'm at it?' asked Jim.

'A coffee would be nice,' answered Carol.

It was not long before Jim was back with a tray so that he could eat informally, alongside Carol. The tray held two coffees and a plate containing a rather bland-looking ready meal of some sort which struggled, and failed, to fill the whole area of the plate. Still, it was functional, thought Jim and, above all quick, and it was not often that Carol left him to fend for himself.

Carol had the television on in the background: that is to say in picture only, having muted the sound by remote control. This was partly out of deference to Jim, but coincided also with the end of the programme that she had been watching. Jim noticed the familiar introduction of the national news bulletin.

'Turn it up if you like, love,' said Jim, 'let's see what's been happening in the world.' Carol looked around for the remote, found it and hit the mute button again, having missed only the opening headlines. Jim was concentrating on his meal, but looked up when the volume came on.

Together, the first they both heard in the familiar tones of the male newsreader was, 'Good evening. Seven people have died so far as a series of fires rage out of control in various parts of the country. Hundreds of square miles of woodland, heath and moorland are ablaze and weathermen say that worse could be to come as the drought intensifies. The army has been called out again in several areas to help with fire-fighting. There have been calls for all public woodland amenity areas to be closed in view of tinderbox conditions.' The screen cut to a map of the whole country with several areas, mainly in the Midlands and South, highlighted by captions and with the newsreader continuing, 'In Wales, there was tragedy on the roads as smoke enveloped motorists and was thought to be responsible for three deaths.' The screen cut to pictures of smashed and burnt-out cars. The bulletin continued with further footage of fire-fighting from different locations.

25

'You don't have to watch this, darling. Turn it off,' said Jim. He had half expected Carol to kill both sound and pictures and was kicking himself for wanting to watch it in the first place.

'No Jim. It's all right. I have to come to terms with what happened to Dad,' said Carol. 'I can't go through life avoiding new bulletins or pretending that fire doesn't exist. I just wish that other people weren't having to suffer in the same way that Dad did.'

They returned their attention to the screen. There was an interview with a politician and someone from the Forestry Commission.

That wrapped up the lead story, but the newsreader promised, 'Later in this bulletin, we'll be looking at the wider implications of the drought and asking the weathermen when it will end. But first, tonight's other stories...'

Jim told Carol what Bill had been saying earlier about how serious the drought was getting. Carol wondered if it would affect her sister Anne and family's boating holiday next month. Jim reckoned not, because he knew that the Norfolk Broads were partly tidal and would not be affected as badly as rivers and canals.

Later, their attention turned back to the television. There was an interview with one of the top weathermen from Bracknell. Jim remarked that Bill probably knew him and he would try to remember his name for the next time they met. The interviewer began by asking how bad this drought was in the context of others.

'Well, there are local variations, as always,' came the response, 'but generally speaking, it is not yet a record-breaker, not quite. In most places, 1976 or 90 or 95 are likely to have been worse in terms of the length of time without rain. What is different, however, is that this is the earliest time of any year to have reached this stage of drought. Of course, that does not necessarily mean that it will continue throughout the summer. We could still end up with a summer of average, or even above average, rainfall. It's still too early to say.'

26

'What are you forecasting for the rest of the summer?' enquired the interviewer.

'Well, we don't forecast that far ahead, as you know,' replied the expert, knowing full well that they had one, but that it was definitely not for public consumption, not yet anyhow. 'What we can predict,' he continued, 'is that very little change is expected in the next week, other than that temperatures will continue to climb slowly. But definitely no sign of rain yet.'

'And what's causing the drought?' came the next question, again with refreshing brevity.

The man from Bracknell was tempted to give the obvious answer, 'No bloody rain.' On reflection, he opted for a more considered response:

'Well, if you mean, where are the rain clouds, then the culprit has to be our old friend here.' He pointed at the large-scale weather map behind him, covering the North Atlantic and most of Europe, and he identified in particular a part of the map, most of it in actuality, that was notable for the absence of lines, or isobars. 'This anti-cyclone has been over us or near us, in one shape or form, for several weeks now. High pressure shows no sign of diminishing. This is having the effect of diverting the westerly winds that bring most of our rain.'

'Is anybody else suffering the same as we are?'

'Yes, certainly. The Low Countries and parts of France are well down on their usual rainfall. In fact, one feature of this high pressure system is not just how it is maintaining its position, but how it is now expanding and growing in strength, as it were. Those viewers with barometers will be aware of readings nearly off the scale. We are approaching record levels and still rising.'

'So the message is then that there is no immediate prospect of an end to the drought and we need to conserve the stocks that we have?'

'Yes. It obviously makes sense to use water sparingly wherever possible. Certainly, if the drought continues our farmers will be among the first to be seriously affected. Another thing to bear in mind is that temperatures are now rising further and this will not only increase usage of water further, but it will also cause the evaporation of lying water. In other words, stocks will reduce at a faster rate.'

Jim was an investigator by profession, and suspicious by nature. He relied a lot on gut feeling. He was uncomfortable about this whole business of the drought, not physically, but in terms of what might develop and the apparent complacency and inaction prevailing. Of course there were the usual platitudes from all concerned, not least the government, that the situation was under control.But he likened his feelings to a sort of animalistic premonition of an impending crisis. He decided he would like to be actively involved rather than sit back and await the inevitable.

*   *   *

As predicted, the drought continued over the following week. Temperatures soared to the low thirties Celsius. No rain fell anywhere in the country, nor indeed anywhere in Western or Central Europe. High pressure continued to dominate the weather map and readings were nearing record levels. In parts of Lincolnshire and Essex there had now been 60 days without rain. Forest fires raged in Staffordshire and parts of Wales. Peat bogs dried up in The Pennines. Hosepipe and sprinkler bans were now widespread. Many stretches of canals in the Midlands were now closed. Depletion of reservoir stocks continued and accelerated as forecast. The whole topic was now at the very top of the political agenda.

Prime Minister John Marner had shown himself to be a worthy and respected leader of party and country during his tenure of office. His plainness and ordinary background had enhanced his appeal to the electorate, especially in his earlier years in control, though he seldom got credit for the political craft and astuteness that he undoubtedly possessed. He had that knack of all successful politicians of being able to stay one step ahead of the game, able to identify and react quickly to the burning issues of the day. A tall, bespectacled man, usually reserved in both speech and dress, nonetheless he projected a solid, respectable and caring image. But no politician of such long-standing could isolate himself from the scheming, image-making and self-preservation that was endemic to the political profession. His government was in the second half of its current term with the next election not too far away. It was necessary now more than ever to keep the lid on problems that had the potential to hamper re-election. Foresight and forward-planning were needed to nip such problems in the bud. Swift and decisive action was the order of the day. John Marner adjudged that the drought dilemma would soon move into his domain and with this in mind he would raise the issue himself at the next Cabinet meeting.

It is strange the way that as the web of life becomes ever more entangled, every now and again, the past puts in an appearance. Connections long since severed and forgotten reappear in a different format. Old acquaintances turn up in unexpected circumstances and locations. These thoughts and others crossed Jim's mind when he answered an early evening knock at the door and encountered a face and expression that was instantly recognizable though he had not seen it for nearly twenty years.

'Trevor Reaney! I don't believe it. What are you doing here?'

'Christ, it is you,' responded the man called Reaney. 'I saw your name on the list but assumed that it was a coincidence. How long have you been living down here?' he asked, in the kind of accent associated with a northerner. Jim did not answer immediately. The sight of Reaney had temporarily thrown him: his mind cast back many years ago to when he used to know both him and his beautiful wife, Kate.

'I could ask the same about you,' he said at last. 'But please, come in, and what list are you on about?'

'The electoral roll, of course' said Reaney, in the same gravelly voice of old, though the Yorkshire accent did not seem quite as pronounced as Jim remembered.

Carol had come out of the kitchen to see who it was. She

saw Jim shaking hands and ushering in a tall, dark-haired man who was about Jim's age, or maybe slightly younger. She always found it difficult to compare other people's ages with Jim's since her husband was one of those fortunate enough to look younger than his years.

'I can't stay long, Jim, because I'm actually working at the moment, believe it or not, but it's a pleasure to see you again. How are you keeping?'

'Just fine, Trevor. But here, introductions are needed.' Jim gestured towards the approaching Carol. 'Trevor Reaney, this is Carol. Talk about a small world,' mused Jim.

'Pleased to meet you,' said Carol, in a friendly fashion, but still bemused as to who this stranger was.

'Trevor and I go back nearly twenty years I should think,' said Jim. 'We worked together in Bradford. Played in the same football team for years. Don't ask me what he's doing in Lichworth because I don't know, but I think we might be about to find out. Not double glazing, Trevor, surely?'

'Jim, I'm surprised at you,' came Reaney's throaty response. 'I always had you down as a public-spirited citizen, a pillar of the community, and all those other clichés. You mean to tell me that you don't know that you are talking to your next Member of Parliament?'

'My God,' exclaimed Jim. 'You mean that you're one of the candidates in this by-election in a couple of weeks' time?' Jim was almost embarrassed by his own ignorance, though perhaps it was not surprising. He had lost interest in party politics and neither was he an avid reader of the local newspaper. Nor was every lamp-post in the district festooned with placards that proclaimed the names of the combatants. Everyone had been caught unprepared by the short notice of the calling of the election. They had barely had time to bury the recently deceased former Member.

'I never realized that you were into politics, Trevor,' continued Jim. By now the three were comfortably seated in the sun-trap conservatory with ice-cold drinks. Jim's mind was still turning over old times. 'Knowing you of old, I can't believe you're the Tory candidate.'

'Correct. I am seeking to become a representative of Her Majesty's Opposition,' declared Reaney in mock formal tones, although a less formal person, with fewer airs and graces, would be difficult to find.

'Yes, but which opposition party?' asked Jim.

'Labour, of course.'

'But this is a Conservative seat,' interjected Carol. 'Do you think you've got a realistic chance?'

'Certainly. We've got a good chance. We'll capture the protest vote and we're hoping for some tactical voting from Liberals. And, of course,' said Reaney with an exaggerated tub-thumping action, 'we have the right policies.'

Reaney stayed longer than intended, before returning to his canvassing. He and Jim swapped a few anecdotes about the old days. Neither seemed to the other to have changed much. Carol listened to most of it with interest and some of it with amusement. She was not so sure that the two of them had been great friends and Jim was later to confirm this, although he seemed somewhat reticent about elaborating on the reasons. Nevertheless, they seemed pleased to see one another again and now that their paths had crossed once more they would endeavour to keep in touch on a more regular basis. Telephone numbers were swapped, along with promises to make contact soon.

'Seems a bit of a rough diamond,' reflected Carol afterwards, 'especially for a politician, or is that because he's Labour?'

'New Labour they call themselves now, darling. At least it will help to give Parliament a good cross-section of the community; if he should get in that is. I don't think he'll be famed for diplomacy or tact, though, if I know him. At the same time, I think he could give a few people a shake-up, get things done. I actually think that he could make it as an MP. He's got one other good thing going for him as well.'

'What's that?' asked Carol.

'A good woman behind him,' he said, playfully embracing Carol round the shoulders.

'So you'll be voting for him then, will you?' she asked.

31

'Oh, I don't know if I would go that far,' he chuckled.

Lichworth was not a big place, though populated enough to have three supermarkets to choose from and most, but not all, the national retailers to be found in most towns. It was a place where there was always a good chance of bumping into someone you knew. Carol had not seen Mandy for a while, which was not that unusual since Mandy's hours at the hospital were often unsociable and irregular, but they used the same supermarket and this was often an unplanned meeting place.

'Hi, Carol. Feeding the five thousand again?' joked Mandy. Carol struggled to redirect her bulging three able-wheeled trolley, the fourth wheel apparently independent of the others and totally uncooperative.

'You'd think so wouldn't you?' she answered.

'You're not the one responsible for clearing the shelves of bottled water by any chance are you?'

'No. why? I didn't know it was in such demand,' replied Carol.

'Neither did I,' said Mandy, 'but you see if you can find any in Lichworth. I've tried everywhere. There's not a drop to be had.'

'Why don't you ask this chap with the clipboard coming towards us?' suggested Carol. A good idea thought Mandy and she raised the matter with the fit-looking young chap who was probably a trainee manager.

'Sorry, madam,' came the polite reply, 'we simply can't get it from the suppliers. Apparently the French stuff has dried up all together, if you see what I mean. They can't meet the demand from their own market so it seems. As for the rest, they just can't keep up with demand.' Mandy thanked him and she and Carol carried on shopping.

'I don't know what this place is coming to,' she complained to Carol. 'Even the fresh veg shelves are bare and have you seen the prices for what there is?'

'Jim reckons that the drought will have a serious effect on food production and when the supply goes down and demand is high, up go the prices. Market forces they call it.'

'Bloody scandalous, I call it' said Mandy.

They heard the sound of shattering glass, followed soon after by raised voices. They rounded the bottom of the aisle in tandem, though Carol had to take an extra wide berth as she struggled to control her overflowing chariot of fare. As they straightened up and made their way up the soft drinks aisle they saw the young trainee manager again. This time he was trying to placate two irate and rather large female customers, whilst an even younger assistant scuttled off in a hurry. He returned seconds later armed with brush and pan and started to sweep up a large number of glass shards that were sat in a pool of liquid. With their way ahead blocked and soon tiring of what seemed a silly argument over who saw the last bottle of some soft drink or other first, Carol and Mandy doubled back and then headed towards the check-out by a different route.

'It must be the hot weather,' said Mandy. 'People seem so irritable.'

'It must be the hot weather,' thought Reaney. People seemed so apathetic. He was finding that political canvassing was a hard slog at the best of times. Those who were not apathetic were downright aggressive, particularly when the knock at the door interrupted a meal or coincided with the end of a favourite television programme or, worse still, ruined a moment of intense passion. Still, he took some encouragement from what returns they had. He was convinced that the more effort he put in, the more dividend there would be. The by-election result was by no means settled. The deceased previous Member had a strong personal vote within his respectable majority. The party committee was split over the choice of successor, eventually being leaned on by Central Office to take on the ex-member for Taverton, whom they wanted to help back into Westminster after he had lost his seat there at the last general election. He had not got off to a good start, though, mispronouncing local place names and showing a general lack of knowledge about the area. The local paper had latched onto it in that week's edition. He was coming across as smug and overconfident to the relatively small portion of the electorate with whom he had so far come into contact. Reaney knew that he was in with a chance. All he needed, he felt, was for a couple of controversial issues to go his way, one perhaps local, and maybe one national, and the whole election could then be wide open. He was already taking a keen interest in the proposed route of the new western bypass. What reactions he had got on the doorsteps were split between that and the hosepipe and sprinkler ban which could well ruin the hard work of many a keen amateur gardener. He could do with a point on mortgage rates or some bad news on inflation or unemployment to give some added momentum to his campaign. He gained some perverse satisfaction from an article in *The Mail* that morning forecasting sky-high food prices as a result of the drought. This augered well for the female vote, although time was short before polling day. Reaney was ambitious and dedicated. He was still young in political terms and he regarded the pursuit of high office as more than just a flight of fancy. Why should he not aspire to being prime minister? After all, his credentials could be no more threadbare than the present incumbent. These were the things he would tell himself when the doors slammed in his face, or the dog was let loose to chase him up the path.

* * *

It had been a successful Wednesday Cabinet meeting. John Marner was reviewing this and various other matters with his aides over a light buffet lunch. He was a naturally slim man, the sort who could eat ample quantities without apparent effect on his shape. The meeting had not thrown up any major dilemmas. At home, the economy was continuing its improving trend and with a bit of luck, his government was still on course to supply the feel-good factor in good time for the next general election, whilst, abroad, the foreign secretary reported on the increasingly serious situation in Turkey. The European scene was relatively quiet, with controversy stifled for the time being as the Germans prepared for their elections.

The topic of most interest to the prime minister was the drought. He reminded his ministers of the need to avoid the kind of cock-ups that had so marred their performance in the last few years. He would personally take an interest in overseeing their handling of this potentially crucial matter. To demonstrate his seriousness, he set in motion a number of initiatives which were aimed at monitoring the situation, supplying projections and laying down contingency plans. Most importantly, he let it be known that he would be appointing one of his ministers to coordinate matters. Firstly though, he would await reports and review at the next Cabinet meeting.

Of most immediate concern, however, were two other issues: firstly, details needed to be finalized for his flying visit to Lichworth, where he would lend support to the by-election candidate. From what he heard so far, he did not deserve such support but, nevertheless, the visit would be personally useful to him. It always did his personal image and his ratings good to be seen amongst the people and, to be fair and unlike most politicians, he wished that he could do it more often than the trappings of his high office permitted: Secondly, he was concerned that his rapidly filling diary would prevent him from seeing a sufficient quota of Test Match action. He had been looking forward to seeing Lara in action again.

Another week of scorching temperatures and sunny, calm days went by. The sensible were seeking shade wherever they could, but the hospitals, clinics and surgeries were still packed with victims of sunburn and sunstroke. Brown bodies were in abundance everywhere. Soft drinks and ice cream manufacturers could not keep up with demand.

One of the more likeable aspects of Jim's job was the opportunity it presented, quite frequently, to get out of the office to undertake claims investigations. It took him away from the paperwork and brought him into contact from time to time with some interesting people. There were only two things wrong with outside calls: firstly inevitably, the paperwork was always still waiting for him afterwards and, secondly, on days as hot and sunny as these, being stuck in a car was no pleasure; in fact, it was purgatory, especially clad in suit and tie, albeit with jacket removed and car windows and sunroof open. Roads were melting as never before. Overheated cars were commonplace and traffic jams became a nightmare to equal the Black Hole of Calcutta. At these times he longed for the air-conditioning of his office, when it was working effectively that was, not to mention the stock of ice-cold drinks from the canteen fridge.

Jim's seniority meant that it was usually the larger or more potentially serious claims that he got involved with, often in association with loss adjusters. He was more likely to be visiting commercial rather than domestic properties, but sometimes he had reason to call on the ordinary policyholder, especially if he was in the area anyway on other business.

On the day in question, he was rounding off a series of calls south and west of Birmingham with two domestic cases in one of the more exclusive commuting villages. One claim was for potential subsidence damage and though it had already been looked into by structural engineers, Jim wanted to take a look for himself whilst in the area. The other matter was a substantial theft from a big detached residence that had been unoccupied at the time, with the owner away on business.

As it turned out, his first call did not detain him long, although it might have done had it not been for the iron-willed self-discipline for which he was supposedly renowned. Whilst he could have made do with a brief visual and external inspection of the affected parts of the property, he obviously felt obliged first to check if anyone was in residence and make his presence known. He knocked on the solid front door after deducing that the doorbell was out of action or, at least to him, inaudible. There was no response. Jim looked at the plans he had in his hand and moved off in the direction of the corner of the building that was said to be most affected. Whilst he soon identified a significant crack in the rendering running up to the eaves, he really needed access to the rear of the building too, but this was fenced off. He tried the clasp on the wooden gate and with a gentle push it opened. Jim felt strangely guilty, despite being on official business. Just a quick inspection he thought, and then away. When he got to a right-angled corner of the building, a partial view of the rear garden opened up and provided him with quite an eye-opener.

The garden was picturesque, with extensive lawns giving way in the distance to a wooded area, but it was the immediate foreground that attracted Jim's riveted attention; not the elegant patio-surrounded figure-of-eight-shaped swimming pool *per se*, so much as the stunning beauty at the poolside. Blonde and bronzed, straddling a white relaxer chair fixed in the upright position, she was busy applying lotion to her outstretched arms, her firm and rounded breasts outstanding in every sense. She seemed completely nude. 'My God,' Jim thought to himself, 'what a cracker!' He was mesmerized. It was only after a few moments drinking in the view that he began to feel vulnerable, wondering what might be thought if he were caught acting like a peeping Tom. It was true that if he were younger he would probably regard this as one of the perks of the job, but, of course, he was a mature and happily married man. But Carol knew more than anyone that her husband was a full-blooded male and no one would be more surprised than her if he had not stopped to admire the ravishing, perfectly-formed female body that was currently within his sights.

As Jim was trying to decide quickly whether to just go, thereby postponing his official business, or whether to make another attempt to introduce himself, he almost unknowingly hid himself partly round the corner. He would indeed have looked suspicious now to any onlooker. From the information he had, Jim assumed that the gorgeous girl was the owner's daughter, or maybe it was a Swedish *au pair*. As he mused over the situation, she stood erect, though still straddling the extended chair and it became evident that, in fact, she was not totally naked: the briefest of triangular coverings was clinging tightly below her flat waist. Its thin side straps became invisible though, as she both turned and bent down to apply lotion to her lower left leg. Not more than twenty yards away, Jim stared admiringly from this new angle, the breasts now pendulous, the figure curved and slender. He just managed to stifle a whistle of incredulity. 'Now come on' he thought, trying to get a grip of himself. He almost had to force himself to turn away, but not before the pulsating beauty had swung the balance of her body onto the other leg, presenting Jim with a spine-tingling view of her barely-covered rear end.

Jim retraced his steps with the silence of a Wild West scout. He felt a mixture of stimulation, awe and guilt. It was the latter that gave a quickness to his step and then to his driving, to which a passing cyclist would have testified. Little could he have imagined, though, the cause of the carelessness.

By the time he was signalling to enter the driveway of his second port of call, Jim was more or less back in control and ready for the more mundane matters in hand. This time he had a pre-arranged appointment with a policyholder by the name of Ben Johnson. According to records, Ben was a free-lance journalist. His recent theft claim was well-advanced but assessors had commented on the possibility of under-insurance. Because Ben's brokers had an exceptionally important account, and this was a particularly high worth policy, Jim thought it better to check it out himself.

Mr Johnson was a youngish-looking man, probably three or four years younger than Jim, and of similar build, tall, dark-haired and quite fit-looking. He was well-tanned, though nowadays that was not difficult to attain. Despite the potential problem with his claim, he was very charming. Well-spoken, he had an easygoing accent, possibly transatlantic in origin. Jim found him easy to get on with. They discussed matters whilst sat outside at a large rectangular patio table.

Though Jim did not wish to settle the claim there and then, he was soon forming a view that here seemed an honest but busy man, given perhaps more to carelessness than deceit. Neither, it emerged from the conversation, did the underinsurance seem as large as had been thought. All in all, it was a very civilized and relaxed meeting and the business part of it was over quite quickly. Given also that his previous call had turned out to be a very brief one, Jim found himself ahead of the clock for once.

He took his time over the coffee that had kindly been served and conversation turned to other matters. As usual, the weather seemed a good ice-breaking topic.

'You look as though you've been taking advantage of the great British weather, or have you got your tan abroad, if you don't mind me asking?' remarked Jim.

'Not at all. Portugal actually,' replied the host. 'I have a villa over there.'

'Oh, whereabouts?' asked Jim.

'On the Algarve. Have you been there?'

'Yes, indeed' replied Jim. 'Carol and I, that's my wife, we have very happy memories of the Algarve. We stayed in a villa in Vilamoura just before we were married and we've been back twice since. We loved the place, although, to be honest, we think it's become overcommercialized in parts and the time-share sharks don't help, either. It's a few years now since we were there.'

'Yes, I know what you mean,' said Ben Johnson. 'Fortunately, my place is a bit off the beaten track, just up the coast from Vilamoura, and a little bit inland. It's still a delightful place out of season and, in summer, well, it's a question of knowing the right places. I like to eat out a lot. Portugal is great for that. Did you try the *cataplana* whilst you were there?' he asked.

'Yes, loved it' replied Jim, settling back in his comfortable patio chair. 'Not to mention the grilled sardine suppers. Yes, we had some happy times there. Mind you, I think the local firewater helped as well.'

'Ah, the *medronho*,' said Ben, knowingly.

'That's right. Very relaxing,' reflected Jim.

'A very relaxing place. I need that in my line of work,' added Ben.

'Forgive me, but I couldn't help noticing from our files that you are a freelance journalist. That must be a very interesting job. Whom do you write for, if you don't mind me asking?'

'Anybody and everybody, in a sense,' replied Ben. 'Obviously, after a while your name gets known, once you've had acceptances. You're right, it is an interesting job in a lot of respects but, like everyone else, I have bills to pay and villas in the Algarve don't come cheap. In fact, I bought that on the strength of some book royalties a few years ago. I'm working on ideas for another book at the moment. Meanwhile, articles in the Sunday supplements help to keep the wolf from the door. Which Sunday paper do you take, Jim?' asked Ben, now comfortable with first name terms.

'Usually just *The Times*,' answered Jim.

'You might have seen my article a few weeks ago then, in the magazine.'

'I'm not sure,' replied Jim.' Do you use a pseudonym?'

'On that occasion, no.'

'What was it about?'

'Bird migration.'

'Now that you mention it,' said Jim after brief thought, 'it does ring a bell. Although, if it's the weekend I'm thinking of, Carol and I were rather preoccupied with other matters. I don't think the papers got much attention at all that day. I'll dig it out when I get home. We've probably got the back copies still.'

'Please, Jim, not on my account. I only mentioned it in passing,' interjected Ben with a wave of the hand.

'No, I will, though I can't pretend to be an expert on birds, mind you,' insisted Jim.

'Nor me, either,' responded Ben. 'It wasn't so much an interest in birds themselves that attracted me to write the piece, so much as some strange happenings in The States.'

'Strange in what way?' asked Jim.

'It was to do with migration patterns that have suddenly changed after thousands of years and nobody is quite sure why. Stop me if I'm boring you,' said Johnson.

40

'No, please, this is much more interesting than insurance,' said Jim, jocularly. 'Please go on.'

'Well, apparently the birds' sense of direction has simply gone haywire. Last season, for example, Canadian snowgeese from my neck of the woods turned up hundreds of miles west of their usual Gulf Coast habitats.' Jim was listening intently, having placed Ben Johnson's accent at last. 'Golden plovers were unable to find the north coast of South America. North Pacific albatrosses were landing in the Philippines instead of Japan. It's even spread to the insect world, with monarch butterflies straying miles from their African habitats. Now it's always been accepted as incredible how these creatures return to the same places year after year with such pinpoint accuracy, but the fact is that they did. So why does that ability suddenly disappear?'

'Any theories?' asked an intrigued Jim.

'Oh, plenty. The weather. Pollution. Radiation. The earth's magnetic field. To mention but a few. I'll tell you what, Jim. If you're interested, let me get you a copy of the article. I have some inside.'

'OK,' said Jim, 'if it's no trouble. You've got my interest now. Then I really must be on my way, with apologies for having taken up your time.'

'Not at all, my pleasure,' called out Ben, now just inside the main house, which he had entered by the opened patio doors. In no time he was making his way back towards Jim.

'Obviously we'll be in touch again shortly about the claim,' said Jim, by now on his feet. 'Between the two of us,' he continued, 'I'm sure that there's no problem that can't be resolved. Meanwhile, it's been a pleasure to meet you.'

'Likewise, I'm sure,' responded Ben, handing Jim the three-page photocopy of his article. 'Maybe our paths may cross again sometime,' he added, 'hopefully for different reasons.' He was anxious not to give the impression that he would be a frequent claimant. 'In fact I was thinking not so long ago of doing an article on insurance claims investigators. You must have a few good stories to tell.'

'Er, yes, quite a few,' said Jim. 'I'm not so sure that they would be interesting enough to sell any newspapers, though. Still, here's my card.' Jim offered the card he had got out of his briefcase just a few moments earlier. As he made his way back to the car, he had the feeling that their paths might indeed cross in the future.

*   *   *

There was just less than a week to go to polling day, and John Marner was in Lichworth where he was lending his support somewhat reluctantly to his ailing party colleague. Recent canvass returns had not been good and there was a distinct danger that the local electorate was going to give the government a kick up the proverbial backside. The Liberal vote was crumbling according to reports, local issues were not going in the Tory candidate's favour and whilst fine weather could usually be relied upon to favour the incumbent party, the recent oppressive heat and accompanying water restrictions had made people irritable. It was time to inject a national presence into the fray and for the prime minister to impose his own importance.

'Hello, hello, nice to meet you. Thank you. Good luck to you too. Hello, how are you? Can we count on your support? Hello, nice to see you.' A word here and a word there, interspersed with handshakes and, always, the famous prime-ministerial grin. John Marner was a plain, unassuming man, not having the type of personality that radiated warmth, and yet always apparently cheerful and friendly. Of course, he was aware of the accompanying cameramen and sound technicians, and the pressing media mob, and this was an outright PR exercise after all, and yet he still came across as an ordinary person for all that.

Reaney was aware, naturally, of the PM's visit, but he was determined to turn it to his own advantage. The tide was running his way and he had no intention of allowing himself to be upstaged at this juncture. Not noted for his subtlety, he decided that the best course of action was to confront Marner head-on, gaining prime TV exposure and blunting his rival's secret weapon. He had already tipped off some members of the media but nothing had filtered back to his rival's advisors. They would be caught ill-informed and unprepared.

As the PM and his entourage made their way without too much difficulty through the crowds, whose numbers were considerably swollen by the media presence, they turned the corner into the market square. Emerging with impeccable timing from a side alley, hand in hand with two sweet and unassuming old ladies, one either side, Reaney confronted the prime minister. He was barely ten feet away and directly in the path of the oncoming group.

'Prime Minister, Prime Minister,' barked Reaney. 'Have you something to say to these two grand old ladies?' Instinctively, the PM's entourage, almost as one unit, tried to veer off to the right to avoid this noisy, unwelcome and inconvenient obstruction. At the same time, the prime-ministerial ear was being whispered into, by way of explanation of the identity of this intruder. 'Come, come, Mr Marner,' said Reaney, having upped the volume, 'don't be shy. We've come here specially to see you.' By now, the cameras were clicking or whirring and a mild jostle broke out in media ranks. Marner resisted the gentle nudges and pushes from his own supporters that were aimed at guiding him away from this obstacle. His natural enjoyment and feel for the hurly-burly of the hustings was coming to the fore.

'Mr Reaney,' he responded, 'I don't know what your problem is, but gimmicks in the street in front of the television cameras will not win you this election, not that you have any chance anyway, if I may say so,' retorted Marner.

'These ladies want to know why they are being evicted from the homes they have lived in all their lives, to make way for an hare-brained road scheme that nobody wants, nobody needs, and is supported by your lapdog here,' explained Reaney at only a slightly lower decibel level.

'It is not for me or my colleague to interfere in matters which can be solved democratically through the proper channels,' came the formal reply. Marner was trying to distance himself from the issue. He was aware that there had been a lot of local controversy and that their candidate had not handled a previous interview on the subject very well.

'Do you support the road, or not?' shouted Reaney, as the prime minister began to move off to greet a couple of potential supporters in a shop doorway.

'Answer the question,' persisted Reaney. 'Are you for or against it?'

'You can't stand in the way of progress,' said the PM, almost immediately wishing that he had not used such an apparently uncaring expression.

'How can you be so heartless?' chirped in one of the old dears in a quiet local accent. But by now Marner was moving on with his entourage, but realizing that he had not handled the incident with his usual aplomb.

'Well, at least now we know,' cried Reaney after him. 'Roads first, people second,' he taunted. 'The caring party? Don't make me laugh. The only thing Tories care about is money.'

It was an insignificant little incident in the general scheme of things but it assured Reaney of his airtime on the local TV and radio and perhaps even a snippet on the national news. If it did no more than niggle his opponent it would have been worthwhile, he thought. The PM had been right, of course: it was no more than a gimmick, but even if it won over a handful of voters that could prove vital in a contest looking increasingly tight.

On the train back to the capital, John Marner was irritable. It had not been a particularly enjoyable or successful day. He normally relished the cut and thrust of electioneering, but now and then he got frustrated with the British political scene and its confrontationalism, just as he had in his early political life when he almost jacked it all in and emigrated to The States. The annoying Reaney had contributed to his demeanour, or was it more to do with the endless sun and heat? Was that making him irascible, as it was so many others? Still, he needed to snap out of it. The commitment required from someone in his high office was very great. His country was very demanding of him. Once back in the capital, it would be straight into a meeting with the Secretary of State for the Environment to consider some follow-up reports to Wednesday's Cabinet discussion of the drought. But really, it was Lord's tomorrow afternoon that he was looking forward to. He had been getting score flashes all day. It was a good wicket. England were batting and hopefully they would really start to rattle the scoreboard along tomorrow he thought.

The early evening TV news was full of drought-related stories again: another day, another week without measurable rainfall. A number of new drought orders had been granted. Up to twelve million people in different parts of the country, though mainly the South, the East and the Midlands were now covered by orders. Whilst they were essentially enabling orders, aimed at putting the powers in place in case of need, there were nevertheless a number of areas now being subjected to various conservation measures. As the TV report revealed, in parts of the Home Counties, the Three Valleys Water Co. had closed automatic car washes, put a stop to the watering of sports pitches and banned the filling of private swimming pools. All government and municipal fountains were turned off throughout the country lest such frivolous use of water gave offence. Millions of lawns were already showing the effects of sprinkler and hosepipe bans. Full page ads in the press were urging householders to save by recycling washing-up water, reducing loo-flushing, putting a brick in the cistern and so on. There were dire warnings of the consequences of not making economies. Then there were the pictures of the standpipes being made ready. Surely that would put the fear of God into the consumers and make them eke out reserves until the inevitable deluge came.

The bulletin went on to outline the equally serious scene developing in France, the Low Countries and a wide area of Western Europe, all sitting under an increasingly large and dominating high pressure system that was breaking all records for both its duration and its atmospheric pressure level.

'What do you think would happen if it never rained again?' asked Jim, turning to Carol as they sat together, coffees in hand, listening and watching the bulletin unfurl.

'Well, I suppose we'd end up eventually like those poor people in Ethiopia, wouldn't we?' replied Carol, followed by a sip from her cup. 'But that would take months, if not years, for us to get in that state, don't you think?'

'If ever,' replied Jim. 'After all, we are surrounded by water. All right, it's not drinkable in its present condition, but it can't be beyond the wit of man to make it suitable for drinking in double quick time if needs be.'

'Desalination plants,' said Carol.

'Right.'

'But don't they take a long time to come on stream, if you'll pardon the phrase?' asked Carol

'Yes, I think they do, usually. I'm sure that they would speed them up, though if they had to.' There was a slight pause and then Jim continued, 'No, I think the immediate effect will be economic. Farming and industry. Prices going up. Then workers laid off. Then there would be the inconvenience: collecting water by the bucketful, supplies cut off for hours at a time. Not a very good quality of life at all.'

'But just supposing that you were right, though, Jim,' said Carol thoughtfully, resting her head to one side on a clenched hand, 'I mean, if it never rained again. Surely that would be a sign that there was something fundamentally wrong with the planet. You know what I mean?' she asked. 'Maybe other strange things might start to happen as well.'

'Yes, that's occurred to me too. In fact, from a number of things that I've been told lately, I just wonder what is going on. And, if we're thinking like that, don't you suppose that other people are as well? I wouldn't be surprised if the powers that be know a lot more than they are letting on.'

'What do you mean?' asked Carol, sitting back now in the comfort of the armchair. 'Some kind of cover up?'

'Absolutely.'

'So, as mature, intelligent and responsible inhabitants of planet earth, what should we do about it?' posed Carol, her choice of words pseudo-dramatic.

'Three things, in my opinion,' answered Jim, treating her question seriously but not gravely. 'Firstly, I think that we should put off that loan on a new car. Extra financial commitments when the economy is on the blink, we can do without. Apparently the stock market plunged today for the third time in two weeks. Then I suppose we should start to do our bit to conserve water resources. You know, a brick in the cistern, that kind of thing.'

After a pause, Carol asked, 'And the third thing?'

Jim rose from his seat, put down his coffee cup on a nearby table and then turned and went back over to Carol. Slipping one arm behind her back and the other under her knees, he lifted her out of the chair and carried her towards the door.

'If the end of the world is nigh, my darling, we need to take every opportunity left to us to express our love and affection for one another. Love will conquer all,' he added, as he began to climb the stairs with his dumbstruck wife temporarily gawping in amazement. Finally finding her voice, and feigning several thumps to Jim's chest, she admonished him.

'Put me down, you sex maniac.' But her protests were feeble and playful and, in truth, she was enjoying the excitement and the unpredictability of it all. They reached the top of the stairs and by the time they were entering the bathroom, they were giggling. They stripped and showered together.

A short while later, Jim, his passionate urges satisfied for now, rose from the bed and made his way over to the window. He was careful not to part the curtains too widely in view of his state of nudity. He looked over the rear garden. The lawn and those of the neighbours were showing the signs of a chronic lack of watering, natural or otherwise. Birch trees and rhododendrons were beginning to suffer. Uncovered flowerbeds were cracking with dryness. Everybody took it for granted that sooner or later it would rain again and deep down nobody really expected that they could be on the verge off some cataclysmic disaster. But in Jim's mind a theory was gaining momentum and his instincts were still telling him that something major was afoot. Whatever the future held, he and Carol would face it together secure in the knowledge that their deep and affectionate relationship was as strong as ever and that this mutual strength would see them through.

Jim's body shuddered in surprise. He had not heard Carol as she slipped quietly off the bed and crept up behind him. She pressed her naked body against his as he leaned towards the window. He felt her against his buttocks, his skin sensitive to the pubic hair rubbing against him. As she lowered her arms to encircle his lower midriff she soon felt the evidence of his re-awakened passion come up to meet them. In no time, Jim had swivelled and they were back on the bed, their bodies intertwined once more in sublime expression.

* * *

The PM was not liking the information that he was being given by the Secretary of State, not that he had any reason to doubt the accuracy of it, but there were several aspects to it which suggested problems ahead. Wednesday's Cabinet meeting had already addressed a number of these but he had arranged for the young minister to call back at Number Ten that evening to plug a few remaining gaps. John Marner felt that he needed an in-depth awareness of the current developing crisis and its effects, real and imaginary, and the contingency planning. He studied quietly some of the information on the table before him, occasionally sipping from a cup of coffee.

'I don't like these latest MORECS bulletins, Alan, nor the long-range met reports. It's looking serious. Have the water companies really got enough standpipes and tankers to cope with a drought more widespread than any other in modern times? What's the long-term political fallout going to be if rationing goes on for any length of time?' He pressed on before awaiting a reply. 'But it's this latest news that's most worrying me. If this spreads it could be devastating, and not just politically. We need to get every government scientist we've got onto this one, Alan, and quick.' The young Secretary of State nodded in acquiescence, then drained his own coffee cup. 'Alan,' resumed the prime minister quietly,

48

'I think we're really going to have to keep right on top of this. Get in touch if you think that there is anything I should know.'

'Does that mean that you are appointing me the Minister for Drought?' asked the tall young man, half-jokingly, as he started to pack up his briefcase.

'If needs be,' replied Marner, in that matter of fact way of his, 'but you and I both know that it will only be a gimmick anyway, just to quell public anxiety.'

'Enjoy the Test Match,' said Alan, brushing his slightly receding dark hair back with the palm of his right hand as he prepared to leave. 'They tell me the wicket's beginning to take spin already.'

It was ages since Mandy and Bill had been to the cinema. They decided to try the new complex over in Tamfield and they were surprised at how popular it was. Certainly attendances had improved in the last year or so and these huge new complexes with enormous choice and the very best facilities were pulling in the crowds. They had chosen the latest Michael Douglas movie and they had not been disappointed. The sex scenes were explicit and the language was foul in parts, but then that seemed par for the course nowadays and no worse than on the telly.

They came out arm in arm afterwards, threading their way through the throng. Seemingly several films had all finished about the same time, judging by the density of the crowd.

'Did you enjoy it then, love?' asked Bill.

'Yes, I did,' said Mandy. 'It was a nice change and not a bad film. Did you enjoy it?'

'Yes, very good. We must do it again sometime.'

'And as for Michael Douglas,' added Mandy, 'what a lovely bum.'

'Cheeky,' said Bill, and they made their way through the car park in high spirits.

Bill took the driving seat and they were soon in the exit queue. They would make their way through the town centre to link up with the Lichworth road. As they got underway they couldn't help but notice the large number of people milling around. Perhaps some of them had come from the emptying cinema throng. Bill was attentive in his driving with so many people about, recognizing that a fair proportion of them at that time of night, whether on foot or at the wheel, would not be at their most sober or disciplined. One particularly dense gathering was becoming rather agitated. They were youths mainly, noisy and gesticulating and spilling onto the road. Bill slowed right down. The car in front also slowed, after first sounding the horn, and then it just managed to stop as a gangling, gawky looking youth waltzed in front of the car, soon to be followed by a handful of his pals. Mandy cautioned Bill to stop but he already had control of the situation and drew to a halt a few feet behind the other car. The occupant of the first car, a short, rotund and balding middle-aged man resorted to the horn again when it became clear that far from moving, the crowd in front of his car was growing denser. Bill and Mandy eyed the situation anxiously. The crowd was obviously in high spirits and potentially aggressive, though on closer inspection it was not exclusively young hooligans. There seemed to be some older ones too.

The driver in front was becoming increasingly frustrated as the mob ignored not only his horn-blowing but also the cacophony of car hooters from the ever-lengthening queue behind. He opened the driver's door, leaned half out and shouted over the top of the door at the crowd. His words could not be heard fully over the din, but Mandy thought she detected at least a couple of expletives. This had not been a wise move. The crowd seemed to swell further, as if attracted by this vocal outburst. The stationary car was now surrounded by a motley crew of youngish people clad in all manner of shorts, some scruffy but not all, and some with vests and others with bare tops, no doubt reflecting the still barmy evening. The overspill of the crowd was beginning to absorb Bill and Mandy's car too. Where were they all coming from? What was going on?

It was clear by now that vehicles further back in the queue were trying to turn or reverse to escape the mêlée. It was a one-way street and quite narrow. One driver, two cars behind Bill, had lost patience. He managed to pull out from the queue and decided that the best course of action was to force a way through the crowd. Whether under some influencing substance, or merely seeking to confirm the superior image portrayed by his powerful executive model, was not clear. The black car surged forward, horn blaring and headlamps full on. A young girl in front fell to the ground as if squeezed up and spat out by the jostling and pushing of the agitated throng. The irate driver, heading straight for her, at least had the time and sense to swerve out of the way, but in so doing he veered off into one of the ornamental lamp-posts that adorned the street. The solid iron column was dislodged, but not before making its mark deep in the bonnet of the sleek saloon.

By now Bill was very concerned, as much for their own personal safety as for the general situation. The scene was undoubtedly turning uglier, with the boisterous crowd in danger of becoming a rampaging mob. Both the car in front and the executive car were now being manhandled, bounced with the frightened occupants still inside. At the moment Bill and Mandy were still just onlookers, but Bill wondered at what stage he might be physically drawn in if matters continued to escalate. He was not a muscular man, nor aggressive by nature, but he always liked to think that if his own flesh and blood were threatened he would have the courage to respond. He was not sure to what extent he would go to the aid of others, especially if such bravery might then rebound on his own family. The short, fat man from the car in front was now being dragged out through the driver's door by two menacing yobbos. Mandy grabbed Bill's arm for reassurance. The odds were not good. The mob was becoming more threatening.

'Where are the police?' asked Mandy, her voice displaying increasing anxiety. 'Surely they'll break this up soon. Where are they?' As she spoke someone started banging on their roof and there was suddenly a crush of people down the passenger side of their car. Bill made a move to open his door but had barely lifted the release lever before pausing again. A well-built, smartly dressed chap came hurtling past his door, heading for the fracas in front. He was running to the aid of the short fat driver who was by now receiving a thorough kicking on the ground. Two bare-chested youths were responsible, but as Bill eyed up the scene he noticed that another of the onlookers was brandishing a knife.

Events were moving quickly. Bill was caught in a temporary paralysis between thought and action. His almost trance-like state was interrupted by the smashing of the side window, glass showering all over Mandy. Her scream was almost in unison with the cries of the good Samaritan who had flown past Bill's window seconds before and who now lay writhing at the end of the knife Bill had seen.

Bill was out of the car now, both incidents concentrating his attention at the same time. Who was in greater need of his assistance? The knifed Samaritan screamed in agony, but Bill's instincts sent him round the front of the car to confront Mandy's assailants.

Mandy, however, was obeying her own instincts. Oblivious of the danger from broken glass, she clambered across the front seats and emerged through the driver's door, drawn to the screaming and now blood-spurting victim who was in need of her medical skills.

Bill, meanwhile, found himself face to face with a hooligan. Afterwards he recalled having tried to reason with the man, but without being able to remember exactly what had been said. The vision stayed with him, though, of an almost respectable young man, clean-shaven and tanned, but with a deep-glazed expression in the eyes. Notwithstanding that, Bill did recollect that his conversation was peppered with profanities. The only other thing that Bill could remember was a heavy blow to the back of his head, followed by a vague recollection of dull pain in his face and ribs.

It transpired that only seconds later, the mob, almost in unison, as if like a human wave, moved on. It was probably as a result of two realizations: firstly, the knowledge that the knifing incident constituted a serious criminal offence and, secondly, the arrival in force of the police, some by car with sirens wailing, others on foot running towards them. A number of ambulances were to follow almost immediately, with Mandy and Bill set to occupy one of them. As they were driven off at speed to the nearest casualty department, three miles away, they left behind a scene of disarray, anger and bewilderment. Their pleasant evening out had been transformed into a violent nightmare.

Mandy had several lacerations to her arms and legs caused by flying and broken glass, though she had not felt them at the time. She had been more preoccupied with stemming the flow of blood from the man with the deep knife wounds and, whilst she hoped that her actions had helped him to cling to life, his wounds were such that she feared for his ultimate survival. The short, round man to whose aid he had so courageously come was also in a bad way, having taken a fearful beating and kicking.

Bill came round in the ambulance, much to Mandy's relief, though for some time he would feel pain from that bottle smashed over his head. It was also likely that he was suffering from broken ribs and he also had a bruised and bloodied face.

Later, at the hospital, strapped up, bandaged, but still sore, Bill was interviewed by the police. Mandy, too, treated and thankfully without serious damage, was asked to give her version of the night's events. They did their best to recall every detail of what they had witnessed, not least a description of the assailant with the knife. Whilst they would remember what happened for the rest of their lives, nevertheless a lot seemed to have been compressed into a short space of time. It was inevitable that they would omit little details but maybe they would come to mind later. The young policeman knew this and he would delay taking the formal statement until the next day. Meanwhile, he needed some information while it was still fresh and with a view to apprehending the culprits as quickly as possible.

Two plain-clothes officers turned up as the young uniformed policeman was talking to them. One of them, a significantly bald, but smartly dressed detective, in pale cream jacket and matching tie, announced his entry to the room in a somewhat dramatic fashion.

'It's murder, Clive. How are those descriptions coming along?' The news sent a shudder through Mandy and Bill.

'Oh, no!' exclaimed Mandy, with feeling. 'I did what I could for him, but it was a very deep wound,' she added.

'No, luv,' said the smart officer 'not the knife victim. He's still clinging to life, albeit by a thread. It's the other chap I'm afraid. He wasn't very fit you see. His body couldn't take the beating. The doctor says that his heart gave in under the strain.'

'It's shocking,' said Bill.

'Seems as though he may have had a dicky heart anyway,' continued the officer. 'Not that that matters, of course. You take your victims as you find 'em. It's still murder. Unless the court decides otherwise of course,' he advised, in a matter-of-fact, clinical sort of way. 'But first' he resumed after a pause, 'we need to catch whoever did it. So, what have we got on them, Clive?'

The young one in uniform passed on the descriptions that Mandy and Bill had been able to put together, though explaining that they had so far concentrated more on the knife-wielding thug, expecting that he would be the most wanted. The other plain-clothes officer was less abrasive and direct than his colleague. He seemed more methodical and in a quietly-spoken way he suggested that they might all go over everything again to try and tighten up on the descriptions. Bill would have welcomed some respite but, understanding the importance, cooperated in full, as did Mandy. Eventually a young nurse came in.

'Excuse me, gentlemen. I think our patients could do with some rest. I'd have been in earlier if I hadn't been so busy.'

'OK, luv, nearly finished,' said the smart one, 'but we do have some maniacs on the loose and we do need to catch them before they do any more damage.'

'Two more minutes only,' said the nurse, closing the curtain as she left.

When the police interview was complete, Bill and Mandy discussed with the nurse and the duty doctor whether they could go home. They explained that it was normal practice to admit victims of head injuries for observation, so Bill should stay in overnight. Mandy, though, need not be detained and an ambulance was summoned.

It was another baking hot day, though not yet at its hottest. Carol returned to the shaded conservatory with a tray of ice-cold drinks after her foray into the kitchen. Mandy and Bill were grateful for the refreshment, still recovering as they were from the violence of two days ago. Bill's ribs were strapped up and both he and Mandy bore numerous cuts and bruises still. 'Take it easy,' the nurses had said and that was just what they intended to do, not that Bill, in particular, had much choice.

'I still can't believe it,' said Carol. 'What is the world coming to?' she asked rhetorically as she handed out the drinks.

'Bless you,' said Mandy.

'Cheers,' echoed Bill.

'According to the police, this sort of thing is escalating all the time,' said Mandy, picking up on Carol's comments. 'I can vouch for that myself from the nursing standpoint. The hospital figures for woundings are well up this year.'

'Of course, the police blame the weather, you know,' added Bill, perhaps somewhat appropriately. 'The long, hot summer syndrome, increased beer consumption, allied to the usual problems of indiscipline and lack of respect for authority. They reckon that it happens whenever we have a long spell of hot weather.'

'But why must it always end in violence?' asked Carol. 'That's what I don't understand. Too much to drink should make you merry or happy, shouldn't it? It used to do for me. Is it just in this country that it all turns to violence?'

'I'm not sure,' answered Mandy, 'but it can't be just the drink that's causing the violence.'

'Mandy's right,' said Bill. 'It was funny, actually, but being in the middle of all the aggro, well, it was frightening, of course, but if you looked at these people as individuals, face-to-face, some of them almost seemed quite innocent and respectable. It was almost as if they were being carried along by something, part of the herd I suppose.'

'It's certainly one of those things that you need to experience to appreciate fully,' added Mandy. 'But don't get me wrong, I wouldn't wish it on anybody.'

'Ah well,' sighed Carol, 'let's change the subject. You haven't come here to be reminded of the other night. How long is this fine weather going to last, Bill, long enough for me to put the finishing touches to my tan?'

'I wish I knew, Carol. Not that you could improve much on the tan you've got, anyway.' Bill was right. Whilst not being a sun-worshipper, as such, Carol liked the occasional hour in her bikini on the sunlounger in the back garden and it certainly found favour with Jim, not to mention the neighbours. 'Not being at work, I'm confined to watching the TV forecast just like you,' he continued, 'that is when the telly's not on the blink.'

'Oh, sounds as if your TV reception was as bad as ours last night,' said Carol. 'Ours kept breaking up, sound and picture. We gave up and turned it off in the end.'

'It came back later on,' informed Bill, 'complete with apology. They blamed it on the transmitter, another victim of the unusual weather they said.'

'I can't remember getting reception problems in the past around here,' responded Carol.

'This year is exceptional, though,' advised Bill. 'In fact, did you know that atmospheric pressure levels over the UK at the moment are the highest ever recorded? Or that many places are now having their longest ever dry spell? Are you ready for the water shortage?' he asked.

'Do you think that we should get extra containers in?' asked Carol.

'I don't think that it will make any difference. When the tanker draws up at the end of the street, you'll get your allocation, and no more.'

'But I thought we'd have standpipes so that we could all draw as much as we liked,' suggested Mandy.

'Love, there won't be enough standpipes to go round the whole country. It might work to begin with. So might rationing by daily cut-off rotas. But once the hoarding starts they'll bring in the tankers, and the army to maintain control.'

'My God,' exclaimed Carol and then asked Mandy how she thought that they would manage at the hospital. Bill expected that they would get an exemption.

'In fact, I'll bet the civil servants already have the plans ready to dust off,' he added.

'You think that it's that near then?' asked Carol, draining the drink that had long since become devoid of its ice cubes. Bill drained his glass, too, before replying.

'I think that it's a lot closer than most people think.' During the ensuing pause for reflection, Carol rounded up the empty glasses and then had no difficulty in persuading Bill and Mandy to have the same again.

'Better tell Jim that his golfing partner will be out of circulation for a while,' Bill mentioned to Carol on her return.

'He'll just have to practise on his own until you're fit again, Bill,' she said.

'Yes, but not too much. I don't want him getting too good,' he joked. 'Anyway, they tell me that the course is now opening restricted hours to avoid more damage to it during the drought.'

'I'll tell him,' promised Carol. 'Perhaps he can take you out for a drink and a good old natter instead,' she suggested.

'Last time he nattered about the weather all the time,' remarked Bill, light-heartedly. 'Seemed fascinated in a strange sort of a way.'

'I think that it was not long after Dad died' said Carol, 'and whilst most people will look back on this as a wonderful long hot summer, for us it will always be associated with that event.'

Mandy stretched out a hand of consolation as Bill wished that he had not been the cause of unhappy memories resurfacing.

* * *

Ben Johnson had found the conversation that afternoon a while ago stimulating and interesting, not to say intriguing. He had thought that Jim Webb's second visit to his house was on the sole pretext of delivering a cheque in payment of his claim, although it did seem strange that the postal service was not being used.

Jim had been a little embarrassed and apprehensive when he first arrived and saw that Ben was entertaining a stunningly attractive slim brunette seemingly a few years younger than him. She had long shapely legs accentuated by brief, frayed denim shorts, while a deliberately short T-shirt showed off her flat smooth waist to best effect. This, together with Ben's own casual appearance in shorts and T-shirt, led Jim to believe that he might be intruding on a rather intimate scene. A patio table containing evidence of consumed alcoholic drinks added to the ambience. Jim decided that he should just conduct his business and leave, but was pleased when Ben insisted that he stay a while. He was glad, too, when Ben enquired if Jim had read his article yet, because it was that that had really encouraged Jim to make this a personal visit. On no account was Jim interrupting anything, and he should take his jacket off, sit down and grab a Pilsener, in that order. Jim was able to accept these conditions without much difficulty.

The conversation was not very old before it was established that the brunette with the model figure and looks was Ben's younger sister. Ben and she had not seen each other for a while and they had spent a couple of hours catching up on each other's gossip and the latest family news. Joanne, as she was called, had also just returned from a week at Ben's villa in the Algarve. He liked to keep it free for family and friends. He had not bought it as a moneymaker to rent out to all and sundry. The three of them chatted briefly about Portugal. Jim noticed that Joanne's accent was more Anglicized than Ben's. After a while, Joanne excused herself in order to make a telephone call. That enabled Jim and Ben to resume their talk about Ben's article.

By the time they had finished their chat they had indeed given each other food for thought. Ben had been intrigued by Jim's speculations and had promised to pursue aspects with his North American contacts. Jim had been fascinated by some additional information that Ben had been able to give him and which had lent weight to his own ideas. Though both men were curious by nature, Ben was also alive to the prospect of another article and Jim still carried an instinctive urge to delve deeper into matters which both puzzled and worried him.

Joanne returned just as Jim was about to leave.

'Have you been running up my phone bill again, sis?' kidded Ben. 'That must be one of your longest yet. Long-distance as well was it? When are you going to get your mobile fixed?'

'Don't worry, bruv, I've hardly cost you a penny. Well, not in phone charges anyway. I've been having a nice long soak in the bath, for your information, and I've got changed. Can't you tell? Too many beers, eh?' she teased, playfully patting his cheek in a manner which suggested that they had probably been absolute horrors to each other whilst they were younger, but nonetheless part of a happy, close-knit family. Joanne had that cheeky grin and sparkle in the eye that implied that, more often than not, she would have been the instigator. Jim had realized instantly, and most approvingly, that Joanne was now clad in a very smart two-piece white suit that accentuated her curvaceous figure whilst also adding an enormous amount of maturity to her stunning physical attributes. Ben and Joanne's little game had amused Jim and delayed his leaving slightly.

'No, unfortunately I couldn't get through straightaway,' Joanne continued when it became clear that the only retaliation she was going to draw from Ben was a dismissive facial gesture. 'It seemed as though the number was unobtainable. It's as bad as my mobile. Anyway, I've just now tried again but got the most awful line. Still, having established that he's there, I've decided to drive down the motorway like a lunatic and let him take me out for dinner tonight.'

'Oh, good. It will save me having to cook,' said Ben, getting his retaliation in at last.

'Meanwhile, you should get your phone fixed,' she said, heading off as she spoke towards the gleaming all-white cabriolet that Jim had noticed in the drive when he arrived.

She departed with a raised acknowledging hand and her words trailing behind her, 'Goodbye, Jim. Nice to meet you.'

'My pleasure,' said Jim, and he meant it. 'Quite a character,' he said to Ben, when Joanne was out of earshot.

'You're telling me,' responded Ben. 'She has that agent of hers twisted round her little finger.'

'Agent?' said Jim, inquisitively.

'Yes. Our Joanne is a fashion model,' explained Ben, 'and very much in demand at the moment.'

'That I can believe,' said Jim. 'Well, I must be making tracks too. Funny about the phone, Ben. I should get it checked out if I was you.'

'Oh, you mean it might be connected to what we were talking about?'

'Could be.'

'Stay in touch,' said Ben, his words almost drowned by the screeching of rubber on gravel as Joanne departed. Jim followed more sedately, and deep in thought. Ben went inside and picked up the telephone receiver. It was dead.

* * *

John Marner's Cabinet meetings were much more open and participative than those of his predecessor. He liked to get the collective view. He believed that it encouraged loyalty and he also valued the opinions, expertise and experience of some of his ministerial colleagues. It had to be said, though, that the calibre of Cabinet ministers, like the current standard of members of parliament generally, had deteriorated alarmingly. When deprived of their entourage of civil service advisers, the knowledge and contribution of some of them was little short of scandalous. For too long previously the party had been dominated by an autocratic leader who had used her ministers as little more than acquiescent underlings and the present prime minister had been striving for some time to change that by drafting new, more modern thinkers into his government. Few, however, seemed to have the same grip on political realities that he had, nor the common touch that he was sure he possessed.

The Cabinet discussion on the drought and related matters had meandered around the peripheries. Time was running on and it had reached the point where the prime minister had to bring the debate back to the cogent points.

'Gentlemen, and ladies, we have had a very detailed brief of the current state of affairs from Alan, whom we thank, and our thanks also to David for apprising us of the agricultural implications. Clearly, we ... the country ... faces a difficult situation likely to cause, at best, significant inconvenience and, at worst, disasters of varying proportion across a range of social and economic fronts. We could very soon be faced with urgent short-term problems and whilst there is always the possibility of Mother Earth providing a solution literally overnight, there is also the prospect of lasting damage to the country and its economy in the medium term, not to mention the worrying fear of possible longer term effects. To put it simply, preservation of water supply, arrangements for emergency distribution of resources and future provision of supply are now very firmly at the top of our agenda. You can rely on Alan, David, the home secretary, the defence secretary and myself to keep you fully briefed on our sub-committee activity. Alan will coordinate matters in my absence. Obviously we will also be liaising closely with all bodies concerned, both private and statutory.'

Alan Hunter, the young Environment Secretary, had the advantage of sitting close to the prime minister. He wondered if, before concluding his remarks to Cabinet, the PM would comment on the brief report that Alan had slipped him just before the meeting began. But Alan could see that this still lay in the same folder, closed and partially covered by other documents, whether deliberately or not.

'You will be aware,' resumed John Marner, 'that the first meeting of this special subcommittee will be immediately

61

after this meeting. Meanwhile, we must press on. I know that the home secretary has an urgent report for us on the inner-city violence of last weekend, not to mention the latest on the hippy convoy. Over to you, Michael . . . '

Reaney was studying the latest canvassing returns at his election headquarters. It was a functional, cramped and untidy room, hired solely for the duration of the campaign, after which it would return to its former status on the offices to let register. It may have been his lack of respect for the refinements of life, or possibly an attempt to rest his overworked feet, but he did not look out of place with his feet up on the second-hand desk, a mug of coffee in one hand, and a set of papers in the other. The unbuttoned collar of his white shirt and the loosened tie were not so much in deference to the hot weather and stuffy room, as a testimony to his informality, though some regarded it as a lack of style. The telephone rang and as Reaney swung his legs off the desk to wheel his chair nearer to the apparatus, he spilt hot coffee down the front of his shirt.

'*Shit!*', he cursed, picking up the receiver. His caller was somewhat taken aback, although gathering that the remark was not aimed directly into the microphone and assumed that it was not intended for him. As a member of the gutter press, however, he did not find it sufficiently remarkable to query anyway. Instead, he launched straight away into a pre-prepared question, which was to seek the parliamentary candidate's comments on a statement by his rival at his press conference earlier that his canvassing returns were now showing a clear and unassailable lead. 'It is clear' the rival had allegedly said, 'that as the reality of polling day approaches, many voters are not prepared to experiment with an unsuitable and unqualified candidate.'

'*Bollocks!*' retorted Reaney in a response that contained brevity and anger and was on the level he thought appropriate for the tawdry tabloid involved. The reporter, though he preferred to be called a journalist, was totally unmoved by the content of the response, though caught unawares by the brevity of it. After a pause, his follow-up question went into a little more detail. The gist of it was to seek Reaney's reaction to his rival's decision to home in on their respective educational backgrounds and academic qualifications, or in Reaney's case, the lack of them.

'*Bastards!*' was Reaney's even more venomous response this time, accompanied by a slamming down of the telephone.

'Trevor, anybody observing and listening to you in the last two minutes could be forgiven for thinking that you had a very limited and obscene vocabulary.' It was Reaney's agent speaking, a balding, middle-aged man with an acerbic wit honed by a hard-bitten political background. His drawn features and small stature made him more suited to the backroom than to candidature in today's image-conscious world, but he had contributed in no small measure to the successful campaign. 'All I've heard from you are three words,' he continued 'and none was suitable for mixed company. One thing is for sure, if you ever do become an MP you won't get invited on Question Time. Who the bloody hell were you talking to, for God's sake?'

'Frank, give me a bit of credit will you?' answered Reaney. 'I wouldn't talk like that to anyone important. It was some young kid from a downmarket rag.'

'Never underestimate the power of the press, Trevor. That young kid might be an editor one day.'

'I'll be the prime minister first,' quipped Reaney.

'One step at a time,' said Frank, 'and we'll know about the first step soon enough, in about thirty-six hours to be precise,' he said, looking at his watch as he spoke.

'I'll tell you something, Frank,' said Reaney, 'looking at these canvass returns, I think it's going to be mighty close, a real nail-biter.' For all his bluff it was evident that Reaney was now beginning to feel the tension as the campaign was drawing to a close. The result would indeed not be long in coming.

John Marner had managed to get the Cabinet meeting completed in reasonable time, with only a slight overrun. He was anxious to get down to the more crucial business of the emergency subcommittee and, in particular, Alan Hunter's report. The participants had remained seated round the large oval table but had shuffled up to form a more compact grouping, closing ranks as Marner had termed it.

'Gentlemen,' as the prime minister began the new session 'I think it best that we take up from where the general Cabinet meeting has just left off. I don't think that there is anything to be gained by repeating matters of general knowledge. As you know, Alan is coordinating and liaising between departments as becomes necessary. It goes without saying, almost, but time is a valuable commodity and another one, incidentally, that is in very short supply, I might add.' The last comment struck a chord with all those present. In addition to the prime minister and his young environment secretary, there was David Mallow, the round-faced, bespectacled agriculture minister, who looked upon every new challenge with relish only because it gave him another chance to get a leg-up the ladder of personal political ambition. The home secretary, Michael Hazeldean, was there, all guile and gusto, with his flowing golden locks in need of a barber's scissors as usual. He had needed all his gushing self-confidence recently to cope with the seemingly endless flow of problems landing on his desk: from inner-city violence to hippy convoys to prison riots to media controls and much more. And the final minister, the oldest and most circumspect of those present, the pin-stripe suited, grey-haired Clive Marchant, from the defence ministry, whose resources were always at the disposal of the nation in time of crisis.

'Without further ado then,' concluded the prime minister, 'I will hand over to Alan.'

'Thank you, Prime Minister,' began the confident young secretary of state whose meteoric rise through the ranks had been one the most significant political developments of the last two years. 'As if the potential problems of a record-breaking and seemingly never-ending drought were not sufficient cause for concern in themselves, there are two additional and related problems to advise you of, both of which may considerably exacerbate the current situation.' Hunter, as ever, was concise and accurate in his communication, and like John Marner, with whom he had chatted prior to the meeting, he was careful in his choice of words. This was not so much because he was pedantic, but because the two of them had agreed in advance to limit the release of certain information at this stage. 'We have talked in Cabinet,' he continued, 'about the water levels in our reservoirs and the remaining water supply. We have talked about depletion rates, including measures to curb and reduce consumption. We have considered also the low water-tables and soil mois- ture deficiency levels, which will seriously impact on agri- cultural and commercial users not dependent on reservoir supply. What we have on the horizon,' he said, coming to the crux of the matter, 'are two additional factors which have the potential to decimate even the present dwindling resources, thereby playing havoc with our contingency planning, to put it mildly. Gentlemen, in a nutshell, we are talking about nitrates and algae.'

For years governments had been warned by ecologists and scientists about the increasing danger from nitrates being washed into rivers and ultimately the water supply. As the pressure for higher agricultural yields mounted, so did the increased use of fertilizers. The lack of conducive growing weather had intensified their use even more. What everyone should have learnt from the 76 drought in particular was that falling river levels increase the concentration of nitrates and other harmful effluents in any given body of water. From time to time there was public outrage, usually following some catastrophic decimation of fish population, but more often than not it was deemed to be a local problem. Legislation existed, with powers vested in the minister of agriculture, but it was rarely invoked. And it was not just fish that were at risk, but humans too. As always, it was the most vulnerable in society who were at most potential risk. Infantile cyanosis in babies gave most cause for concern. Blue baby syndrome, as it was known, once diagnosed, necessitated a switch to the use of bottled water. For the poor in society, that was not regarded as an essential commodity. The middle classes could not only afford it but were also more aware of the debate on water quality. There had been speculation recently, for example, that linked nitrates in water to stomach cancer. It was true that additional water treatment plants were coming on stream in some areas but there was still no consensus on their effectiveness anyway. The usual noises were made about the lack of capital and research spending now that the industry was privatized. The perceived weakness of the regulators in the early years after the 89 release from state control had left much catching up to be done and the problem of nitrates was still a very real one, especially when drought conditions returned.

Hunter assured his fellow ministers that intensified sampling and analysis was being carried out and reports would be studied carefully. It had apparently been reported that two major sources of water supply were currently indicating more than 100 milligrams per litre and this information was being urgently corroborated. But even much lower levels than this would have the environmentalists literally screaming blue murder, if they knew.

If the nitrate situation was worrying, what Alan Hunter had to say about algae was alarming. For the benefit of those present who did not have a scientific or biological bent he explained the background, again in calm, but authoritative tones.

'There are fifteen hundred known species of blue-green algae. It is endemic to all parts of the world and tolerant of extremes of conditions. One of the most primitive of organisms, they have been around for three thousand million years, that's longer than any other living organism, apart from bacteria. In many ways they resemble bacteria, certainly in their reproductive and physiological behaviour. Although more common in the seas and oceans they are also found in freshwater and, indeed, they can appear in any body of water. It is well known that many strains are toxic, although there is not always a regular pattern to the toxicity. In other words, within the same species of algae some strains are poisonous and some are not. There are many recorded cases of toxic algae being responsible for widespread and catastrophic deaths of fish, cattle, horses, swine and other smaller creatures. However, phycotoxicologists, as the experts in this field call themselves, assure us that the adverse effects in humans are usually limited to gastroenteritis. The most common problems arise from algae known as anacystis cyanea or anabaena flos-asquae, both of which are rapidly acting neurotoxins, potentially fatal to creatures, but not humans ... until now.'

Hunter paused for the first time and took a sip from his glass of water, bottled of course, and pure, out of a deep underground well in France. His last words had caused his listeners to sit up a bit straighter, and he thought he heard one of them mutter, 'Oh, my God' under his breath. But there was worse to come.

'Both strands had also been capable of being dealt with by filtration plants ... until now,' he added, then paused again, but this time not for a drink. 'I regret to have to tell you that two deaths with a potential link to a new strain of highly toxic blue-green algae are currently being urgently investigated. It is also being postulated that spores are being found in drinking water and, almost incredibly, as with some types of bacteria, pre-boiling of water is not always an effective defence against these amazingly tolerant organisms. It is known, for example, that some forms of algae thrive in volcanic springs. It remains to be seen what the final conclusions of the investigations will be, of course, but the cause for alarm that I mentioned earlier stems from a report delivered to me this morning. This stated that initial surveys are suggesting a very widespread infestation, if that is the right expression. Naturally, all possible measures will be taken to identify, alleviate and eliminate the problem with the utmost urgency. However, I have to warn that the immediate repercussions from both this and the nitrates issue are that we are likely to be left with further decimation of already severely stretched stocks of water of acceptable quality. Indeed, in certain well-populated areas, we may have a supply that instead of being measured in weeks may now have to be counted in days, in terms of what is safe and usable.'

An explosion of questions followed from the small but worried gathering. How could this happen? What had gone wrong with monitoring procedures? What were the regulators playing at? Who else knew about the current situation? Who were the experts looking into the issues? When could they expect a solution? How would all this affect the contingency planning? What were the implications for agriculture, for the economy as a whole, for the whole social fabric, for that matter; oh, and of course, most importantly of all, for the government's re-election?

'Gentlemen, your concerns are understandable and laudable,' interrupted the prime minister firmly, but as ever politely, and with an expression which as usual gave no clue to his degree of concern, rather like the disguised delivery of a clever spin bowler in his beloved game of cricket. 'We have little time and possibly little room for manoeuvre but, as I see it, the most urgent priority is to gather and corroborate the facts. Alan has already alluded to the report being only a few hours old and this will be followed up with the utmost vigour. We must know exactly what we are dealing with. I reckon that we have a few days. Inevitably the media will get hold of it eventually, although we must guard against public alarm. We must also consider when to brief our Cabinet colleagues and, of course, the House. However, for the time being, gentlemen, I implore all those present in this room to maintain complete secrecy in this matter. Furthermore, I would like you all to cancel all out-of-town appointments until further notice. I may need to call another meeting at short notice. I think it likely that we may have to make some very quick decisions.'

* * *

'I, Samuel Albert Collyweston, being the duly appointed returning officer for the parliamentary constituency of Lichworth, hereby declare that the number of votes cast for each candidate in the by-election for the said constituency, is as follows...' The hush that had fallen on the civic hall was indicative of the tense and expectant atmosphere. The candidates, lined up on stage, looked sufficiently respectful of the occasion with the exception of the candidate for the Clown Party. His temporarily straight face seemed strangely at odds with his huge rosette, his ridiculous brightly coloured garb, and a big red hooter. Reaney's thoughts drifted momentarily to the times he had watched such occasions on the television, almost disbelieving that his name was on the list of real candidates about to be read out. He refocused his mind as the returning officer was completing his pronouncement on the second of the joke candidates. As the alphabet would have it, Reaney was last on the list, his Conservative opponent immediately before him, and the three stooges, as he described them, were first. The declaration continued ...

'James Fortesque Deed-poll Glum, Clown Party,' an idiotic cretin whose painted face now came to life in celebration of the high point of his existence, as he considered it, '...twelve votes.' How could there be another eleven as stupid as him? thought Reaney ... but now down to the important business. 'Oliver Michael Popplewell, Conservative Party, twenty-five thousand and twelve votes.' The muted reaction of the modest gathering was insufficient to interrupt the stride that the official had now got into. 'Trevor Anthony Reaney, Labour Party, twenty-five thousand and ni...' There were gasps from the crowd, 'Sorry ... er ... twenty-five thousand nine hundred and nine votes,' he finally splurted out, '... and I hereby declare that the said Trevor Anthony ...' but his remaining words were drowned out by the cheers of Reaney's supporters. The victor raised both hands above his head to acknowledge his success and his toothy grin almost eclipsed that of the Clown Party candidate, though the latter had the advantage of a considerable quantity of make-up, much of it now smudged and runny.

So, Reaney had done it, against the expectation of most of the national pundits and commentators, but not his own. His majority was low, as might be expected, but just enough to see off the need for a recount. It might well prove difficult to defend at a general election, when the seat would be more likely to revert to national trends and would be deprived of the mid-term protest vote. But that was a long way from his mind at the moment, as he savoured his victory. His joy was there for all to see, but he adopted a more serious countenance as he approached the microphone to give the traditional thanks to the returning officer and his staff.

Jim reached for the remote control. He had stayed up late to catch the result but was not interested in the acceptance speeches, nor the verdicts that would follow from the pompous politicians back in the studio. If truth be told, he had also been hoping to catch sight of Kate, Reaney's beautiful wife, and in that he had not been disappointed. He had not seen her for many years and though the odd glimpse through a television screen could be no substitute for seeing her in the flesh, it was enough to remind him of times past, before even he had met his own wife, Carol, who had been safely tucked up in bed for an hour or more by now.

While Jim still had doubts about the calibre of Reaney as a worthy MP, he was pleased for him in a way, for old times' sake. It also meant that he now knew a member of that most exclusive of clubs, the House of Commons, not that Jim was the sort who went in for name-dropping, but he had a feeling that such a contact could prove very useful to him. He would have to move quickly, though, if he had anything in mind in the short term, as he had heard the TV presenter mention that the victor would scarcely have time to take up his seat in the House before the summer recess.

Carol seemed to be asleep as Jim eased himself into bed, trying not to disturb her, but evidently it was not a very deep sleep.

'Did he win then?' she asked drowsily.

'Yes, he did, by nearly a thousand,' replied Jim, slightly surprised by her question.

'Are you pleased?'

'In a way, I suppose I am,' said Jim.

'You'll have to get in touch,' said Carol, still struggling to show enthusiasm. 'Maybe he'll give us a conducted tour of Parliament sometime.'

'Yes, he might at that,' replied Jim. 'I think I'll offer him my congratulations tomorrow, if I can get in touch with him that is. I think that he could prove very useful in more ways than one.'

'Mmmm . . . ,' murmured Carol, giving up the fight to keep the conversation going and too tired to have enquired deeper about Jim's last comment. The last thing she remembered before entering the land of dreams was the warmth of Jim's near naked body against hers.

'Damn that working-class hero from an age gone by,' spat David Mallow, with a venom that almost penetrated the TV screen. If political standing was measured on the Richter scale, he would rate Reaney no greater than a mild tremor, whilst he himself would have the potential impact of another San Francisco earthquake. There were two things that upset him about the Lichworth result. Firstly, Olly Popplewell was a pal from years back who had sponsored him when he was a new boy, and before Olly had lost his seat at the last general election. Secondly, Reaney needled him, reminding Mallow of the old style, flat-capped socialists he had so hated in his youth and who had helped persuade him into politics in the first place. The incident with the prime minister in the constituency had, to Mallow's mind, confirmed the kind of scheming crass individual that Reaney was.

It had not been a good day all round. Following yesterday's post-Cabinet emergency subcommittee meeting, a number of searching questions were being tossed his way about his rôle and involvement in the nitrates' issue. Under the Water Resources Act he had power to limit any farming activities involving the use of nitrates that might endanger the water supply quality. Despite some recent reports which had landed on his desk, calling for action, he had not appreciated the significance of them and had done nothing. He had

71

spent the morning going over them and trying to cover his tracks. Then, he had been late for a lunch appointment and his afternoon had been marred by telephone problems preventing him from making a number of important calls. He had been told that there was a general problem with telephone links in the capital. It had been yet another hot and sultry day, which he had spent mainly indoors in sticky, uncomfortable surroundings. He was glad, therefore, of the opportunity to unwind at his Pimlico flat.

He had phoned home to let the dutiful Mrs Mallow know that he would be in town another night due to pressure of work, but he would definitely be back home the next day, Saturday afternoon. In fact, his work, piled high though it was at the ministry and bulging in his briefcase, was not his preoccupation at all that evening. Instead, he had been enjoying the most agreeable French cuisine and excellent wine, in the company of a charming companion, who now joined him back at the well-furnished flat.

'Come on, Marshy,' uttered the soft young voice from behind, 'this is no time for business,' and at that moment, as he sat back on the deep-buttoned sofa, feet up on pouffe, with her bare comforting arms gently around his neck, and gin and tonic in his hand, his animosity towards the imbecile on the screen in front of him suddenly become irrelevant. He was relaxed now after the rigours of the day, as he so often was in the company of his mistress. Using his free hand, he touched her gently on her heavily tanned arm as she bent forward, standing behind but leaning over the sofa.

'I take it that you are ready for bed then, my darling,' he said.

'Well, what does it look like?' came the teasing, mischievous reply and with that Mallow craned his neck to look over his shoulder. Still mostly masked by the sofa, her upper body only was visible and it was completely devoid of clothing. She was tall, dark and slender, as tall as Mallow, but considerably lighter. That and her already inclined angle meant that he had no difficulty in pulling her over and down on to the sofa with him, but the momentum generated saw them both roll off onto the plush deep-pile carpet. Despite the soft landing Mallow was temporarily jolted.

'Oh, I'm getting too old for this sort of frolicking,' he exclaimed in feigned agony. In fact, he was not old for a senior politician, although you had to wonder what attractive young women saw in him. Previous experience suggested that it must be power and prestige that attracted them. In Mallow's case, it was most certainly unlikely to be his physical attractions. The same could not be said for his mistress, as she lay on her back next to him on the burgundy carpet, clad only in a triangle of white silk cloth over her most intimate parts. Her arms were stretched out above her head where she had left them, in a deliberately exaggerated fashion, as though to indicate how she had come to rest following the rough and tumble. In so doing, her breasts tightened to form two pointed and fleshy peaks, each topped by a hard red nipple pointing up to the ornate ceiling. Her normally flat hard waist was now indented by her prostrate position and her long shapely legs were spreadeagled. They both laughed. If this was what came with the power and the job, then Mallow was indeed a lucky man, despite his current tribulations. Pompous and reactionary; someone had called him in the House earlier that week. If only they could see him now, he thought.

Once the formalities and then the interviews were over, Reaney went down amongst his supporters to show his gratitude and share their delight. Many returned with him to his headquarters for a small celebratory reception. Whether or not it was the anticlimax following the result, or the relief at the end of a hectic campaign, or maybe the considerations of the implications of the result, he was not sure, but he seemed to be in a more reflective and pensive mood. The instinctively raucous and ebullient nature seemed subdued. Certainly, he was happy and smiling as he posed with his arms around Kate and his agent, Frank, but he seemed strangely contemplative. The familiar gravelly tones were still there, though, as, flanked by Kate and Frank, he made an off-the-cuff speech:

'Friends and supporters, what can I say? I'm overcome with gratitude. A thousand thanks for all your support. This outcome would not have been possible without you. I feel very humble.' At this point applause broke out and mingled with cheers and shouts of congratulation. Reaney went on to thank several individuals by name, with the two standing beside him at the top of the list. He regained some of his bubbling enthusiasm as he drew his little speech to a close. 'I'll leave you with a message, and let it be a promise to you and the people of Lichworth. I'll serve you to the best of my ability and I'm determined not to hold the Palace of Westminster in awe, nor let it suck me into complacent respectability. I'll give it to them straight between the eyes, and the sooner the better. You can rely on that.'

There was no reason to doubt that Reaney would be true to his words or that he was likely to be one of the more active, involved and forthright members of the ancient institution.

'Darling, I'm right out of Perrier. What else can I get you?'

'Oh, just a glass of ordinary tap water will do,' said Mallow's mistress, by now ensconced in the quilted comfort of the luxurious king-size bed in the master bedroom of the minister's flat. The satin sheets lay soft against her bronzed and still naked body, recovering now from its exertions both inside and outside the bedroom. 'Marshy' Mallow returned with two drinks.

'I don't know how you can drink tap water,' he said. 'Filthy stuff, full of nitrates and algae and God knows what else.'

'But I thought our drinking water was the envy of the world,' she replied. 'Don't drink it abroad they used to tell you. It's not as good as ours.' Mallow removed his dressing gown, to reveal a frontage in need of reshaping and tightening, his limp sex organ showing no enthusiasm for any further activity. He scoffed at the suggestion that had just been made as he too climbed into bed.

'Darling, take it from me, as a man who knows, that there are things in our drinking water that should not be there.'

74

'You are putting me right off,' she responded. 'So how do I know if I have any of these nasties in my glass?' she asked. 'These nitrates and allergies.'

'Algae, actually,' corrected Mallow, never one to let an error pass without comment, however pedantic. 'And you won't see either by just looking, unless you happen to have a microscope with you,' whereupon she stopped studying the contents of the glass. 'Seriously, though,' he continued, 'promise me that you will stop drinking the stuff when you get home. We've had some bad reports from your part of the country.'

'I'll promise if you tell me what it's all about, Marshy. What sort of reports are you talking about?' she asked.

Mallow saw no harm in giving her a potted version of the previous day's discussion in committee because he was genuinely concerned for her health and, in any case, everyone would be told in a few days. There was no way that they could keep that kind of information bottled up, as it were, for long. The glass of tap water by her bedside remained undisturbed throughout the night.

*　*　*

It was another scorching Saturday. The pleasantly warm early morning had given way to another baking hot cloudless day long before noon. The forecasters were more confident than ever that the 100 Celsius mark would be reached, and possibly in more than one location, despite the fact that they had predicted it, without success, earlier in the week. Everyone's limited energy was devoted to finding ways of keeping cool. Activity of a voluntary kind was minimal. Supplies of electric fans had long since run out.

Jim had to get in touch with Reaney urgently if he wanted to make use of his services and to set up the gathering that he was now planning. He had failed to get through to him the previous day but must give it one more try. In fact, there was always the danger that Reaney might have left town now that the election was over but, as it turned out, Jim was lucky. He tried the telephone number of the election HQ again and this time was pleasantly surprised to find that the ringing was answered.

'Hello, Trevor Reaney MP at your service.'

'Oh, very grand,' said Jim. 'Many congratulations on your victory, Trevor. Saw it on the telly. You must be well chuffed.'

'Jim Webb, nice of you to ring. Hope you voted for me.'

'Now that would be telling, Trevor. Not that you needed it anyway. But I'd like to buy you that drink we promised ourselves and perhaps to talk over old times again.'

'I'd love to, Jim,' replied Reaney, 'but I have to say I don't know how I'm going to fit it in with my diary. For a start, I've got a little appointment at Westminster next week. That's why you've caught me here today. I'm trying to tie up loose ends before going down to London.'

'You're not wasting any time taking up your seat then,' observed Jim.

'Can't afford to,' replied Reaney. 'The summer recess is coming up. I've got to get sponsored and introduced in record time.'

'I hesitate to delay you then, Trevor, but if you could spare the time for a brief chat there might be something to interest and benefit you, from a professional point of view, that is,' said Jim, arousing Reaney's curiosity.

'About what?' asked Reaney, succinctly, illustrating that he was slightly puzzled.

'Well, let's just say certain facts and speculation concerning a major national issue which, in the opinion of myself and some of my friends, should be receiving greater political prominence. Just the sort of thing to give a vigorous new member such as yourself a flying start,' explained Jim.

'This all sounds very mysterious,' responded the thoughtful and somewhat surprised politician. 'You wouldn't be pulling my leg by any chance, would you?' he added.

'No, Trevor. Honestly,' assured Jim. 'This is all on the level and, indeed, potentially a very serious matter. If you could find time to pop round to my house, say tomorrow afternoon, I'll have an ice-cold drink for you and a promise not to waste your time.'

'OK, I'll see you at about four o'clock, but you'll have to excuse me if I can't stay for long,' said Reaney. There was crackling on the line as the final niceties were exchanged and Reaney put the telephone down thoughtfully, pouting his lips in puzzlement. Was this a wind-up? What issue of major national importance could Jim and his friends be involved with, he thought as he wafted himself with a file of papers to create a draught in the oppressively hot environment. The forecasters had got it right again, it seemed. It was turning into an overbearing, energy sapping, record-breaking day.

Having confirmed Reaney's attendance, Jim went on to finalize arrangements with the others, having already had provisional acceptances from them.

It was almost a week since Mandy and Bill had been caught up in the violence in Tamfield. They were both feeling and looking much better, though Bill, in particular, was still somewhat bruised and sore.

The police had made little or no progress in apprehending their assailants. In fact, the local bobbies continued to be fully stretched with isolated but unusual outbreaks of violence, and not just from rampaging mobs. Violent domestic squabbles had risen alarmingly, as had incidents of road rage, as it had become known. Nationally, many commentators were reporting on racial disturbances, though some of the experts said that it went much wider than that, encompassing the socially deprived of all groupings. Others even produced evidence to show that well-off youngsters and wage earners were amongst those arrested, demonstrating that this was a behavioural phenomenon, ranging from lack of respect for authority to outright anarchy, possibly organized anarchy if that were not a contradiction in terms. Of course, drink and the weather were identified as the catalysts, as might be expected, and no doubt with some justification. Other factors were less easy to explain away: the surprising number of more mature, seemingly respectable persons being dragged into disturbances and disputes of a violent kind and the wide yet apparently unconnected geographical spread of the incidents. What was becoming evident, however, was a rising level of violence, touching on many aspects of life, a level which seemed to be a reversal of the recent trend, albeit slight, of a reduction in violent crimes; a level which the police were becoming increasingly unable to cope with and a level which was still escalating. The general consensus of opinion was that violent conduct in society was now reaching a new and higher plane than ever previously attained. Television and the media would inevitably accentuate the dilemma, of course, and, in the view of many, create an alarmist view. But no amount of pictures could substitute for direct involvement and Mandy and Bill were among many who could testify to that. Was it really a coincidence or perhaps a convenient excuse that the surge of violence was accompanying the extremes of climate? Or was it the culmination of years of indiscipline and moral decline? People continued to disagree over the causes but many felt that society was in the midst of a fundamental and not so subtle change of direction. Of course, there were many more who had no time for what they regarded as so much claptrap and who went about their normal daily lives oblivious of such theories.

Carol was eager to help Mandy get her life back in the groove again that Saturday afternoon. Bill stayed at home with his feet up, watching the cricket. Though he was bored by his inactivity, the weather was again not conducive to anything energetic anyway. In fact, his liking for televised sport would have won the day, in all probability, in normal circumstances. Unfortunately for him, however, his enjoyment was destined to be plagued by yet more interference in the transmission.

Carol would permit no such inactivity for Mandy. Using the principle that the best reaction to falling off a bike was to get straight back on again and that the best way to overcome a car accident was to get back behind the wheel as soon as possible, she persuaded Mandy that she needed to venture out into the wide world again and mingle with some crowds. What's more, she advised, it should be in Tamfield. Notwithstanding the heat, a shopping expedition was the order of the day. Mandy's confidence in public had been understandably sapped by the previous week's events. An element of shock was not unusual in such cases. But she was a fighter by instinct and would not allow her life to be disrupted by the actions of yobbos. All the same, she was grateful to be visiting Tamfield by day and not at night.

They set off in Carol's car, her old faithful as she called it, on the short journey from Lichworth to Tamfield. She told Mandy how Jim was reluctant at the moment to put his hand in his pocket for a new car and how it was all right for him with his low mileage company model. It was a half-hearted moan, as she remained very fond of her reliable old servant, not least for all the happy memories that were associated with it. With windows full open and speed gathered, there was a refreshing blast of air through the car to counteract the almost unbearable heat as the thermometer again climbed inexorably. Carol, dressed befittingly lightly in white shorts and low-necked T-shirt, rested her bare arm on the door ledge as they paused at the first roundabout on their journey. Her bronzed, fetching appearance brought whistles of approval from an open-top sports model full of young men that drew alongside. For a moment it embarrassed Carol, but then brought chuckles of amusement from both her and Mandy which increased in volume once the other car had safely sped away in a different direction to theirs.

Carol decided to take the back roads, preferring the country lanes and villages to the main trunk road. It took them behind the army barracks and through a shady and hopefully cooler wooded area before it rejoined the main road not too far from Tamfield. Just off the road, on either side, were numerous minor roads leading to the army firing ranges that took up a large part of this area. There were warning notices at frequent intervals:

WARNING! MOD PROPERTY! KEEP OUT!
DANGER! FIRING RANGES! KEEP CLEAR!
MOD PROPERTY! NO ACCESS!

Some of the ranges were visible from the roadside and it was not unusual to hear the sound of gunfire. Indeed, firing times were published in the local paper for the benefit of the local populace. It was not even unusual for these activities to take place at weekends, often to accommodate the practice needs of part-time, reservist soldiers.

With a modest speed and windows down it was not particularly surprising, therefore, to Mandy and Carol when the apparent sound of gunfire greeted them as they approached this area. What did surprise and alarm them, however, was the group of people dashing across the road not fifty yards ahead of them, some waving and others aiming and firing handguns. It soon became apparent to them that this was not the orderly and disciplined firing practice that they had seen on previous occasions.

'Do you think it's some kind of exercise?' Mandy asked Carol, rapidly seeking a rational explanation for what was going on.

'What, on public roads?' replied Carol, not allowing the conversation to distract her from her prime objective of slowing down the car quickly in readiness to stop. 'Besides, those don't look like full army uniforms to me, at least not all of them. Why aren't they in full gear?'

'Oh, my God,' yelled Mandy, moving her hand to her mouth. 'They're not firing blanks either.' It soon became apparent to both, as the scene unfurled, that live ammunition was being used and at least two bodies lay stricken as a result, one of which crumpled up in agony before their eyes. Both victims came from the chasing group, some 50 yards to their right. Any thought that this might be an exercise striving for increased realism was quickly discounted by the sound of desperate and agonized screams and the sight of spurting blood. It was all happening so quickly. Mandy did not have time to consider what she had done to deserve being caught up in violence for a second consecutive week, nor time to ponder the astronomical odds. Carol, with the car now at a more comfortable speed, acted instinctively. Seeing that her present course would take them between the warring parties and through a hail of bullets, she turned off to the left onto a minor single track road. The alternative would have been to stop and then attempt a three-point turn before heading back in the reverse direction, but that was not a manoeuvre she would have been comfortable with in the time she judged was available. Simply reversing at speed was not one of her stronger skills either, particularly on a narrow road. She hoped that the minor track would take them at speed away from the danger, although inevitably it was a gamble. It was a narrow, private road, in fact, which led to the firing ranges and not one that she was familiar with or, indeed, had any right to be on.

In seconds, Carol knew that the gamble had failed. Fooled by the part of the road that was initially visible, it soon doubled back on itself, taking them back in the direction they were trying to avoid. Then matters got worse.

'Oh, my God,' exclaimed Mandy again.

'Shit!' said Carol, unthinkingly, for she was not and never had been given to the habitual use of bad language. The whole width of the road was barred by a thick, heavy-looking horizontal pole resting on vertical metal struts, red like the warning notices all around that threatened all those who went beyond this point. This time there was no possibility of turning in the road and the prospect of reversing, however slowly, was not attractive either. Perhaps the pole could be moved, manually or mechanically, or simply dislodged from its support and pushed aside. Their little detour could not have put much distance between them and the first group they saw and yet Carol was still acting instinctively, looking for an effective escape route, as she leapt out of the car. Without consulting Mandy, she had decided that the removal of the barrier in front of them could be the only means of fleeing the danger they found themselves in. She hurried towards it.

Carol's whole body shuddered when, as if from nowhere, a rough heavy hand clamped itself around her nose and mouth, whilst her delicate thinly-clad waist was wrapped in a vice-like grip by another arm, on the end of which, not inches from her body, was a handgun. Partly from the shock and partly from the physical jolt of the assault, Carol staggered backwards, but she was held so firmly that there was no likelihood of her falling. Nor was there any immediate prospect of freeing herself. The assailant turned her round to face others who were running towards them and, breathlessly, he spoke to them.

'I think that we might have found ourselves a hostage. What do you say, boss?'

'Maybe, Andy. Maybe,' said the apparent leader of the troop, a big, well-set young man dressed in army trousers and in shirt sleeves, an automatic weapon slung over his shoulder. 'But the car we can definitely use,' he added. All eyes switched to the car, motor still running and seemingly empty.

'Get the barrier up. Phil, help him,' barked the leader, with authority. As the man called Andy released his iron grip on Carol, the leader grabbed her slender forearm, so tightly that she felt he could probably break it if he had a mind to or if an excuse presented itself. The two men successfully moved the heavy pole. The leader turned towards Carol.

'Listen, luv,' he said, in a surprisingly quiet and calm voice, tinged with a north country accent of a type not unfamiliar to her, 'just do as we ask and we won't hurt you.' Then, he added, after a slight pause and equally surprisingly in the circumstances, 'Please.'

Carol had so far acted instinctively and with the sound of bullets being fired nearby she could see only the need to escape the area quickly. She had neither the time nor the information to assess what might happen later or what further dangers might be lurking. She was also concerned about Mandy. Was she still in the car, lying on the floor? Carol did not resist as she was ushered back towards the car by the two men known as Andy and Phil. Their leader had gone off in the opposite direction, through the bushes and, shortly afterwards, from that same area, came the noise of increased gunfire and then a lull. The young leader re-emerged from the bushes with another colleague stumbling and scampering behind him. They made straight for the car where Carol was now firmly esconced in the back. The new man, breathless, sweaty and pale-looking, dived in alongside, to the left of Carol who had Phil at her other side. Andy was at the wheel and his young superior took the front passenger seat. He ordered his driver to take off and that he did, with the roar and screech of a speedway rider.

'What about Jack and Degsy?' came the anxious enquiry from Phil in the rear. There was stunned silence save only for the still heavy breathing of the man on Carol's left and the increasing engine noise of Carol's pride and joy, as Andy pushed the revs rapidly round the dial. 'You can't just leave them. You said we were all in this together, didn't you?' implored the distraught young man, in rising tones. 'We have to go back.'

'No, Phil,' said the leader firmly and then, more quietly, 'there's no point, they're dead.' Phil let out a loud groan. Head in hands he broke down, sobbing loudly. Carol wondered what on earth these young men had got involved with and, strangely, despite her predicament, she was not afraid. Before she could offer any comfort to the distressed figure on her right, however, the one on her left slumped forward. His head butted into the seat in front, which stopped him from sliding down. Carol noticed for the first time that a large part of his clothing was bloodstained, probably from wounds on his left-hand side. As his mouth fell open, the trickle of blood suggested internal injury too.

Mandy watched from the bushes as the red car tore off up the narrow strip of tarmac past the dislodged barrier in a fashion she had never seen it driven before. At that moment she felt a mixture of shock, relief and worry: shock once again at the onset of such sudden and unexpected raw violence; relief at not being in the clutches of armed and dangerous men; worry about what would happen to Carol, but in a strange way that was also tinged with guilt that she had somehow deserted her best friend for her own selfish safety. Yet she did not have time to dwell on any of these emotions before contemplating another worry of more immediate concern. Was she now safe herself as a result of her deft disappearance only a few minutes before? She had to consider that the chasing pack was also armed and dangerous, not least because, as she had seen with her own eyes, two of its members had been cut down. Instinct would suggest that it would be the good guys chasing the bad and not the other way round. But was any armed individual stable in such circumstances, in the heat of battle, aggrieved, frightened and possibly not very experienced in such matters? She could not even be certain that all of the fleeing group had left the scene. Certainly there were only four of them in Carol's car when it took off, but she felt that it was significant that firing in the immediate vicinity had now stopped. There had been some distant cracking of ammunition, but now that too had ceased. There was an eerie silence abounding and Mandy was determined that it would not be broken by any sudden, potentially startling movement on her part. She continued to crouch down in the bushes, pulse still racing, but mind alert, awaiting developments.

The single track tarmac strip had gone on much further than Carol imagined and further than would have been expected by any motorist passing by this small lane on the main road, unless they had cause to know it. Andy had, nevertheless, powered his way along it single-mindedly and silently, oblivious of the wretched state of his colleagues in the back of the car. Despite her dilemma, Carol felt as though she would like to proffer help to them both but was powerless to do so.

'Where to now, boss?' asked Andy, having seen the end of the tarmac coming up and turning his head slightly to pose the question to his front-seat passenger. He, in turn, was sat in a half-turned position, allowing him a wide arc of surveillance covering his passengers, his hostage and any outside pursuers. He held his automatic with his right hand, vertically, with his right arm propped at right angles from the hip. He remained the calmest member of the group, befitting his status as leader. Strong and athletic, but intelligent looking, he exuded an air of refinement. In response to the driver's question, he looked round to his left again, weighing up options and then gave his order.

'Farm track at ten o'clock ... fifty yards.' As they left the tarmac surface with a jolt he looked anxiously behind again. No sign of pursuers yet, but the moment of truth would arrive when they hit the main road and he knew that.

'What's your name?' asked Carol suddenly and unexpectedly but with calm authority.

'They call me Boss. But you can call me Geoff,' came the equally calm reply, despite the bumpy ride they were now having to endure. 'What's yours?'

'Carol.'

'Nice name, and you seem a nice lady. Don't worry, luv, we've no argument with you, so long as you behave that is,' he added menacingly, but without venom.

'Geoff, I'm more concerned about your two colleagues here, one at or near death's door,' said Carol, glancing at the slumped figure on her left, 'the other in a deep state of shock,' looking now at the man called Phil, on her right. Phil had stopped sobbing but was a pathetic, trembling figure with a staring, vacant expression. 'I don't know what this business is all about,' continued Carol, still calm, 'but don't you think they need help ... urgently? You seem an intelligent man. Surely you can see that?'

'Don't patronize me,' blurted Geoff, half-jolted out of his seat by the roughness of the terrain and the speed of the silent Andy's driving. The edge in his voice persuaded Carol to back off a little, at least for the present.

The car had rejoined a farm track now and Geoff turned to watch the road again as Andy accelerated further.

'Fork right at the top,' ordered Geoff as a second track veered off through dark stone pillars and over a cattle grid. He seemed to be familiar with the location. A little further on, through a clump of trees, and they emerged into a farm-yard, scattering clucking hens before them. Andy screeched sharply to a halt, again at Geoff's command. The latter leapt out quickly and went to the rear car door. Here he helped his still bleeding and barely conscious colleague gently out of the car, laying his arm around his neck and then lowering him carefully onto the gravelly surface. Carol was aware for a moment of the opened door, but the potential for escape was not good. As Geoff was uncoiling the man's arm from around his neck he paused to look down at the drawn and bloodied face.

'I'm really sorry, mate. The whole thing just got out of hand. You'll be OK here. Someone will see to you.' Then, as he started to move away, he added, 'Phil, this is where you get out too, mate. Come on, the party's over. But quick about it, we have to move.' Geoff then bent slightly to look through the car window at Andy. 'You staying or going, Andy?' he asked.

'I'm sticking with you, boss. I'm surprised you should ask,' he replied, almost indignantly but never less than respectfully. 'Now I think you'd better dive in and let's get out of here,' added Andy.

Phil, meanwhile quietly departed through the other rear passenger door, mumbling something and then closing the door behind him. He looked for all the world like a walking zombie.

Geoff quickly seated himself in the rear this time. He beckoned to Carol to move up to the other end where he could keep an eye on her, but at an arm's length. He still sat almost sideways on to preserve a wide-angled surveillance again. For the first time, he allowed himself a good look at Carol and he liked what he saw: a physically very attractive lady, young but mature, feminine yet not fragile or weak. As they screeched off on the gravel surface people emerged from the farm buildings, but Geoff's mind was elsewhere at that moment.

'There, are you happier now?' he said, looking at Carol.

'Slightly,' she replied. 'Now can you tell me when the next stop is? When do I get out?'

'We'll see,' said Geoff.

'Directions please, Boss,' interrupted Andy.

'Not much choice at the moment, mate. Carry straight on up this track. Look for an opening to your left in about a hundred yards or so. We need to head over towards those woods, without hitting any public roads.'

After about a hundred and fifty yards Andy turned off through an opened gate into an empty and fairly level field.

Some time had elapsed now since the last shot was fired. Mandy had waited patiently but anxiously. She was frightened but also frustrated at her inability to get help for Carol. Her concern and the continuing quiet eventually persuaded her that she had to make a move. She rose from her crouching position with difficulty after such a long period of immobility. Her immediate concern was to make contact, with the police, with her husband Bill and, of course, with Jim, so she felt that she should try to head in what she thought was the general direction of Whittleton, a little village that could only have been not more than a mile away. It was important, though, she thought, to make as much use as she could of the trees and bushes on the way.

The trouble was that the twists and turns of their evasive detour had muddled Mandy's sense of direction. At least the distance they had covered was not great and she set off as quietly as she could across the track near the barrier and into the cooling shade of more trees on the other side. There was bracken to get through and the ground, whilst dry and hard in the almost barren conditions beginning to take over some localities, was more suited to robust footwear. However, Mandy was more concerned in looking out for people, whether armed or otherwise, then concentrating on the placing of her every footstep. Despite her slow and deliberate movement she stubbed her toe painfully on a hard protruding tree root, lost her balance and cursed out loud as a throbbing pain shot through her open-toed sandal. Almost immediately she heard voices in conversation. Was it a coincidence, or had she been heard? Who were they? What should she do? Still hobbling, she decided to duck down out of sight, only to lose her balance again, but this time in a deep hollow, causing her to roll over and over, ending up somewhat ungainly in the undergrowth. Her momentum ceased when she came to rest against a bulky, solid object. When she regained her composure and lifted her head, Mandy found that she was looking straight into a pair of petrified, terror-stricken staring eyes not more than a few inches away from her face. She let out a shriek that could have been heard in Lichworth. This time there was no doubt of the interest that she had aroused, as a flurry of shouted orders testified, but her instinctive reaction was understandable, faced with the awful sight and touch of the mortally wounded body lying alongside her.

Oblivious now of the dangers, and without knowing why, Mandy pulled herself to her feet and trudged the few yards that took her into a little clearing in the wood. Perhaps her nursing instinct was sending her for help for the stricken body, although it was clearly a lost cause. She was fortunate that before anyone could open fire on her, a voice barked out an order not to fire, her now blood-stained and forlorn appearance signalling that she posed no threat. Cautiously at first, but then more quickly, a number of figures dashed towards her from different directions, some from nearby and some a little further away. It was quickly evident that she was now in safe hands.

A short time later, two bodies were found, one just a few yards away from where Mandy had appeared, and who it later transpired was known as Degsy. The other was Jack. There was no sign of anyone else.

'Wait a minute!' shouted Carol urgently, as the sharp briers ripped into her pale blue top and scratched and bloodied her midriff. The thought of being in the clutches of such armed and desperate villains, possibly murderers, seemed to be eclipsed by her annoyance at being almost dragged through the woods they had entered not ten minutes earlier. Her outburst had the desired effect. Geoff halted and released his tight grip on Carol's arm. Andy paused in sympathy.

'All right, take a breather,' ordered Geoff in between deep breaths. He was concerned obviously that they should stay one step ahead. He was puzzled at the absence of any helicopter activity, but he judged that they could spare a few moments rest and thinking time.

Having made their way across several fields in the car, they had abandoned it in a fairly inconspicuous location right at the edge of the wood, partly in bushes and partly covered by some nearby fallen branches and twigs. They had made good progress then through the wood, most of the time avoiding the more worn tracks and thoroughfares. In the confusion and excitement of the afternoon's events, the unbearable heat from the record-breaking temperatures had not seemed to affect them. They put their profuse amounts of sweat down to their hectic exertions. The wood they were in had stood up better than many in the country to the ravages of the hot dry weather. Though very dry, there was still plenty of undergrowth and ground cover to negotiate.

Carol was in a sorry state: shabby, unkempt, sweaty and breathless. She had cuts to her legs as well as her midriff but she saw little alternative at present but to go along with her captors' wishes. She thought that she knew vaguely where they were but wondered just what the man called Geoff had in mind. So far he had acted decisively and, where necessary, swiftly and he seemed to know the area.

'Geoff, what is all this about?' asked Carol, now steadily regaining her composure. 'I realize, with all the shooting that's been going on, though God knows why ...,' she continued, pausing occasionally for breath, and with arms akimbo, '... that you must be in fear of your lives ... but this futile attempt to escape is bound to fail. You might as well stop this charade and give yourselves up to the authorities now ... if that's who they are.' She added the last comment as an afterthought for she could not be other than confused by who and what was involved.

'Come on! Move!' said Geoff and she felt his big strong hand clamping her lower arm and jerking her forward again. She had to comply and they all set off again at a frantic pace, Andy bringing up the rear. Geoff, constantly alert, looking all around him, had simply ignored Carol's plea, being more concerned with finding his bearings again and setting off in a slightly different direction.

They must have spent at least another twenty minutes

dodging and darting through the trees and the under-growth. On one occasion they passed close to an elderly couple who had strayed off the public path. In fact, they should not have been in the woods at all had they obeyed the Forestry Commission exclusion notices posted as a result of the drought. Before Carol could even think about raising the alarm those big hands again held her tightly, clamping her mouth this time. In any case, she would have doubted what benefit could have accrued from involving such a harmless, innocent looking pair. Maybe they could have reported a sighting, eventually, but that assumed that Geoff and Andy would have allowed them to go freely on their way. Overall, she was surprised that she had not reacted to her capture in a more frightened manner but the two men, despite the threat of their strength and their weapons, simply did not fill her with dread. She even wondered at one stage if the whole rig-marole could be one incredibly realistic army exercise. But there was no faking by Phil, nor by his heavily blood-stained colleague they had left behind them at the farm. Perhaps, then, it was all a dream, or rather a nightmare. If only that could be true. Certainly the bumping, stumbling and scratching felt real enough before they finally came to a halt at the far edge of the wood.

It was late afternoon before Jim returned home from a brief outing into town. Like most others, he was anxious to keep out of the sun and the heat as much as possible. A cool shower could well be the next order of the day he was think-ing as he pulled into The Close. He was unprepared for the police presence, just as Carol had been a few weeks earlier. However, he was even more unprepared for and astounded by the news that awaited him. Those sentiments were to be submerged quickly though by heart-stopping fear and dread for the consequences for his beloved Carol.

A mixture of incredulity and shock continued to fill Jim's mind as he was driven to the scene of the carnage and the abduction, at his insistence, at considerable speed. Roads were now closed off. Large numbers of police and army personnel were milling about. He soon found himself in a police control unit where, before being briefed, he was able to meet up with the ashen-faced Mandy, who now had Bill with her. They embraced and exchanged words of disbelief.

A helicopter clattered overhead. Police radio crackled. There was much activity. It was only a matter of time before Carol was found, thought Jim. He prayed to God that she would be unharmed. Five had died already, including a man found at a nearby farm.

'Joanne,' said Ben, with a faint air of surprise as his enormously attractive sister entered quietly through the open patio door. 'I heard the screech of gravel and the car door slam, but I wasn't expecting you tonight. Not that you aren't welcome as always, of course,' he added with the usual overemphasized politeness that passed for affection between them. But Joanne was not in the mood to retaliate. She looked stunningly beautiful in a low-necked white mini-dress but her appearance was marred by a glum-looking face and eyes that were devoid of the usual sparkle. Her car journey north had apparently not improved her demeanour.

'Hello, bruv,' she said despondently as she parked herself languidly in the favourite leather armchair she always occupied when visiting her brother Ben's home.

'OK,' responded Ben after a slight pause, 'in your own time, sis. Tell your long-suffering older brother all about it.' It was often to Ben that Joanne turned when she had relationship problems, not that her mother would be unsympathetic, but somehow she did not always appreciate the pressures and strains of the modern kind of relationships that Joanne got involved with, and nor did she understand or have experience of the circles in which Joanne now moved. On the other hand, Ben had always been very close and they often confided in each other. 'But before you start,' continued Ben, 'shall I pour us both a drink? You must be ready for one after travelling in this heat.'

'Why not?' replied Joanne. 'I'll have my usual, please.' In no time at all Ben was back with the drinks and he eased himself into a nearby armchair, one which was a little closer to Joanne than his previous one. They sipped their drinks in silence for a while, Joanne in particular being quite thirsty. 'Why are men such bastards?' she began at last, and somewhat shockingly.

'Present company excepted, I hope,' commented Ben, though Joanne was now too deep in thought to react. Ben was not surprised. He had been through this before, several times. If his vulnerable and sometimes naive little sister wanted to use him to give vent to her feelings and clear her chest as well as her mind, then so be it. That is what families are for, he thought, and he was happy for her to turn to him in times of trouble.

'What I object to most, is being used,' continued Joanne, now gathering pace. 'How can you be the centre of someone's world one minute, and then ... and then ... a little bit on the side the next? Men are so dishonest!' Ben decided not to interrupt her flow now. 'They say they love you, they act as if they love you, and then, without any warning, they tell you they have to go shopping with their wives. Shopping, for Christ's sake. It's so bloody hypocritical.'

'Joanne, what have I told you about messing with married men?' said Ben, unable to restrain himself. 'Will you never learn?' he continued. 'Someone always gets hurt, and usually very badly.'

Undaunted, though, Joanne went on.

'Last night we fell asleep in each other's arms. This morning, I wake up and before I can wipe the sleep out of my eyes, he is telling me that he has promised to spend the rest of the weekend being the dutiful husband. Not a word the night before, though, when he was busy getting his leg over and fulfilling his sexual fantasies with yours truly.' She paused. 'I thought it was different this time,' she sighed. 'He's not the best physical specimen of a man in the world, but there seemed to be this attraction between us. You know, Ben, the kind of feeling that is just there but you can't explain. I know it's difficult when he has a marriage and a family to think of, not to mention a high profile career,' continued Joanne before Ben could respond to her previous point, 'but love has to win through, surely, if that's what it is,' she concluded dolefully.

'Only you can decide whether it's the real thing or not,' said Ben, 'but don't expect it to run smoothly. All relationships have problems to solve. But have you identified them together and can you tackle them together? Is your love strong enough to surmount them, however insoluble they might seem? And whilst you're thinking over those little snippets of advice from your agony uncle brother, would you like another drink?' he asked, rising from his chair. Joanne drained her glass and answered in the affirmative. 'Back in a jiffy then. I need to top up the water jug,' said Ben.

'Watered down whisky. That's unusual for you,' commented Joanne, at last reacting to something other than her own introspective thoughts.

'I'm drinking so much liquid today with this blasted heat, that I'm having to dilute my alcohol,' replied Ben, his voice tailing off as he went into the kitchen area.

When Ben re-emerged with his replenished jug he found that Joanne had got up out of her seat and was coming towards him with a rather anxious look on her face.

'That's tap water isn't it?' she asked.

'Full marks for observation,' said Ben, puzzled and with Joanne still coming towards him.

'Don't you dare drink it,' she said.

The light was beginning to fade and with it some of the sting was being drawn from the overpowering heat. A magnificent deep red sunset was in prospect, heralding another dry and sunny and no doubt oppressively hot day tomorrow. Jim had dismounted from the military Land Rover that had brought him to the site of Carol's abandoned car. For reasons that had been only partly explained to him, the investigation was being jointly handled by police and army, and the military involvement was believed to be responsible for the news blackout that had been imposed. At this moment, however, all this was of little significance to Jim as he walked, with trepidation, across the field and towards the car. He was flanked by an inspector on one side and a colonel on the other.

Jim already knew that the car had been found empty but he peered anxiously in for clues or signs of reassurance about his beloved Carol. The inspector asked him not to get too close for fear of disturbing potential forensic evidence but Jim could not fail to notice the heavily blood-stained rear seats. It was clear that there had been significant loss of blood and whilst those present knew that the body recovered at the farm was probably responsible, at least for much of it, it would be foolhardy to deduce that this was the only victim. For a time Jim was shaken by the prospect of it all and became oblivious of what was going on around him. Photographs were being taken and there was much activity and chatter.

'Haven't the helicopters found anything yet?' asked Jim, eventually.

'I'm afraid there's been a problem,' said Inspector Childs, the balding, smartly-dressed officer who had become familiar to Bill and Mandy the week before.

'What sort of a problem, Inspector?'

'There's a malfunction on the thermal imager,' came the reply, 'and with the light fading it's going to make an aerial search very difficult.'

'What do you mean ... what problem ... I don't understand ... what are you going to do?' Jim could hardly get his anxious words out quickly enough.

'Searching woods in the dark is hopeless. Normally technology can do it for us, but with this problem, we're stuck.'

'Get another helicopter,' said Jim, succinctly.

'Not so easy I'm afraid, sir. There's all hell let loose tonight apparently. Civil disturbances in Birmingham I believe.' Jim shook his head in disbelief.

'We can't just stand here,' said Jim. 'Let's get searching.'

'In which direction, sir,' asked the inspector.

'In the woods of course,' replied Jim. 'Isn't that the obvious place?'

'Maybe,' said the inspector, coming closer, 'but have you

94

any idea how extensive these woods are? We need back-up. We need coordination, to ensure that we cover every inch, if needs be. Then again, sir, the woods could be a decoy. With a head start they could have risked heading off in a different direction.'

'But is that likely, Inspector, with a helicopter buzzing about?' asked Jim, 'Even without its thermal imager. Surely they need the cover. If we leave it much longer we are going to lose the light, aren't we?' he added anxiously.

'Our immediate concern is to find some evidence of the direction in which they are heading.'

'What sort of evidence?' asked Jim, curtly.

'Drops of blood, torn clothing, shoes, flattened grass, that kind of thing. Meanwhile, we are searching the immediate area, and have called the helicopter in to a tighter radius. We have a watch on all the usual exits to the woods. We have road blocks on all roads in the area in case they try to hijack another car or in case passing motorists spot anything and we also plan to check every single dwelling in the vicinity. Believe me, sir,' concluded the inspector, 'we are doing all we can.'

'I'm sure you feel that you are, Inspector, but it's my wife in there,' said Jim, nodding towards the darkening interior of the woods, 'and God knows what kind of state she's in. I feel so bloody helpless.'

'We'll get these people, sir, and I promise you that in doing so, we won't do anything to put your wife's life in danger.'

'Just who are they, Inspector?' asked Jim.

'Well, the military boys don't want me to say too much, you understand, but it seems as though the ringleader has flipped, gone off his rocker. He has some sort of grudge and he and his mates decided to exact some revenge. Security at the armoury was too slack. The escapade got out of hand. Panic set in. You can piece together the rest,' said the inspector.

'But we are talking about a disciplined military establishment aren't we?' said Jim, somewhat stunned by this version of events. 'This sort of thing just can't happen can it? It's not some kind of kids' cops and robbers game we are talking about.'

The inspector moved closer, aware that he was about to divulge sensitive, if not classified, information, but he felt that in the circumstances it was wrong to cover it up. He spoke quietly, 'What you may not know is that indiscipline has been rife at the barracks for some time but it has not been deemed a danger to the public because it has not gone off limits. The army are very secretive about this sort of thing, which is why you will hear and see nothing in the media about tonight's events.'

'My wife is abducted by armed lunatics and all that matters is protecting the army's image. Is that what you are saying?' asked Jim, incredulously. 'And what about my wife's friend, Mandy, and her husband? Are you going to put some kind of gag on them, or lock them up?'

'They have kindly agreed to go along with our request not to discuss the incident for the time being,' replied the inspector quietly. 'As far as your wife is concerned, we cannot guarantee anything, of course, but we have no reason to think that she will be a target for their violence. They have no grudge against her. They may be intending to use her as a shield or a hostage. That is a possibility. But I assure you that her safety will be our paramount consideration.'

Jim was baffled and bemused, angry and stunned, and yet the inspector seemed an articulate, competent and experienced man. Despite the bizarre and frightening events that had taken place, somehow he had been reassured by his calm authority. Jim could understand that a heavy-handed, all guns blazing approach would probably bring the opposite result to what they were seeking, but the thought of Carol in the presence of these armed and murderous hooligans, plus his own feeling of helplessness, were eating away at his insides.

'God, my head hurts,' said the man called Geoff, and for a moment it fell heavily into his two propped hands as he sat forward on the convertible bed-settee in one of the forward cabins of the long narrowboat. He did not allow himself to dwell in this position for too long and nor did he permit his weapon to be far from his grasp. Whilst the attractive lady who said she was called Carol had not caused trouble, and even though, at his insistence, she was seated at a comfortable distance away from him, he was not prepared to reduce his vigilance any more than absolutely necessary. He knew that Carol would have to get past him if she made any attempt at escape.

'Then why don't you call a halt to this charade, give yourself up, and get some treatment?' said Carol. 'What's happened today would be enough to give anyone severe shock and trauma.'

'I've had it for days,' was Geoff's short and dismissive reply, 'but I don't blame you for trying to get me to give myself up,' he added.

Geoff and his loyal pal Andy had been lucky in several respects in their attempt to distance themselves from their pursuers. Firstly, they had stumbled across the woman with the car, providing them with transport just when they needed it and a hostage they could use if things went wrong. Secondly, after dumping and hiding the car, it had taken longer than expected for it to be found. Thirdly, they were under the cover of the trees before the aerial search started, and the heat-seeking equipment needed to flush them out was slow arriving. Finally, they were chugging away in their hijacked canal boat before the net could be closed and, in any case, Geoff had correctly reasoned that no one would immediately suspect the canal as a potential hiding place for armed bandits, let alone a means of escape. But they would eventually realize, thought Geoff, that this water course skirted the far corner of the wood. Luckiest of all, however, for Geoff and Andy was the fact that this was one of the few significant stretches of canal in the region with an adequate water level and which was lock-free for miles and, not least, which had an inviting, fuelled and inadequately secured boat just waiting to be borrowed. The cover of darkness now added to their good fortune.

The safe haven, temporary though it probably would be, gave Geoff a chance to reflect whilst Andy was up top doing the steering and whilst his hostage was comfortably under control.

'You might as well give yourself up,' continued Carol. 'You can't sail this thing to the open sea, you know.' Geoff raised his head and looked across at Carol. She was older than him and he admired her maturity and her calmness in the situation in which she found herself. He also found her physically very attractive. Her scant and now somewhat tattered and dirty clothing barely concealed a trim-looking figure with tanned and healthy skin. A less respectable and civilized person than he would have taken advantage of her by now.

'Why don't you have a look round and see if you can find something to eat?' suggested Geoff, 'or maybe some warmer clothes? It looks like being quite a temperature drop tonight.'

'Boss,' came a sudden shout from up above, before Carol had time to answer, and immediately Geoff was transformed, as alert as a dog with pricked ears and raised hackles. He moved towards the stern end quickly.

'What is it, Andy?' he called.

'Come and look at this,' replied Andy.

When Geoff emerged into the night air he was confronted by a most spectacular sight. The dark, clear star-studded sky was now ablaze with a mass of brilliant colours in strange shapes and forms. They had all seen the colourful sunset earlier, not an unusual sight in this summer of hot settled weather, but this was different, much different. This was certainly not the mere remnants of a setting sun. Instead, huge tracks of the sky were being filled with strange spiralling shapes, set at first against a deep green background. The vista was constantly changing. Brilliant white lights with tinges of other colours at the fringes were dancing like flames in another corner of the sky, but these were no ordinary flames, and from no terrestrial fire. The luminescence from all this activity was intense, almost turning a part of the night sky into day. The clarity and brilliance of the colours was breathtaking. The scale of the activity seemed cosmic.

'How long has this been going on?' asked Geoff.

'Its been building up for a while, and then suddenly it filled the sky,' replied Andy, in wonderment. 'It just keeps changing all the time. I've never seen anything like it. I thought you'd like to see it. What do you think it is?'

'I don't understand it, Andy,' said Geoff, 'but it's not doing my head any good. I can't stand it.' Geoff went back down below, clutching his head as though it was bursting apart and he was trying to hold it together.

Carol had moved closer to the staircase and saw Geoff come back down, his face now white and contorted.

'What is it?' she asked.

'Go up and have a look for yourself,' said Geoff, for the first time relaxing his guard, without apparent concern for security. He seemed unimpressed by the phenomena outside and concerned more, in a pathetic sort of way, for his own well-being.

'My God, that's beautiful,' said Carol, almost instinctively, as she emerged from the open hatch. She forgot for a moment the chill of the rapidly cooling night air that had earlier caused her to rub her bare arms for warmth. 'The colours. They're so pure and deep,' she continued, as though she were talking to her captors like long lost friends, 'and the shapes are weird, not like anything I've ever seen before.'

'But ... what is it?' asked Andy. 'And can you feel it, inside your head?'

'What?' said Carol. 'Not you as well.'

Jim had reluctantly returned to the police control room. The police, and the army advisers, were convinced that the two armed men, with their hostage, were holed up in the wood. There was still a delay in getting in the heat-seeking equipment. Someone would get a rollicking for that. They were confident, though, that they could pen them in by covering all the exits and patrolling the perimeter. At this time of year first light would also come early. Meanwhile, they would also continue with other avenues of enquiry. It was thought significant that no reports had been received of any vehicle theft in the area. The conclusion was that there was a limit to how far these people could get on foot.

'Has the other man had anything to say for himself?' Jim asked the inspector, referring to the one called Phil who had been found at the farm along with his dying colleague.

'Not a dickie bird,' replied the inspector who, like Jim, was refreshing himself with a mug of coffee. 'Completely shell-shocked,' he added, after a sip from his blue and white hooped beaker. 'The doctor's given him something and he'll be held at the barracks for the time being.'

Jim stared out of the mobile control room side window, gazing at the sky. He noticed some strange and vivid colouring in the distance. It seemed rather odd, but his thoughts were elsewhere.

'Please be safe, my darling,' he said aloud, and with a moistness in his eyes, he added, 'I love you.'

Some miles further south, and a little bit later in the evening, Ben Johnson was also gazing out into the dark night. He had a number of things on his mind. He was concerned for his sister's unhappiness and had been quite startled to learn of her lover's identity; or was it her ex-lover? Not even Joanne appeared to be certain of their present status. He had been even more shocked to hear the information she had to impart about the nation's dwindling but contaminated water supplies.

Ben was turning his thoughts also to the short trip up to Lichworth tomorrow. He was looking forward to meeting Jim again, this time on his own territory, as it were. It should be a pleasant outing, though, like everyone else, he now longed for the edge to be taken off these ridiculous temperatures. 'Oh for some long, cold rain,' he thought to himself, 'or even some warm rain for that matter,' and then again, he reflected, 'oh for some pure, clean rainwater.'

As he was looking in a northerly direction, towards the Birmingham metropolis, he too was struck by strange coloured shapes in the sky. He looked for several minutes. Had it been earlier in the evening he might have thought it was the remnants of a spectacular, but nonetheless unusual sunset. Perhaps there had been some gigantic firework display somewhere, leaving its traces in the night sky, though he was not convinced of that.

The headache that had bothered him, on and off all evening, had eased a little now. It was a peculiar type of inner pain, not the usual type of headache at all. He really must cut back on the booze he thought, or perhaps there really was something in the water.

It was the middle of the night, or the early hours of the morning, the distinction being of no consequence, and although Jim had been persuaded to return home, it was not for the purpose of sleeping, since that would have been impossible. Instead, he pondered whether or not to inform their closest relatives and friends of Carol's dilemma. He plied himself with more coffee as he sat in his favourite armchair and deliberated. He decided against, partly because of the lateness of the hour and partly because of the secrecy that had been requested. Another consideration was the need to keep the telephone free so that he would not lose a minute when the police rang to inform him that Carol was free and safe and well. How he longed for that call to come and the more he longed for it, the longer the night became, so that the darkness seemed never-ending.

Despite his lonely contemplation, Jim was unable to turn his mind to other matters. It was almost as if his train of thought was being dictated and superimposed. It must have been his subconscious, therefore, that had planted in his mind a reminder about the get-together that was due to take place at his house tomorrow, or by now, later that same day. And yet, he pushed that to the back of his mind again, since his next concern would be to rejoin the search for Carol at daybreak. The other matter could take care of itself and in a strange way he believed that it would, as though events were now running to a timetable of their own making and as if he was now part of something that had been set in motion and he was powerless to stop.

* * *

During the course of the night, Geoff and Andy exchanged one form of diesel transport for another. The chugging boat gave way to a turbo-charged four-by-four that they quickly pointed at the nearest motorway. They had had decisions to make: whether to give themselves up to the authorities and face serious charges or to continue defiance; whether to hide or to run; where to run to and how to get there; and whether or not to take their hostage with them. Going to ground had certain attractions but it was too dangerous unless they could distance themselves from the various stolen modes of transport that they were first using and then dumping. They had to assume that these would be searched for and eventually found and it would be better if they were found both empty and a long way away. And just where would they hide anyway? 'Must keep one step ahead. Must keep one step ahead,' Geoff kept telling himself, in throbbing unison with his still pounding head. And as for their hostage, well, they might as well keep her in tow, so long as she did not prove a hindrance.

They had driven for about an hour since acquiring the vehicle from the farm-cum-estate that had adjoined the canal near its junction with another branch. They were thankful that in these rural areas, security of vehicles sometimes received no more than lip-service still. The first light of day was dawning and bringing with it the first traces of what would be another relentless rise in temperatures. In the night's last vestiges of darkness they had driven cautiously so as not to arouse any suspicion, should any police patrols have been lurking, but the elevated platforms and the bridges were empty. They were heading east and by now running out of motorway if they wanted to maintain that direction. The plan was to transfer to less conspicuous roads.

Carol, whilst obviously worried and concerned, was slightly more confident of her safety, though she was sensible enough to realize that the acid test was probably yet to come.

At least she thought that her personal integrity was not in immediate danger of violation. She wished that she could get a message to Jim to give him at least these reassurances.

The three of them were all somewhat worse for wear after a night of snatched but shallow sleep. The two men would have benefited from a shave and a wash, whilst Carol looked tired and weary. Her hair was unkempt and she was wearing an ill-fitting navy blue pullover that she had discovered on the boat and wore to keep out the night chill. It would quickly become redundant as the heat of the day emerged, were it not for the fact that it was serving a dual purpose, acting also as a cover for the now filthy and tattered T-shirt that had turned out so unsuitable for the unpredictable events of the previous day. Carol and Geoff were in the back of the car, with Andy, as ever at the wheel.

'I'd like to stop at the next telephone and speak to my husband,' said Carol. 'He will be worried sick.' The comments were aimed at Geoff, alongside her yet slightly apart, the gun no longer in a permanent state of readiness now that there was no sign of immediate pursuit, and confident in the knowledge that he could subdue Carol if necessary without the need of weaponry. 'Please be reasonable,' added Carol, after her earlier comment drew no response.

'OK,' ventured Geoff, at last. 'You keep asking and I keep saying no, but if I let you speak to him it must be on my conditions.' The feeling of relief for Carol was almost tangible.

'Thank you very much,' she said and she meant it, almost as if she had no right to expect such generosity.

'I will choose the place,' said Geoff, 'and tell you what to say and I will terminate the call. If you put one foot out of place,' warned Geoff, finger wagging, 'you will pay for it. Do you understand?' Carol concurred and as they turned off the motorway she looked anxiously for a phone box, not realizing that he intended to use the mobile phone he had found earlier in the glove compartment.

The telephone had barely completed the first ring before Jim snatched up the handset. Was this the call that he had been waiting for all night? He had not even given himself time to consider whether it might be the precursor of bad news.

'Hello, Mr Webb. This is Inspector Childs,' said the now familiar voice with tiredness and no sense of urgency.

'Any news?' asked Jim quickly, trying to hurry along the process.

'No as far as Mrs Webb is concerned,' came the reply, 'but I wanted you to know that we are about to launch the full-scale search of the woods now that we have daylight and sufficient manpower. I know that you said you wanted to join in that and I can send a car to pick you up and bring you here. However, there is the question of whether or not it would be more worth your while to stay by the telephone in case of contact being made.'

'But they aren't likely to ring me from the woods, are they Inspector?' interjected Jim. 'Or is this your way of telling me that you no longer think they are there? In other words,' said Jim, standing up now as though to give greater emphasis to his words, 'that you have let them get away,' he said pointedly.

'No, sir,' replied the inspector calmly, ' we still think the balance of probability is that they are in there. Our search of surrounding properties has yielded nothing. There are no reports of stolen vehicles in the vicinity and we have no sightings. It is difficult to see where else they can be.' The inspector did not mention that the special equipment brought in had failed to locate them. 'It is unlikely that they would ring, I agree, even if they had a mobile, but it is always possible,' he added.

'I wouldn't have thought that they would make contact unless they felt that they were backed into a corner. Meanwhile, I can't see them wanting to give their position away,' responded Jim.

'You are probably right, sir. We'll send a car for you then. Oh, and sir . . .' asked the inspector.

'Yes?' enquired Jim.

'The matter is still, shall we say, confidential, and it is probably better for your wife's safety that it stays that way. You haven't said anything to anybody, have you, Mr Webb?'

'No, Inspector. Not yet,' replied Jim, his words barely concealing a thinly veiled threat.

A car arrived twenty minutes later and Jim was whisked away long before any of his neighbours had their curtains undrawn.

About thirty minutes after that the telephone rang, but there was nobody there to answer it. About ten minutes later it rang again, and again it went unanswered.

'No reply,' said Bill to Mandy. 'I'll bet the poor fellow's still not home.'

'Nor is he likely to be,' said Mandy, 'with Carol still out there somewhere, in the clutches of murderers. God, I hope she's safe and unharmed. I still feel guilty about not being there with her,' she added, clutching the mug of black coffee.

'Perhaps I should go round,' said Bill, 'or do you think that I should leave it until later?' he asked Mandy.

'I don't know, Bill. I would have thought that poor Jim has so much on his mind that he has forgotten all about what he had planned for today.' She sipped from her cup. 'At least the police have confirmed that they haven't found a body,' said Mandy, her thoughts once again returning to Carol. 'We should be grateful for that. No news is good news,' she added, now draining her drink.

'I'm sure you're right, darling,' said Bill, consolingly, now standing closer and with his hand on her shoulder. He couldn't help but wonder, though, how forthcoming the police would be over the telephone. 'And as far as today is concerned, I'll probably go round later as arranged. It's not far after all. But that's only if you're going to be OK without me for a while,' he added.

'Yes, of course, Bill. Jean is coming round at lunch time and I'll know where you are if I need you. That's provided that Jim returns home. God knows what agonies the poor man is going through,' and with that Mandy began to weep again, although there was not yet the uncontrollable flood of tears that had gushed forth earlier. Bill appreciated that it was a good thing for the body to release its pent-up emotions. He just wished Mandy had not had cause to do it so frequently as in the last two weeks. All things considered, she had borne up to the strain remarkably well and her nurse's training must have been an important factor in that.

Carol was more depressed than frightened. She had finally persuaded Geoff to let her make contact with Jim, only for the telephone to ring out unanswered. She wanted to stop and try again but Geoff grew impatient and refused to allow any further interruptions to their journey. It seemed as though he had reconsidered his generosity, at least for the time being. Maybe she would try again later.

The news bulletins on the car radio failed to give any clues. There was not a mention of the horrendous events of the previous day. Being a Sunday, the bulletins were irregular, but nonetheless predictable, consisting mainly of details of another weekend of violence and law-breaking up and down the country, together with the continuing saga of the record-breaking, and now thoroughly unpleasant heatwave, with its attendant fears of water rationing. One of the more laid-back summaries, on a music channel, had a tail piece about strange celestial phenomena being reported from various northern parts of the country.

They were well off the beaten track now, though still heading east to judge by the position of the sun. Geoff was doing a rare stint of driving with Andy keeping Carol company in the back. He was in similar clothing to Geoff, army camouflage trousers and a now grubby white shirt. He seemed a bit younger than Geoff and did not have the same northern accent. Until now, Carol had seen little more than the back of his head. Peeved with Geoff's attitude over contacting Jim, nevertheless, Carol still had the good sense to try to maintain a rapport with the two men. She rightly judged that it would be best for her personal safety to develop as friendly a relationship as circumstances would allow. At first, the quiet and subservient Andy was a frightening threat. Now that Carol was able to study him more closely, she saw a young man who perhaps was very impressionable and who maybe had been dragged into a situation that had simply got out of control. He did not seem a vicious or nasty person.

'How's your head?' Carol enquired.

'A bit better,' said the young man of few words, not quite sure whether the boss would approve of him conversing.

'Does it come and go?' asked Carol, persevering.

'What do you mean?' replied Andy.

'Is it the same pain that you've had ... continuously ... since last night?' continued Carol, struggling to keep the conversation going.

'I suppose so,' mumbled Andy, after which there was silence for a while.

Meantime, Geoff, oblivious of the mumblings in the back, or so it seemed, took another turning onto a lower grade road still. He gave the impression that he knew where he was heading but the roads seemed to get slower and more devious. Carol was watching out for the signposts. They were still heading east.

Andy had been thinking during the pause in the conversation, if it could be called that, about the unusual sky the night before. For a time then he had come out of his shell and had become quite excitable almost, putting his serious predicament behind him for a short time. Geoff had demonstrated no interest at all, but the woman, thought Andy, had shared his wonderment, until, that is, Geoff called her back down below.

'What was that all about last night?' ventured Andy, taking the initiative now with his question directed to Carol, who stared back at him. 'You know ... in the sky,' he added. 'You know what it was about, don't you?' he said.

'Aurora borealis,' answered Carol and then, after a pause, 'I think.'

'Come again,' said a perplexed Andy.

'Northern lights,' interjected Geoff and Carol turned her attention forward.

'Do you agree then?' she asked, in Geoff's direction.

'I knew instantly,' he replied.

'But it's unusual isn't it, in this country, so far south?' asked Carol.

'Unheard of,' was Geoff's prompt reply, and then, 'never known before, I shouldn't wonder.' He slowed to take in a sharp bend.

'Then how can you be sure that's what it was?' Carol asked, intrigued, notwithstanding the traumatic circumstances in which she found herself: held hostage by two armed and desperate men, heading she knew not where, with no help or rescue in sight, and here she was, discussing atmospheric phenomena.

'Believe me, I know,' said Geoff in a definite and deliberate tone. 'And believe me, it's bad news,' he added. 'Now let's drop the subject and have a bit of quiet. I need to concentrate on where we're going.'

Carol thought that Geoff was a very authoritative person, almost to the point of commanding respect, though that might be something to do with the menacing firearm currently lying on the front passenger seat and which was never far from his grasp. She thought also about his pale and contorted face the night before and his throbbing headaches and his seeming familiarity with the phenomenon they had seen. She suspected that there was some connection between it all somewhere.

A little further on Geoff stopped the car and asked Andy to take over the driving. He needed to consult his maps, the ones he had found in the glove compartment, that is. The navigation was becoming more complex as he sought to maintain a certain direction, but without using the main roads. It was Carol's suspicion that his head was causing him some pain again.

It was approaching late morning now on this midsummer Sunday with temperatures already racing up to the upper 20s Celsius and with plenty of mileage in them yet. It would soon be siesta time for the mass of British people as they began to adopt continental ways of dealing with the Saharan-like heat. In other years a stroll in the woods on a warm summer Sunday would be a pleasure; it was one of those images that helped to cheer people up in the dark winter months, an occasion for family outings or maybe a romantic interlude. But this year was very different. The public was barred. The woods were merely a fire hazard waiting to claim more death and destruction. For Jim, however, it was worse still. He gained no enjoyment from his Sunday morning outing. It was clear by now that the birds had flown the nest. There would be no early reunion with his beloved Carol.

'What next, Inspector?' enquired Jim, as they stood together next to one of a number of patrol cars assembled at one of the main entrances to the wood. Though the helicopter searches had thrown up nothing encouraging they had still felt it necessary to reinforce these with a manual search, if only because of the inspector stubbornly refusing to accept that their quarry could have slipped through the net. If only the thermal imager on the helicopter had not malfunctioned. If only a back-up machine had been available sooner. If only the manual search had thrown up some evidence of their presence in the wood. He had been hopeful of that, at least. He knew that Jim Webb had a right to expect better.

'What next, sir?' repeated the inspector. 'Well, we continue to widen the search area. There has to be a limit to how far they've got.'

'Admit it, Inspector,' said Jim, scathingly, 'you botched it. They could be anywhere.'

The inspector was temporarily lost for words.

'I understand your concern, sir,' he replied at last. 'We have to be careful in hostage situations. We had to think of your wife's safety. It was essential to wait for the right kind of equipment and back-up. I still don't understand where they've disappeared to,' he said, shaking his head.

'Well, then I suggest that you get your thinking cap on and step up the whole search effort,' rapped Jim.

'I promise you that we'll do all we can. You have my word

on that,' said Inspector Childs. 'Meanwhile, could I suggest that you might want to return home again in case of contact being made. It could be very important.' Jim couldn't see what else he could do. He asked for some transport home, and the inspector gestured in the direction of a patrol car. The driver came towards them.

'If you go with this officer, sir, he'll get you home,' said the inspector. 'And, oh, by the way,' he added, as Jim made to move, 'don't be shocked or offended if you find an officer already in the house when you get there.'

'What?' said Jim, slightly puzzled.

'Well,' resumed the inspector, 'I realized this morning that you wanted to be here and that was understandable, but at the same time it was essential to have someone at the house ... not just for the telephone ... but in case Mrs Webb should return, with or without her assailants.' Then he added, almost as an afterthought, 'I'm sure that access will have been gained without any damage, sir.'

Jim sat quietly in the back of the patrol car as they began the relatively short journey to his home. As he reflected on the desperate situation, he tried to dwell on the positive things. There had been no evidence of further violence or injury. He had to believe that Carol was alive and well and, he prayed to God, unharmed and unmolested. If she was to be of any use to her abductors as a hostage they would have to keep her alive, at least until it came to a final confrontation. Unless, of course, they decided to be clever and make a ransom demand, with the aim of trading Carol for money or a means of transport. But might they have transport already and how far could they have got by now? If only he knew where they were. He had to stay optimistic, he told himself.

'Have you got family or perhaps friends who could keep you company this afternoon, sir?' asked the young driver, somewhat startling Jim after his quiet period of contemplation. 'It might be better than just sitting alone, dwelling on the situation,' added the officer, half turning round for as long as safety would permit. There was a pause before Jim answered.

'Yes, as a matter of fact we have got some friends calling

this afternoon,' he replied, staring straight ahead, and without appreciating his inappropriate use of the word 'we'. It had dawned on him, as he looked now at his wristwatch, that he had indeed some very important visitors calling that afternoon. They were coming for a meeting.

The short journey to Jim's house seemed to take longer than expected. On arrival, he found it occupied, which seemed strange. At least it was a friendly and sympathetic face that greeted him. It was Bill. The constable had let him in just a few minutes previously. Bill could see that Jim's face was etched with concern and worry, exacerbated by tiredness and, once again, the overbearing heat developing.

'Any news?' Bill asked simply.

'They've not found them yet, Bill,' replied Jim. 'I'm trying to convince myself that no news is good news,' he added in a quietly spoken voice and then, in the same low tones, 'The police have botched it, Bill.' He suddenly realized that the young copper posted on house-sitting duties was within earshot. 'Nothing personal, mate,' Jim said in his direction, but it was the fresh-faced young constable who was embarrassed. 'Any phone calls?' Jim asked him.

'No, sir, none at all,' he replied dutifully and then began to apologize for his being there in the first place, until Jim interrupted him and dismissed it as being unimportant in the present circumstances.

Before long Bill was pressing a black coffee into Jim's hands, commenting that he looked in need of it.

'Have you remembered the meeting you set up for this afternoon, Jim?' asked Bill.

'Strangely enough, yes, Bill. It's crossed my mind a couple of times.'

'Do you want me to ring round and cancel it?' enquired Bill.

'No, I think I'll let it take its course,' responded Jim. 'Nobody is coming from any great distance. And I'm sure they'll understand if I have to leave suddenly for urgent personal reasons. Besides,' he added, 'it's a bit late now.'

'It might not be a bad idea,' said Bill. 'It will help, I'm sure, if you keep occupied.'

'Bill, forgive me. How's Mandy?'

'Just fine, Jim, in the circumstances. Worried, of course, about Carol, but you know Mandy. Resilient, as always. My God, she's needed to be these last two weeks.'

'Christ, it's so hot again, Bill,' said Jim, after sipping his black coffee. 'It's like being in a living hell.'

Bill pressed on with more practical matters, hoping to take Jim's mind off his understandably more depressing concerns.

'If we are going ahead with this meeting this afternoon,' he said, 'we'll need to think about organizing some refreshments and I'm sure that you could do with some food inside you as well. Mandy has offered to put together a few things for a buffet. You know, sandwiches and sausage rolls, that kind of thing. What she hasn't got fresh, she'll have in the freezer. Shall I ring her and get her to organize it?'

'That would be great. I can't thank you enough, mate.' Jim clasped Bill's shoulder firmly for just a few seconds, long enough though to demonstrate not just gratitude but friendship.

* * *

John Marner had always been proud of his humble origins and the trappings of high office held no great significance for him. He was not one of those politicians who felt the pull of destiny, nor did he sense that fate had decreed that he was to be a chosen one, expected to lay down the best years of his life in the service of his country. That was not to say that he was not ambitious, which he had been, nor that he was not proud to serve his country in the highest capacity, which undoubtedly he was, nor that he was anything other than hardworking and conscientious, which intensely he was. However, foremost of all, he was a family man and he valued his private life enormously and guarded it jealously. For this reason, it was usual to find him taking Sunday lunch, and a traditional one at that, in the confines of his own home, with his loyal wife Ursula, and his teenage son and daughter, when they could be in attendance. Many in the media poked fun at the grey and mundane image he projected. He was a nice man, if not, like most politicians, misguided a lot of the time. He had soon come to realize, after attaining the leadership of his country, that he would be the object of widespread and regular criticism, often stinging and virulent in nature and sometimes unnecessarily personal. He would gladly throttle those who had the obscenity to attack his wife and family and it was that aspect more than any other that had caused him to consider his position very closely on at least a couple of occasions in the last few years. Usually, however, on encountering difficulties, it was to the family that he looked for renewed strength and this Sunday was one of those occasions.

Though the prime minister did not make full use of his official residencies, he could not escape all the trappings of office. Retreat to his family home though he may, there was still no escape from the interruptions, the messages, the red boxes, and the decision making. At least he found the pressure easier to handle in his home surroundings. On this particular scorching Sunday, he had been determined to enjoy the company of his family and what better way before the cloudless morning turned into a breathless midday, than a short stroll around the country lanes near their home? For a short while they could even try to forget the ever-present security that shadowed their every move. Before returning home they would also partake of liquid refreshment at the village pub, The Green Man, though some had unkindly retitled it The Grey Man in honour of their most distinguished customer. Ursula and daughter left early to put the finishing touches to the lunch, with prime minister and son staying on for an extra drink. The security guard split accordingly.

When John Marner got back home with his son, the Sunday roast was just about ready. The prime minister was in his element: family, fresh air, Fullers, food and fulfilment. He decided that he would not return the telephone call that had been made to him whilst he was out, until after his lunch, even if it was from the president of the United States of America.

PART TWO

Jim and Bill did their best to prepare a cool environment, although in the prevailing extreme weather conditions the usual method of opened doors and windows had little effect. The two portable fans that Bill had brought with him would provide some alleviation of the heat. The nourishment on offer, courtesy of Mandy, was laid out but covered, in the lounge which was where Jim decided that he would convene his meeting. He rearranged the seating into a more compact formation, placing the two deep-cushioned armchairs opposite the settee, the whole forming a kind of square, but with a mahogany coffee table in the middle. On that Jim had placed some notes and papers that he had prepared over the last few days and which would act as an *aide-mémoire*. A copy of Ben's article was amongst them. He intended that he and Bill would occupy the settee with Ben and Trevor in the armchairs. Jim could not pretend for a moment that his mind was focused on the meeting, but he had at least reassured himself that there was nothing further to report in respect of Carol and for the time being, at least, nothing that he could be usefully doing to contribute to her rescue. The young constable would be asked to confine himself to the rear of the house from where he could continue with his monitoring role and Jim had thoughtfully supplied him with some sustenance. The fact that his was an unmarked police car would help to avoid unnecessary suspicion amongst the arriving guests.

Though his was a wider drive than the average in The Close, it was still not enough, despite the absence of Carol's car, to accommodate all the vehicles without resorting to use of the verge. Still, it presented no undue hazard in this quiet, sun-drenched *cul-de-sac*. Inside, preliminary introductions were informal and friendly and took place around the buffet table. The food was gratefully but sparingly accepted, whilst the ice-cold drinks were gulped down with a vengeance. Ben Johnson was introduced by Jim as a friend and thanked for coming from the other side of Birmingham, whilst Trevor Reaney was welcomed as the country's newest Member of Parliament and as an even older acquaintance. Both were introduced to Bill, as well as to each other. It was casual, with shirt sleeves the necessary order of the day. Jim initially parried their questions about why they were all there together until after they had partaken of drinks and snacks, thus lending a little bit of formality and organization to the proceedings. In the preliminary small talk, he made excuses for Carol, notwithstanding the real reason for her absence being the persistent cause of his insides being eaten away.

Eventually, the four men were seated in the format Jim had designed, with Bill to his left on the settee, Ben directly opposite Jim in an armchair and Trevor diagonally across in the other armchair. The table with Jim's notes was nearer the settee than the chairs, though a handy repository for all four cold drinks.

'Thank you all once again for coming,' began Jim, 'on yet another scorcher of a day. Please excuse any formality. There is a specific purpose to inviting you all here together which I hope will become clear very shortly. I promise not to take up too much of your time. Meanwhile, please make yourselves at home. I hope that we can regard this as a meeting of friends who may or may not have a common interest by the end of the proceedings, if that's the right word.'

'Take your time, Jim. We're enjoying the hospitality,' ventured Ben.

'Very well then,' continued Jim, 'down to business. Let me run past you a sequence of events and please bear with me if some of this is blindingly obvious. We are currently enjoying, if it can be called enjoyment, probably the hottest spell of

118

weather in this country since records began. We are also still in the throes of certainly one of the longest periods of dry weather ever recorded. My good friend, Bill, here,' Jim gestured with a slightly raised left hand, 'happens to be an expert meteorologist. He has convinced me that we are potentially in the grip of a situation that could be far worse than the great drought of 1976, or the one in 95 that affected some parts of the country in such a bad way. This is going to be the worst ever. Is that right, Bill?'

'I'm sure it is,' said Bill, leaning forward, 'and before you ask why, the reason is the extraordinarily high atmospheric pressure sitting over both this country and most of Europe. I'm sure that you've seen and heard reference to that in the media these last few days but no one has really laid it on the line just how significant and crucial that is. There is no previous experience of shifting an anticyclone as massive as this. I think that it has been building up for the best part of twelve months, a period that has seen unusual weather patterns in many parts of the world.' Bill paused momentarily for a sip of his lemonade.

'Please don't take this the wrong way, Bill,' said Trevor Reaney in his usual gravelly tones, 'but where have you acquired your expert knowledge?'

'Twenty years working for the Meteorological Office, so far,' said Bill, 'and currently as a special projects manager at the regional office.'

'Fine,' said Reaney succinctly, happily acknowledging Bill's credentials.

'By the way, ' added Bill, 'I'm not here in any official capacity. But I'm worried enough to stick my neck out and tell you that if current medium and long-term forecasts are correct, we will be entering a period of weather the like of which has never been experienced in this country before, since records began, that is.'

'Bill, again please don't take this the wrong way,' it was Reaney again, 'but have twenty years with the Met Office possibly given you a slightly biased view of the standard of their forecasting, especially the longer term ones?'

'It's probably made him more sceptical,' interjected Jim on Bill's behalf and causing Bill to chuckle, 'but there are good reasons for trusting the accuracy of current forecasts, which Bill may elucidate later.' Bill nodded. 'For the time being, though,' continued Jim, 'can I return to my scenario? We have a unique climatic situation and we can all see the day-to-day repercussions of that, much of it trivial admittedly, from increased ice cream sales to supermarket scuffles over bottled water; but sometimes, more serious, from forest fires to bankrupted businesses, and potentially more serious still as we now enter uncharted waters. So what is my interest in it, you may ask, apart from the normal Englishman's curiosity about the weather? Well, a few weeks ago my father-in-law was driving home to his country bungalow in the early evening when he got caught up in a forest fire that was raging out of control. He skidded off the road and ended up losing his life in the most horrible of circumstances.' Jim paused for a second or two during which silence prevailed. 'A tragic accident, of course,' he continued, 'but somehow the futility of it all drew me into a deeper awareness generally of what was going on and it has also generated a need to pursue my inquisitive instincts. Of course, many other people have died, too, in drought or weather-related incidents. We accept that the forces of nature can take lives. But then I got talking to Bill about previous droughts, like the one in 76 and then about weather patterns, like the fact that heating up of the planet has resulted in sea levels rising seven inches this century; that more recently six of the last seventeen months have been the respective warmest on record, and every month that passes seems to bring some new extreme of weather in some part of the world. I respected Bill's gut feeling that something unusual was happening. What is the significance of the record atmospheric pressure level? Is it a record merely because our weather readings do not go back far enough in relation to the vast age of the planet, or are we seeing some delicate shift in the balance of nature, some small but subtle change in cosmic terms but profound in earthly terms?'

Jim paused for a drink and the lack of interruption from

his small audience he took as a sign of their interest. So he ploughed on.

'So let me continue with my speculations if I may,' he said. 'We may be experiencing subtle changes to both our atmosphere and our biosphere. If we are, then what will be the effects on human civilization and behaviour? Might we already be seeing some of these effects, both tangible and intangible? If so, what are they, who has recognized them and what is being done about it? What could people like us do?' Once again Jim's question was rhetorical. Leaning forward as he had been doing from the start, he continued. 'The more I have delved into these matters the more curious I have become. You see, if you research into the history of the planet, you soon discover that any idea of a steady and progressive development from the primordial soup to the pinnacle of civilization we see today is a total myth. Evolution? Yes. But no way has it been planned and orderly. Palaeontologists will tell you that the geological evidence points to a stop/start situation, and there are lots of examples of this.' Jim was in full flow now, though still a little uncertain as to whether or not his guests were listening quietly out of fascination or good manners. Undoubtedly, it could not have been what they expected the afternoon to be about. He carried on, with some examples to illustrate his last point.

'I'm talking about sudden climatic changes, like the ice ages, but sometimes not quite so extreme. I'm talking about chemical elements in the earth's rocks sometimes being in abundance but at other times being virtually absent. Then there are the huge drops in atmospheric pressure, like the so-called Maunder Minimum in the seventeenth century when sun spots all but disappeared and it gave rise to a mini ice age. Then there are the species that disappear overnight, and I don't just mean the dinosaurs, but vast numbers of land and sea creatures, plants and organisms. The earth's past is littered with catastrophes. Speculation about the causes is rife, from being struck by meteors and comets, to tilts in the earth's axis, huge volcanic eruptions and so on. I would suggest that only one thing is certain, that changes to the climate are not so much the cause as the symptom of the problem. Therefore, if we are seeing significant climatic change now, it could be a reflection of something much more fundamental taking place. But I haven't asked you here just to listen to my pontifications about the weather. There is much more to this business. A short time ago, in a professional capacity I bumped into Ben Johnson. Now you may know of Ben by his real name through his writing or you may not, but without wishing to embarrass him, let me tell you that he is a prolific and respected writer, sometimes under pseudonym, of international repute, on current affairs. What I have learnt from him is absolutely fascinating and may, I think, be connected with what I have just been talking about. Ben?'

'Well, I'm not sure about that just yet,' cautioned Ben, after a moment's hesitation. 'Let's just say that we have opened up some interesting areas for investigation.' Ben was quite relaxed talking, as he leaned back in his armchair, with his customary matter-of-fact North American lilt. Jim, meanwhile, as he topped up his glass with more ice-cold orange juice from the jug, noticed how attentive Reaney and Bill were. 'It just so happens that I did an article recently,' continued Ben, 'that resulted from some information I picked up in The States, and mainly concerned some rather weird behaviour in the animal kingdom.' He paused before adding, 'Unique behaviour, in fact, and to do with strange migratory patterns.'

'The article's here, by the way, if anyone wants to read it in full later,' interjected Jim. 'Go on, Ben.'

'Well, it's Jim's belief that this behaviour may be linked to the strange climatic effects being experienced not just in the UK and Europe, but in parts of the USA as well. After all, it is well-documented that birds are very sensitive to atmospheric changes and somehow have the ability to guide themselves from more than just sight alone, in some cases over many thousands of miles. Now, Jim's theory is that whilst birds might be a species which is super-sensitive, if there was a significant and fundamental change going on, might there be evidence of odd behaviour in other species too?' Ben had a marvellously relaxed style of narrative, which is no doubt why he was also such a good read too. He stood up and with a nod and a gesture towards Jim he then made his way towards the buffet table, but he continued his story as he went. 'So I promised that I would make some enquiries with some of my contacts in The States and, fortunately, being a well-travelled man and having lived for a spell over there, I do have a lot of contacts, some of whom, I'm pleased to say, either occupy or have access to high places. And believe me, in my profession that is invaluable. Let me tell you that in the US scientific fraternity there is great curiosity at the moment in odd animal behavioural patterns, so much so, in fact, and my friends in the political fraternity have confirmed this, that a top secret report has just gone to the president. Now, say what you like about me, but I can smell a scoop from here on the other side of The Atlantic. Needless to say, I am doing my level best to get a copy of this report. At the moment I know only that the word is that there are strange phenomena in the upper atmosphere.'

'What sort of phenomena?' asked Bill.

'I don't know,' replied Ben, by now taking his seat again, with drink in hand.

'What sort of animals are we talking about?' asked Reaney on his left.

'Farm animals, I believe. Low milk yields, I suspect. That kind of thing,' replied Ben. 'There are a lot of strange reports in the newspapers about odd happenings with domestic pets as well, some of which you may have seen in the papers over here. Zoo animals also tend to be closely monitored. Dolphins and whales are behaving strangely. I'll know a lot more when I can get hold of a copy of this report, which I am hopeful of, fairly soon.'

'But odd animal behaviour is not unheard of' said Reaney. 'What makes you think that the current situation is all that special?'

'You're right,' said Ben. 'Animals do sometimes behave strangely, but often it is a premonition, if you like, or a warning of something significant. Perhaps they are closer to nature than we are. They get the news first. And what's special about this time?' asked Ben, rhetorically. 'Well, the scale of it, by all accounts, especially across species, plus the consternation amongst the scientists, top secret presidential reports, and the one thing that we journalists can always identify.'

'And what's that?' asked Reaney.

'The all pervading stench of a cover-up,' replied Ben.

'Just the sort of thing to interest a young ambitious politician sceptical of world leadership, Trevor,' suggested Jim. Reaney sat back and grinned.

'Mind if I smoke?' he asked.

'Not if you must,' replied Jim, but without venom and he offered to get an ashtray. This took only a few seconds.

The through draught created by the fans lifted Reaney's obnoxious fumes out through the opened doors and wafted them into the garden.

'Let me take this speculation a little further,' continued Jim, now seated again. 'If atmospheric changes are causing odd behavioural patterns in birds and animals, is it not rather naive, not to say arrogant, to believe that humans would be totally unaffected? And if human behaviour is modified by its environment, how would we expect it to show up? Could the significant upsurge in violence here in the UK be a symptom? Are we really to believe that it is just down to sun and booze?' For a few seconds there was just the background hum of the fans.

'I'm not so sure that this is the stuff of maiden speeches,' reacted a sceptical Reaney. 'We seem to be jumping some big chasms with little or no evidence,' he said, easing back slightly in his chair and encouraging a passing bee to continue on its journey with a waft of his hand. 'If there is something going on in the earth's upper atmosphere, what is it and how can it be linked to our current weather, let alone something as complex as human behaviour?'

'It's not quite so far-fetched as it might sound,' said Ben, rejoining the discussion. 'There has been some interesting research about links between health and the atmosphere and let's not lose sight of the most obvious link of all, the gap in the ozone layer, letting in harmful ultraviolet rays. But there are other rays out there too. A body of opinion suggests that cosmic rays are capable of affecting human health if the earth's deflecting mechanisms fail. As I say, there has been research, though as yet not conclusive. It's a subject requiring a much bigger research effort. Certainly I know that there is a belief that cosmic rays may cause mutations. It is not beyond the bounds of possibility that human behaviour could also be influenced by this kind of phenomenon.'

'You talk about mutations, Ben' responded Reaney, using first name terms to help temper his persistent scepticism. 'Are you suggesting that we could be on the verge of some kind of evolutionary sea change here, one of Jim's catastrophes maybe?' He flicked cigarette ash into the ashtray. 'Again I have to ask: where is the evidence?' Before Ben could reply, Bill leaned forward to give an opinion.

'There is no doubt that there is a lot of ignorance about some atmospheric processes and the link between atmosphere, climate and health and behaviour. We moan about extremes of weather, though it is usually within human resourcefulness to adapt. Yet there we are, looking at very, very minor and subtle changes in the cosmic scale of things. We have no right to assume that we can always expect to be faced with only such narrow bands of cosmic activity. Our whole ecosystem is more fragile than people realize. We are no more than pawns on the cosmic chessboard. For example, just a slight change in the earth's orbit, or the gravitational pulls within our solar system, or indeed the interactions within our atmosphere, could all have catastrophic effects. We are so complacent,' Bill concluded, settling back now in his chair.

'But how come our civilization has got so far?' questioned Reaney. 'Why haven't we been thrown off course before now?' he asked.

'What makes you think we haven't?' asked Jim. 'I've talked about the stop/start theory of evolution. Consider for a moment one of the strangest things I have uncovered in my own limited research. That is, the sudden, total and inexplicable reversals of the earth's magnetic field. Believe me, this is not science fiction I'm talking here, but well-proven hard scientific fact, backed by the mainstream palaeontologists. What is speculative is their cause and also the effects they might have had on climate and life. It is even postulated that reversals can happen almost literally overnight, with some kind of magnetic flip. So far, science has failed to ascribe any pattern to them or the intervals in between them.' Jim had a quick sip of his drink. 'Possibly not unconnected with these events is the behaviour of that part of the atmosphere known as the magnetosphere. Is this the area, I wonder, that is the subject of Ben's secret report?' asked Jim. 'Are we seeing changes taking place there that can have a knock-on effect on the troposphere in the lower part of the atmosphere and which is the place where our weather is made? If so, might these changes also affect the lifeforms most susceptible to magnetic activity, like the birds and the bees. But if the changes are more significant, could they also affect other animals and, just maybe, the behavioural patterns of man as well?'

'Jim, if I may just interrupt here,' said Ben, 'and this may support your theory, I'm not sure, but during my research it became clear that the strange behaviour of birds, for example, was thought to be due not necessarily to significantly larger doses of magnetic forces, as it were, so much as the subtle change in them. In other words, there have been experiments in the past that showed that birds recognize magnetic field strength within quite a narrow band. It would take little change to alter their behaviour, whilst substantial change up or down, as it were, might have no immediate effect. I suppose that if that's true, it shows once again that nature's forces are in a very delicate state of balance.'

'Thanks, Ben' resumed Jim. 'I think that illustrates how vulnerable we may all be to subtle changes. Certainly the more I've researched these matters, the more intrigued I've become and the more questions arise. If there is increased activity in the magnetosphere, what is causing it?' It was another of Jim's rhetorical questions, which the others had become used to by now. 'Well, there is a proven link between increased solar activity and magnetic storms on earth. Huge solar flares have an impact on our atmosphere between twelve and thirty hours later, with the assistance of the solar wind. Did you know that the sun is currently more active than at any time since Galileo? In March 1989 huge solar flares were thought to be linked to severe electrical storms which caused power surges in Canada and Sweden. Navigation systems were thrown out by ten per cent. Huge electrical charges ran through pipelines. It led to the setting up of solar flare prediction centres in Colorado and in France, Germany and Russia. Sunspot activity has soared, over one hundred reported this year already. In the last few weeks the US National Oceanic and Atmospheric Association has spotted X-class solar flares, the most violent category known.' Jim paused. He looked up from the notes he had been using intermittently. 'These are the facts, Trevor,' he joked, casting a glance under raised eyebrows in Reaney's direction and Reaney chuckled. 'Now we know that all this activity has an effect on the upper atmosphere but it is not quite clear yet how it reacts with the lower atmosphere and the weather systems that form there. It is also speculated that increased sunspot activity has a link with certain medical conditions, like thrombosis and maybe even cancer. Are the rising cancer rates of recent years just coincidental with increased solar activity?' Again, Jim was leaving no room for answers to his questions. 'And then, there is the latest research coming out of The States, but so far inconclusive, which suggests that the human nervous system is conducive to increased magnetic fields. How soon before a link with behavioural patterns emerges, I wonder. Maybe the chasm is not that wide, Trevor.'

'It is beginning to sound more convincing, Jim,' responded Reaney, 'but I have to say that such evidence as there is can only be described at best as circumstantial . . . and thin.'

'What new theories don't start off with thin evidence?'

asked Jim. 'And sometimes, isn't even circumstantial evidence so overwhelming as to demand deeper investigation at the very least?' Bill nodded in agreement, and then he rejoined the discussion himself.

'Another thing you have to remember is that research into the solar wind has only really taken off, as it were, in the satellite age. It wasn't even discovered until the sixties. And when you think that the output of solar wind from the sun is three hundred thousand tons per second and can reach the earth in two to five days, I think that you have to sit up and take notice when activity increases.'

'Thanks for that information, Bill,' said Jim. 'Let me also give you a quotation that I came across recently from one of the most eminent scientists in this field, Professor Thadheus Nowakowski of Boston, who said "Scientists are only just beginning to unravel the physical details of the interactions of the solar wind with the earth's magnetic field."'

'Another fact.' It was Bill again, continuing to lend support to Jim although this had not been pre-planned. 'There is no doubt that weather patterns and pressure systems are gradually moving westwards, which largely explains why there is a blocking action on the wet westerly winds that normally batter the UK and the result is the long dry periods of recent years. The interesting thing is that if you draw up isomagnetic charts for the same period you will find the same pattern of movement in the earth's magnetic field.'

'So what have we got?' asked Jim, once again rhetorically and with a quiet self assurance, all the more staggering because of the devastating personal circumstances which, so far, he had successfully pushed from the forefront of his mind. Leaning forward he ticked off on his fingers one item after another. 'We have increased solar activity on a massive scale. We know that this will lead to magnetic disturbances. We know that that will impact on climate, though not the precise mechanisms involved. It is also probably impacting on animal behaviour. It may be affecting illness and disease rates. And what is it doing to us?'

'Just to come in on the magnetic disturbances, Jim' It was

Ben this time in his easy-going manner. 'Are you aware of the increased auroral activity, which, of course, is a corollary of magnetic activity in the upper atmosphere?'

'You mean the Northern Lights,' said Reaney.

'Or the Southern Lights' said Ben, 'depending where you stand. It's something that has increased a lot in the last couple of years.'

'Quite right, Ben,' said Jim. 'I talked about the fantastic events of March 89 earlier. They were accompanied by amazing auroral displays apparently. And it wasn't just a light show. It was linked to the communication and power problems too. I know that Norway and Canada have reported spectacular shows as well. It's not surprising really. These activities generate a million amps of current in the upper atmosphere and although a lot of that has dwindled away by the time it reaches the surface of the earth, there is plenty of power left when solar activity is at its highest.'

'Is this the cause of my TV going on the blink?' asked Reaney.

'Don't mock it,' responded Bill, leaning forward. 'It is quite probably the cause. In fact, it sounds as if none of you can have seen the auroral display last night.'

'Where?' asked Ben.

'Right here,' replied Bill, 'in the Midlands.'

'But I thought that they were usually confined to northern latitudes,' said Ben. 'You know, sort of Oslo and north.'

'Quite right, Ben,' said Bill. 'Although, remarkably, in 89 they were seen as far south as Portugal and the West Indies. Usually, though, it's unheard of in this part of the UK. But having witnessed it with my own eyes last night, I decided to check with some of my Met Office colleagues this morning. There's no doubt that there was an auroral display and quite a spectacular and colourful one at that. It all goes to confirm the theory that there is something mighty unusual going on up in the heavens.'

'And I thought that it was just fireworks,' mumbled Ben, almost inaudibly, although his view of the previous night's events had obviously been a more distant one.

'I didn't venture out last night,' was Reaney's excuse.

'My God,' said Jim, suddenly realizing that his subconscious had recorded the vestiges of the auroral display. He had stared at it the previous night whilst looking out of the police control room. It did not mean much to him at the time. The pictures came back, as did the reason for him being there, not that Carol's plight had ever been out of his mind.

The others sensed that something was up. Jim got up and went to the table, apparently to replenish his drink, but actually to compose himself. Bill realized that his friend was under stress and, of course, he knew why. He got up also and went to the table to stand next to Jim.

'Why don't you tell them?' said Bill quietly. 'I'm sure that you can trust them not to breach the confidence.' After a pause, Bill added, 'It might help if you tell them.' Jim had shown signs of becoming distraught but was just managing to keep himself under control. As he returned to the others, he followed Bill's advice.

'Ben, Trevor, I have something to tell you,' and he proceeded to recount some of the events of the previous day. He was careful not to divulge the military aspect, however, not wishing to breach the confidentiality with which he had been entrusted. But he did mention the presence of the police officer in the house.

The disclosures brought forth genuine expressions of shock and sympathy from Ben and Trevor. It also put into sharper perspective some of the things that Jim had been saying.

After a while, Jim felt more composed again, perhaps being subconsciously grateful for the opportunity to share his dilemma. He felt the need to pull the meeting back to its purpose as he saw it.

'I thank you for your sympathy,' he continued, 'and I could understand it if you felt that first my father-in-law's death and then Carol's violent abduction meant that my judgement was unbalanced in an attempt to link somehow these events together. All I would say to you is that these events do have a common denominator, if you like, but they have served only to galvanize my actions rather than be the cause of them. All around me, whether it be from my job, my friends, the environment, the media, I have this gut feeling that something abnormal is going on. Trevor is right. It may all be circumstantial, but, please, just reconsider the list again: unusual weather patterns all over the globe … a unique weather spell in this country … record atmospheric pressure … strange atmospheric phenomena … distorted directional systems in birds … odd behavioural patterns in other animals … and then … what of human behaviour? … A degree of lawlessness and violence escalating way beyond even the record levels of recent years … and perhaps a sense that the violence is occurring across a wider spectrum of society than ever before … a potential drift into anarchy maybe? I'm sorry, but I just can't believe that all this is unconnected.'

'You may well be right, Jim,' intoned Reaney in his usual gravelly delivery but in a slightly less blunt manner than usual, 'but I would suggest that we need a lot more information on the causes of aggression and violence in society. My party would say, and who am I as a good party man to disagree, that unemployment, poor housing and social deprivation are the root causes of antisocial behaviour.'

'I would not dismiss those theories,' said Ben, 'but there's also the theory of the bored rich kids who have no respect for other people or property, no discipline, and plenty of money to afford to get high on drugs. On the whole, I think that Jim is right about a higher plane of violence across a broader range of society. The old theories may still be valid, but maybe not enough on their own any more.'

'Right…,' said Jim, but before he could continue further Ben was anxious to follow through his point.

'I just wanted to say also that some research in The States…'

'Why is it always The States?' quipped Reaney.

'Because they spend more on research than anywhere else,' replied Ben, but then returned to his central point.

131

'Some research is suggesting that there is a link between human behaviour, and after all, that is what violence is, an antisocial, physically aggressive form of behaviour, between that and the universal atmospheric environment all around us. The truth of the matter is that we are all the product of the stuff of the universe. That is what we are all made of and no amount of man-made tinkering can alter that fact. It stands to reason, so the argument goes, that if there are fundamental changes in the basic constituents of the universe, or in the balance or reactions between those constituents, then all living things must be affected, to some degree.'

'I have enough constituents to worry about,' said Reaney light-heartedly.

'You obviously remain sceptical, Trevor,' said Jim.

'You could put it that way,' came the reply, 'but I would never dismiss the possibilities of what you are saying.'

'Could I suggest then that there is at least room for some investigation and research? Would you agree with that?' asked Jim.

'Yes, there is probably enough circumstantial evidence and logic to these theories to make it worthwhile for a few boffins to have a look for any links between these matters and come up with a report or an expert opinion,' answered Reaney.

'You see, Trevor,' said Jim, standing up now and strolling towards the patio doors with hands clasped behind his back, 'I think that there has already been a report by the boffins, as you call them, and Ben here confirms something similar in The States too. I think that we, and people like us, should ensure that there is no cover-up.'

'Well, now, from my point of view,' responded Reaney, directing his words at Jim's back, 'that would be more interesting, not least because if there is one thing that I intend to speak up about, and this was something of a personal initiative in my election campaign, it is the lack of openness in government.'

Jim turned round now, encouraged by Reaney's positive words, believing that he could play a key part in what was now

132

developing for Jim into some kind of crusade. As if to illustrate this, Jim spread his arms wide, almost in a beseeching sort of way.

'It's our planet', he said. 'We have a right to know what is going on in our atmosphere, what the analyses, the measurements and the research are showing, what the problems are and the causes, where it will all end and, above all, what we can and should do about it.'

'I could not agree more,' said Reaney, 'but let's not lose sight of the fact that you still have to tie in somehow the violence aspect, accepting, as we do, that it is increasing and running out of control. I am interested in this theory of it involving a wider cross-section of society and it may be possible to substantiate that, but how do we take this forward?'

'Well, as far as this meeting is concerned, I think that I can take it forward a little,' said Bill, causing Trevor and Ben to cast their glances in his direction. Bill then recounted the events of just over a week ago and from which he still bore some physical scars. He told of the sort of people who seemed to be attached to this marauding gang, the almost robotic behaviour of some of them, not to mention the almost anarchic violence. He told of the police version of the events and their opinion generally on the rising tide of criminality and violence in the area. He touched again on the terrifying events of the previous day involving Mandy and, in particular, Carol.

They all knew also of other incidents which seemed to fill the pages of the national press on virtually a daily basis, not to mention the television screens.

'Clearly,' said Jim, 'there is an urgent need for some kind of public enquiry into the volume, the scope and causes of the rapidly escalating levels of violent behaviour in our society. It should consider the link between these levels of violence and extraterrestrial influences, including magnetic forces and solar influences. Probably it should also look at other types of behaviour and, maybe, I would venture to suggest, at some of the modern illnesses that have developed or have been identified in recent years and which have caused

133

such puzzlement … I am thinking here of ME and RBD.'

'I am familiar with the first of those but not the second,' said Reaney.

'RBD stands for Recurrent Brief Depression syndrome,' explained Jim. 'It's a condition, now well-documented, where people become almost suicidally depressed, but for no apparent reason. It may last a few days, go away, and then come back again. Sometimes the periods in between are longer. It does not appear to be linked to traumatic periods or events in people's lives. Is it coincidence that diseases such as these arrive on the scene and then thrive at the same time as excessive solar and magnetic activity? And aren't conditions such as these linked to the human nervous system and the brain, the same centres that control and influence human behaviour, including aggression?'

'Questions, questions,' was Reaney's response.

'And not a lot of answers in sight,' commented Ben.

'Unless they are being hidden from view,' said Jim, bringing a thoughtful mumble from Reaney, who followed it with a more considered and intelligible comment.

'What you seem to be implying or suggesting then, Jim, is that something in our atmosphere, which has become more prevalent in recent times, may trigger certain types of behaviour, though it may affect different people in different ways, to the extent of nervous or mental illness in some, aggression in others, and possibly no discernible effect at all in the rest. Is that a fair summary?'

Jim thought about Reaney's summary for a few seconds, his head slightly in the air, before replying, 'I suppose that I am suggesting something like that, in circumstances where the atmospheric culprit, if I can put it that way, becomes out of balance with the other forces of nature.'

'In fact,' said Bill, rejoining the discussion, 'this theory is not so far removed from views expressed in recent years about links between the weather and certain diseases. It is said that arthritis sufferers are sensitive to tiny changes in barometric pressure. Biometeorologists are examining links between climate change and meningitis. Doctors at the

Environmental Health Center in Dallas have linked mood changes, headaches and allergies to storms and I believe we have a doctor in Hertfordshire who supports this. As usual, much more research needs to be done, but I think all of these things lend support to Jim's view that we are likely to be very sensitive to atmospheric changes or imbalance. I don't think it is jumping too big a chasm, as Trevor put it earlier, to envisage a link with violent human behaviour,' he concluded.

'And if the phenomenon is increasing,' said Ben, 'whatever it is, then the level of violence and, for that matter, illness will also increase.' Ben narrowed his eyes before continuing. 'Maybe the biggest threat to human existence is not the AIDS problem but atmospheric change. Do you think those could be related?' he asked no one in particular.

'But at least, even if not cured yet, AIDS is an identified problem,' commented Reaney.

'Precisely,' concurred Jim. 'And that has helped to contain it and direct enormous research towards it.'

'Which you fear will not happen or is not happening with your theories?' enquired Reaney.

'I suppose so,' answered Jim and, then, on the front edge of his seat, 'I would like to convince people that though this might sound a bit like science fiction, so did many other theories until the final strands of proof fell into place. I believe that there is a common thread to all that we have been talking about. We are all a product of the universe. We are totally dependent on the sun. Recently increased solar output, solar flares, sunspots are all proven facts. These things are bound to affect our lives and, for that matter, the lives of all inhabitants of the planet to some extent. It will affect our atmosphere, which also serves us as a shield. What happens if the shield is insufficient to cope with enormously increased solar wind activity? Isn't human health, physical and mental, and human behaviour bound to be affected? There is much more to this than just a drought. All that is, is a symptom, a forerunner of something much more devastating. Call it intuition, call it the vivid imagination of an investigator's mind, or perhaps my personal traumas have unbalanced my thought processes, but somehow I keep getting driven to the conclusion that I have to do something about it all. It would be pretentious to suggest that I feel that it is my destiny, but maybe that word might help to explain how I feel about things.'

Jim finally paused. He leaned back as though to say, 'I rest my case' and there was a silent acknowledgement from the others. There had been a lot of talking on a hot sticky afternoon, but the real crux of the reason for them being there was now being reached. Jim leaned forward again.

'I asked you all to come here today as friends, but also because you all are, or could be, people with influence. What I would really like to ask you is: will you help me? When I set up this little get-together, I could never have envisaged the events of the last twenty-four hours but in a strange way that has actually reinforced my determination to pursue these theories and blast open the establishment cover-up. Will you help me to solve at least one of my dilemmas?'

Jim sat back again and this time he had concluded. There were some finer details best left until later. It was odd how his thoughts about the puzzling events they had been discussing were coming to a head at the same time as the personal trauma he was suffering as the result of Carol's abduction; his two dilemmas, as he called them, coinciding and somehow linked. He waited for his guests to respond.

It was Ben who volunteered the first response, speaking in his customarily relaxed manner.

'I think that Jim's on to something. I believe that there is some natural force, if you like, that is modifying behavioural patterns, certainly in the animal world and, yes, it is feasible in the human world too. All right, maybe it is a bit of a jump to link in human aggression and violence but I'm not sure whether or not Trevor's chasm is the right analogy. For sure, there are a lot of unanswered questions. We're all professionals in one field or other. My professional instincts tell me that there is a scoop to be had and when my Washington contacts come up with the goods on this report, I'll know where we're headed.'

'Do you think that you'd go into print on it, Ben?' asked Jim.

'Certainly. With a bit more substance on the cover-up aspect, I could definitely sell this to the nationals. Even without that, I'd think about doing a general interest article and touting it round.'

'Thanks, Ben,' said Jim, wondering who might be next to proffer an opinion. There was a brief silence, broken eventually by Bill.

'Speaking as a meteorologist, and trying to be objective,' he said thoughtfully with head down, 'like Ben, I have a gut feeling that something unusual is happening. There is no doubt that modern weather and pressure records are being broken, but I would caution here that these are only modern records, because statistics don't go back that far in the grander scale of things. Having said that, neither do accurate descriptions of the environment. Nevertheless, if all my years in the business have taught me one thing, it is to respect the forces of nature. No matter how sophisticated and civilized we have become, we are still unable accurately to predict events very far ahead, let alone influence them. We are still almost completely at the mercy of the cosmos and the atmosphere and we probably always will be. I think what you and Ben are saying,' continued Bill, looking now at Jim next to him on the settee, 'is very plausible and it needs very carefully evaluating and, yes, if needs be, some publicity.'

'Publicity is all very well, but only at the right time,' ventured Reaney in his guttural tones.

The other three awaited his views keenly, aware that if this blunt sceptic could be converted, then Jim's theories may indeed have substance. And Jim was all too aware of the national and political influence that his old friend could have, even though he was yet to set foot in the Palace of Westminster. Reaney mopped his brow with his hand in the increasingly uncomfortable heat, studying the results on his upturned palm before going on.

'Going off at half-cock now might give you some temporary publicity but you need to be sure of your facts.'

'But sometimes, Trevor,' responded Jim, 'a dose of publicity can act like a good kick up the pants. It can stimulate governments and officialdom into action.'

'That's right,' added Ben, supportively. 'Never underestimate the power of the press, even the tawdry tabloids.'

'Especially the tabloids,' agreed Bill.

'OK,' said Reaney. 'All I am saying is, delve a little deeper if you don't want to run the risk of being a one day wonder.'

'And what about the cover-up aspect?' asked Ben.

'Now that's a different matter,' enthused the politician. 'Give me a whiff of a cover-up and I'm your man. I'll be on to it in a trice and I'll ferret out the truth for you.'

'But be honest, Trevor,' said Jim in a quietly enquiring, almost imploring voice. 'What do you think about what you have heard this afternoon? About my theories? About the violence? About the gut feelings we all have? What's your opinion? What can you do to help us? Do you want to become involved? Or have we wasted your valuable time?'

Reaney grinned in his inimitable fashion, a full-toothed grin, happy to be in the limelight and intent on transferring that importance to the national stage.

'Questions, questions,' was his initial response, but then came the specific answers. 'No, you have not wasted my time, Jim. Far from it. There is no doubt that we are living through an unusual time. Is it a long-term trend? I don't know. Does it have serious repercussions for us all, for the whole world even? It would be a brave man to say, "No", and a stupid man who tries to predict the future.' Reaney leaned forward and looked straight ahead at Jim. 'Let's just say that a lot of things I have heard this afternoon have interested me greatly and I would very much like to be kept in touch with any developments. However, I'm sure that you will appreciate that things are rather hectic for me at the moment. Maybe I can be of some help to you, if not now, then in the near future.'

'Thank you for that offer, Trevor,' said Jim. 'I have a feeling that we may yet take you up on it. In summary, can I take it that you would like to be associated with our efforts but not yet in an official or public capacity?'

'I think that's a fair summary,' replied Reaney. 'Or, to put it another way, I do not feel that what you have so far would constitute maiden speech material.' There was a chuckle from Jim and Bill, but not from Ben, who took up Reaney's last comment.

'Then let me offer you some more suitable material.' Ben drew the full attention of the others, and continued, 'If I were to tell you that water supplies in many parts of the country, already severely depleted and receding rapidly due to the drought, were contaminated to the extent that a large proportion of what is left is not and cannot be made fit for human consumption, would you be interested? Furthermore, the government is keeping this information secret to avoid public panic even to the extent of covering up deaths arising from the contamination. And if I told you that this information has come direct from a member of John Marner's cabinet, would you be even more interested?'

Reaney was aghast and astonished at this information and was temporarily struck dumb, as were Jim and Bill. When the ever sceptical politician eventually found the right words, he expressed a profound interest in the matter and implored Ben to tell him more. With apologies to Jim for stealing his thunder, Ben proceeded to put more flesh on the bones of his story. Acting in true journalistic tradition, he was determined, at least for the time being, not to divulge the sources of the information, including the name of the minister who blabbed. But he gave what information he had, though he had not come to the meeting with the express intention of doing so. It was just the way things had developed. All he had previously decided, once Joanne had taken him into her confidence, was that somehow or other the story must come out. Ben had not known that Reaney would be here, nor that he would develop a cautious respect for him, but he believed that Jim's blunt friend could help him.

Jim was called out just before the end of Ben's exposition to take a telephone call from the police inspector. Having feared the worst, it turned out to be only routine. Nevertheless, it served to remind Jim once again, not that it was necessary, of the more traumatic personal matter hanging over him. The afternoon's events had seemed somehow to grab his concentration and acted as a sort of cocoon from reality, but it was indeed a fragile shell. When he rejoined the others, he returned their enquiries about Carol politely and reassuringly, but it soon became apparent that his previous enthusiasm was lacking. Jim was understandably feeling, and now beginning to show, the strain of it all.

The others talked on for a while, with Reaney in particular gleaning information from Ben and giving every indication that this was a matter that he was going to be very proactive about, one that could get his fledgling Westminster career off to a flying start. Ben, aware of Jim's new demeanour and conscious that he was now the one centre stage, discussed with Reaney how they could progress this issue between them and how to keep in touch. There was a general wish to keep in touch by telephone and fax and that they should try for another meeting soon. Again, in deference to Jim, Ben offered himself as coordinator if Jim was understandably absent and he offered his own home as a possible next venue.

Not long afterwards, the meeting broke up. All offered sympathy to Jim and expressed the wish that the search for Carol would be speedily and successfully concluded. As Ben was chatting to Reaney as they made their way in the hot and stifling conditions to their respective cars, he could begin to feel again the onset of a dull throbbing pain inside his skull.

PART THREE

Even in the oppressive heat of another afternoon of record-breaking proportions, it was an idyllic setting that they had found: shaded by trees and soothed by the sound of sometimes swirling water. They were back in the vehicle now so familiar to them, parked up on the once-grassy verge of a wide bend in an otherwise narrow and winding country lane. A few yards away was the lych-gate and path that led to the imposing and impressive part-Norman church, peaceful and deserted, apart from the crowd of surrounding tombstones. From this vantage point Geoff could see yards down the river, as far as the wharf that was used as a tie-up for boats off-loading visitors to the church or, more usually, to The Red Lion further back down the lane, but hidden from their sight.

They had seemed to have been there an age and Carol had earlier regarded it as a minor victory when she had persuaded them to leave the vehicle temporarily for the sake of some physical, if not mental, exercise. Geoff had agreed on condition that Carol behaved herself and he permitted her to wander round the interior of the historical church under the supervision of Andy, whilst he meanwhile went off on a reconnoitring mission. It was not long though before he returned to collect them from the back of the church.

'A fine church,' said Geoff, looking around.

'You like churches?' asked Carol, who was close by with Andy.

'I like the feeling you get from old ones like this. You can almost touch the history of them,' replied Geoff. 'It's a pity so many of them are locked up now.' In some ways Carol thought that this was an odd comment from a man who apparently was capable of killing and kidnapping. 'Come on. Back to the vehicle,' he ordered. Andy moved towards the door but Carol hesitated.

'I'm coming,' she said. 'I just wanted to have a look in the visitors' book.' Andy and Geoff wandered outside, confident that Carol would follow within a few seconds.

Outside, with Carol out of earshot, Andy quizzed his leader about the current situation. Geoff pondered his reply. He was obviously a student of human behaviour. Whilst some would have taken the view that they had so far successfully eluded capture through a sequence of fortunate events, he would have none of it. Whilst most people believed that lack of respect for others' property was a crime of epidemic proportions, he blamed the property owners too for a matching lack of care. In other words, if you waited long enough, and often that would not be very long at all, cars would present themselves with doors open and keys in the ignition, not to mention barges and boats, especially in areas where a relaxed holiday atmosphere prevailed, and vessels were more than likely hired rather than owned. It was all a question of opportunism, he explained to Andy, plus the knack of trying to ensure a situation where the loss would not be reported for a while and a location which offered a variety of escape permutations.

'Give it another couple of hours,' he explained, 'and you'll have half a dozen boats tied up at the wharf, out of sight of their guzzling occupants. I guarantee that at least one will be suitable for our requirements.'

'But why not stick to the car?' asked Andy. 'It's faster.'

'Trust me,' was Geoff's reply. 'The trick is to outwit the opposition, not to be predictable, to keep one step ahead.' After a pause he added, in a voice designed to assert his authority, 'Now find out what our friend is doing.'

When Andy popped his head back inside the main door of the church, Carol was nowhere to be seen. He scampered quickly down the aisle, looking all around constantly as he went.

'She's gone, she's gone,' he shouted in agitated fashion.

The thick stone walls prevented Geoff from hearing Andy's shouts, but it mattered not. Geoff had already anticipated a problem and was by now sprinting round towards the north-west corner of the building. The fleeing Carol was already in his sights. By now she was thirty yards from the church, picking her way through the gravestones. Geoff saw a more direct route. He must head her off, he thought, before she reached The Red Lion, which appeared to be her general direction. In her desperation, Carol did not help her cause by losing her footing as she tried to clamber over the modest stone boundary wall. She was not aware of the resultant trickle of blood down her shin. It was at this point, however, that she realized that Geoff was in hot pursuit, ahead of Andy, who had just emerged from the north entrance that she had also used.

Immediately over the wall there was a stretch of grass interspersed with the occasional bush and sapling and, beyond that, the outhouses in the grounds of the public house. Her chance to raise the alarm was within her grasp but in the balance.

Carol was barely a few yards into this no man's land when a huge weight descended on her from behind, pinning her to the ground. Andy, the only witness, was later to describe Geoff's leap as being worthy of Jonah Lomu powering in for a try at Twickenham.

Geoff completed the manoeuvre by gripping Carol tightly and rolling the both of them over as if one unit, and by one and a half revolutions to the left. This had the effect of partially hiding them from view behind an azalea bush and ended with Carol now lying on her back with Geoff on top of her. In this position their bodies were pressed tightly together. It may have been his physical presence, aided perhaps by the thrill of the chase and, no doubt, fuelled by subconscious desires, that aroused Geoff considerably. Carol could feel his heart pounding against her thinly covered breast, the both of them panting heavily, whilst lower down she could feel his bone hard appendage pressing against her.

Geoff found himself maintaining this position for longer than was strictly necessary until, oddly, he seemed rather embarrassed by it all. He raised himself, but only to a kneeling position, still straddling Carol. Andy was now standing behind them, but he quickly ducked down to a crouch at Geoff's insistence.

'I wondered how long it would be before you made a run for it,' said Geoff, looking down at Carol.

'All I want is to contact my Jim,' gasped Carol, still catching her breath. 'Is that too much to ask?'

'Why didn't you think of it before, Inspector?' asked Jim.

'It's easier with the benefit of hindsight I'm afraid,' he replied, somewhat uncomfortably, arms folded and looking down at his boots. 'After all, who would expect fleeing criminals to make their getaway by canal?'

'And what makes you so sure that they have, then?' asked Jim, by now sceptical of police activity.

'Simply the location of the boat and the time that it must have gone missing,' answered Inspector Childs. 'It seems to be too much of a coincidence otherwise.'

'Shouldn't it have been found by now?' queried Jim, his face now showing tiredness as he stood in his own hallway, facing the hard-pressed law officer.

Jim's telephone rang.

'Maybe it has been found,' said the inspector hopefully, and grateful for the interruption. Jim picked up the receiver and identified himself in a brief and subdued manner.

'Hello, Jim.' In a split second Jim's facial expression changed and his heart lifted. Elation replaced depression. Anxiety was traded for hope. His demeanour communicated the identity of the caller to the inspector an instant before Jim called her name out loud and the policeman gave the nod to his colleague with the headphones.

Carol continued, 'Darling, I have only a limited time. I must do as I am told. I am all right. I have not been harmed. I can ring you again in two days' time if I behave. I love you.'

'Sweetheart, I love you. Should I stay by the phone? I have

a mobile you can ring me on.' Jim spoke quickly and loudly, sensing that the call may be ending.

'It's as broad as long,' said Carol, her voice tailing away before the call was suddenly disconnected. No amount of calling out by Jim could coax the line back into life.

The inspector waited anxiously, but not too long before it became clear that the call was untraceable. Evidently the call had been made from a mobile of the old type. It was possibly one that had been stolen and its owner was not yet aware of the fact.

At least the inspector felt that they had something to work with. A willingness to communicate had been demonstrated. He was grateful for any break at this stage. They would run over the tape again and again for some clue.

Complete silence had prevailed as Carol had made her call but it terminated with the phone being snatched violently from her grasp, accompanied by a raised voice.

'What the hell do you think you are doing?' barked Geoff. 'I said no more than ten words, not the bloody Gettysburg Address. What was all that about at the end? What was he asking you?'

Before Carol could answer, Geoff gabbed her by the wrist and jerked her out from the shade into the hot bright sunshine and back towards the vehicle, where Andy, wiping sweat from his brow, was waiting.

* * *

Dennis Plimmer had earned a rebellious reputation for himself in his eight years in Parliament. Many regarded him as rude, lacking in respect for others, uneducated, ill-mannered and obnoxious, and he was noted for keeping the Speaker and the Sergeant-at-arms busy with his ill-tempered outbursts in The House. His notoriety had earned him the status of folk hero or subversive, according to point of view, but with no in-between. Being sponsored by him meant that Reaney was nailing his colours well and truly to the mast.

Sponsorship was just one of the requirements of a new

Member. A multiplicity of arrangements had to be made, from accommodation to post collection. Then, there were all the formalities and niceties of Parliamentary procedures. Even finding the way around in the labyrinth of Westminster was a feat. Many a new Member had come to this seat of democracy full of euphoria and healthy scepticism only to be sucked in and overwhelmed by the awesome history and complexity of it all. Plimmer was one of the few who could genuinely claim that the place had not changed him, and if that was what Reaney wanted, he had chosen his mentor well.

It was unusual for a new Member to take his seat in The Commons so soon after his election but in Reaney's case it was necessary because the Parliamentary summer recess was not far away. He would have to learn the ropes quickly and he listened attentively to Plimmer's words of wisdom while seated in a comfortable armchair in the latter's cramped and shared office.

'You see, they don't like it in this place, Trevor, when you break their nice little rules,' said the short and stocky Plimmer in his inimitable fashion, that was in danger of making Reaney seem refined. 'You can only speak at certain times. You have to make your maiden speech in a certain way. You have to call everybody by daft titles. And woe betide you if you don't conform to the proper procedures. The men with the funny breeches will come and get you.'

'You make it sound like school,' said Reaney.

'That's exactly it,' replied Plimmer. 'And you either get ticked off like a naughty public school boy or expelled, or sometimes something in-between.'

'So, what do I have to do then,' asked the new boy, 'if I want to raise a matter of national importance with the prime minister?'

'What, straight away, you mean?' asked a somewhat incredulous Plimmer.

'Today,' said Reaney.

'Trevor, you're a man after my own heart,' was the response of his sponsor after he had paused to take in breath and he accompanied these words with a solid pat on the shoulder. 'I fear that you'll 'ave to wait until tomorrow, though,' he added, going on to explain that the PM would not be in The House until then.

'So, what's the procedure then, Dennis?' asked Reaney.

'Well, normally you 'ave to table a question for a verbal reply with two days' notice,' replied Plimmer, 'but there's no guarantee of it being called. Alternatively, you could ask for an emergency debate at the end of Question Time and they give you a couple of minutes for a full-scale debate the following day. It depends 'ow much you 'ave to say and what it's all about. By the way, controversy is very much frowned upon in maiden speeches. You're expected to say nice things about your predecessor and the constituency, and all that twaddle,' he added, with a dismissive wave of the hand.

'Is there any precedent for anything controversial?' asked Reaney.

'Oh, aye,' came the reply, 'that Bernadette Devlin, as was, the Irish woman. She made a big speech on 'er first day in The Commons years ago now that broke all the rules of the club. Very controversial, but it was 'eard in total silence throughout. Even Maggie Thatcher used 'er maiden speech to bring in a bill.'

'Why don't I just jump to my feet and say what I have to say?' enquired the House's newest Member.

'Well, the danger is that you will either be ignored or ejected ... or both, if that's possible.' Plimmer rubbed his chin thoughtfully. 'There is another way you can do this, in a conventional manner, I mean.'

'What's that?' asked Reaney eagerly.

'There's something called a private notice question. It can be raised at the end of Question Time, but only with the consent of the Speaker. I think that the best thing to do is for you to tell me what it is that you want to get off your chest, lad, and then we can consider the best way to go about it.'

The conversation continued intently, nourished by additional cups of tea, with Dennis Plimmer in the unlikely role of mother.

*   *   *

149

Jim had gained renewed hope and strength from that briefest of telephone conversations the previous evening. The thought that Carol had sounded reasonably normal and was able to promise another call later were grounds for optimism. When the police subsequently found the boat and then linked in the theft of the Range Rover in the immediate vicinity, it further encouraged confidence. Inspector Childs decided not to call the number of the mobile phone that was stolen with it, for fear of revealing their hand too soon. Of course, Jim was concerned still for Carol's safety but there was at least a glimmer of hope. For the time being, he would go along with the renewed request of the authorities for secrecy.

Jim could not face another day of sitting waiting for something to happen. Suitably reassured that immediate contact would be made with him if there was anything to report, he decided that he would try at least to fulfil an appointment he had previously made. This was nothing to do with his profession. He had already made arrangements to take a few days off work. It was to do with the matters that had been under discussion at Sunday's meeting.

Many of Jim's claims investigations involved accident victims and this often brought him into contact with medical experts. Over the years he had made several acquaintances he could rely on for independent advice, often specialists but sometimes with a wider range of expertise. He decided that it was time that he made use of one at least of these contacts, but this time not to meet his professional needs.

Hamish McDonald he counted as a friend whom he had first met in a professional capacity many years ago, though their paths had not crossed recently. The tall and affable Scot had been something of an expert on head injuries but his talents had spread beyond mere diagnostic and surgical skills. He had been drawn to the fascinations of pure research and the intricacies and complexities of psychological disorders; in general the workings of the inner mind. He had moved to Cambridge, which had partly accounted for their lack of contact in recent years. Jim was delighted when Hamish found time to see him out of his busy schedule.

The rougher edges of his mother tongue had long since been rounded off but there was still no mistaking the Scottish lilt of this tall gangling man as he stooped to offer Jim his cup of tea.

'No matter what the weather, you'll never part the English from their tea,' he said. Jim gratefully acknowledged it from his low armchair in Hamish's study, his position having caused Hamish to exaggerate his stoop.

'I can only think that it must fulfil some psychological need, Hamish.'

'More likely a chemical one, I fear,' responded the Scot, now seated in an equally low and comfortable chair. 'Delighted to see you again, Jim' he continued, after a slight pause, 'though I got the impression that there might just be a professional angle to it,' he suggested.

'You always were perceptive,' said Jim. 'Can I tell you a story?'

Geoff was not a happy young man. His hijacking plans of the previous evening had been thwarted by unexpectedly vigilant boat owners. An uncomfortable night spent in the car had done little to solve his chronic tiredness. Instead, it had added stiffness of back and limb to his general lack of well-being. Worst of all, however, his numbing headache had returned with a vengeance, not that he had had much respite from it for days now. He was unshaven and unkempt and he looked thoroughly demoralized.

Carol had sensed that this might be a dangerous time to push him too far, but had gently suggested once again that he ought to seek medical advice. She had also tried to persuade him, again unsuccessfully, of the futility of his actions. He seemed to have some master plan, possibly involving escape by water-borne transport once again. Perhaps he was going to sail through The Broads up to Yarmouth and out into the North Sea. But where then? And what would they do for food, money and clothing? She could only bide her time once more, without attempting any foolish escapes this time.

151

Geoff had decided to risk venturing into the little Norfolk village of Dorning, not far from their overnight halt. After parking inconspicuously just off the High street, Andy had left the car and disappeared round the corner. The next time they saw him he was on the other side of the road, driving past in one of those middle-of-the range saloon cars that looked the same the world over. It was a red one. Geoff set off in the four-by-four in pursuit, Carol in the rear and behaving herself as ordered.

The change of car had been plan B as far as Geoff was concerned. Now they must find somewhere isolated to stash the Range Rover that had served them so well.

'It's an interesting theory,' said the tall Scot, uncrossing his long gangling legs and wafting himself with a handy pamphlet to create a cooling fan effect in the high temperatures of the late morning. 'It certainly takes you into the area of whether or not man is programmed to be aggressive, how aggression is triggered, and how it is suppressed. Some scientists believe that there is a fund of aggression waiting to be discharged. That's why you always get a rush to enlist when a country calls its citizens to arms. In peacetime, of course, there are lots of outlets, in combat games, and crime, and so on. Some see it as being similar to the orgasm you get from sexual activity and, in fact, these two functions are very close together in the brain.'

'So you can identify a certain part of the brain as being responsible for violence and aggression then, can you?' asked Jim, fascinated.

'Oh, yes,' replied Hamish. 'Generally it is believed to be a part of the old core brain, the hypothalmus. The modern view is that the more recently evolved sections of the brain, in the cortex, would suppress the function.'

'You sound very clinical about the brain's function, Hamish,' observed Jim.

'Well, from the clinician's point of view, it has its functions and its components and its chemicals. That doesn't prevent it from being tremendously complex, of course, but we are becoming more knowledgeable about it all the time. What may never be quantifiable and understandable is the way in which social and environmental matters affect the brain function, not to mention the influence of those strange and unscientific factors that people refer to as the mind or, indeed, the soul.' Hamish stood up and went over to what looked like a pile of books on a small box but turned out to be one of those table top mini-fridges, but a very well-concealed one. 'Ice-cold beer?' he enquired. After a slight pause, he added, 'They're only little ones.'

'Yes, please,' answered Jim. 'So how does this grab you then, Hamish, as a possible scenario . . . man has an inherent aggressive streak . . .'

'OK,' nodded the Scot, pouring the first beer into a tankard.

'It can be triggered as both a physiological or a biological function . . .' continued Jim.

'Possible,' said Hamish, still bartending.

'But more often it is likely to be triggered for social or environmental reasons,' said Jim.

'More likely,' commented Hamish.

'If triggered biologically it could even be suppressed by behavioural or social considerations.'

'And usually is,' said Hamish, now supplying Jim with his drink.

'So, if there is a biological trigger,' asked Jim, 'what would it be? How does it work? Would it always be suppressed?'

'More than one question,' replied his tall host, 'but the answers may be connected. The key may lie in the brain's chemicals or, to be more precise, an imbalance in them.' He completed pouring his own drink and returned to his seat, opposite Jim. 'You see, it is known that nerve cells in the brain prepare for aggression by secreting monoamines. Adrenalin is one that might be more familiar to you. The chemical can differ according to the precise function. For example, aggression might arise for different reasons . . . instincts, if you like: territorial, predatory, defence mechanisms and so on. An excess of dopamine has been identified as a potential precursor to aggression with violence. If there are errors in the monoamine system it might lead to aggression also.'

'Have there been any experiments to support these views?' asked Jim.

'In animals, yes. Rats mainly. Although in tests on violent alcoholics, an increase in dopamine has been found.'

'Now be honest, Hamish,' said Jim.

'Aren't I always?' he quipped.

'What are the chances of unusual atmospheric activity affecting chemical imbalances in the brain?' asked Jim, getting to the nub of the issue. Hamish was anxious to give a considered response and paused for thought momentarily.

'It cannot be ruled out,' he replied. 'I know of experiments with monkeys which have successfully demonstrated that electric shock treatment to a certain part of the brain can disrupt the balance of amines and lead to excessive aggression. Atmospheric disturbance is slightly different but I believe that it could be just about feasible.'

'Especially, perhaps, if there were disturbances to the electromagnetic field of the atmosphere,' added Jim, seeking approval.

'I suppose that would be a possibility, subject maybe to the scale of the activity,' responded Hamish, again thoughtfully. 'The biological effects of electromagnetic fields is a fast developing science in its own right.'

'Really,' said Jim. 'That's interesting. So you wouldn't dismiss the theory as wild and fanciful speculation, then?'

'Of course not, Jim. But I fancy that you have two very big obstacles to overcome. Firstly, you have to find the link between atmospheric and brain activity and, secondly, you have to demonstrate that the current levels of atmospheric activity are unique, to the extent that the force it is generating is sufficient to overcome, or at least dilute, millions of years of human brain evolution. A tall order indeed,' concluded Hamish.

Tall orders did not bother Jim. His mind was already moving on to his next step. He had to speak to Bill, but before that he would have more pressing matters to attend to.

'Are you sure, sir?' asked the smart, balding Inspector Childs, in his methodical way.

'Believe me, Inspector, it is not a phrase that I have ever heard Carol use before,' said Jim, 'and in the context of the conversation we were having,' he continued, 'the expression "as broad as long" seemed completely out of place. I am sure that it is this which has been niggling and puzzling me ever since last night.'

'So you think then that your wife is trying to point us in the direction of the Norfolk Broads?' asked the inspector.

'I'm convinced of it,' replied Jim, at the other end of the telephone. A pause suggested that the police officer was still being hesitant about the situation. He was fed up with being second-guessed by the two fugitives. It might be worth a shot, he thought, to put some extra effort into the area. Just the police this time, though. He could not risk involving the military on just a hunch. Meanwhile, there was a nationwide watch in force for the vehicle and the abductors, though the full background was still being withheld.

'OK then, sir. We'll go for it. We'll concentrate extra manpower in that area and we'll make some appropriate noises to the local forces. Bear in mind, though,' added the inspector, as a rider, 'that we are still talking about a large area and we still have to tread with great care.'

'Believe me,' responded Jim, 'nobody is more aware of that than me, Inspector. I just wish that you would be a bit more positive and reassuring about it all.'

'I understand your feelings, sir. Just trust me. I do have experience in these matters. We will get Mrs Webb back, and safely. You have my word.'

'I hope so, Inspector, I hope so.'

When the line went dead both men cursed another of the breakdowns in telecommunications which had become more prevalent in recent days, but at least on this occasion it coincided more or less with the natural end of the conversation.

155

The inspector reflected on the promise that he had just made and wondered why he had allowed himself to make such a commitment.

Jim was also reflective, but he was soon to be interrupted by an incoming call. A now familiar voice with a gentle North American accent identified itself.

'Ben, I'm glad you phoned. I was wondering if I could make use of your friends in the American scientific community.'

'Of course ... such as ... are,' came a reply that was both distant and breaking up, seemingly due to yet another bad connection. 'B... first, I though ... like to know ... faxes I've ... States ... all day to ... 'ms as though ... cation problems wi... side of ... lantic ... Something ... with ... tellites ...'

'Pardon? What? Eh?' Jim was struggling to make sense of it all.

After three attempts, Jim finally got it across to Ben for him to come over and see him instead. Jim thought that it would be a good opportunity for them to compare notes and the distance wasn't far.

Jim went back into contemplation. Sat in his favourite armchair, there were only two topics occupying his mind. Firstly, his continuing determination to resolve the strange events that were unfurling all around him and, secondly, his constant distress and concern about Carol. The latter required no effort of thought. It was a situation continually eating away inside him, which understandably would not go away, no matter how absorbed and involved he became in the other matter. His brave face, his protective shell, was in danger of collapsing, though. He was not sure how much longer he could maintain it.

Jim was oblivious of the sound and pictures emanating from the television set in the corner that he had turned on a few minutes earlier. The content of the news bulletin did not register; not the violent scenes surrounding the industrial action at several Midlands car factories, nor the sinking of a French fishing boat in conflict with their Cornish equivalents, nor the chaos in the City caused by yet another break-

156

down in the Stock Exchange computer. Neither did the all too familiar weather forecast register despite its unusual format due to both computer and satellite problems. All in all, anyone who had tuned in and devoted attention to the bulletin could have been forgiven for thinking that many of the component parts of modern civilization were collapsing under stress.

Joanne was stretched to her full height in the shower, arms above head, rubbing each one in turn with a warm soapy lather. From time to time she would incline her head backwards under the full force of the spray, allowing the hot beads of water to cascade invigoratingly down her face, then onto her upper chest and then dividing into rivulets, two of which ran down and off her nipple-pointed breasts like sensuous miniature waterfalls. Immersed in the noise and pleasure of her showering, she had not heard Mallow unlocking the door and letting himself back into his flat, nor his entry into the bathroom, where he stood ogling her wet slender body. In no time at all the vision before him transmitted a message so erotic that it disturbed the tailored cut of his trousers. Just what Joanne saw in him, however, would always remain a mystery and over the weekend she had begun to wonder herself. Her brother Ben had persuaded her to return to London, but for a specific purpose. She would accomplish that if she could and then extricate herself from the politician's plans.

Joanne gasped in surprise when she realized that Mallow was there and made as though to cover up, though there could scarcely be a morsel of flesh left that he had not seen, touched and groped several times over. Perhaps her instinctive reaction was indicative of changed feelings towards him.

'It's only me, Jojo. Are you coming out? Let me get a towel and dry you. I've missed you terribly this weekend, darling. It's been awful without you.'

All the usual superficial crap, thought Joanne to herself, and then, out loud, 'No, it's all right, darling, I can manage.' She stepped out of the shower and picked up a large white towel quickly and protectively. 'You're late tonight,' she continued. 'I was beginning to think that you were out of town or had some other engagement.'

'Nothing that I couldn't get out of, thank God,' responded the grumpy minister, still eyeing his mistress's body intently.

'Would you like me to rustle up some supper when I'm finished, darling?' she asked, towelling her front and with one eye on the distance between them still.

'That would be fantastic,' said Mallow, making his way now through into the lounge, tossing his briefcase aside with one hand and loosening his striped tie with the other, his voice trailing away as he went. 'How could I exist without you, my sweetheart? You make my life worth living. Just wait 'til I get you between the sheets tonight ... ' Joanne could not quite detect the rest as it tailed away, but thought that there was some crude reference to an intimate part of her anatomy.

They passed a quiet late evening. Despite his earlier ebullience, Mallow seemed tired and drained and Joanne no longer had any enthusiasm for their relationship. Perhaps she would stay in contact with him, to use him and his accommodation and his contacts, to her own ends, but only if she could back off the physical side of the relationship. Meanwhile, she had promised Ben.

Mallow reluctantly but finally accepted that Joanne's headache was genuine. She was potentially a good actress as well as a good model. He resigned himself to no more than a quick read before lights out.

'I could do with a good night's sleep, anyhow,' he said, but without conviction.

'Have you not been sleeping well?' asked Joanne, by now under the sheets, though there was still plenty of residual heat from another breathlessly baking hot day in the capital. Not long ago she would have displayed her naked attributes, at various angles, on top of the bed clothes, but tonight they were under wraps.

'Yes, but it was tomorrow that I was thinking of,' responded Mallow. 'The brown stuff is really going to hit the fan. The PM has been running around like a blue-arsed fly all day.

158

Something else has happened over the weekend. The US president is involved. We've all been told to stand by for an urgent meeting either tomorrow morning or afternoon. All out of town appointments cancelled.'

'What's it all about?' asked Joanne.

'It's bound to be tied in with this bloody drinking water emergency,' said the minister, tetchily, the subject clearly not sitting well with him. Perhaps that was due, at least in part, to his own contribution to the matter through neglect of his ministerial duties.

'But where does the president of the United States come into the equation?' she asked, showing interest but trying not to appear too inquisitive.

'Could be a global climate problem,' mused Mallow. 'Or something to do with the algae contamination. All I know for sure is that their top scientists have uncovered something of significance. We'll know soon enough,' he added, in a matter-of-fact way. He was not going to lose too much sleep over the situation though. 'Are you around tomorrow, darling?' he asked. 'I might need you.'

Joanne leaned over to switch off the bedside lamp before answering.

'Yes, I'll be here, though I will have to head back north later on possibly.'

'We must get our bodies together before you go,' he suggested.

Joanne did not respond.

* * *

There was no such thing as a perfect world. Poor people yearned for wealth. Lonely people longed for a partner. City dwellers dreamed of a life in the country. In reality, it was often the dream that was important, for the reality was never usually quite the same. Escaping the rat race to run a country store came fairly close to fulfilling Keith and Elaine Bentley's dreams, but commercial pressures now reached all corners of the land, even if their inheritance had left them more or less comfortable for life. The countryside could also be a lonely place, sometimes even isolated. At night there was a darkness and quietness that could encourage a feeling of vulnerability. Of course, in the country urban levels of crime seemed remote, but, then, so were the officers of the law.

If anyone had been positioned inside the closed dark shop they would scarcely have noticed the slow silent uplift of the door latch, followed by the barely discernible opening of the door itself. An old-fashioned bell over the top of the door was muted by an intruding hand. The main protection against a break-in was in the form of a visible but unsophisticated alarm that proved no more than a token defence, the wire being cut courtesy of some small sharp cutters found in the extensive tool box in the boot of the stolen red saloon car. An outer porch door had soon succumbed to the attentions of a tyre lever and, once inside, Andy had been able to demonstrate his skills with the inner door. His locksmith apprenticeship from years ago had proved, not for the first time, to be invaluable. It was an added bonus when the door opened slowly without meeting the resistance of any bolts. In any other location the absence of such a basic security measure would have been viewed by an insurer as tantamount to complicity. In fact, the bolts were there but not in use that night, Elaine having locked up at closing time, secure in the knowledge that Keith always did a routine double-check later on. He did not do so that night; a simple break in routine of the sort that happened from time to time and which usually counted for nothing. To Geoff, though, it would have reinforced his theory that victims of crime were often authors of their own destinies.

Once inside, Geoff soon found an empty cardboard box and he and Andy proceeded to fill it with a selection of fresh and tinned food, operating in a stealthy and efficient manner. A few bottles of Bells found their way into the container, too. Geoff thought that it would help his headaches.

Keith Bentley, though now well into middle age, was still quite a fit-looking and agile man. He generally slept well, though that had not always been the case when he was a city dweller. However, like many others currently, whether in town or country, he was finding that unbearable daytime heat was lingering on to make conditions for sleeping uncomfortable at night. It was true that there was still a considerable diurnal temperature range but this tended not to become noticeable until late in the night. So, whilst his black-haired and bearded face lay on its pillow, his eyelids closed and breathing slow, he had not yet succeeded in crossing the threshold from light sleep to deep slumber. In the quiet country environment, his senses were still receptive to the slightest noise. With wife Elaine apparently sound asleep, he crept quietly out of the bedroom to investigate.

Whenever danger threatened, Geoff's military training inevitably took over but allied to a frightening aggression that had been so dominant in him back at the camp recently. When he saw the half-clothed figure spring out of the shadows to grab Andy in a stranglehold from behind, Geoff acted instinctively and decisively. Clenching his hands together and swinging them high above his head to gain momentum, he brought them crashing down on the side of the shopkeeper's neck with the force of a human sledgehammer, knocking him almost instantly to the ground. Geoff had hardly been aware that he accompanied his action with a blood-curdling yell, acting as a kind of focus of his power like a crazed karate expert. However, he did hear the sickening thud, as Keith Bentley caught his head on the metal edge of the meat counter, diverting his slump to the thinly covered concrete floor.

'I think that you might have overdone it, Boss,' said Andy, now recovered and bent over examining the crumpled bare-topped shopkeeper. The lifeless body lay almost sideways, the face wide-eyed and open-mouthed, with blood from the head wound spilling onto the beige linoleum.

'What did you expect me to do?' raged Geoff. 'Shake his hand and offer him my calling card? Don't you dare question my actions,' he added menacingly, pointing a rigid, jabbing finger in the direction of Andy's face. Andy bent lower and put his ear to the man's mouth, placing two fingers on his neck at the same time, to check for a pulse.

'I think he's dead,' said Andy, then raising himself to full height again. Geoff made no immediate comment but went back to the box of food on one of the counters. After quickly and quietly throwing in a few more articles, he turned to Andy, who was still standing his ground near the body, numbed at the thought of the futile loss of life.

'Are you still with me or not?' asked Geoff. Andy paused before answering in a subdued fashion.

'I'm with you Boss, but what do we do now?' he asked.

'We do what I decide. I've never let you down before, have I?' replied Geoff.

'No, Boss,' said Andy, now back in subservient mode.

The two men left the shop without further ado, unaware that they were being watched. However, Elaine Bentley would regret for the rest of her life that she had merely spied on her husband's killers and not challenged them.

Carol's hopes were momentarily raised when she heard noises approaching, only to be dashed when it became clear that it was her two unwelcome fellow travellers returning. At least, she hoped, it would hasten her release from the tightly-bound tow rope that had been rubbing against the delicate skin of her wrists and would lead to the removal from her mouth of the hideous sticky tape that was more suited to the sealing of radiator hoses. She felt sweaty and dirty and depressed. She could do with a change of underwear, not to mention other clothing, though she still retained the pullover that she had found on the narrowboat. In her current predicament, though, she could not afford to be too ambitious about the finer points of life. Physically, she had still not been significantly harmed or violated, so far. She missed Jim terribly. They rarely spent nights apart, let alone in such circumstances as these.

After loading a box in the car Geoff shuffled off again, leaving Andy to untie Carol.

'Turn round and then keep still,' ordered Andy, 'whilst I get you out of this.'

'Mmm ... mmm ... mmm ...,' uttered Carol and after a few seconds it dawned on Andy that she was trying to get him to remove the gag. He duly ripped it off unceremoniously and painfully.

'I didn't think you were the vindictive type,' said Carol after catching her breath and enduring the stinging pain around her mouth.

'Believe me, it's better taken off quickly rather than slowly,' said Andy. 'You ask a nurse.'

'I don't know any nurses who have been put through this ordeal,' responded Carol, then thinking to herself, 'Thank God that Mandy managed to avoid capture.' It was hardly likely that the two of them would have been taken along for the ride, which meant that one or both would have been dumped, but in what state, alive or dead?

'So, where have you been then?' continued Carol.

'Oh, not so far,' replied Andy, still struggling with the ropes and causing her to grimace occasionally.

'And what's in the boxes?' she asked.

'You'll find out soon enough.'

'Where's Geoff gone? He didn't seem in a very good mood,' observed Carol.

'What an awful lot of questions,' said Andy, finally making some progress in unravelling the knot.

'Something's wrong, Andy, isn't it? Tell me what it is, please,' she urged.

In response, Andy got a few short sentences out, but edgily, whilst looking over his shoulder constantly for Geoff's return.

'Give it up,' said Carol. 'You know that this is crazy. Give it up now before it gets any worse.'

'It can't get any worse,' thundered a voice from behind, startling Carol and Andy. Having attended to his call of nature, Geoff had then emerged out of the darkness from a different direction.

Carol was now free of her bindings. The latest revelation by Andy stung her into action. She moved towards the gun that Andy had laid on the back seat whilst he was untying her. Geoff realized quickly what was happening. He reached over and smashed her fingers hard with the butt of his own weapon. Andy reacted almost instinctively with seething anger, grabbing Geoff viciously around the neck in a stranglehold and forcing him backwards and down onto the ground. Andy's patience had finally snapped. His decency had got the better of him, in the light of Geoff's cowardly treatment of Carol. Perhaps, also, it was a delayed reaction to earlier events. He went for the same gun as Carol had. No sooner had he grabbed it and turned to face the grounded Geoff, though, than he felt, at the same time as he saw and heard, the blast from Geoff's automatic. His consciousness melted away almost instantaneously.

Carol froze, mouth agape but soundless. For a few seconds she was oblivious of the pain from her bleeding fingers. Her ears were ringing. When she eventually moved it was to raise her hands to her face in horror at the bloodied mass of Andy's face. Undoubtedly he was dead, at the hands of the person he had most respected in life. When Carol was eventually able to bring herself to look at that person, all she saw was a monstrous zombie with mad staring eyes. Her horror was now mixed with genuine fear. Geoff was moaning and holding one side of his head. As Carol looked across at him, the black sky in the background was once again beginning to fill with bright dancing lights, although this time, she thought, like the flickering flames of hell.

Plimmer had been astounded by Reaney's information and saw immediately both the implications and the urgency of the situation. However, Parliamentary procedures meant that the issue could not be raised as quickly as Reaney would wish, at least not by Reaney himself. As a newcomer, he would first have to be installed as a Member and that, too, was steeped in tradition and formality. New Members could not take their seat as they pleased. There was an orderly pattern to the Parliamentary day, from morning prayers onwards. The installing of new Members was well down the list. It meant that Reaney would not be *in situ* when questions were called. Of course, there were alternatives. He could ask someone else to make the revelations, perhaps Plimmer. He could break the news outside The House. He might even make himself heard from the public gallery. Plimmer was no respecter of tradition, nor procedural niceties, but he was so excited by the prospect of the prime minister being made to squirm, and so aware of the potential, perhaps fatal political damage, that on this occasion he decided to do something that was very foreign to him. He decided to pay a visit to Madam Speaker to enlist her cooperation.

It was not clear whether it was the shock of this apparent conformity by the stocky and forthright member for the East Midlands' mining community, or whether it was the shock of the information to be revealed, or indeed just an example of the Speaker's enlightened approach, but the upshot was that Reaney was inaugurated on the Monday and ready to reveal all by private notice question on the Tuesday. This was not before the expected protestations from government supporters, but the Speaker stood firm.

The prime minister had his by now customary rough ride at questions, fielding criticism on crime and drought-related matters. It was nothing, however, to the bombshell that Reaney was about to deliver. When the new Member for Lichworth was called upon to speak, John Marner glanced to his right with the minimum of head movement. He recalled the recent acrimonious meeting in Reaney's constituency and suspected now that there was more of the same to come, but this time he was on home ground.

'Don't worry about the nerves. It's natural. Use the adrenalin pumping through your body to your advantage,' thought Reaney, recalling Plimmer's earlier words of encouragement. He had been psyching himself up for several minutes now and concentrating on what he was going to say. It was a big moment for him and he was shaking inside with anticipation. Plimmer gave him an encouraging pat on the arm as he rose to speak.

'Madam Speaker,' his voice was loud and confident, but even more gravelly than usual, 'would the prime minister tell this House and the people of this country, how he can justify presiding over his government with a clear conscience, knowing that the majority of the country's already scarce and dwindling drinking water supplies are poisoned? When is he going to lift the veil of secrecy surrounding the deaths from contaminated water in the East Midlands and Greater Manchester? Why does he deny the people of this country information on potentially one of the worst natural disasters it has ever faced?' By now Reaney was into full stride but he was struggling to get his fourth question out as a crescendo of babble and noise began to rise from the chamber. At his side he could hear Plimmer, by now no longer able to contain what passed for political repartee.

'Come on, you heartless prat, answer the question,' he said.

'Shut up, you idiot,' came a rejoinder from the opposite benches.

'Point of order,' came another voice from the government side.

Lots of localized chat developed, adding to the trading of insults from one side of The House to the other, with Members up and down like yo-yos trying to attract The Speaker's attention. A cynical observer from the public gallery could be forgiven for wondering what the hell was going on, whilst the seasoned political commentators saw nothing too out of the ordinary in the increasingly raucous proceedings. Reaney had to struggle to make his final words heard.

'Just how long,' he shouted, 'did the prime minister feel that he could maintain this cover-up and, more to the point,' raising his voice again, 'what is he doing about this life-threatening situation?' He finally sat down, attracting a congratulatory pat and a 'Well done, lad,' from Plimmer.

The bedlam quietened, encouraged by the persistence of The Speaker, and a hushed feeling of expectation replaced the game show atmosphere. The prime minister was ashen-faced and seemed shaken and slow to respond, but he was still a professional. He was nothing if not phlegmatic and he chose his words carefully.

'The honourable gentleman is new to this House. Let me assure him that neither I nor any member of my government will come to this despatch box with statements on such matters without due investigation, not least out of deference to the feelings and sensitivities of any injured parties. That is not "cover-up". It is diligence and duty. Madam Speaker, exaggerated scaremongering and abusive remarks will not further the standards of this House.'

Reaney was allowed a supplementary question.

'So, when will the prime minister be making a statement on this matter and how many more will die as we wait?' The government benches reacted to the truculent nature of Reaney's question with jeers, though, at least, he had been succinct, a trait often found in newer Members who were yet to succumb to Parliament's tedious traditions.

'I would hope that a statement can be made to The House before the end of business today,' replied Marner quickly and not long afterwards he was headed for the exit with agitated voices ringing round his ears. The word was quickly passed round the members of the inner Cabinet to convene immediately in the prime minister's room.

A crowd gathered around Reaney. Primarily they wanted to congratulate him. Then they wanted to know his next move. Would he release more information? How serious was the situation? What and who were his sources? An early press conference and media interviews seemed inevitable.

John Marner was known for being an even-tempered and outwardly calm, even passionless, man in public, but those closer to him were more aware of his acerbic tongue. Nevertheless, this was a time to demonstrate his implacability, that steady hand on the tiller in time of crisis. Not five minutes earlier he had been on the receiving end of a Commons mauling instigated by an opponent he thought particularly distasteful and irritating, who had come by information that should only have been the privilege of a few. He was bound to wonder just who it was who could not be trusted, but he could not afford to dwell on that. There were problems to solve and the ones just outlined by the Member for Lichworth were not necessarily the most paramount, despite

167

their gravity, and nor were they the ones that had preoccupied his several discussions in the last 48 hours with the president of the United States. So there was a lot for John Marner to contemplate as he adjusted his broad-rimmed spectacles and waited for his inner Cabinet to file into the room past his outwardly calm gaze.

The sunroof and windows of the inspector's Rover were open to their fullest extent, the ventilation system alone being totally inadequate to cope with the never-ending heatwave. As they sped east on the main trunk road from the Midlands they discussed the current climatic crisis. Jim expounded his theories. The more tangible effects were all too visible to them: the scorched scenery, the shimmering heat, and the melting roads. It was the intangible effects that most worried Jim, though every so often these did manifest themselves, in the form of road rage and the like. Patience was dead, and not just on the roads.

It was dual carriageway for most of the journey and they were making good progress towards their destination, but as they came hurtling round one of the sharper bends the inspector was forced to slam his brake and clutch pedals to the floor, bringing the unmarked police car to a screeching halt. In front of them, a queue of stationary traffic was beginning to form, seemingly as a result of a herd of cows blocking the road. But this was no ordinary herd being taken for milking, or indeed being taken anywhere else, for that matter. Their movement was slow and aimless and, above all constrained. Placards were being held aloft and voices were being raised, sometimes in unison.

'That's all we need,' said the inspector, 'a farmers' demonstration.' He covered the wheel with both arms and bowed his balding head on top of them, in exasperation. Slowly, he raised his head again to gaze at the activity ahead of them, weighing up the situation.

'Mad cow disease,' said Jim out loud, but not necessarily directed at the inspector.

'I beg your pardon,' said Inspector Childs.

168

'Bovine spongiform encephalopathy. Another modern phenomenon,' responded Jim, staring directly ahead, blankly. The inspector looked at Jim and then out through the windscreen again towards the demonstrators.

'Look at the placards,' added Jim. 'Some of the cattle look none too healthy either.'

'Don't they slaughter them if they are diseased?' asked the inspector.

'Supposedly, yes,' answered Jim, 'but now it seems that there is a row over the amount of compensation. Hence the placards and the road block.'

'So do you think that this is another chain in your theory, Mr Webb?' enquired the police officer, now leaning back in his seat.

'Well, it makes you wonder. The government thought the outbreak had peaked but it shows no sign of going away. Over fifty thousand cattle slaughtered already, I believe.'

'So that explains no doubt the tightening up on compensation,' observed Childs.

'Maybe,' said Jim, 'but the main issue is not the cost but the cause. When first diagnosed over ten years ago, it was blamed on contaminated feed. That was banned but it still hasn't solved the problem. You see, this is another brain disease, and with a strong body of opinion in the scientific community believing it can be passed on to humans in the form of Creutzfeldt-Jakob disease, as it's called.'

'So what do they believe is the cause?' asked the inspector.

'I don't know precisely, but I believe that malfunction of brain chemicals is being explored,' replied Jim.

There was a screech of tyres from behind, followed by that silent pause that heralds the crashing of dented metal and smashed glass. A few cars back, the latest member to join the queue had announced his arrival in a rather abrupt and violent fashion, being unable to react in time to the unexpected congestion on an otherwise fast road. Fortunately, contact had been kept to a minimum, the brakes only just failing their ultimate test. Seat belts had ensured no lasting injury to the occupants of the car, nor the one in front, nor indeed the

169

one in front of that which had suffered from the concertina effect.

The inspector was just about to yield to his natural policing instincts to intervene in the situation, when his police car radio burst into life. The message was for him and sought to divert him from his present destination to another location slightly nearer. Evidently there had been a further development.

Jim felt both encouraged and worried at the same time; encouraged by the expectation that he would be closer to a reunion with Carol, worried by the possibility of her being found dead or injured. It made escape from their present hemmed in position paramount. Fortunately, there were signs of movement up ahead. The cattle had proved difficult to control and were straying onto the other carriageway. This opened up one lane and the possibility that some cars might get through before the farmers got organized again. The inspector clamped his mobile flashing blue light on the roof to ensure that their car was one of the few that succeeded in getting through. Behind them there was confusion, firstly from those who were hoping the sign of a flashing blue light would signify some action to clear the road and, secondly, from the drivers of the cars that had collided, who momentarily wondered if their jostling was going to be the subject of police intervention. On both counts expectations were dashed as the inspector first edged his way through the disorganized herd and then, once clear, accelerated rapidly away.

* * *

Ben loved London pubs. He found them characterful and also diverse, provided that you were selective. Over the years he had made a point of seeking out some of the best. It might be the design, or the surroundings, or just the location that attracted him. It might be for the quality of the food or, indeed, the quality of the ale, for he was partial to a decent pint or two, now and again. He liked nothing more than to use them as meeting places for both his business and social acquaintances.

The Lamb was a delightful hostelry, still true to the old traditions, ornate and panelled, with different sections and levels affording privacy and intimacy. The decor was tasteful, the embellishments antique, with engraved glass panels and Hogarth prints on the walls. The sparkling beer pumps offered up a fine choice of real ales. The Lamb had been one of Ben's favourite places from years back when he had lived for a time in Bloomsbury. He spent many a relaxing Sunday thumbing through the papers in the back room, putting the world to rights with friends in convivial surroundings. He liked to revisit from time to time, even though the area was one that he now seldom had reason to be in, his old friends having moved on too. When he arranged to meet sister Joanne there for lunch and a chat after she had concluded a business appointment, it turned out to be a not too inconvenient halfway house.

By mid to late afternoon they had been there for a while and were almost ready to go their separate ways again. However, neither was in a rush to desert the leisurely surroundings that had steadily become emptier and quieter.

'I don't know if I trust you, brother,' said the beautiful Joanne, resplendent in her two-piece floral suit and looking every inch the professional model she was. Her moderately long dark hair was no longer tied up, as it was on occasions, but framed her increasingly photographed face. Most of The Lamb's customers that afternoon held Ben in envious regard.

'Do you really believe Jim's theories,' she continued, 'or is this your famous eye for a good article again, once written to be confined to the memory bank to make way for the next story?'

'You'd laugh if I said that I believed every word of it,' replied Ben, half-empty pint glass in hand, 'but I know that I can say that to you without it being regarded as a load of bull. And shall I tell you why I believe it?' he asked, middle finger raised in Joanne's direction.

'Please do,' answered his sister, her plain English accent contrasting with her brother's gentle Canadian twang, belying their close relationship.

'Because for this story,' continued Ben, 'I have more than one source and, what's more, they are all impeccable. Above all, though, I have that journalistic instinct, that gut feeling that I am on to something big, much more than a one article wonder.' He then proceeded to drain most of the remaining ale in his glass.

'So have you got the follow-up already lined up in the word processor then?' asked Joanne in her inimitably cheeky way.

'Not quite,' said Ben. 'I just have one or two gaps to fill and there I think that you might to be able to help me, sister.' Joanne looked at Ben with raised eyebrows. 'Are you seeing your Cabinet minister friend tonight, by any chance?' he asked.

'Possibly,' she said, letting the word out slowly and cagily. 'I do hope that you're not going to ask me to prostitute myself again,' she added, disdainfully.

'If I know you, and I do,' said Ben, 'I'm sure that you can get what you want without having to go that far.'

Though they had not realized it, the place was by now deserted. Even the barman had temporarily disappeared. And yet Ben still found the need to lean over and spell out to Joanne in whispers exactly what help it was that he was seeking.

The Range Rover had been found, but the radio call had diverted the inspector and Jim to a small village just a few miles to the east of where it had been abandoned. When they arrived in the small community, their attention was immediately drawn to the marked police car stationed outside the village store-cum-post office. It was situated, not surprisingly, on the main street, at a junction with a narrow country lane, not that the main street was particularly wide or much frequented by traffic. This was a small village with clusters of disorganized housing, and well off the beaten track. Its church, its pub and its village shop bound its inhabitants together, helping to foster that community spirit that was so difficult to generate in more populous areas. An affront to one villager was an affront to them all. News of the fatal killing of Keith

172

Bentley sank in and was greeted firstly with stunned disbelief and then a mixture of deep sympathy for his widow, Elaine, and angry determination to do all they could to identify and apprehend the culprits. The villagers were aware that levels of violence, misbehaviour and crime were running out of control in the big cities and spreading to the larger villages. Undoubtedly, the perpetrators would be outsiders.

The inspector's car had been directed into a space just round the corner, off the main street. He suggested that Jim remain in the car, at least until he was certain what it was all about. If there was any news of Carol he would, of course, brief him immediately. Jim gestured agreement with a nod of the head, but somewhat unconvincingly, and he watched as the inspector got out of the car and made his way towards the shop, stopping at the door momentarily for a few words with the sergeant before entering.

Jim soon got restless. Being in a well-ventilated moving car in high temperatures was just bearable. Sitting in a stationary one, especially without the benefit of any overhead screening from the sun, was like being baked in a metal oven. He got out and strolled over to where two women were standing, conversing, one in late middle age in a floral dress, the other a young mum sensibly kitted out in shorts and T-shirt and wide-brimmed hat. The young mum's offspring was thankfully well-shaded and protected from the heat and the scorching of a sun that seemed to get bigger and hotter by the day. Jim wiped perspiration off his neck with a handkerchief as he approached them.

'Do you know what's happened over there?' he asked quietly, nodding his head towards the post office store, feigning ignorance.

'There's been a murder, according to our local bobby,' said the older woman, with a touch of a Norfolk accent.

'I thought perhaps you might know what had happened,' said the younger woman, addressing Jim. 'I couldn't help noticing your colleague was let straight in by the sergeant. I thought you must be police or something.'

'Well, my colleague, as you put it, he is a police inspector,'

173

replied Jim, 'but I'm not. I just happen to be with him on another matter. At least it may be a different matter. I'm not making much sense am I?' The ladies smiled politely. 'So, you don't know what's happened then?' persisted Jim.

'No,' replied the older woman, 'but here comes someone who might.'

Crossing the lane from the direction of the store was another woman, of similar age to the one who had just spoken, but plumper, her red face indicating discomfort in the blistering heat. She nodded at the strange man stood with her friends but didn't allow his presence to inhibit her.

'According to Sergeant Anderson, they are looking for two men,' she said. 'Seems as though they were after food and things rather than cash. Very odd, apparently. But poor Elaine,' she continued, stressing the adjective and sounding genuinely concerned, 'the poor girl is so distraught.' She held her hand over her eyes and was comforted by the others. Though from her accent she was not a local, she was undoubtedly part of this close-knit community.

'I'm sorry to intrude,' said Jim, sympathetically, 'but could I ask if any of you have seen any strangers around in the last day or two? Not just the two men implicated, but also a woman with them?' He went on to describe Carol to them, but his enquiry drew a blank. Perhaps the inspector was gleaning more information from the victim's widow. Jim tried in vain to shut out from his mind the possibility that Carol had now been discarded in some kind of cruel and gruesome fashion. He sensed that their reunion was a step nearer.

Emerging from his thoughts, Jim caught the tail-end of the conversation between the three ladies, which culminated in the young one making her excuses to be on her way. Jim, too, thanked them for their information and made to cross the road. His immediate target was the red telephone box, one of the old type that was still defying conversion to the glass shower cubicle type that was nowadays more common. He had to ring Ben. He must see him that night. He had to settle for leaving a message and hoped that that would be enough.

Making his way back across the road to the village store, it wasn't long before Sergeant Anderson emerged and Jim managed to intervene as he made to go over and see a colleague in another police car.

'Excuse me, Sergeant.' The uniformed officer looked round. 'Any news of my wife?' The officer paused.

'You must be Mr Webb,' he said.

'That's right,' answered Jim.

'I'm very sorry, sir, but we have no sightings of her; at least not in connection with the incident here.'

'But is it the same men?' asked Jim, anxiously.

'Er ... we think so, but I think it would be better if you spoke to the inspector. He shouldn't be long,' added the policeman. 'Unfortunately, I've been called away to another incident. Please excuse me.' The sergeant raised his hand in apologetic manner and went on to the door of the waiting car.

Jim did not have long to wait, however, before the inspector emerged and he, too, seemed to be in a bit of a hurry.

'Mr Webb,' said the inspector, not entirely surprised to find him immediately outside the shop doorway, 'there's been another development,' he continued. He gestured Jim to walk with him back towards the car. 'It seems that another body has been found not far from here,' he added.

Jim pulled at the inspector's arm, forcefully enough to stop him in his tracks.

'Who, for God's sake?' asked Jim, with alarm.

'No, not your wife, sir,' answered the inspector hurriedly, suddenly realizing that Jim Webb had feared the worst. 'It's apparently a man who fits one of the descriptions given to us by Mrs Bentley. It also resembles the description of our friend Andy,' he added, looking at Jim. 'I'm told he has been found dead, with gunshot wounds,' he said, matter-of-factly.

'Oh my God, whatever next?' exclaimed Jim, the news of another killing rekindling all his fears for Carol. He silently prayed for her well-being but said nothing as they set off in the car.

*   *   *

175

'I'm home,' announced Bill, somewhat perkily, fresh from his first session back at the office since the assault.

'I'm here,' called Mandy from the kitchen.

'Any news?' enquired Bill.

'Not about Carol, I'm afraid,' replied Mandy, sat at the pine table, propped on her elbows, with coffee in one hand and an eye on the television monitor in the corner. 'I've not been able to speak to Jim today but I gather that he's with the inspector. There may have been a development. I just pray for the best, Bill.'

'That's all we can do, darling,' said Bill.

'How did work go?' she asked, trying not to dwell morbidly on the other matter.

'Oh, fine,' came Bill's reply. 'As I told the doctor, there was no need for me to stay off any longer. I'm better off being occupied.' Bill put down the briefcase and the jacket that had been over his arm. He could tell that Mandy was still pre-occupied, understandably, with Carol's situation.

'Any other news?' he asked, glancing across at the TV.

'Well, our new MP has made a name for himself,' replied Mandy, jogged back into conversation. 'His revelations are filling the early evening news, which won't surprise you. There's some coffee in the pot, darling, or a cold drink in the fridge if you prefer.'

'No, coffee will be fine,' said Bill, enticed by the aroma if not its temperature. 'Yes, we expected that Reaney would be spilling the beans,' he continued. 'What's the official re-action been?' he asked.

'Oh, the usual politician's babble to start with, but the government have promised a more detailed statement later today. Where's it all going to end, Bill?'

'I fear that the situation will get worse before it gets better,' answered Bill, by now sat down opposite his rather sullen wife.

'No encouraging news from work then?'

'No. The forecast is for more of the same. Record high pressure levels are set to continue. Scorching temperatures. No sign of any weather systems penetrating western Europe.

I know other things have been happening whist I've been off, though. High altitude atmospheric testing and lots of special data have been collected. There've been a number of high level meetings between the government and our boys in Bracknell, which I should find out more about tomorrow.' Bill took a sip of his coffee. 'I'll tell you what,' he continued, 'I'm glad that we got that fitted,' he said, looking up at the ceiling-fitted fan that was straining to convert the hot air into something more bearable.

'Do you think that we should invest in a water purifier?' asked Mandy, but barely had she completed the sentence than the telephone warbled.

'I think that we should,' answered Bill as Mandy walked by him on the way to pick up the hall telephone. It was generally Mandy who took the calls, even though Bill was sometimes nearer.

'Two-nine-five-o-two,' acknowledged Mandy in a slightly trepidatious voice that mirrored her current outlook on life.

'Listen very carefully, Mandy, but don't interrupt,' said the familiar voice at the other end of the line. Mandy's heart leapt joyously in relief, but she obeyed the command to be silent, with difficulty. Carol appeared calm and normal yet almost methodical as she continued.

'I am safe and I am well. I cannot say where I am but it is a long way from home. Please don't worry about me. I have been told I will come to no harm if I do as I am told. Please give my love to Jim and to everybody.'

There was a click and the message was over. It was so brief and matter-of-fact that it seemed unreal. Mandy found herself still standing there, in the hall, receiver to her ear, half expecting that the call would resume. The sound of Carol's voice had made a deep impression on her. She could not accept that there was no more to be heard.

It was Bill eventually who took the receiver from her grasp, placed it to his own ear and then replaced it quietly on its holder. Mandy turned to him and after a short pause threw her arms around him, at the same time bursting into tears in a release from her shock-induced trance. Her shock would

177

have been even more pronounced had she known that for the whole of the brief conversation Carol had been reading a statement, verbatim, and under the discomfort of a gun barrel pressed harshly into her rib cage.

Mandy's head pounded as she clung to Bill for dear life.

Jim rearranged the items on his plate, subconsciously nudging a morsel here and a mouthful there, but without showing any great enthusiasm to transfer them in the direction of his mouth. He was deep in thought and though he had not eaten well in recent days, his hunger was suppressed.

It was a pleasant enough environment they were in: the characterful and comparatively cool interior of a rural Norfolk inn, sheltered from the oppressive early evening heat, with an appealing cold platter and the best local ale before them. But Jim's thoughts were elsewhere.

'You should try to eat a little. You look pale and drawn.'

The inspector was right. Despite the seemingly endless days of hot unbroken sunshine, Jim's off-white complexion stood out like a sallow beacon amongst the swarthier looking faces around. But the inspector's advice was easier given than accepted.

'The next proper meal I have will be with Carol,' said Jim, at last. 'Until then, I'll get by.'

'I hope that we won't have long to wait now,' said the inspector, tucking in more enthusiastically and enjoying just a half of the cask conditioned ale. 'Though I must caution that Norfolk is a big county, with lots of byways. We can't put a road block on every route in and out.' Deep down, though, the police officer was now seriously worried about Geoff's instability. Whilst there was some doubt about the shop-keeper's death, there was no doubt that Andy's had been a callous killing from close range. Both men knew that it was now a race against time to get to Carol whilst she was still apparently unharmed.

'We should have tried to make contact on the mobile whilst he had it,' said Jim. It was puzzling in a way why Geoff had given it up and left it with the Range Rover. The telephone call from Carol then came as even more of a surprise, Geoff no doubt insisting, they thought, that the call be made to Mandy and Bill's house to lessen the chances of a trace. They knew that Lichworth was one of those areas still without automatic call identification.

'I don't think that it would have made any difference, but then we can't be sure about anything. He's unpredictable. All we can do is try to close the net, cautiously. If they're still mobile, we'll find them, I'm sure. But he may have gone to ground.'

'What, you mean he's stopped running and is holed up somewhere?' asked Jim.

'I wouldn't be surprised,' replied the inspector, dabbing the edge of his mouth with a serviette.

'Why did he let Carol call?' mused Jim after a short pause in the conversation.

'As I say,' responded Childs, 'he's unpredictable. A murderous villain one minute, a caring, sensitive bloke the next.'

'Very reassuring,' commented Jim.

'Sorry, sir. I didn't mean to ...'

'It's all right,' interrupted Jim. 'That's no more than I've been thinking all along. He's acting like some kind of schizophrenic, reacting to some type of mental stimuli, but in an uneven sort of way. In fact,' added Jim, 'his behaviour is very much in a pattern that fits my theories.'

'So what can we do to influence his behaviour? Anything?' asked the inspector. 'If we could make contact, I mean.'

'First,' replied Jim, 'We need to know what's driving him. We have some of the answers. I think most of the other pieces of the jigsaw will fall into place tonight when Ben arrives.'

'This is your friend from London whom you rang earlier,' said the inspector.

'That's right,' said Jim, now making some attempt at taking in at least a small amount of food. 'I've booked us both rooms for the night here.'

'I hope that he finds the place. It's a bit off the beaten track. In fact, it's the kind of place where, in different circumstances, you could spend a very pleasant and peaceful holiday, away from the rat race,' said Childs, nudging his now empty plate to one side in that subconscious way that indicates that it is finished with. 'Yes,' he added, looking round the near empty room, save for two locals drinking at a corner table, 'very peaceful indeed.'

Smash went the glass in that explosive, splintering, shattering fashion that could never be mistaken for anything else. It was the cue for Carol instinctively to hunch her shoulders and cower behind raised arms in self-protection against flying shards; instinctive because the tumbler landed several yards away, not having been aimed directly at her. It hit the wall with significant force, though. It also brought home to Carol in a graphic and emphatic manner, if she did not already know it, that here was a man with whom she could no longer take any liberties. Throughout her short period of captivity she had tried to talk to her captors, develop a relationship with them, reason with them. Geoff's frenzied killing of Andy the previous night should have brought home to her the futility of it all. Of course, anyone committing murder must have an element of madness about them, but Carol should be under no illusions now that here was someone who was sick, genuinely, mentally and, above all, violently. And yet he still retained, at times, an aura of responsibility, though now, worryingly, less and less so.

'Stop telling me what to do,' spat the increasingly unbalanced Geoff, through clenched teeth. 'This is your last warning,' he added, with admonishing finger. 'I've treated you gently. I've respected your body. I've even allowed you your phone call. I will not listen to any more preaching.'

Carol stood motionless in the corner of the back room of the old stone cottage, her bare arms back down by her side, deciding now that discretion was the better part of valour. She brought her hands together in front of her and was idly, nervously picking at her nails. Geoff was becoming an increasingly menacing, desperate-looking fugitive. She must be very careful now about her actions.

'From now on,' said Geoff in a quiet and deliberate voice,

180

'you will be confined to this room. Any backchat or disobedience and you will be bound and gagged. You will not attempt to leave this room without my permission. Do you understand?' he asked, staring at Carol with distant eyes and clearly on edge. After a pause without reply, he added, 'You may speak. Do you understand?'

'I take it that the bare essentials of civilized behaviour will be maintained,' she ventured, resilient still.

'Such as?'

'The calls of nature, the need to eat,' she replied.

'That depends on whether or not you behave yourself,' said Geoff and he turned and left the room, taking his always menacing weapon with him.

Carol looked around the small back room. It was comfortably but not luxuriously fitted out. It had two deep, green covered armchairs, occupying adjoining corners, and a couple of low level tables, one in between the armchairs and one, slightly longer and larger, more towards the centre of the room. There was a four-shelved bookcase running along much of the length of one wall. Carol had not yet had the time or inclination to discern the type of books that more than half-filled the shelves. However, she did notice two framed photographs sat on top, one near each end. One was a picture of a happy twosome embracing in some warm looking holiday destination, stood on a little rock, with some spectacular scenery behind them. The other had the same couple, a few years older, leaning over a five-bar gate with a field beyond, but this time with two young children, one girl, one boy, making up a contented looking quartet. The man's face looked familiar to Carol.

On the opposite wall was the only window in the room, set fairly high up and about four feet wide. It offered a generous view of the hedged and lawned back garden which rose in height away from the house, restricting the view out and, from Geoff's point of view more usefully, discouraging any prying eyes from looking in. Even if Carol were able to overcome the window locks or smash the pane, there was little chance of her escaping or, indeed, attracting any attention.

There were a few other artefacts adorning the walls, an attractive beamed ceiling and the only other item of note was a pair of folding camp beds, or maybe sunloungers, occupying the remaining corner. It seemed that the room could well be one held in reserve for unexpected guests. As the solid connecting door to the hall was slammed shut, Carol could only contemplate that her occupation here was equally unexpected, but she could only wonder for how long she would be treated in the manner of a guest. She sat in the nearest armchair and lowered her head into her hands and thought of Jim.

The last week had been the most hectic of Trevor Reaney's life: an election victory, a political scoop, a Parliamentary triumph and international fame and recognition via press and television. His face was now known to millions. He was the centre of attention. It was both barely credible and totally unpredictable. Despite the gravity of the national situation, it was difficult for him not to bask in the glare of personal success. His ego was at an historical high, just the moment when life usually bites back with a vengeance.

Reaney, his agent Frank, who had travelled down from the Midlands during the course of the day, and Dennis Plimmer, were joined for some sustenance by Barry Haddock, one of the most senior and influential members of Her Majesty's Opposition. Though not having a shadow ministerial role, it was well-known that he was a close confidant of the leader of the opposition and one of his chief advisers. It had been Plimmer's idea to adjourn to a nearby eaterie, not more than a stone's throw from Westminster, once the packed and lively press conference had finished and before the next television commitments were due. It was Haddock's idea to tag along, no doubt on the instructions of his mentor. Plimmer was none too happy. He had never seen eye to eye with the right-wing Haddock and his faction, but Frank was delighted and Reaney was not yet too embroiled with the infighting of the Parliamentary party to raise any doubts. So Haddock came and he took the opportunity to weigh up the credentials of

182

this new colleague who had caused such a stir on his debut in The House.

Plimmer was the last man you would expect to have airs and graces and, as a matter of principle, he did not frequent those fancy restaurants that charged extraordinary prices for puny amounts of 'funny foreign muck'. Barneys was a no-nonsense good value eaterie with a menu that he could understand and with an unpretentious air. He was known there and was usually able to obtain a table in a quiet corner away from the inquisitive public eye. The place was about half full and the four men had ample elbow room round their designated table with no other diners within normal earshot.

'He's got to resign,' said Plimmer, dismissively. 'He's the minister responsible, and if Marner 'ad any guts, he'd go with 'im. We should go for the jugular until they both go.'

Reaney seemed to have done nothing but talk all day long. His throaty delivery had caused his voice to give out on him on more than one occasion during the recent campaign and he had not needed his wife, Kate, to tell him to give it a rest now and again, though she had, several times, and often with glee. He was quite happy to leave it to his three companions to do all the talking.

They had not been there long, however, before Frank's mobile started bleeping. It was Kate, asking to speak to her husband. She knew that if Frank was not actually with Trevor, he would know his whereabouts and, having failed to per-suade Reaney to have his own mobile, ringing Frank was the next best thing when she need him urgently.

When Reaney heard Frank say, 'Hello Kate ...' he held out his left hand in anticipation of the receiver being passed across, but instead, after a momentary pause, Frank simply telescoped the aerial and passed on the message that he had been given. Trevor was to ring her back immediately on their home number, and in privacy. Reaney borrowed the mobile and went off towards the reception area.

Frank realized that Kate's request was unusual, which sug-gested some kind of problem, or perhaps a piece of bad news. He could still see Reaney from where he sat and thought that he detected from the body language that there was indeed a problem. Leaving Plimmer and Haddock to continue their uneasy dialogue, Frank got up and started to make his way over to Trevor. As he got nearer and the lighting became clearer, he could tell that Reaney was indeed subdued and also ashen-faced. He had got barely half way before Reaney came back to meet him. The MP was so lost in his thoughts, however, that he carelessly nudged into a bald and rather rotund diner who was just about to raise a heavily-creamed desert to his lips, causing a rather messy accident. Reaney's apology was distant and unconvincing. Frank met him halfway back to the table, but Reaney spoke first.

'Can you drive me back north, tonight?' he asked quietly.

'What, after the TV interviews, you mean?' asked Frank.

'No, now.'

'And the meal, and our friends here?' said Frank, half turning in the direction of the table. 'And what do you want me to say to the TV people?' he asked.

'Can you make some excuses for me?' asked Reaney. Then, after a short pause, 'I'll see you outside in a few moments.' He turned for the exit, passing an abusive character with cream on his nose on the way. But the abusive remarks fell on deaf ears.

Ben ached all over, but particularly in the rib cage where they had given him a good kicking. As he gradually raised himself to a sitting position in the dusty ditch in which he now found himself, he contemplated the crazy events of the last few minutes. He was as much bemused as battered. It seemed as though this was another symptom of some kind of violent anarchy. It was not as if his attackers could be classed as muggers. They rifled his pockets only, it seemed, as an afterthought. It was as though they were seeking to satisfy some secret craving for violence, but it was coming to something, thought Ben, when attacks of this nature were so brazen as to take place on main trunk roads and apparently without even the need for the cover of darkness.

The girl who flagged him down had actually seemed quite respectable at first, but her apparent decency was soon exposed as a sham when her two male companions sprang on Ben without warning from the cover of a roadside bush. His memory of the whole incident was incomplete. He recalled heavy blows to the back and ribs, some smacking round the face and a particularly painful blow in the crotch. He remembered the sneering, evil laughter of the outwardly decent girl, but not a lot in the way of chat, save a passing exchange over who Ben was and where he might be headed. He remembered, also, that the tall, slim and lightly clad girl was goading the men, urging each to outdo the other. Certainly he remembered the smash on the head prior to landing in the ditch, possibly from a bottle. He only half remembered his attackers bending over him, chuckling and mumbling as they rifled his pockets and he had only a vague recollection of some warm liquid spouting over him, followed by a zipping sound. The whole incident was thoroughly obnoxious and vile. Ben had seen street violence before, in downtown Miami and in New York, but never in the Cambridgeshire countryside.

Ben staggered back to the top of the not very steep bank. It had been high enough, though, to shield his predicament from any other passing motorists, not that the normally well-used road was particularly busy that night. Perhaps that had encouraged the boldness of his misguided and violent assailants. He felt again at his ribs. His shirt was sticking to his back. There was the stench of urine. His spirits rose, however, when he saw that his car was still there, but in what condition, he thought. A quick visual check and a turn of the key suggested no problems and it seemed as though they had afforded more respect to his vehicle than his person. They had their own car, the one that the girl stood beside as she flagged Ben down. It was a blue performance version as he remembered it, the type more often associated with executives. No doubt it was stolen.

After allowing himself ten minutes just sitting quietly in the front of his car, Ben felt sufficiently composed to resume his journey. He could only speculate on what Jim would think of his state. Maybe it would give him another little piece of evidence for his theories.

Ten miles down the road, he drove past a lay-by. Had he been alert, he would have noticed the tail end of a blue car sticking out beyond the parched hedge. If he had realized and if he had been brave enough to approach it, and to look through the rear window, he would have noticed three young, fit and totally naked bodies entwined in a frantic, writhing and heaving bout of sexual activity. He would have seen a beautifully rounded female posterior bouncing up and down like a frenzied piston and two young males undergoing phase two of the evening's examination in primeval urges.

More likely, Ben would have noted the registration number and location for the benefit of the police. In fact, he noted none of these things because he had only the one thought on his mind, the need to reach his destination. This he was determined to do despite his discomforts, to which had now been added a murderous and brain-splitting headache.

Joanne had never seen Mallow so angry.

'Calm down, Marshy,' she urged. 'You are going to give yourself a heart attack.' For all the feigned friendship that she had been showing, at her brother's instigation, she could not help but be worried by his almost delirious, half-crazed outbursts. After all, she had known the man intimately for some time and, no matter that their relationship had deteriorated of late, beneath the surface there must still have been some fondness or sentiment.

'A scapegoat, that's all I am. A bloody scapegoat,' he ranted. Joanne had lost count of the number of times he had used that description since he had stormed through the flat door, hurling his briefcase bad-temperedly, not twenty minutes earlier. 'Spineless bastard,' he continued, prowling round the room like a wounded lion. Joanne thought it best to keep a low profile until the storm blew itself out. Mean-

186

while, she could only speculate on the target of Mallow's abuse.

'Why me, for God's sake?' he asked, arms outstretched and head upturned, as if seeking an answer from the Almighty. It was as if Joanne was not there as he talked at her, around her, and even above her, but not to her. 'He won't win. I promise you that he won't win,' he said, his anger showing signs of turning into determination. 'He will regret this day for the rest of his life,' he added.

There might possibly be a consolation in all this, thought Joanne. Whatever had happened had put her companion and erstwhile lover into such a foul and rebellious mood that he might regard nothing as being sacred. In other words, the task that Ben had set her of coaxing out certain information might be more easily achievable and, better still, attainable without resort to excessive use of her feminine wiles.

The expletives continued at slightly longer intervals. In between Mallow swigged whiskies. Eventually he plonked himself down in front of the television and switched it on just in time to catch a news broadcast. Joanne came and sat with him, but not too close. It soon became evident from the newsreader what had happended to the miserable minister, or ex-minister as he now was. He flicked off the news broadcast before it had ended and before he was tempted to put his foot through the screen.

'The bastard,' he said through gritted teeth. Here we go again, thought Joanne at first, but then she wondered if this time she detected a more calculating rather than abusive tone. 'I'll find a way of getting even, believe me. The phoenix will rise from the ashes,' he vowed on his way over to the booze cabinet for another top-up.

This time he finally acknowledged Joanne's presence by asking her what she wanted to drink. She joined him in a whisky. It was simpler that way. Joanne sensed that now might be the time to offer her elegant shoulder to cry on. Whilst the drinks were being poured she adjusted her position on the left-hand side of the couch, brushed some imaginary specks of dirt off her lap with her hand, though she looked, as always, immaculate, in a tight-fitting, figure-hugging all-white cotton dress, high at the neck and bare at the arm.

'I think it's time you told me everything that's happened,' she said quietly and calmly as Mallow made his way over with the drinks. He blabbed like a child, leaving nothing unsaid, from the uproar in The Commons, to the emergency meeting with the PM, firstly in his room at The House and then, later, and more revealingly, back in Downing Street. Then came the prime minister's huddled meetings with his advisers amidst the apparent outcry from the media and from the party elite, demanding that heads roll. Mallow had been the sacrificial lamb, though it was inevitable that it would only buy a little time, because, undoubtedly, there were greater shocks to come. They would generate a panic and alarm that would eclipse all that had gone before.

Joanne was staggered by the information that Mallow gave her and which he reeled off in such a morose and matter-of-fact fashion without the slightest regard for national security. He no longer cared about confidentiality, it seemed, not that he would ever have considered Joanne as a source of disloyalty. He was too busy using her as an emotional crutch and as a sex object, to worry about what she might be thinking or doing. Like so many politicians, though supposedly serving the common good, he was a career-minded egotist. At this moment he was too wrapped up in his own blubbering to fret about any wider implications.

When Mallow had finished, Joanne knew immediately how important it was to get the information to her brother. It was just the sort of report that he had hoped for, but never dreamed would be so easy to obtain. Nobody was more pleased about the ease of it all than Joanne, but the plan now was to extricate herself from the flat and make contact with Ben. Having pre-warned Mallow that she would be returning north that night, she did not expect her early departure would now arouse suspicion, but she had taken insufficient account of his current mood. His demeanour may also have been influenced by the number of whiskies he had consumed.

'Joanne,' he called from another room. His story-telling complete, Mallow had gone to find a reserve bottle of whisky which had not been in the booze cabinet as he had expected. 'Forgetful as ever,' thought Joanne, already on her way as he called her a second time. She was still half-thinking of how and when to break the news of her departure.

'Where are you, darling?' she called out when she could not see him in the kitchen area.

'In here,' came the reply from the direction of the main bedroom. Still unable to see him, Joanne had to go right into the bedroom, but had not got very far when the door was slammed shut behind her. She turned to see a gleeful Mallow, who was almost salivating at the success of his little ruse and at the prospect of having his wicked way. Joanne used to like his little games, his unpredictability, but not any more. Her feelings had changed.

'Sweetheart,' he said, approaching an apprehensive Joanne, 'what would I do without you?' She thought that she detected some slurring of the words. He stood facing her, placing a hand on each of her shoulders and he planted a soft kiss on her forehead. From there it became an embrace. Joanne stood motionless, not completely without a tinge of pity or sympathy for the fallen politician, but hoping, nevertheless, that she did not have to maintain this position for too long.

Mallow was contented for the first time in ages, standing there, hugging his mistress, running his hands up and down her slim curvaceous figure. He could feel her beautifully shaped hips and allowed his hand to roam further, across her firm straight back, then down to her perfectly rounded bottom. And everywhere the flesh under the sexy white dress was yielding, yet firm. There was still no response from Joanne, at least none visible. In no time Mallow's fumbling fingers found the end of the zip and he proceeded to uncover her bare back.

'No darling, not now,' she responded at last. but her words of discouragement either did not register with him or seemed to be merely a part of the game. He carried on with

189

his attempt to disrobe her, bringing his hands forward now, pulling her dress forward over her shoulders and then lowering it. The verbal approach having failed, this time Joanne pulled back slightly and brought her hands up in between their two bodies. Then she placed her hands on Mallow's shoulders in a sort of restraining action.

'This is not the time, darling,' she said. 'You've had a very stressful day.'

'I can't think of a time when I've ever needed it more,' he replied trying to look deep into her blue eyes. She pulled back again, this time right out of his grasp.

'But you know that I have to go back north tonight,' she said, still outwardly calm and trying to reassemble her dress. 'I told you that yesterday.'

'But that was before ...,' he paused, 'before ... today,' his mouth dropping open. 'You can't possibly desert me now. I need you.'

'What about your wife?' asked Joanne. 'Surely, after all that's happened, she'll be expecting you home.'

'We've already had a long chat over the phone. She thinks that I'm staying over to tie up loose ends, that sort of thing. Anyway, you need not concern yourself with her involvement. I can handle that. It's you I need,' said Mallow.

'I think that what you need is a good night's sleep,' said Joanne. 'Now be a good boy and zip me up again,' she added, back towards him. Mallow grinned wickedly to himself and as she stood there waiting, the only zip that moved was his.

'What are you doing?' asked Joanne, fearing the worst. As he lifted his feet out of the trousers that were now round his ankles, he moved closer to her. Then he pulled the dress apart to expose Joanne's naked back once more, running his fingers up her spine.

'Do you remember our first night of passion?' he asked.

'How could I forget?' replied Joanne, hesitantly.

'Talk about unbridled love,' continued Mallow. 'It was mind-blowing.' He was deep in thought, released at last from the day's torment. Again he eased her dress forward over the shoulders. 'Don't deny me tonight, darling. Not tonight.' He

190

moved up ever closer and wrapped his arms around her now near naked torso, pressing his lower half against her buttocks. Her resistance was low. She did not know if it was through pity, or whether it was for old times' sake, or just the feeling of being wanted. After all, she had her own needs and urges, even if she had seen Mallow less and less as the person to satisfy them. It seemed as though she had resigned herself to accepting his advances, or at least not pushing her rejection too far.

'All right, then Marshy,' she thought to herself, 'but this will be the last time,' and she let her dress continue to fall to the ground. Mallow inwardly rejoiced at the signal.

Ben finally arrived at his destination, his nightmare journey reaching its conclusion in a sparsely populated car park at the rear of an attractive ivy-clad country inn, whose location would have tested the prowess of a circumnavigator of the globe. He crossed his arms over the steering wheel and laid his head to rest on them, allowing himself a few moments to recover and take stock. Now that he had let his concentration drop, he could feel some of his aches and pains returning. In particular, his head was buzzing. 'God knows what it was they hit me with,' he thought. As he looked up and through the windscreen he could see in the distance, high up in the now dark sky, the dancing curtain of multi-coloured lights beginning to form again in their increasingly familiar pattern.

When Ben turned his head, he was immediately startled. There at the driver's door was a tall figure that had suddenly emerged from the darkness and which was now trying the car door handle.

'Ben, where the hell have you been?' asked Jim, opening the door. 'I was beginning to worry about you.'

'Christ, you gave me a fright,' said Ben and as he eased himself out of the car Jim could tell from the look of him under the car's interior lamps, and from the awkward way that he was moving that something was wrong.

'You all right, Ben?' asked Jim, with a concerned voice.

'Not a hundred per cent,' replied Ben, making his way

slowly towards the boot, where his overnight bag was. 'I'll tell you all about it over a drink. I could do with one.' He got his bag, looked up and made his way over towards the back entrance to the inn, in the direction that Jim had indicated.

As Jim followed close behind he cast a glance at the night sky. He paused momentarily to take in the same view that Ben had eyed a few seconds earlier. It was a sight that he expected would become more and more commonplace, and perhaps even more spectacular. But the beauty of it, he thought, belied the life-endangering threat to society that was building.

Carol looked out of the window at the developing night sky. She had watched intrigued as the coloured streaks and shapes that she had first seen from the boat, and then on following nights, had formed again. Tonight they seemed even more stark and dramatic and brilliantly coloured.

She was suffering from a headache that she attributed to the hot, sticky, unventilated atmosphere of the room, together with a general depression about her situation. Geoff had left her alone for most of the time they had been in the cottage, alone to dwell on her predicament. She had glanced at the books on the shelves but had neither the patience nor inclination to take much of an interest in them. She had assessed the security of window and door and had decided against any misplaced bravado at this time. Carol had heard the noise of voices which she thought was the television, in all probability, and she thought that she had detected the clink of bottles or glasses. Only twice had he unlocked the door to make brief appearances. On one of those occasions he had left a plate containing some cheese-flavoured crackers and a glass of water. On the other, he left a bucket by the door, together with the thin remnants of a toilet roll.

Carol thought that she heard a shuffling noise outside the window. She climbed onto the coffee table between the arm-chairs, as she had done several times already, enabling her to see out into the garden and, more importantly, in the hope

192

that she might be seen. But it was too dark for her to see anything.

A few minutes later the door to her room was opened again. It was such a solid door, she thought, and behind it lay the unexpected and the potentially dangerous. When the old lock clunked round and the knob turned, she never knew quite what to expect, what the purpose of its opening was, nor quite how Geoff would be. She had become more frightened of him since Andy's killing. The solitary confinement was also beginning to play on her mind now. She awaited his entrance with trepidation.

Geoff's appearance shocked Carol. Although possibly the worse for drink, he looked ill, his face pale and drawn, his eyes large and staring and red-lined. His trusty weapon was slung over his shoulder, more like a companion than a tool for deterrence. It was a few seconds before he spoke, with a slight slurring of the voice, Carol thought.

'I warned you not to misbehave,' he said menacingly and no longer in the civilized, almost friendly tones that he used when they first met.

'In what way?' asked Carol, puzzled and somewhat apprehensive. 'What do you mean?'

'Trying to make yourself seen by the outside world, that's what I mean,' replied Geoff and as he talked he pulled the smaller of the two tables out into the centre of the room, underneath the light fitting. Taking a grubby white handkerchief from his pocket, he stood up on the table and quickly removed the light bulb. Despite the layer of protection, the bulb was hot and he had to juggle it at first before he could adjust his grip and the positioning of the handkerchief.

'You can't leave me in the dark,' said Carol.

'Can't I?' replied Geoff, operating now by the reflected light from the hall.

'But you promised the bare essentials of civilized behaviour,' she responded, instinctively fighting her corner but perhaps now not quite so boldly as before.

'Such as?' asked Geoff, tersely.

'Something decent to eat and drink, a bathroom to use, a

light to see by, and what I wouldn't give for some fresh, clean, nice clothes to wear.'

'The food you've had. It might get better. I don't know yet. The toilet you've got,' said Geoff, glancing at the bucket and roll. 'You might get more if you behave. Likewise, you might also get the light bulb back. As for the clothes, well, I'll tell you what I'll do,' he said feigning concern. 'I'll wash yours for you. How does that sound?'

'And what have you got in their place?' asked Carol.

'Who said anything about that?' replied Geoff. 'If I give an inch you take a mile. Now give them to me before I change my mind.'

'No, thank you,' said Carol. 'It doesn't matter.'

'Stop messing me about,' roared Geoff, wild-eyed once more with anger. 'I'm fed up with your stupid moaning. My head is bursting. Don't you understand?'

Carol backed off, anxious about his attitude and concerned about his general state of mind. He crossed one hand over to rest on the barrel of his gun, as if threatening to use it.

'Now take them off now and give them to me,' he ordered.

Carol was afraid of what was happening and fearful that Geoff was losing his self-control. She stepped further back into the shadows, hoping that the darkness would swallow her up and make her invisible. Better still, perhaps she would wake from the darkness and find that everything had been a nasty dream, a nightmare.

'Give me your clothes and I'll bring you a sheet back,' added Geoff and Carol suspected that this was the last offer. He then partly closed the door to, shutting out most of the light to preserve her understandable modesty. Resigned to the indignity of it all, she started to disrobe. She began with the navy pullover she had got from the boat, slowly pulling it over her head, but as she did so she started to sob, quietly but just audibly, and very soon uncontrollably. When she was down to her white underwear, she stopped undressing.

'All of it,' barked Geoff, gathering her clothes into a bundle, and unmoved by her distress.

'Please . . . ,' sobbed Carol.

'Come on,' he snapped back. Carol stripped herself completely naked and then cowered by the side of one of the armchairs. Crouching, she wrapped both arms around herself trying to envelop her body and conceal her bareness. She was sobbing still and the flash of light from the hall as Geoff left illuminated her sad pathetic figure.

After a while, Carol climbed into the armchair and curled up, having first carefully turned the chair around to face away from the door. Eventually, she cried herself to sleep in the dark. She never got the promised sheet. Geoff had lain down on the bed for a temporary rest but was soon overwhelmed by chronic weariness himself. Not even his throbbing head could prevent him from giving in to the most basic of human needs.

It was late but Jim had persuaded the proprietor to stay open a little longer despite the absence of other customers. Ben looked a lot better after cleaning himself up, showering and changing, but he bore the bruises of his violent encounter, not to mention the unseen aches and pains. And his head was still hurting, though the throbbing at the back of his head associated with the sizeable lump there was subsiding. Ben had recounted his experience to Jim, though not before he had first enquired of the latest situation with Carol. He still had to decide what steps to take about reporting the incident, but he was anxious that it should not detract from his main purpose in being there.

Ben thanked Jim for the Pils, and the two men sat around a corner table, at right angles to each other. Ben, in particular, was grateful for the firm support offered by the red velvet lined, hard-backed seats.

'I'll probably report it to the police first thing in the morning,' said Ben. 'I can't see that there is much to be gained by calling them out tonight,' he said. 'They must be miles away by now.'

'Well, it's up to you, Ben, obviously, but so long as you don't let the bastards get away with it.'

'Let's talk about more interesting matters,' suggested Ben.

'OK,' agreed Jim, anxious to get news of Ben's latest contacts with Stateside friends.

'Firstly, I have it on good authority from my contacts in NASA that the US government satellite launching programme has been altered. Project SOLEX has been brought forward.'

'This is the project that you were trying to tell me about on the phone, isn't it?' asked Jim.

'That's right,' replied Ben. 'It's been on the cards for some time, in fact since the exceptional auroral activity of 89. Basically, the plan was to launch two satellites to monitor the solar wind, and to X-ray the sun itself. But the plan had been to launch at the very end of the decade.'

'So what do you think is the significance of it being brought forward?' asked Jim.

'Well, these things do happen from time to time due to changes in priorities, or maybe even if earlier projects are delayed and a window becomes available,' replied Ben. 'In this case, however, there is some puzzlement. There is a feeling that the whole project is being rushed through when not quite ready, even to the exclusion of other experiments that are ready.'

'Suggesting some urgency over the need to investigate current solar activity?' enquired Jim.

'Correct.'

'How urgently?'

'Next week, would you believe?' said Ben.

'That's urgent,' agreed Jim, taking a sip of his drink. 'But how can they arrange it so quickly?'

'To the ground crew it's just another launch,' explained Ben. 'They don't need to know the payload. In any case, this is a military launch slot that's being used, so most people know not to ask too many questions.'

'But how can the measuring equipment and the other experiments be ready?'

'Rushed in and untested, I'm told,' answered Ben. 'Maybe they'll be more focused and not quite so sophisticated as originally intended,' he added, tongue in cheek. 'Obviously somebody wants some answers, quick.'

196

'You know a lot of people in The States, Ben. Important people, I mean. What's the feeling there about what's going on? Is there a sense of something unusual, something different, something dangerous happening?' Ben thought for a few seconds before responding, whilst draining most, but not all, of his drink.

'Bill Twinings knows everything there is to know about US military research. He ought to. For years he directed it. When I started poking around and asking him leading questions, even though half of it was no more than speculation on my part, his reaction was "Shit. How did you get on to that?" Sure the Americans have had doubts for years about environmental damage, the delicate balances of nature, if you like. For a time they resisted the European view that the world climate was slowly but inexorably changing. I think that it was the Mississippi flood disaster that finally convinced them that something was going on "up there".' Ben raised his hand and his head in the direction of the ceiling.

'So what do they think is happening?' asked Jim.

'It has to be magnetic,' replied Ben. 'Probably linked to solar activity.'

'So they hope that by gathering more information they will understand the sun that much better and will be able to predict climate change,' said Jim. 'Is that the plan for SOLEX?'

'I think that it's a lot more than just prediction, Jim. I'm sure that they are looking for information that will help them either to control the situation, or at least to resist it, or both.'

'Trying to control the sun, even if it were possible, sounds like the ultimate in playing with fire,' said Jim. 'Even seeking to resist its power sounds like a forlorn hope, not to mention dangerous. Typical bloody Americans,' mocked Jim. 'They may have the best of intentions but, realistically, all they can do is predict, not change. Surely?'

'That won't be enough, Jim,' said Ben.

'What do you mean?'

'Well, it brings me to the second piece of information I have for you,' replied the Canadian, but before he could continue the landlord put in an appearance. He asked if they would be wanting any more drinks and Ben signalled two more of the same, before turning back towards Jim to resume the conversation.

'Have you ever heard of Sanguine?' he asked.

'It's an orange, isn't it?' suggested Jim.

'That's as may be. But what I'm talking about is the low profile experiment with ELF by the US military in the early seventies.'

'I think that I remember some oblique reference to that in some research I did recently,' commented Jim. 'Extremely low frequency magnetic fields, isn't it?'

'That's right. Very low frequency. Lower even than the earth's own magnetic field.'

'But wasn't that research discontinued?' queried Jim.

'That's what most people thought,' went on Ben, 'or rather were encouraged to think. In reality, it has continued at a low budget level and with a small band of scientists. Here...' Ben passed over the table a couple of pages of fax. Jim instinctively pulled it slightly to one side as the landlord returned with the drinks. When he had left Ben resumed.

'What you are reading is part of the conclusion to a top secret report by the USAAF in 1982.'

'"Potential for dealing with terrorist groups, crowd control and security at military establishments, etc."' read Jim. 'And it goes on to say that "ELF could be harnessed into a format that could provide mild to severe physiological disruption or perpetual distortion or disorientation ... they are silent, and counter measures to them may be difficult to develop." So, what they are talking about is some kind of magnetic gun that could be shot at people and would upset the balance of their mind. Is that right?' asked Jim.

'Something like that,' confirmed Ben. 'Now, I have it on good authority that development continued for a while longer but it was then judged politically unwise to take it to its ultimate conclusion. Although, I'm told, the team still meets from time to time, but only a handful of people are aware of the existence of the group, or, should I say, its real purpose.'

'So, you've got low magnetic field activity on the one hand,' said Jim, making his point with arm outstretched in front of him, 'but huge solar activity on the other, on a much grander scale. Is there a tie-up?' he asked.

'Well, you're right to wonder,' said Ben. 'Like so many other scientific break-throughs, though, it's the spin-off knowledge that's gained that is the key. You see, Jim, Sanguine started at a time when the view was that it was magnetic field strengths that were important. No one believed that anything useful would be achieved by researching into fields so weak as to be in the zero to one thousand cycles per second zone of the electro-magnetic spectrum. What the project highlighted was that it was the balance, the frequency and variation in fields that was important and to which human beings were susceptible.' Both men had a sip of their drinks whilst reflecting on the theory. Then Ben continued, 'In other words, we all live in a certain magnetic environment, one which is in a state of delicate balance, just like the other balances of nature, such as the atmosphere we live in and the gravitational forces we have adapted to. Alter the balance and you have a recipe for trouble, even at the very low frequencies we are talking about, as the Sanguine team have discovered. The other thing to bear in mind, as it were, is that this kind of thing will affect different people in different ways, at different times and to different degrees.'

'You realize,' said Jim, 'that this kind of theory would fit in very nicely with my own theories.'

'Precisely,' said Ben.

'Taken to the ultimate, the reversing of magnetic polarity in the earth's history could account for the elimination of species, the ones unable to cope with the magnetic fluctuation.'

'That's right,' agreed Ben. 'Whilst those species not quite so susceptible survived, maybe with some adaptation.'

'And bringing it right up to date, it could help explain changes in behavioural patterns.'

'Right, it fits everything you said last weekend.'

'So what is this Sanguine team actually saying right now?' asked Jim.

Ben handed over another piece of paper, this time a single sheet. In effect, it summarized information said to come from another top secret report. Jim scanned the paper.

'When was this report produced?' he asked Ben, solemnly.

'Within the last week or two. By the way,' Ben added, 'our own prime minister knows about it.' This caused Jim to look up, partly with a look of admiration about Ben's fact-finding ability.

'There he is trying to reassure the country about the water crisis,' said Jim under raised eyebrows, 'when all the time he knows that it is merely a symptom of something potentially earth-shattering, almost literally. I don't know whether to applaud him or feel sorry for him. Is there any chance that the report could be wrong?' asked Jim, handing the sheet of paper back.

'SOLEX will help to confirm it one way or another,' answered Ben.

Jim's mind was still working overtime, tossing around the information that Ben had given him.

'How do they carry out the measurements on people referred to in the report?' was his next question.

'By using a SQUID.'

'Ask a silly question,' said Jim, but Ben produced another, small piece of paper from which he read.

'A superconducting quantum interference detector. This detects the magnetic field produced by the brain from up to several feet away and expresses it in a MEG, a magneto-encephalogram.'

'So what we have then, Ben, is mounting evidence of magnetic distortions and a linkage between that and the effects on people's health and behaviour and behind it all the threat of a global disaster.'

'That just about sums it up,' agreed Ben. 'And then there is the political angle.'

'What do you mean?' asked Jim.

'What John Marner, not to mention Mr President and the

other world leaders in the know, are going to do about it all. I'm still working on that. I may have something for you soon.'

'You never cease to amaze me, Ben. But I still think that there is a missing link.'

'What's that?' asked Ben.

'Well, the theory holds up fine. The pieces are fitting into place and the scientific evidence is mounting. But if we are really to convince people of a major crisis ahead, then I think that we need some more definite evidence on the medical link.'

'I'm told that there is increasing evidence in The States about cancers and other illnesses near power lines, thought to be something to do with localized electromagnetic fields. Could that be connected?' asked Ben.

'Interesting that you should say that,' said Jim and he picked up a thin book from the small collection of papers he had with him. He opened it immediately at a place marked with a protruding marker. 'This is from a book a friend of mine advised me to read,' he continued and then proceeded to read verbatim, ' "I experienced a strange lassitude, headaches ... odd feelings ... some kind of mental barrier between my thoughts and myself ... a mental block ... sometimes it was like being caught in a net." That was from a villager in an area suffering severe distortions to the magnetic field, not just due to power lines, but compounded also by local geomagnetic field variations.' Jim continued with his reading. ' "I often felt better after thunderstorms," he added, the suggestion being that the release of negative ions stabilized the situation. Other villagers take up the story, listing various medical symptoms, "headaches across the eyes, exhaustion, sleeplessness, loss of appetite, heart palpitations, and trembling" and, note this,' added Jim, ' "especially in hot weather." Then, there is this account,' he continued, turning the page, ' "There was a strange occasion when the light seemed to go black, though I could still see, but the clarity was affected, as was what was up and what was down." '

There was a sudden silence. The end of Jim's sentence coincided with the cutting out of a large ceiling fan, of the type that was now almost obligatory indoors in the hot weather. Those establishments caught out by the failure of manufacturers to keep pace with the demand for them had seen trade suffer as a result.

'It's the link to the brain that's important,' continued Jim. 'If we can prove that, we can explain all sorts of things: illnesses, suicide rates, increasing schizophrenia and mental illness, changing behavioural patterns, including increased sex crimes and more aggression and lawlessness in society. I think I know what the key is.'

'Really?' said Ben, leaning forward now, intently.

'A chat to my Scottish friend and medical adviser in the morning is called for.'

'That reminds me,' said Ben. 'What morning paper do you take?'

'*The Telegraph*,' answered Jim.

'Good. Look out for my article if you get time.'

'Oh what?' asked Jim.

'The drought. Its causes. The future. Lots of things that you touched on last Sunday.'

'Soon we will need to decide how we are going to take this matter forward,' said Jim. 'Are you with me on this, Ben? Can you stay here for a day or two?'

'But of course. You've got me riveted on this story as with no other that I've been involved with. And by the way, if I get any more news during the night, do you want me to disturb you with it, or wait until morning?'

'You wouldn't disturb me, Ben. I don't sleep at nights.'

Ben was embarrassed by his stupid insensitivity. Jim was so immersed in this whole business that it was difficult to appreciate that he actually had a much more worrying and pressing personal matter on his mind, one that he was only able to suppress temporarily.

* * *

As the summer had gone on, the lifestyles of millions of people had changed. Staying cool was the aim. Clothing was at a minimum. A siesta mentality had developed. Air-condition-

202

ing was no longer a luxury. Sunbathing had given way to shade hogging. Water conservation, though somewhat late in the day, was now demanded rather than advised.

For many it was the shock of illness, death or depression in an increasingly unhealthy, aggressive, dangerous and unstable society. For others, so far at least, it was just the inconvenience and discomforts, like certain food shortages and not being able to sleep at night. The latter could often be helped by a change of habit, like retiring to bed at a later hour, or sleeping on top of the bedclothes, but that was not always the solution.

For Trevor Reaney, his sleeplessness was more psychological than physical. He should have been worn out after all the exertions and excitement of recent days. The news that had brought him scampering back home was preoccupying his mind, understandably.

Like so many that night, he was staring out into the dark sky, looking at the spectacular, colourful, dancing mosaic. He was slightly startled by the unexpected telephone ring. Clad only in briefs and smoking a cigarette, he made his way to the hall telephone fairly quickly, hoping that he could curtail the ringing before the simultaneous noise of the bedside extension disturbed Kate. It was Frank on the line.

'Any news?' he asked.

'No, I'm afraid not,' replied Reaney.

'Can we talk about other matters?' asked his agent.

'Go ahead,' said Reaney, stubbing out his cigarette in the onyx ashtray on the hall table and exhaling the last vestiges of smoke.

'The PM wants to see you,' said Frank, always straight to the point. There was no immediate reaction from Reaney. 'He made contact via Haddock, not long ago, though not directly, of course.'

'I thought that Haddock was on our side,' reflected the subdued Reaney.

'You will be surprised what goes on behind the scenes, so Plimmer tells me. Anyway, it's not an immediate summons, as it were, but he wonders if you can keep yourself available. He will make contact again tomorrow.'

'I'll be here,' said Reaney, succinctly.

'Trevor, can you let me know if you plan to leave, or at least let Kate know where I can contact you? It sounds like a matter of national importance, as they say. Neil's on stand-by as well.' Reaney had little time for his leader, despite his party allegiance.

'No problem,' he answered and he replaced the receiver.

Reaney went outside for a breath of fresh air, the night cooling at last after the lung-scorching day. He looked up at the strangely patterned sky and reflected on the telephone call and then again on his more personal problem.

'What the hell is going on up there?' he thought to himself. It was giving him a headache.

Ben wanted to be up at a reasonable hour to see how his article looked in *The Telegraph*. It was light when the bedside telephone rang, but barely. It was not the early morning call that he was expecting, however, but the familiar voice of his younger sister, Joanne.

'You tracked me down then,' he said, raising himself onto one elbow.

'Yes, I got the details you left on your answerphone,' replied his rather subdued sister, barely audible through the crackle on the line.

'I didn't expect you to ring so early, though,' ventured Ben, after a quick glance at his watch on the bedside table had surprised him. 'You must have some urgent news for me.'

'Too right,' said Joanne. 'Can I talk?'

'I suppose so,' said Ben. 'Is it sensitive information?'

'Very.'

'Where are you speaking from?' asked Ben.

'Mallow's flat. So, I'll keep it as brief and as quiet as I can.' Joanne looked round, especially in the direction of the bedroom. Nothing stirred, as she sat perched on the edge of the cushioned telephone seat, next to the hall table, clad only in a loosely tied black kimono that just about held her naked top half in, but left her bottom half uncovered almost in its entirety.

'There was an emergency Cabinet meeting yesterday,' she began. 'In fact, there were a series of meetings most of the afternoon and evening . . .'

Ben listened to his sister intently. He had to ask her occasionally to speak up as the line deteriorated badly. An observer would have detected an occasional raised eyebrow, plus one whispered expletive, which was most out of character for Ben.

'Listen,' he said when she had finished her brief report, 'I know I'm asking a lot, but do you think that there is any chance of our friend still having access to classified information and, if so, could you stay on the case?'

'Believe me,' replied Joanne, 'there is no chance. He's finished. Dead as a dodo as far as the corridors of power are concerned.'

Mallow cringed and silently fumed as he stood by the bedroom door listening to what was being said about him. The last few minutes had seen his blood pressure rising steadily. Was there no loyalty? No respect? No justice? He was oblivious of Joanne's final words before she quietly replaced the receiver. By the time she had stood up and straightened her silk kimono, tucking the left-hand side underneath the overlapping right he was right behind her, his bare feet having contributed to the silence of his approach. She turned as she was completing her tie-up, only to be smashed by a sledgehammer blow to the face. Mallow's weighty right hand had powerfully slapped her down before she even had a chance to see him.

'You two-faced slut,' he sneered, as he looked down on her, the scant clothing having fallen open to reveal her naked beauty. For once Mallow had no interest in the exposure of her most intimate parts. Joanne, meanwhile, was too shocked and stunned fully to appreciate her predicament. The side of her head was still numb and the blood flowing from her mouth felt warm. As Mallow turned away and walked back towards the bedroom, she lay there motionless, hurt and blank.

Some minutes later, the ex-minister emerged again, fully

dressed now and with a packed canvas bag. Joanne had by now dragged herself to a nearby armchair where she was slightly more decently covered and holding a wad of tissues, now soaked blood-red, to her rapidly swelling face.

'Drop your key through the letter box when you leave,' said Mallow and, with that, he opened the door and left.

'Automatism,' said Inspector Childs, knocking back his cup of tea in relaxed conversation with his East Anglian opposite number, before getting down to the real business of the day. 'That's what they call it. It's what all the good defence lawyers are claiming nowadays. "My client is not guilty, m'lud, because he was not in control of his faculties at the time he half-slaughtered the defenceless victim."'

'There must be more to it than that,' suggested his colleague, whose office they were using.

'Well, of course, technically it has to be shown that a person was acting unconsciously, a bit like the driver who blacks out at the wheel and is not responsible for mowing down a bus queue. Mind you, if he has had previous blackouts, or an illness that is known to give rise to blackouts, then that's a different matter. It becomes an avoidable event. The defence fails.'

'Sounds a bit like the old "not guilty due to insanity" plea,' said the younger detective.

'Exactly,' said Childs. 'It's a spin-off from that, but you need to show that the mind has been completely taken over, or there has been a total loss of control that could not have been countered.'

'Reminds me of a couple of cases we have had recently though, I must admit. One, a domestic, middle-aged man, respectable pillar of the community, woke up screaming in the middle of the night, strangled his wife, claims to have no recollection of doing it, no motive for it and totally wrecked and devastated by it afterwards. All he can remember is a kind of blackness filling his head after he woke up, and a dull headache.

'And the other one?' asked the inspector.

206

'Younger bloke. A pub fight but he swears blind it was nothing to do with booze.'

'Don't they all?'

'Well, yes, to a point. But how he described the events leading up to it and his feelings afterwards sounded very similar to our other chappie, except that this happened a few days earlier and we rubbished it at first.'

'So, is there a connection?'

'Who knows? We can't find one. We've got a changing society round these parts, though. No doubt about it. There's lots of strange things going on.'

'There's mindless violence all over the country, Nick,' said Childs. 'Nutters wherever you turn.'

'We've still got to catch the buggers, though.'

'Too right, mate,' agreed the inspector. 'Which brings us nicely to the business in hand. I think we need to take stock, review our operation, before the chief super arrives for his breakfast conference. I badly need a result on this one, Nick. It's taking up a lot of time and resources.'

'Tell me about it,' said Nick, rising from his seat. He stretched his arms and back before walking over to stand in front of the big map on the wall. 'It seems to me,' he said, 'that we have to take a view on whether our man is still within this area.' He moved his right hand in a general sweep of that part of the map on which he had been concentrating his attention. This included the pinpoints that marked the location of the two murders and the ditched Range Rover and was broadly within the circle of road blocks that had been in operation the previous day. 'Now,' he continued, 'we'll have just about every available copper in North Norfolk on this again, so we're going to have to think about how to use them to best effect.'

'Three choices, as I see it, Nick,' said the inspector. 'We can widen the area of search, we can constrict it further, or we can leave it as it is. But I agree that we'll need every available copper.'

'What about the army again?' asked Nick.

'They'll want to be involved, I'm sure, because he's one of

207

their own. But if you ask me, it'll be a local bobby who stumbles on them, you mark my words.'

'So you do think they're still in Norfolk.'

'No doubt in my mind,' confirmed the inspector. 'They've gone to ground. Could be another hostage-taking situation. Could be an empty property, a holiday home perhaps.'

'Or a second home,' suggested Nick. 'There's plenty of them in these parts.'

'In which case we would need to widen the search,' said Childs, 'to take in the whole of The Broads and the coast.' Uncrossing his legs, he leaned forward, elbows on knees, head resting on hands in thoughtful pose. 'We need more choppers,' he concluded. 'And more manpower,' he added. 'People can't hide in small towns and villages without the locals knowing.'

'You'd be surprised how many isolated and remote properties there are,' cautioned Nick, 'especially around here,' pointing at the map again. 'Even in the villages there isn't the same community spirit that there used to be, what with all the outsiders and the weekenders.'

'Yeah, we probably ought to mobilize some army help,' conceded the inspector. 'If only we could get a lead on their car. They must have one. It can't have been reported missing yet.'

'Or noticed missing,' said Nick. 'Maybe the owner isn't in a position to report it.'

'Christ, not another corpse, please,' pleaded Childs in mock prayer.

Nick walked over to the window, already full open in readiness for another day of overbearing heat.

'Here comes the chief super and his assistant.'

Jim heard the knock on his door instantly. He had not slept properly since Carol's abduction. Just occasionally, through physical and mental weariness, he dropped into a light drowsy state, but he was ever alert to interruption, always hopeful that the next contact would be from, or about, Carol.

Ben excused his presence at such an early hour but this presented no problem to Jim, who invited him in.

'My contact came through,' said Ben, quietly excited.

'The one in government circles?' asked Jim. Ben nodded.

'We have a new angle on the situation,' continued Ben. 'One that's rather unexpected and very worrying.'

'Oh, really,' responded Jim, surprisingly alert for the hour and slightly taken aback that he might have omitted something of significance from his own previous prognostications.

'I have it from an impeccable source,' said Ben,' that the prime minister is in possession of a file with the highest possible security rating, containing information relayed to him by the president and based on top US scientific advice. The file confirms that there is severe disturbance and imbalance to the earth's magnetic field, which is causing all sorts of problems, and not just weather-related ones.'

'So what's new?' asked Jim, politely as always but tinged with impatience.

'Until now the blame for this has been put down to increased solar wind activity, arising from the gigantic solar flares you know all about, but now it seems that is only part of the answer.'

'So what else would be responsible?' queried Jim, as much to himself as to Ben.

'The other part has to be terrestrial,' continued Ben.

'Of course,' mused Jim.

'It's the balance. The balance of forces,' prompted Ben.

'Of course.'

'We live in a magnetic field that is, in effect, a balance between the incoming particles of the solar wind, aided by the interplanetary magnetic field,' said Ben, 'but all of this is resisted by the earth's own field, the geomagnetic field, which stretches out some sixty-five thousand kilometers into space.'

'The earth's field pushes out the incoming forces into the magnetosphere, forming the Van Allen belts,' said Jim, recalling his own knowledge on the subject.

'Right,' agreed Ben. 'And what we should have realized is

that this balance operates within certain tolerances. Exceed them, and initially you get magnetic storms.'

'And the auroral displays,' added Jim, in a slightly detached fashion, his mind working through Ben's synopsis towards its own conclusions.

'And thereafter we don't know, but perhaps we are now finding out,' suggested Ben.

'So it's not just the strength of the attack, but also the weakness of the defence. So that's what the president's experts are saying.'

'Precisely,' confirmed Ben. 'They know that the geomagnetic field fluctuates anyway but usually only gradually, say over hundreds of years. They know that it has been in decline and that will lead eventually to a polarity reverse. The field is also drifting westwards over the earth's surface.'

'As are the weather systems,' interjected Jim. He walked over to the window, hand rubbing jaw. He barely noticed the view, a landscape looking increasingly parched as each new day dawned. 'So why should it suddenly weaken further?' he asked. 'And how do they know anyway?' he added, turning to face Ben again.

'The second question is more easily answered than the first,' replied the Canadian. 'Isomagnetic charts, magnetographs, and satellite readings.'

'Measured in units with strange sounding names, if I remember,' said Jim, 'like nanotesla, or gauss.'

'Oh, that explains that then,' said Ben.

'Explains what?' asked Jim, now close to Ben again.

'This file of the PM's. Apparently it's titled THE GAUSS FACTOR!'

John Marner had defied all the odds to have remained in Number Ten as long as he had. But he had done so at a price. His life had lost nearly all semblance of normality. He had aged considerably in the job, just like his predecessors. The longer he went on as prime minister and party leader, the more hangers-on there were and the fewer real friends he had. It was physically a hard grind, too: all the paper work, the lack of sleep, the constant meetings. This morning his breakfast was earlier than ever and the briefing he received on the morning press from one of his inner circle of most trusted advisers was enough to give him indigestion over his toast and marmalade.

His advisers were civil servants ostensibly with only their master's wishes and well-being in mind, but it was a considerable mistake to underestimate their power, particularly that of the Cabinet secretary.

John Marner had another visitor, too, that morning, Alan Hunter, the dynamic young environment minister whom some sceptics saw as his main political rival.

'Have you read Ben Johnson's article in *The Telegraph*?' asked Hunter, as the four of them, the two politicians, the Cabinet secretary and the other civil servant sat around the table, helping themselves to toast and tea from the silver tray.

'Just about to,' answered the PM. 'Justin here has given me the gist of it.'

'Very perceptive it is,' added Hunter.

'He usually is when he writes under his real name instead of one of his many aliases,' remarked the prime minister. 'It usually means that he's confident that he is onto something and is quite prepared for his reputation to be on the line.' There was a pause during which those present continued scanning the papers and sipping their tea. It was broken at last by the Cabinet secretary, a balding man with hard-bitten face.

'As far as we can tell then, gentlemen, no one has yet latched onto the nub of the problem. It is important that they don't, for obvious reasons. I'm quite convinced that mass hysteria and anarchy would prevail.'

'God knows, we are going to have enough problems with the panic developing over the water crisis,' added the PM. 'We must control that situation. I want to take that Reaney fellow along with us, loathsome creature that he is. Is he on stand-by? Will he cooperate, Justin?'

'I think so, Prime Minister,' said the younger civil servant.

'What about David?' asked Alan Hunter quietly, directing

211

his look and his question towards Marner.

'It was a mistake briefing him, Alan. A bad one. I still trust him, as a friend, though, strangely enough. I don't think he'll blab.'

'Can we risk it?'

'Probably not.'

'Is there some way we can ... erm ... encourage him to ... lie low for a couple of days?' suggested Hunter, delicately.

'He's being tailed and his phones are tapped,' interjected the Cabinet secretary in a matter-of-fact way. 'We'll do whatever's necessary,' he continued, knowing that he could control the situation through his chairmanship of the PSCIS group.

'When is the president expected to make contact?' asked the young minister, again aiming his question straight at Marner.

'Two o'clock this afternoon,' said the PM. 'Until then we have to find a way to alleviate everybody's anxieties: public, press, Parliament, the Cabinet, and Uncle Tom Cobbleigh and all.'

Electronic tracking had come a long way in the last few years. No longer was surveillance dependent on visual contact. It was easy to place an electronic bug on a vehicle and to conduct a pursuit from many miles away, whilst still being able to pinpoint location within yards. The old business of spotting suspicious looking pursuit cars in the rear view mirror was no more than a romantic image confined to old films. Even civilian car theft had dropped substantially in the last few years through the fitting of these devices.

David Mallow had no reason to suspect that he was being tracked as he headed north and then east from the capital. For sure, in the dramatic events of the last 24 hours he had fallen from grace, but he had not realized that he was being treated as public enemy number one. He could only wonder who Joanne had been speaking to when he violently admonished her, just a short time ago. So upset and distraught was he with the way his life was collapsing all around him that all

212

he wanted to do was get the hell out of it. 'Sod 'em all,' was his illogical but perhaps understandable attitude.

The LED read-out on the dashboard of the unmarked M16 pursuit car, however, meant that his wish for isolation would not be easily achieved.

The inspector had phoned Jim after the breakfast briefing to keep him informed of developments and they arranged for a meeting later in the day. Jim had confirmed that he would not be leaving the area without Carol, one way or another. Meanwhile, he was determined to keep himself busy with his other pre-occupation.

First he rang Bill at his office.

'Jim, what is it? Any news?' Bill asked apprehensively, through yet another crackly line.

'No, Bill. We're still searching. The net is closing, I'm sure of it. But it was some information from you I was after,' said Jim. 'How far back do your weather records go?'

'It depends what you want,' replied Bill.

'Well, I don't really mean records so much as information on climate, I suppose. And I might be talking thousands rather than hundreds of years.'

'For example?'

'Back to the time of the last magnetic flip, say four thousand years ago.'

'You couldn't be more specific, could you?' asked Bill, half jokingly.

'I only wish I could,' said Jim.

'I'll have a poke around in the reference library here for you, Jim. We might have some general information on overall weather patterns at the time. The trouble is that the further back you go in time the longer the period you can examine and averages don't always mean very much. They can mask wide variations.'

'I understand, Bill, but anything that you can come up with would be appreciated.'

'I take it that you're looking for similarities between then and now.'

'Correct,' said Jim. 'And with any other periods of similar magnetic field activity if possible.'

'I'll see what I can do, Jim. It could take some time, though.'

Jim signed off with his thanks and left his contact number. It had been a difficult call with the line breaking up at times and he was hoping that his next call would be on a better quality line. At least Cambridge was not that far away from where he was, so he was hopeful.

'Hamish,' Jim called out with relief both at getting hold of his busy friend and the apparent clarity of the communication. He wasted no time getting down to the purpose of his call. 'Hamish, you remember the other day that we talked about establishing a link between happenings in the atmosphere and behavioural trends?'

'Indeed I do,' came the reply, with that disarmingly gentle Scottish lilt. 'And I've done the research I promised.'

'If I were to tell you that there was now overwhelming evidence of major change to the earth's magnetic field, in what way would you expect that to register in the human body?' asked Jim.

'By "register" do you mean outwardly, in terms of visible or detectable symptoms, as it were?' asked the ever canny Scot.

'Well, not necessarily,' replied Jim, thinking as he spoke, 'although that would be interesting if there were any obvious signs.'

'I'm not so sure about any obvious signs. I think that I'd need time to consider that. If we were talking about major changes arising from a situation that we have never experienced before, then the truthful answer is that we do not know what would happen. Maybe we should look at people who already experience a slightly different magnetic environment.'

'Are there any?' asked Jim.

'Surely,' replied Hamish in that authoritative manner of his. 'Airline pilots and astronauts, for example, spend long periods nearer to the magnetosphere than you or I.'

'Are they any different to the rest of us?'

214

'It has been suggested that prolonged exposure to stronger magnetic fields will have an effect on circulatory systems.'

'What about delicate changes in the balance of the magnetic field?' asked Jim. 'Is there some organ or part of the body that regulates our reaction? Something we can latch onto? Something we can measure or look for?'

'There is a body of opinion that believes that the pineal gland is sensitive to magnetic fluctuation.'

'And where is that, and what is its function?' asked the ever inquisitive Jim.

In reply to your first question, it is more or less situated in the middle of the brain but without being neuronally connected. And in answer to your second, let me pose a question in return: have you ever heard of the third eye?'

'I've heard the expression,' replied Jim.

'Hindus swear by it,' said Hamish. 'They believe that we have a kind of third sensory mechanism between and behind the eyes. It's very much an underresearched organ of the body that no one fully understands. A number of medical papers in recent years have suggested that it is much more important and active than previously realized.'

'In what ways?' asked Jim, believing that he may finally have stumbled on the missing link.

'God, you ask a lot of questions for this time in a morning. I wish half my students had this enthusiasm.'

'Sorry, Hamish. You're my expert on everything medical.'

'I'll tell you what I can, off the top of my head, if you understand my meaning. The pineal gland is implicated in the regulation of the other glands. It produces neurohormones and other chemicals. It may exercise control over...'

'Hang on a minute,' interrupted Jim. 'What chemicals?'

'Melatonin I know of,' came the reply.

'Eureka!' shouted Jim. 'Hasn't that been implicated in some behavioural traits?'

'Schizophrenia may be. There's also serotonin that's been linked to suicide conditions in Norway.'

'Which is a part of the world susceptible to major magnetic

215

disturbances,' commented Jim, thinking out loud as much as anything.

'Serotonin has also been considered a factor in jet lag' added Hamish.

'For airline pilots, read airline passengers,' mused Jim. 'So what have we got?' he asked rhetorically. 'Magnetic disturbances unique in modern times, which send confusing and dangerous signals to the pineal gland, the body's receiving organ. This responds by secreting chemicals, whether as a defence mechanism or as a malfunction. These affect human behaviour, turning on the aggression and violence that are instinctive to the human core brain. In effect, present conditions may be replicating the conditions that prevailed when man only had the core brain.'

'You're painting a frightening picture, Jim,' said Hamish, 'one of prehistoric man suddenly reinhabiting the brain and body of his modern counterpart.'

'But is it plausible, Hamish?'

'Aye, it's plausible all right, feasible if you like, but there are still a few gaps in the theory to fill in, not to mention some cast iron scientific proof.'

'Such as how we are able to sit and talk about it rationally and not be affected by any apparent changes to our own behavioural patterns,' suggested Jim.

'No, that need not be a weakness in the theory,' reassured the genial Scot. 'There is no reason to suspect that it would affect all individuals in exactly the same way, just as now we do not all conform to the same behavioural patterns.'

'So some may be more susceptible than others,' said Jim.

'Quite. It is also known that pineal activity increases and changes at puberty. The increasing aggression may also go hand in hand with heightened sexual activity. Of course, if you are right about current conditions and they do deteriorate further, we could all be affected, but to varying degrees.'

'So we could all become raving schizophrenics,' pondered Jim, now subdued.

'On the other hand,' said Hamish,' it could lead to some very interesting research into the pineal gland. Is this the key to unlock and control human behaviour, always assuming that we would want to? It's the kind of research western governments won't fund unless they can see a pay-off.'

'Or unless they are forced into it, for military or defence purposes,' suggested Jim.

'Jim, this has been a fascinating talk. I'm glad you came to see me the other day. You've got me interested in something potentially very exciting. I'm going to speak to a friend of mine at the University of Surrey. I'll certainly be in touch if I have anything of interest for you.'

'Thank you, Hamish. You've already been an enormous help. I've a feeling that we'll be talking again very soon.'

'Look forward to it, old friend.'

Jim put the receiver down but his brain was still formulating. He had his complete theory, well almost complete. There would be other details to slot in, from Hamish, from Bill, and from others. But what to do next? It was time to go public, time to talk to Ben, perhaps to bring in Reaney again. What did the government know? Above all, what were they doing? Or what would they do? Who else knew what was happening? Surely there must be those in the scientific fraternity with their suspicions and theories. What could anybody do? Above all, what could he himself do to bring home Carol, safe and sound, convinced as he certainly now was that she was an innocent victim of what was a totally unprecedented state of affairs.

The following morning, Carol had thought that she had detected a less menacing side to Geoff. She had slept only in fits and starts. When she awoke finally, she had to look around to remind herself of the unfamiliar surroundings in which she found herself: captively, against her wishes. Almost as an afterthought she remembered the naked state she had been in the previous night and then felt relief at the white sheet that was now covering her. It did not envelop the whole of her body but had been crudely tucked in down the sides of the chair. This could only mean, she realized, that Geoff had intruded during the night. He must have touched her body,

217

if only briefly; but had he taken any greater advantage of her exposed and unguarded state? Carol could not feel or sense anything to suggest that she had been tampered with. She could only hope and pray that her increasingly unstable captor had acted in kindness on this occasion. When she saw the nearby tray, complete with sandwiches and glass of milk, she felt more confident that he had been in one of his more civilized moods. She could only hope that this would now continue. Unfortunately, having seen less of Geoff she had not realized that he was becoming less stable. His overall condition had deteriorated and his provision of the food and drink and the sheet had been no more than an oasis of kindness in a desert of ill will and confusion.

If she could have seen through the thick wall dividing them, Carol would have noticed an increasingly desolate and desperate figure. Geoff sat forward in his armchair, his elbows propped on his knees, and his head slumped low between his arms. Try as he might he could not find a position that would give him any comfort, nor any respite from the constant grinding pain in his head. Though his weary body had finally forced itself to find sleep in the night, it had not been for long. It was as if it had been allowed no more than the bare minimum and for now it would be deprived of any more.

It was on exercises in Norway that Geoff first started with the headaches. Then they went away for a period, only to return more excruciatingly than before. Sometimes it was a throbbing pain, though that was unusual. More often than not it would be a grinding, boring pain, sometimes around the eyes and forehead, sometimes the temples. Migraine was dismissed as a diagnosis. The military doctor likened them to cluster headaches, more common apparently amongst air force pilots than in the other services. It was believed that they could be triggered by climate or temperature changes, that they often went into remission, but were usually difficult to treat. They had been linked to violent behavioural traits by some researchers. For Geoff, all attempts to alleviate the headaches had failed. He was not interested any longer in

218

the speculation and the diagnosis, only in the fact that he was increasingly unable to cope with the excruciating pain. It was dominating his brain and his mind, squeezing out the space he needed to contemplate other thought processes and actions. It was as if he was turning into a zombie, as his vacant red-ringed eyes would testify. He no longer cared about the way he was behaving, or the devastation he was causing because he no longer had the capacity in his mind to care. Just occasionally his palaeomammalian brain would force through a glimpse of a more sensitive side of his nature, but more and more his baser, aggressive, primordial instincts were all that he had left, all that he had space for, other than the constant, needle-tipped agony dominating his head.

Any strange or unexpected sound or activity was a threat as far as Geoff was concerned. It mobilized his heightened aggression and fed his sick body with more adrenalin. The approach of a car, however innocuously, down this quiet country lane, was sufficient to cause him consternation and alarm. When it pulled into the space in front of the cottage it had Geoff up on his feet, grabbing his weapon and darting around like a dervish, straining to see without being seen. It was a large dark-coloured car. He could not safely deduce much more than that. He eventually landed up in the hall-way, still stooping to avoid being seen, despite the lack of win-dows, and with a wild, crazed look in his eyes. He was uncertain. He did not know whether to go forward to the front door to confront or to retreat down the hall to the back room to first check and then grab his hostage. Outside, a car door slammed. Geoff's head screeched inside as his indeci-sion mounted. He fell to one knee in the middle of the hall, unable now to think of any other alternative than to raise and point his gun at whoever might seek to come through the door. A key rattled in the lock and the adrenalin pumped stronger and his trigger finger tightened. It seemed an age before anything else happened, almost as though time had gone into slow motion. When the door eventually swung open Geoff immediately recognized the figure that was framed, almost motionless and disbelieving in the doorway:

the round, bespectacled face, the lank hair, the arrogant stature that was so familiar from the television pictures. Time momentarily slowed to a complete stop. The figure had made only the smallest of steps through the doorway, bags in hands, before freezing. From Geoff's angle it appeared to fill his forward vision and threaten his well-being. His answer, seemingly now his only answer to everything, was to blow away the threat in a thunder of noise. The force of the outburst threw Geoff's shoulder back and he overbalanced onto the hall floor from his previously crouched position. At the same time, the man at the door was hurled backwards under the force of bullets unleashed. He was dead.

Carol slumped heavily against the door with her back. Having strained to hear what was the cause of all the scuttling about, the explosion of firepower told her all she needed to know. It was a sound that was becoming distressingly and desperately familiar to her. She feared that there was the blood of another killing on Geoff's hands. She was not to know at this stage that it was the man at the five-bar gate, who had been staring out at her with his family, since her arrival at the cottage.

'Makes you wonder why we need to be on the road at all,' said the driver. 'With these devices,' he continued, pointing at the dashboard read-out, 'we know exactly where he is all the time.'

'Flexibility,' answered his colleague, the younger of the two, a ginger-headed man, evidence that recruitment to the services continued, despite the cutbacks. 'Means we can follow at a distance but still move in swiftly if needs change.'

'I suppose so,' replied the other man, experienced enough to know the answer anyway, 'but we could be here for hours now that he's at home.'

'Or second home,' corrected the other, pedantically.

'If not third,' quipped the older man back. 'Rich bastard.'

'What's he supposed to have done anyway?' asked ginger-head.

'God knows. You'd be hard pressed to find a Cabinet

220

minister nowadays who lasts five minutes without some scandal or other, but they usually come up smelling of roses at the end of the day. He'll make a few quid on his memoirs, no doubt. I'd have the buggers shot,' concluded the cynical older one.

'You sure you did the right thing coming back after your sick leave?' asked his colleague, dryly, but he drew only a muttered response.

They settled down to await their next call to action, content at least that their surroundings were congenial, not to say restful. They were parked off the main road, within a mile or two of Mallow's cottage. They had taken note of the 'olde worlde' inn just down the road that served traditional 'fayre' at lunchtimes. Their only discomfort was once again the uncomfortable heat that was bubbling up as the day went on. At least they had found some shade whilst they waited.

They were not the only ones awaiting developments. So, too, were the telephone monitoring team. So, too were the officers manning the police checkpoint they had come through a few miles back. So, too, was Inspector Childs. So, too, was Jim Webb, but he had not had time to dwell on it during a morning full of activity.

Telephone communication continued to be difficult, in terms of both availability and quality of connection. Jim and Ben had important calls to make and required perseverance to get their messages through, but they succeeded. The innkeeper could be forgiven for thinking that the two men were conducting some sort of business from their rooms. It was an unlikely location for the culmination of events that could prove to be historic and far-reaching. In other circumstances it would be a charming inn in a typical north Norfolk village, but as the middle of the day approached, the heat and the surroundings became unbearable and the location no more amenable than any other, save for one redeeming feature: the ale was drawn from a deep, cool cellar, and when Jim and Ben met later in the bar that was their first and most important consideration.

'Well, Ben' asked Jim. 'Is he coming?'

'We'll know within a couple of hours,' replied his amiable friend before quaffing a refreshing mouthful of ale.

'Can we rely on your contact reaching his contact reaching the PM?'

'It's simpler than that,' said Ben. 'My contact is the PM's media adviser. And if he can't speak to Marner direct, he has access to the Cabinet secretary.'

'It's not what you know but who you know,' reflected Jim and Ben chuckled.

Every man had his moment and John Marner was soon to be presented with his opportunity to leave his indelible mark on the records of history. In his case, however, the problems he faced had never been encountered before, at least not in modern times, and the danger could not be discounted that there might be few of his subjects remaining to pass judgement on his efforts. That in itself could be the measure of his success or failure.

He had been with his advisers all morning, considering options, releasing statements, receiving information, preparing explanations, discussing contingency plans. All the time he knew that the real action must wait until the president had come back to him. The gathering media gang keeping vigil at Number Ten could not be given much information at this stage. Nor could Parliament. They must be stalled, despite the falling stock markets.

'We have to keep the lid on a bit longer,' he told his advisers, most of whom were involved on a need to know basis. As callers had come and gone during the morning they had emerged tight-lipped.

Then came the shock that the story was out, or as good as, now that Ben Johnson had ferreted out the facts. Who had told him about the Gauss Factor file? It must have been Mallow. And why this strange request from Johnson to meet him and this other chap, in Norfolk, of all places? And yet if he complied he could hope to delay a little further the inevitable mass panic and hysteria that was sure to develop. They would not speak to anybody but the prime minister, so the message had gone. News was already coming in of chaos in those areas affected by the contaminated water scare started by Reaney's revelations in The House. Hospitals and doctors' surgeries were besieged, schools boycotted, water, health and council authorities at full stretch. There had been public order offences in supermarkets and shops and trade union demonstrations. Those currently being served by tanker or standpipe could not even be sure of a pure supply. All the time, indignation and outrage simmered as temperatures rose inexorably and seemingly without limit. The more people thought that something was going wrong with basic fundamentals of civilized life, the less likely they would be to adhere to civilized values and behaviour. The PM knew that mass hysteria and panic could be turned on like a switch if the truth about what was happening to the earth's environment got out. It was not as though Marner regarded himself as a man with a historic mission, but simply that he knew what he had to do. He had to buy time for a solution to be found. He would know more after speaking to the president over the scrambler. After that, if circumstances permitted, and communication channels with the president could be maintained, he would allow himself to be whisked off to Norfolk to meet Johnson and his friend. If Reaney could be persuaded to rendezvous with him there, too, so much the better. National security must take precedence now and he would see to it that his office, through the Cabinet secretary, would spread its tentacles as necessary to make all appropriate arrangements. Oh, and he would need to have Mallow attended to as well. 'Christ,' he thought, 'what a bloody awful business.'

One thing was paramount in Marner's mind: his family. He knew the immense X-class solar flares would hit the earth's weakening magnetic field before nightfall, with spectacular but also possibly devastating effect. For that reason he would be heading for East Anglia later that day since that was the direction of his family home.

Geoff slumped down after the shooting. He eventually

dragged himself back to a wall, which he leaned against, mind in turmoil, gun on lap, a picture of despair and confusion, a physical and mental wreck. It was some time before he thought to go and inspect his victim. He eventually took hold of him by the feet and dragged him, on his back, across the gravel drive. He opened one half of the solid black wooden gates that gave access to the side and back of the cottage and pulled him through. After rifling through his pockets, Geoff then went back to the gate, opened the other half, and then headed for the car. Using the keys found in the pockets he drove it down through the gate and out of sight.

He had felt an instinctive need to remove all obvious trace of his visitor, even to the extent of rearranging with his feet some of the loose gravel to hide blood stains. However, what he did not know was that in a country lane, a few miles down the road, the movement of the car had alerted two observers who were following the vehicle's every move on a sophisticated tracking device. Nor did he know that the man he had just murdered was an ex-Cabinet minister.

Carol had been listening intently to the noises from outside. She was both exasperated from not knowing what was going on, and anxious, inevitably, about her own safety. She was still clad only in the white sheet Geoff had provided during the night.

She jumped with a start when she heard the key go in the lock and she looked round suddenly, fearing the worst. Geoff looked ill, with heavy tired eyes, set deep in a drawn, sallow face. He was clasping his trusty weapon as always and scarcely looked in Carol's direction, other than the briefest of glances to establish that she was at least still there. He checked that the window was secure and that everything in the room seemed as it should be and where it should be. He made no attempt to speak as he completed his circuit of the room. Then, suddenly, as he neared the door again, he turned towards Carol, who was more or less in the middle of the room, clutching her makeshift dress, and he stared menacingly. Carol felt an evil presence, a kind of primitive fear and she shuddered. Though she quickly averted her eyes, she continued to shake and tremble. As she turned away completely she felt the stabbing of his eyes in her back and thought that she was going to cry out loud. It was only when the door slammed shut that she felt a tide of relief wash over her.

PART FOUR

It started in the late afternoon. The cabin temperature reading was an ambient 20 degrees Celsius. It was much more comfortable for those flying at 60,000 feet than it was on the sweltering surface below. The Concorde autopilot was operating and the eastwards transatlantic crossing was on schedule, the graceful queen of the skies piercing the upper reaches of the azure stratosphere like a silver dart. A series of alarms went off in the cockpit virtually simultaneously. It did not need a pilot with the experience of Colin Bradshaw to appreciate rapidly that he needed to take manual control. All measuring instruments and dials had gone haywire, flickering from one end of their respective scales to the other. The computer control was in malfunction. Back-up instrumentation gave no assistance. There was no panic from Bradshaw, a big-set man who exuded confidence and control as he cut back on speed and height as a precaution, pending full assessment. But without proper readings and readouts, any kind of assessment would be difficult, to say the least. As he and his colleagues ran through sequences of checks it became clear that they were facing a novel experience.

They were over halfway on their journey and had experienced no earlier problems. Visible checks revealed no obvious causes of their current dilemma, neither inside nor outside the aircraft. Bradshaw had been warned of reports of possible magnetic interference as part of the pre-flight briefing but it was unusual for instrumentation to malfunction. They were usually shielded against such interference and they were not in the midst of a storm as such. If they had been they could have taken avoiding action. Even Concorde's special radiation detector was out of action. The cause of their problems was invisible. To add to their concerns, their communications were dead, with nothing to suggest that their messages were transmitting, let alone being received. A constant fuzz, with intermittent crackle, was all that could be heard through their headsets.

Bradshaw still saw no reason to panic and did not wish to alarm his supersonic passengers unduly. So he continued to lose height gradually and allied this to a modest directional change, fully expecting that this little local difficulty would be over soon and normal service would then be resumed.

Meanwhile, behind the cockpit, some of the passengers were complaining of severe headaches and the cabin crew were dispensing aspirin like confetti. Some of the crew were affected too.

About ten miles below, the effects of the phenomenon were only momentarily delayed. A few miles was as nothing compared to the immense journey of the solar wind. Satellite communications, subject to so much distortion and interruption in recent weeks, were completely down. Long-distance telephone links, television transmissions and transport communications were lost. Mobile telephones relying on land-based transmitters closely followed suit. Radio and radar systems at airport control centres were on the blink. Emergency services were hampered.

It was the power surge that really brought home the seriousness of the situation. Had it happened a few hours earlier and had it been more widespread, the electrical failures would have brought chaos to the rush hour traffic, not to mention the evening meals of millions of homes in this part of the globe. With many parts of the country eking out water supplies and questioning even the quality and safety of that, a complete electrical failure as well would have caused widespread consternation. It was not just homes, of course, that were affected. Petrol pumps failed to pump. As dusk developed, street lights failed to light. Bank cash dispensers failed to dispense. All aspects of life were affected and were alleviated only to the extent, firstly, that the breakdown was localized, though spreading patchily southwards like a creeping cancer and, secondly, that any physical hardship was tempered by the warm weather. In fact, the late evening and the early night had become the favourite part of the day for most people as the sting was drawn from the overbearing heat of daytime.

The blackout was to come early, however, for some. As Hilary Baker set out in the family Fiesta to pick up her 9-year-old daughter after tea at a friend's house it was hot, sunny and clear, as usual. The friendly Lake District town of Kendwick had, like everywhere else, experienced a record-breaking and seemingly perpetual summer heatwave. In different times it was an area noted for sudden deterioration in the weather. Big, black clouds, heavy with rain would often roll down from the Cumbrian fells to deposit a deluge that now could only be dreamed of. But the blackness that was to engulf them on this day was of a sort not experienced before.

As they drove down the narrow, busy street the traffic had slowed, as a precaution, due to the failure of the traffic lights. People were gathered at shop doorways and corners. As she passed one group slowly with window, as usual wound down, she heard some chatter about 'power cuts'. At that time it was startlingly bright, almost hurtfully so, as though nature had turned up its contrast control. The pace of the traffic picked up a little and Hilary had progressed to a bend at the end of the High Street when the whole world, without warning, turned black. It was as though she saw everything as a photographic negative. She could still make out shapes and objects, though in a manner so strange and unexpected that she could not react to them. There was still an output from her brain but it was as if her normal senses had been overturned by a blinding, eerie blackness, as though its normal functioning had been switched off, and the longer she waited for the switch to be thrown back, the more she feared. The screams of her little girl counted for nothing, as the car, steered now by a zombie-like mother, failed to turn in sympathy with the bend in the road. The downhill gradient and a right foot lying heavily and aimlessly on the accelerator pedal, combined to hasten its departure from the road and the children in its path stood no chance as they were hurled into the air. The car came to a sickening crunching halt against the solid old stone packhorse bridge. As driver and passenger slumped forward another kind of blackness took over.

There were many other victims, both in this immediate area and the general vicinity, before the black power surge moved on. No one in its path could fail to be aware of it, though its effects varied from person to person. But though this fearful phenomenon was bad enough, it was, in fact, only to prove the forerunner of similar surges until eventually there was a complete blanket. Moving steadily down from northern latitudes, the momentum was unstoppable, like an electrically charged black death creeping slowly but ominously onwards.

'Blimey,' exclaimed the jolly barman, 'we've never had such activity, or such important visitors to our little village.'

'I would keep it quiet, though, for the time being, if I were you,' advised one of the two physically intimidating, but smartly dressed detectives. They were a necessary part of the prime minister's ever increasing entourage.

The innkeeper was happy to oblige. His small establishment had been taken over, but not just by anybody. He could not understand what was going on, or why. He did not know why he had been chosen. And it was not just the throng of people but the equipment too. Part of his restaurant had been commandeered to accommodate it. Outside was parked one of those big caravanettes with a swivelling satellite dish on its roof.

As he prepared to meet the prime minister, Jim did not know about the creeping black mass that was edging its way southwards on a global basis. If he had, it would merely have confirmed his worst fears.

John Marner, on the other hand, had been briefed on

some strange happenings in Scotland and the north and had asked to be kept informed, though communication problems were becoming severe. Reports of other worrying events were reaching him too, not least pandemonium on the Stock Exchange. The PM insisted that his chancellor could cope, but his aides were increasingly puzzled that he should make time to see this chap called Jim, even if his colleague was Ben Johnson, the famous and respected freelance journalist. They thought that his place was in Downing Street at the hub of government. On the contrary, John Marner knew that his place was with his family, or at least within a relatively short drive of them. And in any case, the Cabinet secretary would run the show in London, as usual.

They met in a corner of the lounge, the PM making his entrance with an entourage, all but one of whom held back as he went over to the table occupied by Jim and Ben. They stood to greet the prime minister as he approached. Ben had been in John Marner's presence before, though he could hardly count him as an acquaintance. Jim, on the other hand, had never met anyone so grand, but he was not one to be overawed by reputation or position. There were firm handshakes all round and Justin was introduced, a tall, lean and very correct man, and young for the position he held which was firmly within the prime minister's confidence.

'We know about the Gauss Factor,' said Jim, quietly and at the same time as they sat.

'Who was it? Mallow?' asked Marner. After a pause he added, 'Your silence speaks volumes. It was him, wasn't it?'

'Indirectly,' answered Jim. 'But it is not important. We are more concerned with what rather than how, as you must be, too.'

'So, just how much do you know?' asked Justin, sat on the prime minister's left on one of the many red-backed chairs.

'Let's not beat about the bush,' said Jim, leaning forward for effect, but still speaking calmly and quietly. 'The geomagnetic field has weakened to the extent that it can no longer resist the effects of heightened solar wind activity. Our protective screen has gone. Anything can, and already is, happening. We are into uncharted waters. There could even be a geomagnetic flip, and no one can be sure what effect that would have.'

John Marner wiped his brow with a handkerchief as he considered the situation.

'What is your involvement, Ben?' he said at last, turning to face him.

'Like any good journalist, I want to flush out the truth. I want to know what you and your government are doing about the situation ... and quick ... otherwise we go public.'

They were interrupted, whilst an aide came forward and whispered in Justin's ear and, in due course, he relayed the information to the prime minister. Before they could conclude their conversation, however, there were raised voices at the lounge entrance.

'I've not come all this way to see the monkeys, I want to see the organ grinder,' bellowed the gruff northern voice and all the faces at the table looked up. Ben and Jim were surprised to see Reaney striding over towards them, but he was even more taken aback. 'What the bloody hell are you two doing here?' he asked, almost stopping in his tracks.

'We might ask you the same question,' replied Jim.

'I suggest that you pull up a chair,' said Marner, who waited for Reaney to settle before proceeding to brief them all on the situation in which they, the whole country and indeed the whole world found itself. It was couched in more diplomatic and political terms but the message was essentially the same as Jim's. It stopped short, however, of the solution, the action, the bit they all wanted to hear.

'You've surely not dragged me all this way to tell me this without a good reason,' commented the perspiring shirt-sleeved Reaney in his usual blunt manner.

'You three have had the knowledge to blow this thing wide open,' began Marner. 'To cause panic and mass hysteria. Of course, that may happen anyhow but I have a duty, we all do, to lessen the impact, to avoid mayhem, loss of life. That is why I have wanted your cooperation today. That is why I have been trying to keep things calm and show control for the last couple of weeks.'

'But why?' asked Ben, arms spread wide. 'We are all doomed anyway, aren't we? So why shouldn't people know the truth so that they can make their arrangements, be with their families?'

'All I can say, Ben is, trust me,' answered the prime minister.

'To do what?' asked Ben.

'Within the hour I shall be broadcasting to the nation, from right here. After that I will tell you more.'

'We will have to consider our position,' said Jim.

'Very well, but I have to tell you,' continued Marner, whilst looking at another piece of paper he had been handed, 'that events are possibly moving even more rapidly than I had feared.'

'What do you mean?' asked Reaney.

'Severe communications problems are affecting parts of the country and things are happening that we cannot control.'

'We may need to bring the broadcast forward, Prime Minister,' said the starchy Justin.

'Quite,' said the PM.

'What the hell's going on?' blasted Reaney, more forcefully this time.

'What the hell's going on?' shouted the usually cool Bradshaw. In 30 years he had not experienced anything like it. Devoid of navigational and technical aids, out of contact with the ground, no amount of manoeuvring could free him from the invisible menace. Then, when the aircraft was eventually engulfed by a flashing black mass that descended from above like the grab of some alien spacecraft so beloved of science fiction writers, it was virtually the final straw. Those amongst the passengers and crew whose brains were not frazzled by the atmospheric bombardment tried their best to cling on to reality. Bradshaw fought with the controls as only a brilliant and seasoned flier could. But it was like guiding the plane through a thick black soup. Normal aerodynamic laws were suspended. Slowly the aircraft lost its independence. Those still conscious were screaming as their mind controls shorted.

As the fuselage hit the water, Bradshaw was the only one still alive, if that was the correct description, for his eyes stared wide and unflickering like a zombie. Then, he too was gone. The once graceful bird was now all mangled and fragmented, amidst a sea of debris and death. In the blackness, lightning danced on the surface of the water, sparked by a vast chemical reaction.

Geoff did not remember switching on the television. It was possibly done to establish if there were any news items about him, but if so, it was done instinctively, his capacity for premeditated thought having withered away. His soulless expression changed little, if at all, when the image on the box in front of him became that of the prime minister. Millions of others were watching the same image with anticipation. For once, countless others would also have liked to have tuned in to the politician's broadcast, but were unable to get their sets to deliver any picture or sound. Many, many others were completely oblivious of any kind of picture or sound, real or imaginary.

Some of the prime minister's words, delivered in that familiar monotone, entered Geoff's brain 'National emergency ... crisis ... atmosphere ... unprecedented ... stay indoors ... help each other ... keep calm ... measures taken ... off the air ... cooperate with the authorities ... rest assured ... God bless you all ...' But the capacity to interpret them or to give them any significance was sadly lacking. Primeval instinct was the order of the day, and having fed already on violence, Geoff's appetite was now turning to lust. Those neural connectors responsible for superimposing the will of the civilized, newer parts of the brain over the old core, had all but ceased to function; unable to operate in the hostile atmospheric environment not just prevailing, but growing ever more dominant. Aware of the temptations in the adjoining room, there was no longer any shred of decency holding Geoff back from exploiting them.

Carol, as ever, was startled by the loudness of the key in the lock. Positioned on the far side of the room from Geoff, underneath the window, she held her makeshift gown tightly to her, with her arms folded across for added protection, so it seemed. The bravado that had characterized some of her behaviour in the last few days had disappeared. Her feelings now were much more basic. Perhaps she, too, was succumbing to the hostile formulae of the lower atmosphere, now a cauldron of change to which all life had to adapt or die, just as in reality it always had. It was hot again, but somehow Geoff's appearance made her go cold. She awaited his intentions with trepidation, aware that by now he seemed to have given up any attempt at small talk, or indeed conversation of any kind.

Geoff paused at the open door. He had had little respite from the grinding pain in his head, but those occasions when it had eased had coincided with moments of high adrenalin flow, the moments of heightened tension and violence. He felt some easing of it now, just a little. He could not see the frightened, innocent and decent person at the opposite side of the room, only an object of lust that could satisfy a crude and urgent need that was now welling up inside him. He did not bother to close the door. He stood his weapon against the wall on his right-hand side, just to one side of the door. The chance of it being grabbed by his prisoner did not concern him. He began to loosen the buckle holding up his trousers.

Carol was not unduly encouraged that Geoff was temporarily parted from his gun. She harboured no immediate thoughts of snatching it. When she saw his belt coming off, she wondered if this was the precursor to a beating. She did not know why that should be, only that, in the heavy silence, she had an anticipation of something unpleasant about to happen. She wanted to avert herself from his stare as he stood there, belt in hand, no more than a few feet away, but she found it difficult. As Geoff bent down to remove his footwear and then loosen his trousers it was almost as if she

237

felt compelled to watch his methodical disrobing. It was not so much shock that prevented her from moving or talking, as a kind of inner resignation to what was happening. Her captor was now down to red briefs and T-shirt, an unlikely uniform for administering violence, which suggested that he had something else in mind.

Geoff noticed the folding bed to his left and went over towards it. It was a simple matter to unfurl it and set it up and, having done so, he stood to one side. Looking at Carol, he gestured with the hand for her to come place herself on it.

Carol, having been unable to avert her eyes, had followed his every move. When he gestured her to go over she wondered at first if it was an attempt to make her situation more comfortable again. But why did he have to strip half naked? Had he completely flipped? The answer perhaps lay in the tell-tale bulge in his briefs. She still found herself unable to speak and after a pause that seemed longer than it actually was, she moved slowly across the room, because it seemed the right thing to do, probably the only thing to do. As she came within arm's length, Geoff reached out and grabbed her left arm which she had been holding close to her body. She shuddered at his rough, firm grip and became concerned at the loosening of her covering sheet. Tensing her arm as a show of resistance had no effect. With his other arm Geoff pulled at the sheet, which Carol had fashioned into a makeshift sari. His intentions were crystal clear now. Carol found herself strangely unable to speak. Was this some nightmare fantasy she was unable to stop? She squeezed her right arm tightly against her body to make it more difficult for him, but this battle was running away from her. His brute force ripped at the cotton as though it were rice paper and in no time Geoff had achieved what appeared to be his objective of laying her body bare. Only then, as he stood back to admire his handywork, were Carol's hands and arms free to wrap round her exposed private parts like a recoiled spring. She was stooping and crouching now in a half-pathetic cowering position and, Geoff seemed to be hovering over her. He pulled his T-shirt up and over his head revealing his muscular upper torso, the result of years of army training and dedication. His flat stomach, broad hairless chest and leanness were self-evident. Clad now only in his red briefs, his mounting excitement was obvious, his concealed bulge moving unaided as he eyed the beautiful naked body in front of him, within touching distance. Slowly he walked around Carol, pausing when he was directly behind her, and then, out of sight he reached out.

Carol, despite all the circumstances, all that had happened to her, could not deny a pulse of excitement at Geoff's display of sexuality. She stood motionless, and with eyes closed, as he went round behind her. When the contact came she was jolted, as if by an electric shock through her whole body. It settled down to a tingle that ran through her veins. Against all expectation, the touch of Geoff's fingers across her shoulders was so light that it was almost sensual. As they moved down her side the pores in her skin stiffened like the dimples of a golf ball. Lower and lower he went on her unprotected, tensed body as if tracing a line to her most intimate part of all. She found herself frozen. Then he caressed her rear and her buttocks clenched. She threw her head up in mock anguish, eyes still closed, arms still round her front. It was the gentleness she could not understand. She felt Geoff's fingers explore onwards, touching so close now to the seat of her sexuality. Her mind was in turmoil, a mixture of dread and anticipation, but hard as she fought against it, she could not shake off a build-up of arousal. Nor could she find her voice. She had a feeling of guilt at being unable to demonstrate rejection of his advances in either sound or action. This had to be part of a monstrous and harmless dream, otherwise, how could she be deriving a growing amount of sensual gratification? In truth, her brain functions were in disarray, but in that she was by no means alone. A sound finally escaped from her mouth, a low groan, as his finger found the end of its journey.

Geoff withdrew his moist finger and walked slowly round to the front of Carol once more. She slowly opened her eyes. She found herself gasping slightly for breath. As Geoff lowered his briefs she watched as his swollen, throbbing penis was released like a whip, cracking against his midriff before eventually settling at a near vertical angle. He noted that Carol was seemingly unable to avert her fixed, wide-eyed gaze. As she watched the twitching sex organ, not more than a few inches from her body, inexplicably she felt the need to move her hand towards its tip. She made contact with the gentlest of touches from her outstretched finger. It was enough to draw the first traces of sperm.

With his continuing mix of primeval lust but gentle touch, Geoff took hold of Carol and manoeuvred her towards the camp bed that was laid out. Lowering her into the position he wanted he guided his knee between her legs to part them. A part of Carol's mind wanted to resist, but the brain would not relay the appropriate instructions. Geoff was quicker now, sensing that the welling-up was coming to a head. A flicker of resistance came from Carol's pushing arms. Perhaps not all the relevant neural connectors inside her brain were redundant after all, but it was so limited as merely to delay the inevitable. In fact, the momentary delay was crucial. Geoff's excitement was at such fever pitch that he could not prevent premature ejaculation. From a position still two feet above Carol, his seminal fluid flew everywhere. Carol observed with no emotion the strained ecstasy etched on Geoff's face and did not react to the thick warm substance sliding over parts of her naked body. It was only when he finished his thrusting that he might give thought to the possibility of being cheated of the full act.

The awkward silence was broken by the rapping of the old brass door knocker. Geoff's instantaneous reactions to possible danger exemplified again how intensively trained he was. He was up and across the room to where his trusty weapon was lodged in no time, his nakedness being an irrelevance. The knocker went again, and for longer, as if the caller were becoming impatient. It was the ginger-headed man doing the rapping.

Geoff suddenly remembered that he had not locked the door following his previous caller. If his latest visitors should

240

try the handle and enter they would face the same devastating consequences as Mallow.

The cynical, older colleague went back to the car.

'I'll try the radio again,' he called. 'See if we can get the OK to bust in,' he added. He sat in the driver's seat and leaned across for the hand-held mike, grateful that it took him back into the shadows, out of the sun's boiling rays. Ginger-head knocked again, this time looking back towards his colleague in the car at the same time. His friend shook his head and slightly protruded his lower lip. No contact. They would have to act on their own initiative. He tried the round knob on the solid hardwood door and was surprised to find that there was no resistance behind it. As a trained government agent, he was much more alert and aware than Mallow was, but it counted for nothing. His brain had difficulty coming to terms with the last image it was ever to see, that of a wild-eyed naked man down on one knee behind his lethal, bullet-spitting weapon. Watching from the car, his colleague's mouth dropped open at the sight of his ginger-headed friend being blasted backwards through the door, but he soon slipped into the automatic mode gained from years of training and experience. Slamming the gearbox into reverse he shot backwards at speed, back up the lane down which they had come. After fifty yards he swung the car round on the handbrake, tyres screeching and burning, changing into first gear a split second later. His immediate aim was to get himself out of sight, around the next tree-lined bend in the road, where he could take stock, whilst safely out of range. But before he could reach that zone of security, a hail of bullets came smashing through the back window. They scattered and were absorbed through various parts of the car interior, save one which, typifying his wretched year of ill-health and bad luck, threaded its way through the gap between seat and headrest, exploding viciously into the back of his head. Incredibly, as if on automatic, for a while he continued to drive the car, even to the extent of steering, in a fashion, around several bends.

It was on the long straight stretch to the junction with the main road that he slumped forward and finally lost control. Veering off to the left, the up-sloping verge acted like a ramp, hurling the car into the air and tossing it back towards the road. It flipped onto its roof and slid many yards towards the junction up ahead. Its angle, however, took it over to the other verge where, incredibly, it flipped again, back onto its four wheels. The remaining momentum was enough to carry it the few yards to the junction where it came to rest violently against a road sign, this final impact being enough to toss the battered occupant through the space where the windscreen had been.

The sergeant arrived at the scene only seconds later, passing by on his way back to base with his two constables following the dismantling of the road block not far away. Apparently they were being summoned back for an emergency of a different kind.

Initially, they overshot the junction, screeched to a halt and then reversed to the scene. It was a picture of carnage. The vehicle's roof and body were bent, battered and twisted, the grille and bonnet caved in, steam still rising, broken glass and oddments everywhere. Embedded in the front of the vehicle, almost like a sloping spear, was a metal pole with the words GIVE WAY enclosed in a red triangle at its top. A crumpled, bloodied body lay partly on the twisted bonnet and partly entangled round the aptly marked pole.

'Christ almighty,' gasped the first constable, as he approached over crunching glass. 'How the hell has he managed that?'

His sergeant, meanwhile, less easily shocked by such matters, went quietly about his business. Avoiding the protruding jagged edges, he reached over to the man on the bonnet and raised a limp arm at the wrist in a vain attempt to find a pulse. It was only when leaning over further to get a view of the face, that he noticed the flow of blood from the hole in the back of the head.

'I don't think he "managed" anything,' he said to his colleague, at the same time as thinking that from the temperature of the body and state of the blood that the incident had only just happened. The constable moved nearer to see for himself. 'But people just don't get shot in the head whilst they're driving along,' said the constable. 'Not in these parts anyway.'

'Lots of things didn't happen in these parts, until recently,' said the other constable, the driver, who had now joined his colleagues.

'He must have been travelling out of control at some speed, and for some time, to cause this sort of disintegration of the vehicle,' said the sergeant, his mind still very much on the job.

'Gaz' he said, turning to the constable who had been the driver, 'you try and raise that Inspector Childs who briefed us all this morning. I think he might be interested in this.'

'OK, Sarge,' came the reply, 'but I was having trouble getting through just now. I'll try again.'

'Nuttall and I are just going to have a stroll down the road to have a look at these skid marks and see what else we can find,' continued the sergeant.

'What about the other emergency, Sarge?' he asked before his superior got too far away.

'Isn't everything an emergency these days?' answered the sergeant, setting off down the lane with PC Nuttall.

They stopped at intervals to identify and examine bits of car, or marks on the road. They walked quite a way before concluding that there were no more obvious signs. Not a single car had passed them. It was not a through route to anywhere in particular, just a country lane that linked up a couple of small hamlets and the odd country cottage. The two policemen were glad of the shade that protected them from the intense heat and glare of the sun as they stood, out of sight of the junction now, on the edge of a tree-lined bend. Hand on chin, the sergeant looked around. The copse was showing signs of the drought, parched and dry, leaf coverage thin in places. There was a ditch next to the roadside wall which may have been a watercourse in the recent past. There seemed no significance to the area that he could recall. It was

243

off the beaten track. It was extremely unlikely that anyone would have been around to witness what had just gone on up the road. But then it suddenly came to him. 'Wasn't this the area of Mallow's hideaway?' he thought to himself.

'Take a walk round the next bend, constable,' he ordered. 'See if you can see a cottage.' He sat on the stone wall mopping his brow with a handkerchief, whilst his younger colleague set off again.

In fact, it was round a couple of bends before the constable noticed the old stone cottage, set back from the road, on his right. 'The sergeant was right,' he thought to himself. He could see no sign of life or activity in or around the building, which was about a hundred yards further down the road. He was about to turn away when his attention was drawn to an object on the road that was shining in the strong sunlight. He bent down to examine it and found that it was a spent bullet shell, not quite complete. A further quick search of the immediate area brought no further clues but left him even closer to the cottage. He decided that he might as well see if there was anyone in residence. Before approaching the door he had a peep over the side gate. There were two vehicles there. One was the ex-minister's, though he did not know that. The other, though, was the very colour, model, and yes, he was sure, the registration number that was amongst the latest list of stolen vehicles given to them not more than a few hours ago.

This time, the young officer thought, discretion was the better part of valour, even if it had earned him the reputation in the past of being a bit of a plod. He knew his own mind, though, and his judgement was sound more often than not. He decided to report back.

'You've used me, you bastard,' shouted Reaney, through the half-opened door. The prime minister had been isolated in the lounge area whilst broadcasting. Reaney and the others had hung on to his every word, along with millions of others, but they had expected to learn more now that it had finished, just as he had promised them. 'You've dragged me all the way down here, away from my family, just to keep me quiet, and buy yourself time,' he added, in his gruff voice, gesticulating toward Marner with an aggressive wave of his right arm. The fact that events had moved at such an unpredictably rapid pace was neither of concern nor consolation. 'Tell us the whole truth now. That's the least you can do,' demanded Reaney, echoing the thoughts of Ben and Jim, too, who were there with him at the door.

It was not easy to see all that was going on in the room but Jim thought that he caught a view of Inspector Childs in a group of people who were milling around the prime minister. The view was then obscured as Justin came towards them. He was coming to summon them.

'Look, I understand what you're saying,' said the PM with hands held out defensively as they approached. 'I haven't deliberately misled you, any of you. If you have been used, believe me it has been with the best of intentions.'

'Such as?' asked Reaney, apparently the self-elected spokesman now.

'To try to avoid panic, alarmist statements, chaos, futile loss of life,' was Marner's reply.

'And have you?' retorted Reaney, tersely.

'We'll know soon enough,' answered the politician.

'And just what will be happening, Prime Minister?' asked Jim, injecting a calmer but determined approach into the proceedings. 'It's time we knew,' he added. 'It's time you came clean.'

John Marner paused, aware that there was nothing they could do now to stop the action that was being set in motion, aware that half the population could not be communicated with, anyway, and with the other half soon to follow. He looked at his watch.

'In less than two hours from now, there will be a coordinated international military action designed to arrest the changes that are taking place in the earth's environment and atmosphere. Without it we may not be able to survive the pressures that are currently building up.' There was another short period of silence.

'What sort of action?' asked Reaney. 'Are we all in danger?'

'You don't need to know the precise details,' said Marner. 'The world's great powers and their best brains have come up with a possible solution, but there will only be one shot at it. There is nothing you need do, or can do, to protect yourself, except pray. We are all in danger anyway, every one of us.'

Some animated conversation continued, but Jim was oblivious of it. Turning over in his mind what the prime minister had said, he thought that he knew exactly what the concerted action would be. There was little he or anyone else could do now, he thought. There was, in any case, a more important matter for him still to resolve.

'Inspector?' he said, seeking out the balding Childs whilst the others talked. The police officer had been roped into the general mêlée around the prime minister's entourage when he had arrived earlier, somewhat incredulous of the leader's presence. He had even exchanged conversation, including his reasons for being in the area. He manoeuvred around the group in response to Jim's calling.

After a brief chat, with the inspector doing most of the talking, Jim looked more animated than for some time. It seemed that there was news of an incident that just could be connected to the abduction. It gave Jim cause for hope at last. There was no time to lose, but just enough for Ben, who had overheard part of the conversation, to ask if he could come with them.

'Good luck' ventured the prime minister as the three of them left the room, but they did not hear him in their haste.

As Ben had observed on so many occasions, Joanne always came running to him when she had a crisis and he was more than happy for her to do so. He would not have been so happy, however, with the state she was in when she finally landed home earlier that afternoon. After the traumatic events of the morning, the journey home had been arduous for her, with frequent hold-ups in the awful heat. She had tried to get through to Ben again on the telephone but without success.

At least now she was back on home ground and she could envisage that brother Ben would soon be back in his favourite armchair, too, giving out his pearls of wisdom and helping to get her life straightened out once more.

She lifted the receiver once more, but all she could get again was crackle, so bad she could not hold it to her ear. She switched on the TV, hoping to catch a news bulletin but all she could get was a screen full of fuzz. The radio was the same. 'What the hell is going on,' she thought.

It was shortly after, when the electricity supply failed, that she really began to worry. She no longer felt relaxed. A splitting headache had developed that seemed to grow larger and larger until her head seemed as though it would burst. She went over to the opened patio doors and gazed out. Her hands were pressing against her head now as if to contain the pain. Her face was contorting in agony, mouth open, and a strangulated scream forced itself out. Joanne looked out towards the horizon. In the distance there was a black flashing, as though the sky was alternating between black and deep blue. Was this the break in the phenomenal weather? The storm to end all storms? She pressed her head ever harder. The horizon was filling, the blackness more pronounced and extensive. And it was moving so quickly that, whatever it was, it would be upon her soon, very soon . . .

The inspector lost no time in racing to the scene. Jim had said little on the way but he sensed that matters were coming to a head in more ways than one. They both knew, as Ben did, that time was now of the essence.

They slowed at the junction, and even halted momentarily at the sight of the smashed-up car. There was a quick word and gesture from the bobby posted at the scene and they continued on up the lane. Jim noticed the skid marks on the road surface.

They did not have to travel far before they came across the sergeant and his colleague, sheltering from the powerful sun under the shade of the trees. They had been joined by another uniformed officer whose car was parked at the edge of the road. The inspector parked behind and they all got out.

'Ouch!' exclaimed Jim, simultaneously whipping away his left hand from the car door and shaking it. It was as if his hand had been burnt by the hot metal, but that was not the problem. Jim had been stung by a massive charge of static and it shook him momentarily.

There followed a brief conversation between the various police officers. Could this really be their man? How were they going to tackle him? What were the chances of further re-inforcements? The inspector knew that time was short and manpower stretched due to other, even more serious matters developing. He also felt a pressing need to see this matter through. The usual siege procedure was not a possibility here. And yet, none of them was yet armed. Could they wait for that at least? They had to go in now, try something. It could not wait. They moved up the road on foot, stopping where they could safely view the cottage without being seen. Nothing moved. As they crouched the officers deliberated further.

'Have we got any back-up further up the lane, the other side of the cottage?' asked the inspector.

'One mobile, turning back any traffic at the moment,' replied the sergeant. 'I've told them to keep well back.'

They continued to huddle, at the side of the road, on the final bend before the cottage, using the last piece of available shade. The shadows were lengthening but the day remained hot and still. The sergeant thought that they could at least wait until dusk. He was not one for foolish bravado and, as a family man, who could blame him? But the inspector knew that it was now or never. Maybe, after all, it should be the latter. His heart was telling him to act but he had always been a hard-bitten copper with a calculating brain. He knew enough about what was going on up in the skies to appreci-ate that what they were all doing here could turn out to be of purely academic interest. Yet, since his wife had left him and not having been blessed with children, what did he have to run home to? Why not go out in a blaze of glory?

Jim had no such competing thoughts to overcome. Whatever was going to happen to the world in the next few hours was now irrelevant. He sensed that Carol was there, in that cottage, and he was determined that they should be together, even if it was only to share the end of their existence. While the policemen pondered, he slipped away through the trees, giving Ben the excuse that he was merely going to relieve himself. Instead, via a circuitous route, he crept up quietly on the whitewashed buildings, making a final approach from the rear.

When Ben finally realized that Jim was gone, and told the officers, they could guess why and they made their move also, making what use they could of hedges and walls to screen their movement down the lane. Ben was ordered to stay well back. Despite the heat, they scampered and darted about, crouching where necessary, lying flat on occasions. If there had been a crazed gunman in there, standing guard at a door or window, he would have had ample opportunity for target practice. Maybe he was not expecting company. Or maybe he was not there at all. Either way, the lack of any pot-shots gave the inspector and his colleagues confidence.

'You stay there,' said the inspector to the sergeant in a shouted whisper, mouthing the words carefully as they crouched behind the retaining wall within yards now of the cottage front. 'I'll try the side window,' he added. The sergeant nodded.

Any approach across a gap or window opening, no matter how expert, carries a risk of revelation. The inspector flattened himself, his back against the white stone side wall of the cottage. Though the sun had moved round, the stone retained much of the heat of the day. He edged along until he was next to the mullioned side window. When the moment of truth came, the inevitable happened. As he leaned over and peered in, he was met with another face peering out. The shock instinctively sent the inspector diving to the hard ground underneath the window. Above him the casement opened and he feared the worst.

'It's all right, inspector. It's only me,' said Jim.

Inside the hall, Inspector Childs continued dusting himself down, as he made his way to examine the numerous sites of splattered blood that Jim directed him to. There did not seem to be anyone about. As Ben and the other police officers arrived there were five of them altogether and they decided systematically to search the whole property, not forgetting the car that the observant constable had seen.

When Jim walked into the back room he could almost sense that Carol had been there. The camp bed was still in the position that Geoff had put it and there was a discarded sheet nearby. He wandered over to the bookcase and picked up the photograph of the man and his family at the five-bar gate. He was sure he knew that face.

'Inspector, Inspector,' came the shout from the front of the house and after a few seconds the inspector skipped down the stairs and out through the hall and onto the gravel forecourt.

'What is it?' he asked.

'The car's gone,' replied the constable.

'Christ, they must have slipped away in the few minutes we had no surveillance,' commented the newly arrived sergeant, aware that he might have to carry the can for this lapse.

'Worse though, I'm afraid,' added the constable. 'We've found a body.' The three of them crunched over the noisy gravel, through the side gate and down to the far corner of the modest cottage grounds.

'What the hell!' exclaimed the inspector.

When he returned to the cottage he found Jim and Ben in conversation, apparently discussing a photoframe in Jim's hand.

'May I?' asked the inspector, holding out his hand. 'Yes, it's him all right,' he said.

'David Mallow, Inspector,' advised Jim. 'Ex-Cabinet minister now, I'm told.'

'Ex in more ways than one, sir. He's currently lying face down in the vegetable patch. That is to say, what's left of his face,' he added somewhat morbidly.

'I don't understand it, ' said Ben, vacantly and with mouth

agape, hoping that by saying the words somebody could help him to grasp what was going on. One minute Mallow was his sister's lover, then a government leak, and now entangled in Carol's abduction. It all baffled him. 'How could he be involved in this?' he asked no one in particular.

'I am wondering the same thing,' said the inspector.

'Come on. We must find Carol,' said Jim. 'We can sort out the whys and the wherefors later.'

'Firstly, are we absolutely certain that she's been here?' asked the inspector. Jim held up a small red earring with the miniscule design of a Cornish pixie on it, as if to confirm her presence. He had found it in the back room near the photo.

'They can't have been long gone,' continued Jim, 'and they can only have gone in one direction. Let's get after them.'

The inspector waved up the patrol car that had been hanging back up the lane.

'You realize the dangers involved, don't you,' he said, turning to Jim. 'There's little chance of any back-up.'

'Of course. Let's go,' replied Jim, unhesitatingly, but then, turning to Ben, he added, 'It's not your problem, Ben, I'll understand if you want to keep out of it.'

'Try and stop me,' said Ben.

As the three of them were about to get into the car, the inspector gave the sergeant some instructions.

'There's not a lot you can do here and radio communications are probably still down and likely to stay down,' he said. 'I suggest that you all head back to central command. If you take the Hellingham road back, keep an eye open for our friends in the red saloon. I don't think there'll be much other traffic on the road.'

As the car pulled away, the patrolman at the wheel, the sergeant watched them go. He let out a sigh and wiped his brow, feeling the effects of another long hot day. Looking up at the sky, he saw a thin band of darkness low on the horizon and thought that he could detect flashing far into the distance. He wished somebody would tell him what the hell was

251

going on. Perhaps he would get a proper briefing back at central command.

The car occupants said little. Deep down, even though they were giving chase, it all seemed rather forlorn. Always they had been one step behind, and often more. They were unprepared for what lay round a sharp bend about half a mile up the lane from the cottage.

The inspector was right about traffic being light. Amongst the few cars on the road however was the prime minister's. It was heading south-west in the direction of Marner's family home before time ran out. He would make full use of the protective bunker underneath it.

Marner had Reaney with him. He had to admit to feeling a little guilty about dragging the gruff adversary away from his family at such a time. Genuinely, events had moved faster than they had all imagined. In an effort at least partially to atone, he offered Reaney the use of his private bunker, not so much for his own self-preservation, though that was not a factor to be scoffed at, but for the use of its sophisticated communications system. The prime minister was not to know that the fail-safe system had failed. The PM would also let Reaney take the ministerial car, if he wanted, and he promised that he would do all he could to get his wife Kate contacted and looked after.

Reaney had also asked about the leader of the opposition and why he had not been taken into the prime minister's confidence. It transpired that he was not well and, though he had expressed a wish to be informed of developments, apparently it was rumoured that he had left the capital for his Welsh home.

The car was headed in a direction that would take it past the scene of carnage near Mallow's cottage, an area the PM knew well. Mallow had been his friend, in as much as people of his exalted position and in his profession had friends. He was soon ditched when the going got tough, but that was not an unusual occurrence in politics. Self-preservation was the name of the game. Nevertheless, he had in the past been a social caller at Mallow's cottage. He ordered the driver to slow down as they approached the scene of the incident.

The sergeant was heading back to base, as instructed, but stopped off on the way to brief the constable who was still supervising the crash scene. It was a surprise, to say the least, when he was summoned to brief the prime minister, who just happened to be passing by, so he thought.

By now a cover had been thrown over the corpse on the bonnet and it was no longer so obvious. Marner was shocked to hear of the car driver's death, but not half so shocked as to discover what had led to it and totally bemused and distraught to learn that his erstwhile friend and Cabinet minister had been murdered. Forgetting for a moment the urgency of his journey, he paused to consider the confusion of it all and deliberated what he should do next.

Meanwhile, Reaney began to take an interest in the affair, picking the sergeant up on a piece of detail in the story he had just recounted to them.

'How do you know it was a military weapon?' he asked, leaning across from his seat in the rear of the car, where he was still sat next to the prime minister.

'The inspector told us there was a military connection,' replied the sergeant, 'and we found some spent shells.'

Reaney leaned back in his seat now.

'Surely there can't be any connection,' he said quietly but out loud, and to no one in particular. 'I'd like to take a look,' he said, turning now and addressing his remarks to the PM.

'Yes, so would I,' said Marner, whose response was governed more by his interest in Mallow. He did not think to question what Reaney's interest might be.

The order was given to drive on, up the lane, to the cottage.

The young police driver liked nothing more than the excitement of a chase and ordinarily had the speed of reactions to match. When faced with another vehicle slewed across the road in front of him as he came out of a sharp bend at speed, his braking was almost instantaneous. Nevertheless, the surface was slippy from the incessant sun melting the tarmacadam. He could not avoid loss of traction. The driver braced himself, as did his passengers. The first smack was on the nearside door as they slid horizontally into the stationary vehicle. But their forward momentum was still too great to bring them to a halt. Instead, they were spun round like a propeller blade. The struggle to control direction was lost. A stone wall loomed to catch those who strayed off the road surface.

The angle of impact could not have been worse. Hitting sideways on, it was as if the heavy stones had been catapulted through the windows. Afterwards Jim remembered only vaguely how he regained consciousness and somehow extricated himself from the nearside rear door, struggling through bodies, blood and glass in the process. He must have dragged himself to the verge at the other side of the road, where he sat for a few moments. His head began to clear slowly. Everything appeared calm and still but there was a sort of eerie feeling, almost as though you could reach out and touch the air but be punished for it if you did, a bit like the shock Jim got from the static on the car door. There was no background noise. No birds. No animals. No wind. Nothing.

The silence was broken by the screech of tyres. Another unwary motorist was being lured into the trap, but this time the speed was lower and, with careful manoeuvring, a collision was avoided. The ministerial car pulled up just past the police car. Three occupants leapt out to survey the carnage and a fourth exited more circumspectly. There were concerned voices, one of them somewhat gruffer than the others.

Jim felt strong enough to get to his feet. He surveyed the scene, looking back to the car that had been slewed across the road in the first instance. It, too, was a police car.

'Carol!' he thought, and spoke aloud, though too quiet to be heard by others. 'Carol. I must find Carol,' as if reminding himself of why he was there. He needed to know the relevance of the slewed police car and he walked slowly back towards it. Jim's strength and clarity were beginning to return, though it was only on the second shout that he heard Reaney calling out to him and then saw him scampering over. They reached the car almost together.

'Christ!' gasped Reaney, distorting his face in anguish at the sight of the slumped, bloodied and bullet-ridden body of the police officer lying across the front seats. Jim had seen it, too, but had made no exclamation. Unlike Reaney, he was now becoming almost immune to the brutal events that had dogged this investigation at every turn. His revulsion was tempered by the fact that it could have been Carol. Moreover, his mind was now both preoccupied and disciplined. 'I must find Carol,' he thought.

There was a private track almost adjacent to where they were. Jim thought that he noticed something gleaming in the light of the now lowering sun. He moved a little closer. The gleam was from an object on the floor of what had been a lush tree-shaded thoroughfare before the drought had baked and cracked its surface. It was a policeman's hat with its silver badge. Jim began to search for its owner. Reaney followed.

They did not have to venture far down the track. Jim saw it first. Another body. Another corpse. Another piece of savagery to add to the catalogue. What kind of monster were they dealing with? The body was partially covered by sparse undergrowth, but not deliberately so. The young officer had just fallen that way.

Reaney vomited behind a nearby tree. He had no idea of the butchery that had been going on. His mind was having difficulty in coming to terms with his worst fears. He would have to see it through, though.

Jim carried on walking. 'I must find Carol,' he repeated to himself, over and over. It was getting darker, partly because of the shade and the sun being lower in the sky, but it was all happening quicker than might usually be expected.

A little further on, there was a right-hand bend. Jim began to canter now. He wanted to get there quickly. He had to see what lay beyond.

The anxious Reaney was following at a slower pace now, one which allowed him to be more observant of his surroundings. He noticed the bark damaged on a couple of trees. Undergrowth, sparse and stunted though it was, had been flattened in places. Fallen, dead twigs on the track had been snapped. As he paused to mop his sweating brow with the rolled up white sleeve of his shirt, he looked ahead. Jim was at the bend now, but suddenly he darted to the right-hand side and partly hid himself behind a gnarled old oak. Clearly he had seen something, or someone. Reaney had the sense not to call out but to sneak up quietly, keeping to the right. His sudden presence caused Jim to shudder.

'Is that the car?' asked Reaney, as quietly as his gravelly voice would allow.

'I would say so,' replied Jim, equally quietly, but softly, and without lifting his gaze. The red car had bounced off one tree too many on this stony, rutted part of the track, coming to rest uncomfortably against a huge protruding boulder. Like some stony iceberg, the greater part of the rock was underground, giving it the solidness and strength to cause significant damage to the front nearside of the car. Most importantly, it had crushed the wheel arch against the tyre, and the vehicle was obviously going nowhere in a hurry.

'Any sign of the occupants?' asked Reaney.

'No, nothing,' was Jim's reply.

Inside, Jim was clearly elated at being one step nearer to locating Carol, but Reaney cautioned him about the dangers ahead, restraining him from racing forward without taking sufficient care. It was several minutes before, with a mixture of stealth and cunning, and encouraged by lack of any noise ahead, that they reached the car. It was empty, which was a great relief to Jim who knew that if he had found a body slumped over the seats this time, in all probability it would have been Carol's.

Reaney lingered for a while, making a full examination of the vehicle, but Jim pressed on. He was convinced that Carol was still being held hostage and as his pursuit continued, all the time it was getting darker and darker. There was a five-bar gate not far down the track. Whoever had last passed through had not closed it completely. It flitted through his mind that this gate and its setting were not unfamiliar. It was the one in the picture he had held in his hand not that many minutes ago, though now it seemed ages.

When, with due care, Jim reached the gate, the vista opened up, and he saw for the first time in a while the open sky. It was no ordinary darkness that was encroaching. This was not a fading light. In fact, there was a clear, sharp brightness, almost blinding in contrast, in the unaffected part of the sky. It was as though a flawless straight line divided this from a void of the deepest, darkest imaginable blackness. A sheet of black. Then suddenly, in the middle distance, the sky flashed an alternate brilliant white. Not just a flash of lightning, not merely a break in the pattern, and the brilliance of it was so intense that, even at this distance, Jim had to avert his eyes. A pain developed in Jim's head. It felt as if an iron bar had been inserted in it and was being twisted round and round. He had never experienced anything like it before.

When the flashing stopped, Reaney appeared, running now, and out of breath, and he too was clutching his head in pain.

'What the hell was that?' he yelled. But Jim's eyes returned to the track ahead, following its progress through a walled but not so wide field that might have grown corn but for the drought. Beyond it lay a smattering of buildings that between them could constitute no more than a hamlet. One imposing building in particular attracted his attention: an old church, much larger and grander than it had any right to be in such a location. No doubt it had been the focal point of country life for miles around in years gone by. In this day and age, it was more likely to be locked up tight save for the occasional service by a roving vicar from another parish. The church must have been a few hundred yards away at least, beyond another gate set in the wall on the other side of the field.

'Run for it,' Jim shouted, as he pushed open the gate to enter the field. In the sweltering heat the two of them sprinted down the continuing track as it crossed the field.

They dared not look upwards for fear that the blinding, pain-bearing phenomenon would return.

They were well over half way to their goal when the middle horizon turned itself inside out again. With it, the iron bars ground in their heads once more. The combination of this and the hard, dry uneven ground caused the unfit Reaney to lose his footing. Jim crouched down beside him until the flashing in the distance stopped again. Fleetingly, the old times ran through Jim's mind: him, and Reaney, and Kate, especially Kate. Helping Reaney to his feet, they made the few yards further to the comparative safety of the stone wall and the other, partially opened, gate. It was not far now to the church itself, but they needed to take care with their final approach.

After a few moments' observation, Jim quietly and swiftly scampered over the ground, reaching and taking refuge in the porch. Again, a few moments to consider the lie of the land and then he signalled the less nimble Reaney to follow.

The door was old and heavy and difficult to dislodge, but it was not locked, responding eventually to a gradual increase in pressure. They went through, Jim in the lead, and were thankful to discover that they were not immediately visible from the main body of the church. It was a splendid building, large and high, well beyond what might be expected for such a sparsely populated area. The ceiling was marvellously crafted, the floor solid stone, the wooden pews ornately carved and the whole aura was one of calm reassurance against the chaotic and mysterious goings-on outside.

Jim gestured Reaney to get down, and they both crouched on all fours.

'What is it?' whispered Reaney.

'Voices. Listen!'

'You will do as I say,' they heard, in a menacing tone.

'But don't you understand that something strange is happening? To you. To me. To everybody,' said Carol in a voice that was not as loud as the previous one but which, to Jim, was crystal clear and heart-stopping. But before Jim could react, it was Reaney who was on his feet, oblivious of any danger.

Reaney's eyes saw what his voice had heard, and what his brain had been telling him now for some time. He walked slowly forward, down the aisle.

'Give it up, Geoffrey. It's your Dad,' said Reaney, in a clear firm voice.

Geoff was startled at the noise of an intruder and he had instinctively turned and raised his weapon in readiness. It was the last word that tempered his actions and prevented what could have been another fatal blast of fire. Geoff lowered the gun, but seemed confused. Reaney carried on walking, slowly.

'That's far enough,' said Geoff, his left arm outstretched and fingers spread as if to emphasize the point.

Jim, meanwhile, still well to one side of the church, had risen to his feet slowly and quietly. Using the cover of a stone column to keep him out of sight of the man who was apparently Reaney's son, he tried to attract the attention of Carol whom he could see now at the front.

Carol was watching Reaney and Geoff intently. She would love to ask Reaney if Jim was near by. Then, out of the corner of her eye, she detected some movement at the back of the church and she turned slightly to scan the background. Her heart leapt. She raised a hand to her mouth that barely contained a gasp of joy and excitement. With a hand movement Jim gestured for her to edge further away from Reaney, whilst he was preoccupied.

'I haven't got a father,' said Geoff to the now stationary Reaney. Amidst all the confusion and pain in his head, Geoff was finally faced with a topic he could relate to, one that had run through his life like a thread. Unhappy in his childhood, Geoff had yearned for a sympathetic, sensitive and understanding father, but instead had been blessed with one who was seemingly unloving and uncaring. Reaney was of the sort who found it hard to display emotion, the sort who found it easier to criticize than to encourage. He was from a part of the world where those traits were still very widespread, and whilst they might be suited to a politician, they were of no comfort to a young lad who was underachiev-

259

ing at school. When Geoff left home to join the army he found security and confidence, but the rift with his father deepened. Then, just as it looked as though Geoff was making a success of his military career, along came the Scandinavian business. To his father, by now deep into the political ego trip, it was further evidence of a son who was a failure.

'You've always had a father, son,' said Reaney. 'I only wish that you'd listened to me. Then maybe we wouldn't have been in this situation now.' But Geoff shook his head slowly and deliberately from side to side. For all the trauma and turmoil of the last few days, his mind was cleared and his thoughts now concise and focused.

'You don't understand do you?' said Geoff. 'You just don't understand.'

Reaney began to move forward again but a split second later the whole church was engulfed in darkness, a total blackout, not a chink of light. Geoff's turmoil returned almost instantly, but this time mixed with an impatience and anger from the words that had gone before. In this confusion, Geoff knew only what his last vision had told him, that his uncaring, unloving critical father was once more taking him to task, trying to humiliate him. His head could not cope. He resorted once more to the only solution he now knew. At least, so it seemed to him, it was the only effective solution.

Jim was already taking advantage of the blackness to get closer to Carol, when the whole church reverberated to the burst of fire from Geoff's automatic. He recoiled even more at the blood-curdling cry that followed. His hesitation was only brief though, for it was now even more urgent that he reach his beloved. Jim still could not see the hands in front of his face. He felt his way, pew by pew, down the ends of the rows towards the direction where Carol had been. Surely, if he could not see, neither could he be seen? And, surely, the gunman would have shot in the direction he was facing and, surely, the cries were not Carol's. Yet nothing could be assumed, save only that the all-pervading blackness spread uncertainty and fear. But it was the next, short but seemingly amplified blast of gunfire that really caused Jim such agonizing alarm. Had there been any visibility, his fear would have been self-evident from the contortion of his face, causing him to cry out in desperation.

'Carol! Carol!' Jim called. He no longer cared that his cries might be offering the gunman an easier target. He redoubled his blind struggle to get nearer Carol. She had not answered his call. He stumbled on. There was a blinding flash, but, thankfully, not this time from the point of a gun. Outside, the total blackness turned instantly to a brilliant white and the brightness flooded through the stained glass windows. In the momentary illumination of the interior, a white robed figure could be seen emerging from the area near the confessional box. There was darkness, and then the next flash came. This time the robed figure neared the altar. Then blackness again and Jim carried on fumbling for the next wooden seat. But this time he felt only black air. His feet made contact with something solid, however, causing him to fall forward. He had expected to hit the stone floor but instead his fall was cushioned by whatever he had walked into.

'Jim? ... Jim?,' came the hesitant but instantly recognizable voice. 'I'm here. I'm here.' Scrambling around still in the dark, Jim felt for Carol and in no time at all she was in his embrace.

'My darling, my sweetheart,' he said and he hugged her with a tightness he had longed for. 'I thought...' he said, his voice breaking, 'when you didn't shout...'

'I couldn't get the words out,' explained Carol. 'I didn't know if I had been shot ... if I was alive even.' The traumatic events of recent days had taken their toll on Carol. Battered, bemused and in mental turmoil she had not known reality from nightmare. Now, at last, as Jim's touch brought blessed relief, she sensed some normality returning. She squeezed him in a sort of silent euphoria.

Suddenly, the comforting soft glow of candlelight emerged from the blackness. It was as though it signalled the lifting of an ordeal. It was a light offering not just comfort,

261

but also protection against whatever else might be thrown at them.

'Did you know them?' questioned the soft voice with an Irish lilt, from a few yards away. Visible now in the candlelight, the robed priest was knelt down, examining the crumpled, bloodied bodies at the end of the centre aisle. Jim and Carol, still united in embrace, looked across as he moved from one body to the other a little further down the aisle.

'Both dead, I'm afraid,' said the priest and he made his way back towards Jim and Carol, walking in the dignified way that priests do, notwithstanding the fact that the world outside, above and around them, was having its very existence challenged. In these circumstances, there was a lot to be said for being at peace with one's Maker.

Carol began to sob, understandably, yet quietly and in a controlled manner. Reaching them, the priest put a consoling hand on her shoulder.

'Come and pray with me, my dear,' he said, and she found herself being led ever so gently away.

Jim parted temporarily from Carol and walked over to the two bodies. Geoff was on his back, though his legs seemed to be bent awkwardly beneath him as though he had fallen in an uncontrolled fashion. His head lay in a pool of blood and he seemed to have suffered severe damage to one side of his face. Jim could see into his eyes, though, and thought he detected a look of relief that, at long last, he had been freed from the merciless pain in his head.

Reaney was less splattered, but equally dead. Jim would keep Carol away from the bodies. They needed covering as soon as possible. Firstly, though, he made his way back to the altar, to join the others.

After a few minutes of prayer the three of them rose from their knees, lifted up their heads once more and looked at each other in the glow of the candlelight.

'Will we be safe here, Father?' asked Carol, with a tearful edge to her voice still, though her sobbing had mainly subsided now.

"I can think of nowhere safer, my child,' replied the elderly, round-faced man, greying at the temples. Carol felt reassured by his words.

Barely had these words been uttered than there came the smash of broken glass, a surge of air, and they were plunged into total darkness again. Instinctively, they all ducked and began to cast their eyes dartingly around for the source and cause of the damage. Suddenly, illuminating the blackness, came a blindingly intense ball of light. It was round, like a cricket ball, but never had one been thrown with such venom or power, nor moved in such an erratic manner. Coming at first directly towards them, it veered off on an irregular path like that of a deflating balloon. Then came another. And another. Soon there were many of them, all flying in chaotic orbit round the black interior of the church. The three of them found it painful to look at them and were frightened by their unpredictable presence. They lay flat on the stone floor and allowed the frenetic, dazzling spheres to dance above their heads. It seemed that they were all searching for an outlet, some contact that would utilize and absorb their concentrated energy mass. Some banged against the thick stone walls and eventually diminished in intensity. Others crashed noisily into pews and ornaments, causing damage. There was cracking and flashing as their light extinguished and power expired.

After a while, the situation calmed down, as though one wave of an attack perhaps was spent, but leaving in its wake both confusion and uncertainty as to what might follow next, and with what intensity. The three of them at least felt able to pick themselves up off the floor. The priest fumbled around and shortly had another candle lit. They all huddled round its glow, not for warmth but for the security it somehow symbolized.

'Ball lightning,' said Jim, quietly. 'I've read about it. It's not seen very often. Not understood.'

'What's happening, Jim?' asked Carol.

'The planet is under attack,' he replied. 'At the moment we are no more than pawns in a cosmic game.'

'What game?' she asked, staying close and holding tight, valuing every precious moment of contact.

'The balance of nature, if you like,' answered Jim. 'The earth's magnetic field is not strong enough to fend off an enormous surge of energy from the sun.'

'Is this something to do with the unusual weather?' she asked.

'Yes, darling. Though we now know that is no more than a sideshow to the real problem.'

'For behold...,' said the priest, '... the day cometh, the sun shall fall out of the sky, and there shall be only circles of light. And it shall come to pass that the dust will inherit the earth.' The others looked at him. 'The Book of Isaiah,' he added.

'I'm not so sure about that,' said Jim, 'but I do know that we all face immense danger.'

'And you are in the safest place to face it, my son,' said the priest.

'You may be right,' said Jim, looking round at the blackness surrounding their little niche of flickering candlelight and giving Carol another reassuring squeeze from the arm he held round her shoulder.

'Why do you think that churches have always been the place of last refuge?' asked the priest.

'Fear of the unknown? Of death?' suggested Carol, looking up at the priest from her previously head-bowed position.

'And maybe for protection also,' suggested the priest in his soft Irish tones.

'Through faith, you mean?' asked Jim.

'Ultimately, of course,' agreed the priest, 'but maybe a wider sort of protection than you think.'

'What do you mean?' asked Jim, intrigued.

'Geopathic zones.'

'I think that I've come across those somewhere in my research,' said Jim.

'They are zones with special powers,' explained the priest. 'In scientific speak, it is claimed they offer extra resistance to electromagnetic fields. They are frequently the site of old stone churches that act as a shield against such elements. Stone circles are believed to operate in a similar way.'

'A fluke of nature?' queried Jim.

'Believe that if you wish,' replied the man of religion, gently. 'But there are many who believe that they perform in such a way by design. The most quoted example is the magnificent cathedral at Chartres, a place of great and special qualities.'

'That would not be incompatible with the view that the earth has been through similar experiences in the past,' mused Jim, pensively, hand on chin.

They were interrupted by more blinding white flashes from outside and, very soon after, there was another burst of ball lightning, if that was what it was, inside the church. This time the priest said prayers in defiance and Jim and Carol bowed their heads in support. This wave was no more intense than the first and after a while they relit their candles and were able to continue their earlier conversation.

'What you were saying has substance,' resumed the priest, turning to look at Jim.

'You think that our ancestors have been here before?' asked Jim.

'Why not?' came the reply. 'We all underestimate the strength of the faith.'

'The wisdom of the ancients,' commented Jim.

'Quite.'

'But how can anyone control the forces you are talking about?' asked Carol, directing the question at neither one of them specifically.

'This time may be different,' said Jim. 'We may not be at the mercy of the forces of the universe.'

'A brave statement,' said the priest, 'but in what way can we resist such forces?'

'Provided that there has been no late disruption to the plans, there is to be a coordinated sequence of huge underground nuclear explosions, at various locations, the like and magnitude of which has never been seen before,' explained Jim. 'At least,' he added, 'not by man-made means.'

265

'What?' exclaimed the priest, incredulously. 'What could that possibly achieve?'

'And how do you know?' asked Carol.

'It's a long story, darling,' said Jim, answering his wife first, but then turning to the priest, "but believe me, it is happening and the effect should be to strengthen the earth's magnetic field.'

'It seems a little ridiculous,' responded the man of the cloth, 'but, more than that, highly dangerous, if it is true.'

'Not quite so daft as it seems, Father,' answered Jim, 'though I agree that it is dangerous in the extreme. You see, the scientists say that the centre of our planet has a spinning molten core, and its torque is increased by the accumulation of disturbances above it ... earthquakes, in effect, which are happening all the time, most of them under the sea or in unpopulated areas, so they tend to go unreported.'

'So why would we need to add to it?' asked Carol.

'Because,' said Jim, 'earthquakes have declined in number over the centuries, leading to a gradual but nevertheless significant effect on the core. In a quirky sort of way, the enormous amount of nuclear testing in the 50s, 60s and 70s may actually have helped to delay the slowing down. Even the French, God bless them, may have helped more recently to delay the process.'

'So nuclear testing is good for you,' declared the priest in somewhat mocking tones.

'Sounds all very wrong, doesn't it?' said Jim, 'but huge nuclear explosions under the ground do cause tremors and subterranean movements over very wide areas and that could have the desired effect on the torque of the spinning core. Of course, the computer calculations will have been made to determine the exact coordinates and timings. Like everything else in nature, it is the balance of things that is important. Surely you would agree with that, Father?'

'It is playing with fire, my son. And if what you say is true, we can only pray to God that man's tinkering will not finish us all off.'

With the priest's words of warning still lingering, there

was a huge crash from the back of the church and a deep rumbling sound from beneath them. There was a sensation of swaying that would be familiar to those who had experience of earthquake zones. They were in total blackness again now. But Jim and Carol and the priest were close enough to touch and hold each other as they tried to gain some stability and strength. Their heads swam and their senses became blurred. Above the noise from within and outside the church could be heard the Lord's Prayer, until even that disappeared as their minds were swept up into a maelstrom of frenzied attrition deep in their heads. Moments from their past experiences, images of years gone by, were swirling around, as if being sucked into a spiralling black hole. Unable to think or move independently, they were now at the complete mercy of the black unknown.

EPILOGUE

Six weeks after the event, Jim stood at the open door of the cottage, admiring and enjoying the cool steady downpour. They had been lucky to get it at such short notice, he mused, but he had correctly deduced that the holiday letting programme was severely riddled with cancellations after the recent happenings.

Some aspects of life were beginning to return to normal. The powers of recovery of nature and all its species were, indeed, remarkable. It had taken nearly 36 hours for the atmosphere to regain its equilibrium and acquire a semblance of normality. It was a week in most places before the first rains came to begin the long task of easing the drought. But physical discomforts were surmountable. It was the mental scars, suffered by so many, that would not be easily overcome and which would be evident perhaps for generations to come. These ranged from antisocial personality traits to, in many cases, severe brain damage. Many of those in the latter category would perhaps have wished that they had instead joined the thousands who had perished altogether, their brain functions having been totally nullified by the hostile environment. The least affected were fortunate through location or, to be more precise, they were protected by the counter-effect of neutron flux, predominantly in geopathic zones.

Fate had been no respector of reputation or class. A general election would be held soon to find a new government and prime minister. But the country's institutions had been resilient in the main.

Jim's job was still there, always provided the insurance industry survived the greatest natural disaster it had ever known. Not surprisingly, there would be interminable argument and delay over liability and compensation.

Though the frameworks of western life were just about intact and recovering, society would never be quite the same again within the lifetime of the current generation. There would need to be constant vigilance over the balances of nature and, in particular, the forces of the incoming solar wind and the resistance of the earth's geomagnetic field. The impact of the massive nuclear explosions, 150 kilotons a time, would disturb the earthquake zones for generations to come. But they had had the desired effect of increasing the defensive field and fate had, at last, intervened to reduce the incoming solar attack. The balance had tipped the right way again, at least for now. It was the damage done to genetic behavioural patterns that was potentially the most dangerous matter of all, however, and the most deep-seated.

Jim felt the gentle embrace of Carol from behind, her soft sweet-smelling towelling-robed body close up against him. Life was good again.

'Did you get through to Ben, darling?' she asked quietly and with concern, whilst snuggling ever closer from behind.

'No,' replied Jim, stirring slowly from the depths of concentration. 'Communications are still down. It'll take ages to build up the complex web we had before.'

'Perhaps we can call at the hospital again on the way home next week,' suggested Carol. Jim and Carol's close relatives and friends had fared better than most in terms of the after-effects of the event but Ben, who they now classed as a very close friend, was the one who had suffered. They prayed that his schizophrenic tendencies would be controllable and short-lived, but the prognosis was not reassuring.

'What are you thinking about?' asked Carol, still clinging closely. Jim answered, without lowering his gaze over the distant rain-sodden fields.

'I was just thinking that a lot has happened in the short time since we were last here.'

'The fields are certainly a lot greener,' said Carol, looking in the same direction.

'I was meaning deeper things.'

'I do know what you mean, my darling,' said Carol. 'How can it all be explained?' she asked.

'Who knows?' replied Jim. 'It gives a whole new meaning to the phrase "life's mysteries", that's for sure. It's a universal mystery, without a doubt.'

'But it's all so strange,' continued Carol. 'You meeting Reaney again, after all those years. That was coincidence enough. And then for me to be abducted by his very own son ... and then everything ending up as it did ... it just beggars belief.'

Jim was becoming uneasy about the whole business again, but he did not want to show it.

'I felt sorry for Geoff,' said Carol, pensively.

'Why?' asked Jim.

'I don't think he was a bad person. It was as though something possessed his body.' Carol wished that she had not used the last word. It reminded her again of Geoff's behaviour in the cottage and the guilt that she still felt about her sexual arousal. She had not told Jim about that aspect and probably never would. She blushed slightly and was glad that Jim still had his back to her. It was not the first time that she had been distracted by such thoughts, so much so that when Jim said something in return, it just did not register. Instead, Carol continued as though he had not spoken at all.

'Sometimes I felt that I could identify closely with him,' she said. 'Strangely enough, he was like you in some ways, my darling,' she added.

Jim cringed at the thought. When he had looked down into Geoff's eyes, as he lay motionless in the pool of blood on the cold stone floor of the church, he, too, had noticed a likeness. In fact, it was an affinity that struck him like a radar-locked Exocet missile. With Kate Reaney having succumbed to the ranks of those who did not survive the events of six weeks ago, he would probably never know if his deep-seated belief was true or not. For certain, he knew only that it was possible, that Geoff Reaney could have been his son.

'Come on, darling,' called Carol, more distant now. Jim had not realized that she had gone from his side. He was relieved that she seemed more relaxed now and able to talk about what had happened. He turned round towards the direction of her voice. Suddenly he was jolted. Everything went totally black.

The robe that Carol had so accurately tossed onto his head from the top of the staircase slowly fell and he could see again. As he looked up, he could just see her naked body slowly disappearing from view. He paused, pensively, before climbing the stairs. Only the future mattered now, he thought.